Altered Creatures Epic Adventures
Book 4 of the Thorik Dain Series

# Rise of

# Rummon

**Historical Date 4.0650.1001**
(4th Age, 650th Year, 10th Month, 1st Day)

Copyright © 2012 by Anthony G. Wedgeworth

Published by Anthony G. Wedgeworth

Artwork by Frederick L. Wedgeworth

ISBN 978-1-4681346-9-8

Library of Congress Control Number: 2012913296


**Altered Creatures Epic Adventures**
**Historical Date 4.0650.1001**
**Thorik Dain Series**
**Book 4, Revision 1.2**
**Rise of Rummon**
www.AlteredCreatures.com


Printed in the United States of America

No thrashers or chuttlebeasts were harmed in the making of this book.

# Dedication:

I dedicate this book to all the past and present
men and women in our armed forces
who have dedicated their lives to give us the
freedoms we have come to enjoy.
They are our real heroes.

# Acknowledgments:

Thanks to the following people who have been willing to join me on
this journey and help me see what I've overlooked. They have added
depth and flow to this book that I am eternally greatful for.

Thank you for your labor of love and friendship:
JoAnn Cegon, Alexander Wedgeworth, Tami Wedgeworth,
Darci Knapp, Kelly Gochenaur, Pat Mulhern, Jacob Vrieze,
Josh Crawford, Freelance Journalist & Writer Lyle Ernst,
and my dear friend and business mentor Dennis Shurson.

**Altered Creatures Epic Adventures continues with the following books:**

**Nums of Shoreview Series
(Pre-teen, Ages 7 to 12)**
Stolen Orb
Unfair Trade
Slave Trade
Baka's Curse
Haunted Secrets
Rodent Buttes

**Thorik Dain Series
(Young Adult and Adult)**
Fate of Thorik
Sacrifice of Ericc
Essence of Gluic
Rise of Rummon
Prey of Ambrosius
Plea of Avanda

# Rise of Rummon

by

**Anthony G. Wedgeworth**

# Prologue
# October 1ˢᵗ of the 650ᵗʰ year, 4ᵗʰ age

*Ergrauth, the demon of those living upon the land, leads his army toward war. Unbeknownst to him, his namesake city has been destroyed by a young Polenum named Thorik Dain. The once towering dark red crystal city rested on the pure white dunes at the base of a great desert lake. However, Thorik's act to release the souls which kept the city's crystals strong and tall, caused the city to shatter and coat the once clean dunes with red blood, pooling in the small valleys between each mound. Victorious in the destruction of the City of Ergrauth, Thorik is now tasked with releasing the great dragon, Rummon, in order to stop Ergrauth's war. In spite of this noble quest, Thorik must first escape the wrath of the city's angry residents who no longer have structures to live within.*

Chapter 1
# City of Ergrauth

Thorik pushed Avanda and Emilen behind him as a large angry crowd of Altered Creatures moved toward them. Raising his hands, he attempted to calm the mob of growling, drooling, and snorting beasts. "If everyone would settle down, I can explain."

A tall fiery-red two-legged creature with massive arm and torso muscles, thick wolf-like legs, and a wide hairless wolf head stepped forward from the pack. Blothruds were the military leaders of the Del'Unday clan of Altered Creatures. This one was old and walked with a limp, but he could still prevail in a fight with nearly any other type of creature who crossed his path. "Kill the outsiders," the Blothrud grumbled.

Thorik and the two young women cautiously backed up toward the lake; their feet dragging trails of white sand with them from the open dune desert. Held firmly at his side, he pointed his spear at the beast who had stepped forward. With the wooden shaft of the spear missing, the metal end of the large spear fit perfectly for Thorik's small size.

Shuffling his feet backward, Thorik looked over his shoulder to see how much farther the docks were. To his dismay, they were still nearly a hundred yards. "Hold onto me," he said to Avanda and Emilen.

Snapping his head back toward the Blothrud who continued to lead the aggressive mob toward them, Thorik shifted the pack on his back before standing his ground. "Stay back! Or I shall slay you as I have done to the once majestic spires of your city!" He had spoken in the most authoritative voice he could muster, hoping they couldn't tell that his body was shaking with fear.

The destroyed city of Ergrauth lay in rubble behind the Del'Unday residents. An hour ago it was a grand symbol of the achievements of the Altered Creatures. Now the ruins of the bone colored towers lay coated with red blood and the surrounding pristine white dunes marked with pieces of flesh as blood settled within the valleys between the dunes. The sight of their city stirred anger in their hearts against all those who were not Del'Unday.

Thrusting his thick sculpted arms out to his sides, the Blothrud clinched his fists and bent his knees. The sharp spikes on his shoulders clapped against each other as his shoulder blades pinched together. He was prepared to leap across the sand dune and land on Thorik.

Swinging his spear straight down into the sand with both hands, Thorik screamed, "Rummon, Attack!"

The desert dunes immediately shifted, knocking everyone off their feet, except for Thorik and his friends who hung onto him. Waves of sand pulled and lurched toward and away from the point where the spear touched the dune. Without exception, the Del'Unday mob had been flattened. Many had been washed away in the waves of sand. Others were covered up and swallowed by the dunes. The strongest only fell to the desert floor in the uncontrollable footing.

"Run!" Thorik shouted. Pulling the spear back out of the sand, he turned and began to sprint with his companions toward the docks.

Loose sand splashed with each step, slowing their progress as the three sped toward the boats at the docks. Their speed and agility was half that of when they were on hard terrain. In spite of this challenge, they were closing the gap to freedom, and that was all they were concerned with at the moment.

Blasting up from a sand dune, the Blothrud spun around to see which way the three outsiders had run. "Charge!" Yelling his command, he quickly took to the chase.

Other Altered Creature species shook free of the sand and followed the Blothrud's command. Eel-like creatures folded back the hundreds of needles across their bodies and began to swim beneath the dunes, a few small thin-faced green dragons launched into the air, and several four-legged species collected their footing for their stampede forward. It was now a race to the lake.

Reaching the top of the first dune, Avanda tripped on the loose sandy crest and rolled down the far side into the small pond of blood at the bottom. Thorik's long strides matched her descent and he quickly pulled her up to her feet. However, Emilen also lost her footing on her way down and ran into both of them, knocking her companions into the red liquid with a widespread splash.

"You idiot!" yelled Avanda, giving Emilen an evil eye.

Thorik turned to see who had hit him, only to find Emilen frozen in horror as she stood in the shallow pool of blood at the base of the dune. In addition, he saw the sand vibrate behind her. Before

Thorik could warn her, an eel-like creature sprang forth from the dune in an attack on his friend.

Thorik rolled and kicked the back of Emilen's knees, making her fall, and causing the creature to overshoot its target and miss her. Instead, it splashed into the thick liquid and disappeared below the surface.

Thorik jumped back onto his feet. "Get up! Run!"

Helping his two companions up, they began running to the far side of the shallow pond as the wolf-faced Blothrud reached the dune crest. Others soon followed.

"Awww!" Emilen screamed just as they reached the sand of the next dune. Stepping out of the blood, they could all see the eel-like creature had wrapped itself around her leg and raising its needles, piercing her leg with dozens of its tiny hard skewers.

Reaching down to pull it off, Emilen was nearly bitten by the fangs of the creature. Even if she could get past its head and sharp teeth, grabbing its body would be like grabbing a ball of needles. She'd never be able to grasp it in order to pull it off. Limping from the pain, she looked to Thorik for help.

Thorik immediately looked at her leg and became frustrated that she was going to slow them down. His eyes then went to Avanda who waved him on to leave Emilen and race over the dune to safety. As much as he wanted to escape, he couldn't leave anyone stranded to be killed by the Del'Unday.

Picking up Emilen's petite body, Thorik attempted to scale the next dune with her in his arms. Her arms wrapped around his neck and shoulder, as he could feel Emilen pull her body tightly against his. He hoped to make the docks and deal with the eel-like creature later. "Avanda! Give us more time."

Already at the top of the dune, Avanda glared at the sight of Thorik holding Emilen so tight. Pulling away from the scene, she looked up and saw the horde of Del'Unday reach the bloody pond. Thinking quickly, she recalled a spell her master, Bryus Grum, had taught her. Collecting the correct items from her purse, she swiftly smashed chunks of brown roots and other magical components together in her hands to make a paste before throwing the wad at the lead Blothrud.

Reaching the sandy shore, the Blothrud easily swatted the thrown roots from hitting his face before stepping out of the blood and onto the red stained sand. Roaring at the outsiders, he flexed his muscles before preparing to leap up at Thorik and Emilen.

As he did so, the wad of roots splashed into the blood and immediately began growing at an amazing rate, engulfing the pond and wrapping around the legs of everyone who stood in the red liquid. All of the creatures within it were immediately rooted in their place. As quickly as it spread, within the pond, the roots also reached out of the blood along the shore, one batch snaring the Blothrud's ankle.

The Blothrud flexed his mighty legs and leaped forward toward Thorik. Tightening and stretching roots caused his jump to land far short of his plans. In spite of this, he was able to knock the Num's feet out from under him.

Thorik fell hard onto Emilen and into the side of the dune, their faces pressed together and they both had the wind knocked out of them. Once deeply in love, his heart still raced when he looked upon her, even though she had betrayed him. Logic told him to stay clear but, as his first love, she would always hold onto a piece of his heart. However, he knew the moment of feelings had to end in order to survive.

The Blothrud reached out and grabbed Thorik before the roots began to drag the beast back into the pond, pulling the Nums with him.

Emilen screamed and broke free of Thorik's grasp before dragging her eel-wrapped leg up the side of the dune. Nearing the top, she reached a hand out for Avanda's help.

Avanda slapped her hand away, after seeing how she had pushed free from Thorik instead of helping. Her anger with Emilen for returning into their lives was obvious. She despised the curly red haired Num, and didn't mix words about it. "Get away from me, you traitor!" Grabbing on to Emilen, she attempted to push her back down the dune.

Standing on the top of the dune crest the two female Nums struggled until they fell down the far side, out of sight, away from Thorik and the Del'Unday mob.

Thorik kicked at the Blothrud's massive hand with his other boot. If he didn't break free soon, the Del'Unday would easily get a hold on both of his feet.

As though the creature had read his mind, the Blothrud reached up with his other hand and slapped it onto Thorik's other boot.

Ignoring the roots, which were dragging him back down the dune, he quickly pulled the Num down to view him eye to eye.

"Your magic is no match for Delz. We are always victorious in the end." Snarling, he pulled his elbow back as he prepared for a deadly punch into the young man's chest.

Thorik's eyes widened as the thick red fist of the Blothrud came flying toward him. Twisting his body to avoid the powerful blast, his backpack took the impact and exploded onto the sand. The ripped fabric exposed a wooden coffer as cooking tools and a few runestones scattered from the opened sack.

The two continued to be dragged down to the pool as the roots wrapped farther up the Blothrud's body and then began latching onto one of Thorik's boots.

A second deadly punch from the Blothrud ended deep into the sand, as Thorik twisted back the opposite way.

Kicking at the roots in a futile attempt to free himself, Thorik rolled back and forth dodging the Blothrud's attacks. As they thrashed about, he used the few seconds between attacks to grab for the scattered runestones before they became buried beneath the surface.

Another strong punch hit hard into the sand, this time catching Thorik along his side. The spikes, which extended from the back of the Blothrud's fist, carved several slashes through the Num's clothes and skin. Blood immediately began pouring out of skin-deep cuts in Thorik's side. The jagged blades from the Blothrud had caused a non-fatal tearing slash, which was much more agonizing than a clean cut.

Clutching one of the free runestones in pain, he brought it up to his chest and held onto it with both hands. Wincing from the injury, he instinctively closed his eyes and screamed. His body went ridged and he braced himself for the Blothrud's final attack. The suffering was too much and he momentarily withdrew from reality in an effort to cope with it.

But the moment lasted longer than he had expected.

Opening his eyes, Thorik found the Blothrud gasping for air, and struggling to get away.

The gem in the center of the runestone, which the Num held, was glowing a bright green.

Releasing the young man, the Blothrud fell backward, slapping his back hard against the pool of blood at the base of the dune. The splash barely had enough time to wash back toward him before the roots began wrapping around his chest and neck, dragging him under.

There was no time for Thorik to relax as more roots moved toward him. Kicking off the few small roots that had started clinging to his boot, he quickly turned and crawled up to the top to the dune. He rolled over the top and slid down the other side of the tall wave of sand only to find Emilen and Avanda wrestling at the bottom.

Rolling to his feet at the dune's base, he rushed over and wrapped his arms around Emilen's waist and pulled her off of Avanda and to her feet, allowing Avanda to jump up from the sand. He had fallen in love with Avanda over time and never thought he would see Emilen again. Now, with her sudden return, he was unsure how to handle it. Realizing he was still holding Emilen, he released her and yelled, "Not now, you two! Run for the boats at the dock!"

The three sprinted the final distance to the docks that were filled with fishing vessels of all sizes.

"Disable the boats, so they can't come after us!" Thorik yelled to Avanda. He had fallen behind her as he helped Emilen limp to the dock. "We'll take the rowboat on the end."

Avanda looked over her shoulder and saw his arm around Emilen as he helped her run with the needle-backed creature still wrapped around her leg. The sight of Emilen grabbing onto his hand for support further infuriated her.

Reaching into her sack of magical components, Avanda cursed Emilen's name. "How dare you touch Thorik with those hands of betrayal," she said under her breath. "Once we're safe, you're going to wish the Del'Undays had captured you."

Quickly laying out the components on the dock, she mixed them while chanting her verbal commands. Completed, she looked up to see no effect from the spell she was creating.

Waiting for some explosion or event to sink the other ships, Thorik questioned their ability to escape the rest of the mob not captured by the magical roots. "What's wrong?" Panic was evident in his voice.

Avanda looked the components over again, as Thorik and Emilen ran past her toward the rowboat on the very end of the dock. "I don't know. I watched Master Grum do this once. I'm sure this is right."

"Apparently not!" Thorik looked back at the mob of Del'Unday emerging over the dunes. "It's too late! Run for it!"

"No." Her focus was on the components before her. "I just need to remember what I'm missing from this spell. I have the right components, and the right verbal commands. I must have missed a physical gesture or something."

Three small green dragons flew in front of the mob toward the three outsiders. One headed for Avanda and the other two headed for Thorik and Emilen. The mob was close behind, approaching the docks at a hastened pace.

The first dragon dove down at Avanda, shrieking upon its descent. The creature's leathery thin green face was outlined with yellow thorn-like horns along its jaw and over its bright yellow eyes. Normally wide to the dragon's side, the leathery wings were now folded against his body to dive upon its prey.

"Avanda!" Thorik screamed as he noticed the attack on his friend.

Before she could respond, the dragon had swooped down and grabbed her hair, pulling her off to the side of the dock and away from the components she had laid out.

Swatting at the dragon, she was able to get its sharp claws out of her hair and push it away for a brief moment. She quickly pushed herself off of a pile of coiled rope and back up to her feet. Taking a step toward her inactivated spell, she paused and looked back down at the coiled rope. Ropes from every boat were tied onto the dock with extra length coiled up. "That's what I forgot," she muttered.

The dragon dove a second time but missed her as she ducked out of the way. By doing so, she left her purse of magical components in her exposed pack. The dragon's talons clasped onto her backpack and pulled it away from her. Struggling from the weight of the pack, the small dragon barely remained airborne.

"NO!" she screamed. However, the sight of the mob entering the dock caused her to forget the stolen items in her pack. Instead, she quickly grabbed two handfuls of her mixed components and sprinkled them onto the ropes from each of the ships and small boats as she quickly made her way toward Thorik and Emilen.

Meanwhile, two small dragons were providing Thorik with a challenge. He swung his wooden coffer at them while giving Emilen instructions on launching the rowboat.

It wasn't long before the two dragons were working together and quickly clipped him behind the knees while the other pushed him backward from a frontal attack.

Thorik fell onto his back on the end of the small boat, nearly tipping it over. His backpack, runestones, and gear were now dispersed all over the boat's bottom, and his spear was pinned behind him. Both thin dragons were less than a third of Thorik's size, but their thick skin and their sharp claws gave them the advantage. Protecting his face with one arm, he reached for anything to use as a weapon with his free hand.

Emilen quickly grabbed a coil of rope and started swinging it. Her balance was off, due to the eel still wrapped around her leg, as she swung and knocked one of the dragons off Thorik and into the water.

This victory was short lived as the dragon sprang back up out of the water and landed on top of her, knocking her off the other side of the boat. They both fell with a splash into the warm lake.

Now, with only one green dragon to contend with, Thorik was able to hold off the creature while standing up and grabbing his weapon. Pulling the Spear of Rummon forward, he instantly changed the dragon's desire. Instead of wanting to attack, all it wanted to do was escape, as Thorik held the spear firmly. Heat rose from the weapon and a low voice could be heard from deep within the spear.

Whether the dragon understood the voice or not, it released Thorik and immediately flew off toward the fallen city of Ergrauth with due haste.

While sighing with relief, Thorik suddenly realized Emilen was still underwater with the other dragon in their own fight. Leaning over the edge, he shoved his spear into the water near them. The water bubbled and boiled around the spear for a moment, scaring off the second attacker and releasing Emilen to return to the surface.

Free of enemies for the moment, he pulled the spear back out and set it into the boat before reaching down to help Emilen out of the water. But as he lifted her out, he felt the boat move. Someone or something else was now in the small craft with them.

Dropping Emilen back into the water, Thorik spun around and grabbed his spear, only to find out that Avanda had just jumped into the boat with them.

"You made it!" he said before looking behind her at the Del'Unday crowd moving toward them on the dock. Thorik looked for any opportunity to escape, but none appeared. His grip on the Spear of Rummon shifted as he wondered how far the weapon would get him. Yet, he knew that he could not fend off an entire city.

Emilen swam to the surface of the water, grabbed the side of the little boat, and watched the parade of creatures move toward them. "Thorik, what's our next move?"

His only response was a slight shaking of the head in disbelief. He honestly had thought that they could escape.

Slowing, reaching the rowboat at very end of the dock, the Del'Undays knew that there was nowhere for the outsiders to run. The boats and ships that lined both sides of the dock could easily outrun and outmaneuver the little boat.

Emilen still waited for Thorik to save them, however she could see in his eyes that he didn't have a plan.

Thorik's mind raced for options, adjusting his grip on his spear. Using the weapon on the dock could blow the Del'Unday into the water, while tossing himself and his companions out of the small unstable rowboat. All he had was a bluff of using it.

"We surrender!" Emilen shouted.

"No we don't!" Avanda yelled out. "This is your last chance, Delz. Either leave us alone or we will have to wipe the land clear of you."

Stopping the Del'Unday in their tracks, many began to laugh.

Knowing how Avanda tended to underestimate her opponents, Thorik held his spear firm and pointed it at the front of the mob. Leaning over, he whispered, "What are you doing? Don't make this any worse than it is."

"No!" she shouted with confidence at the approaching Del'Unday. "This is our time to leave, with or without their consent."

A moment of silence followed before one of the Del'Unday spoke up. "She is a warrior! Excellent!"

Avanda smiled at the comment.

The Del'Unday continued with a grin. "Kill her first."

"Tu'cal Oon'dar!" Avanda yelled as loud as she could. The words triggered the spell she had established. Realizing what she had forgotten, she had taken the mixed components and placed some on the end of the ropes from each ship. It was the lack of touching the ropes that caused the spell not to work the first time.

As the Del'Unday filled the dock, ropes from ships on both sides of the docks sprang to life and the ends flew across the docks to the opposite side, immediately tying themselves into knots.

This rope trick knocked a few Del'Unday from their feet and even one off the dock, but it had accomplished nothing more than to spook a few and anger the rest. They growled at her on their final approach.

Emilen sunk down behind the side of the rowboat and Thorik stepped away from the dock to the side of the boat as he heard the moaning of tightening ropes and stressed wooden boards. "Avanda, what have you done?"

"I did warn them," she said with a sinister smile.

Seconds before the first Del'Unday reached for Avanda, the cracking began. Dock boards buckled and sides of ships began to bow inward as the ropes that spanned the docks continued to pull on each other. The ships were being pulled together as the enchanted ropes continued to make more knots with more unenchanted ropes and at a faster pace.

Without warning, a smaller boat shattered into pieces as it was flung across the dock toward the other side. This was quickly followed by a second and then a third. Pieces of wood sprayed across the docks, coating the mob with thousands of sharp projectiles. Chaos quickly ensued as the Del'Unday pushed each other in an attempt to escape and get off the collapsing dock.

Planks beneath their feet buckled and split from the pressure of the ropes pulling the boats toward one another. Many sections began to collapse while others burst upward, knocking Delz off the dock and into the water.

Larger ships now moaned and tipped from the escalating tension as more ropes sprang across the way and pulled on more ropes from other ships. The front ripped off one ship, cleaning off a large section of Delz from the dock as it flew to the other side.

Thorik gathered his wits long enough to know they needed to get some distance from the dock before the spell affected them as well. He quickly pushed off before helping Emilen out of the water, and back into the boat. Avanda, however, continued to watch the spell's reaction with great interest and some pride.

More snapping of large beams could be heard over the screaming locals who were trying to escape. Moments later there was an unexpected collective gasp as all went eerily silent. It was quickly followed by a sudden rush of ships crashing into each other, taking out the dock and all those on it. It was as though an invisible giant had clapped his hands together with the ships and dock in between them.

Heavy timbers from the dock and vessels shot up into the air in every direction, spraying the water and sand dunes with wooden fragments.

Large beams and posts splashed down near Thorik's rowboat while he attempted to row away. Only by sheer luck and the virtue of having a small boat were they able to survive the aerial attack of wood debris with nothing more than being drenched by the splashes they created.

## Chapter 2
# Pheosco

Thorik rowed until his arms and back couldn't row any more. They had distanced themselves from the destroyed city and dock, which were now long out of visual range. The cuts along his side had stopped bleeding after Avanda had applied a wrap, but his skin was still tender.

Emilen was also still in pain, however hers was from the eel wrapped around her leg. The needles on its body had locked tightly into her skin. Avanda had cut off the eel's head and killed it, but Emilen refused to allow Avanda to help remove it. She had hoped to have Thorik spend the time with her while removing each needle.

"Keep it on there for all I care," Avanda said with a shrug.

Emilen traded benches and moved next to Thorik. Tilting her head, she batted her soft eyes at him. "Now that we're safe, can you help me with my calf?" Lifting both legs up, she gently set one on his lap while the other hovered near his face. In doing so, her dress fell back, exposing her knee and much of her thigh. Several long dark tan lines swirled down and around her legs. These areas of sensitive skin were known as soul-markings and most Nums had them.

Avanda's face turned red at the obvious flirting. "*I* could have had that eel off already."

Emilen smiled at Thorik and then looked back at Avanda before her face turned sour. "Why do you look so old? Last time I saw you, you were a lot younger than me. Now you look as old as my mother."

"Well, last time I saw you I thought you had just stabbed Thorik and the rest of us in the back!" The sting in her statement was obvious.

"What? No. You misunderstood." Emilen looked back and forth from Thorik and Avanda before resting her gaze on Thorik. "I was under Darkmere's control. I wanted to help, but his powers were too much for me."

The soul-markings on Avanda's neck and arms turned a deep red as she stared at Emilen's legs on Thorik's lap, while he cradled her injured leg with his left hand as he began pulling each of the eel's needles out with the other. "You chose to leave us in Woodlen and then chose to help Darkmere in his attempt to destroy our lands. And now here you are, conveniently in the same location we are, far from any safe location." She crossed her arms and scowled. "What are you up to this time, you back-stabbing Fesh?"

"Avanda! That's enough!" Thorik had stayed silent long enough. Regardless if he believed Emilen or not, they had no choice but to get along until they had reached a safe environment. In general, Thorik wanted to believe most people were trying to do good. Perhaps they were just misguided. Even with that said, he began feeling uncomfortable with Emilen's leg on his lap. He didn't know why. He wasn't doing anything wrong. In fact, he was simply helping someone who was injured. Yet it still felt wrong, as though he was violating some trust with Avanda. His last statement to her didn't help much.

"Ouch!" Emilen cried out. Her pain was caused by another needle being pulled out by Thorik. She adjusted her position and a single tear ran down her face. "I can't believe that you both thought I was against you on purpose. It's been so long since I have seen you and I have had so many dreams of finding you both alive."

Collecting Thorik's hands from her leg, Emilen held both of them within hers. "My thoughts of you were what kept me going," she said with a heart-felt tone. "Our memories are so dear to me, and all I could think of was how fortunate I would be to find you once again. Now, here you are."

Avanda's blood was boiling. "Thorik, this is a game to her. Don't fall for it!"

Thorik pulled a hand free and held it up to Avanda in order to calm her. "Let's hear her out. Emilen, how exactly did you break free and then end up way out here in the Ergrauthian Valley?"

"I was under his spell for so long. It's hard to say when I finally realized what I had done. There were several of us that helped him spread the word about the Terra King in order to infiltrate the Dovenar Kingdom. We eventually ended up in the city of Corrock, where Darkmere rallied his Del'Unday troops."

Thorik nodded as he listened, knowing that Darkmere was known to call Corrock one of his main homes.

She leaned forward, closer to Thorik's face. "It was then that the trance began to lose hold. We had been held in a private location secured from the Del'Unday while Darkmere was gone. He had left on a mission by himself, which was odd for him to do. Even more unusual was that he didn't return. I don't know how long he was gone, but after a while, his charm started to fade. After several failed attempts to escape, the Del'Unday decided to get rid of us, seeing that Darkmere wasn't coming back for us. They gathered us all up and sent us across the mountains and into the Ergrauthian Valley to be absorbed into the city itself." More tears began to flow. "Oh, Thorik, do you have any idea how scared I was to know I was going to die before I ever had a chance to see you again?"

"That's all Fesh talk!" Avanda's voice was bitter and sharp.

"Avanda!" Thorik shot back. "That's not appropriate. Besides, neither of us were there. We can't say that it's not the truth." Defending Emilen's right to tell them what had happened, he felt he was being squeezed in a vise. He had to watch everything he said in order not to pick one side or the other. In some way he felt sorry for Emilen, at least he and Avanda had each other. She was out here alone.

A wide smile appeared on Emilen's face after hearing Thorik's comment.

Even though he felt sorry for her, he still wasn't going to forget everything she had done. "However, by not being there, it also means that we don't know that it *is* the truth," Thorik said.

The new smile softened as she nodded, accepting his point. "I understand. It will take time to establish trust again." Not turning her head, she glanced over at Avanda. "I have the rest of my life to do so." Continuing before anyone commented on her last statement, she added a deep sigh of relief before saying, "So, which way home?"

Thorik looked up at the sun and then pointed past the left side of the boat. "I would guess that way."

Taking a moment to look at the horizon in front of them and then to the side of them, she finally asked the obvious question. "Then why aren't we heading in that direction?"

"We're not heading home."

"Why not?"

"Because I have some unfinished business to take care of."

Looking past the front of the boat, Emilen could see a mountain range with many of its tall peaks snowcapped. Some, however, were black from base to cone. Smoke billowed from a few. "Business?"

Grabbing his spear, Thorik displayed it proudly. "This is the Spear of Rummon."

Nodding, she waited for more information.

"I am going to take this spear and return it to Rummon's lair. He is the demon of all that fly and his soul is alive within this spear."

"We're returning it to destroy it?"

"No, you misunderstand. I am returning it to find his trapped body and reunite them. We're going to free him after being held for years in his captive state." Thorik was visibly excited about it and accidently bumped her leg which still had many needles in it.

"Ouch!" She quickly moved her leg to prevent being bumped again. "Are you talking about Rummon the Dragon? The dragon responsible for the killing of the Mountain King? Why would you bring the creature back to life after he murdered our spiritual leader?"

"I've made a promise to do this, and I believe this is the right thing to do. Rummon can help us against the evils of the other demons, Ergrauth & Bakalor."

"Even if he would, how are you going to do such a thing? You have no powers to transfer his soul from this weapon. Avanda doesn't possess the magical skills either. I don't even think Darkmere himself could do such a thing since Rummon has been out of his body for so many years."

Thorik shook his head. "We have something Darkmere doesn't have. We have Vesik, the most powerful spellbook ever. The Death Witch, Irluk, created this book. It not only tells Avanda how to create the magic, but the book is a component within the spells. It funnels vast powers through it and intensifies it. Its influence is great. We intend to be very cautious when using it, for such great power also brings great danger. So we plan to use it sparingly, and reviving Rummon is one of these times. He can help us stop the pending war, Emilen. I just know he can." His eyes beamed as he talked about the opportunity they had because of it.

Avanda, on the other hand, held her head low as she looked at the bottom of the boat.

"Avanda, show Vesik to Emilen. Show her what you have. I know how important it is to you."

"I can't."

"Sure you can. She won't harm it."

"No, it's not that. It's just that while we were on the dock, that little green dragon snatched it from me. It's in my pack."

Thorik froze with shock and stared right through Avanda. After muttering a few undetermined words, he finally said, "You can still do it. You remember the spell. You performed it on Gluic. You recall the words and gestures, right?"

Avanda shook her head.

Thorik nodded his. "Yes, you do. You just have to try. Just try." His voice continued to grow louder as he watched her shake her head no. "Just try! What could it hurt?"

"Even if I could perform it without Vesik, it might hurt us. If I do it wrong, we could all be dead before we had a chance to realize something was going amiss."

"How could you let this happen? How will we release Rummon without Vesik?" The words came out sharper than he had expected. He knew she didn't lose it on purpose. He was just frustrated at the news that they no longer had a plan to stop the war.

Emilen placed a hand on Thorik's back. "It's okay, Thorik. If it's that important to you, we'll come up with something. It's not the first time Avanda has let you down. We've always been able to get through challenges together with or without help."

Her touch felt annoying. A touch from anyone at this moment would have irritated him in his current agitated state. Pulling away from her hand, Thorik leaned forward and dropped his head. "I can't believe this."

Avanda struggled with her inner emotions after having let Thorik down as well as Emilen taking advantage of the situation. "I'm sorry! I did the best I could." Her head only rose to look at him for a brief moment, but the pain from the sight of his obvious disappointment crushed her heart, causing her to quickly turn away from him.

"Well," Emilen said, "We all know what that gets us." Turning back to Thorik, she rubbed his back with one hand. "Who did you promise to make this happen? Who would ask so much of you and only give you Avanda to help on such a quest?"

"I did," squawked a large bird from behind Emilen.

Frightened by the unexpected voice, Emilen jumped forward and landed in the center of the boat.

There, flapping its long wings was a large brightly colored red, green and orange bird. Its head was orange and white with eyes far too large for its head as each eye moved in different directions. "I asked him to," the bird said as it prepared for landing while carrying a small thin limp green dragon in its talons.

Dropping the creature on the base of the boat, the bird landed on one of the seats and looked down at the green creature. Short green fur covered most of the dragon's body, except where patches had been ripped out during a struggle. The fine fur coated its neck and the crown of its head before giving way to a leathery skin on the thin face of the dragon. "I think you owe someone an apology," said the bird.

Emilen recoiled and stared at the bird in confusion.

"Sorr...," came from the mouth of the dragon. Tired and battered, the dragon looked like it had lost a fight with a chuttlebeast. The second attempt came after clearing its throat and was successful. "Sorry." It then slowly moved off of what it had been carrying; Avanda's pack with a large old book peaking out.

"Granna! You made it!" Thorik shouted to the bird.

"Gluic, you found it!" Avanda screamed, grabbing Vesik.

"Well, of course, dear. It didn't take much to chase him; weighted down with that book and all."

"Gluic?" Emilen asked, keeping her distance from the bird and the dragon.

"Yes?" Gluic replied.

Emilen looked for clarification from Thorik. "This is your grandmother?"

With eyes rolling around like marbles and her head snapping back and forth, the bird replied to Emilen's question directed to Thorik. "I have been all of his life, dear. Don't you recognize me?"

"No. Last time I saw you, you were…"

"Less feathery?" Gluic said, rustling her feathers across her shoulders and neck.

"Um, no. Dead."

"Oh, that. Yes. That was unfortunate. I should have seen that coming."

"I don't understand. Darkmere killed you in Woodlen, while he performed as the Terra King."

"Dear, if death is the worst thing that happens to me, then life has been pretty good."

"What?"

Gluic craned her neck to the side and tilted her head sideways, moving it closer to Emilen. "Are you hard of hearing? The underestimation of Darkmere, which caused my death, was obviously not the last time I would see my life come to an end."

"But how? How did you survive?"

"Well, I simply…" Gluic's head stopped cold and both of her eyes rotated to the same location. A school of small fish were near the surface of the water several yards away. "Supper!" Spreading her large wings, she flapped them hard a few times to lift off the boat before flying over and diving into the water for some fish.

Swinging her gaze to Thorik, Emilen was clearly looking for an explanation which made sense. She had received nothing of the kind from Gluic.

By this point Avanda had rifled through the book of magic to ensure that it was undamaged. In doing so, she almost missed the sly green dragon make an attempt to escape. While Thorik, Emilen, and Gluic had been talking, the dragon had regained his strength and made a leap off the boat.

Avanda wouldn't allow him to escape that easy. Springing her leg forward, she stepped on his tail, preventing his leap from becoming a successful flight. "Oh no you don't," Avanda said with a vindictive grin. "You owe me for taking my pack."

Injured and tired, the dragon slumped back down and waited for a better opportunity to leave.

Thorik smiled at Avanda, while helping Emilen back up to one of the benches. "Looks like you found yourself a new pet."

Avanda smiled and nodded. "I wonder what I'll call him."

The dragon growled slightly. "I'm no one's pet! Especially for short humans such as yourselves."

"We're not human," Avanda said.

Emilen added to her comment. "She's right. We're Polenums. More often known as Nums…Well, I'm not exactly sure what Gluic is, but the rest of us are Nums."

Squinting his eyes, the dragon leaned toward Emilen. "I don't care what you are. I'm not a pet!"

Just as he finished his statement, Avanda tossed a loop of thick twine over his head and onto his neck. "I'm thinking about calling him Ralph."

"Very creative," Thorik laughed.

"My name is not Ralph. It's Pheosco."

"Sit, Ralph. Stay," Avanda said seriously.

"Pheosco!" the dragon corrected again.

Avanda leaned forward. "Ralph, if you're good, I won't experiment with any spells on you. How does that sound?"

Thorik laughed. "Like the time you blew a hole in Captain Dare Mensley's ship, or attached a tree limb to Bryus Grum's shoulder, or nearly exploded his face right off?"

Avanda smiled, "Yeah, like those times. The only way to learn what works is by experimenting. What do you think, Ralph?"

Pheosco lowered his head and grumbled, "Pheosco."

Finally calmed down, after the arrivals of Gluic and Pheosco, Emilen began asking Thorik questions. They had been bottled up inside her since she had met up with Thorik and Avanda moments prior to the Del'Unday mob chasing them out of the city. "So Thorik, how did you survive Darkmere's attack at Weirfortus? How did you get to the City of Ergrauth? How did your grandmother become a bird?"

"Slow down." Thorik stopped her before additional questions came pouring out. "Lift your leg up here so I can finish getting the rest of the eel needles out of your leg and I'll tell you."

Lifting her leg, she placed it in front of him and waited.

"First of all, we didn't *all* survive. Wess didn't make it, and Ambrosius sacrificed himself to save the rest of us." Thorik thought for a second before continuing. "Well, I thought he did."

"Ambrosius is still alive?"

"Thorik!" Avanda shouted. "She could still be an agent of Darkmere. Don't tell her anything."

"It's alright, Avanda. She's with us now. She has no way to communicate with the Dark Lord even if she wanted to." Pulling a few more needles out of Emilen's leg, he considered telling Emilen more information in order to assess her truthfulness. "We've heard rumors of Ambrosius surviving Darkmere's attack. But we haven't seen him ourselves." Wanting to be able to trust Emilen again, he felt compelled to test her honesty. He needed to give her information that could be useful to Darkmere without giving the Dark Lord an advantage over his own plans. The question was, what bait should be used on the hook? Until he had this figured out, he would have to get her to trust him in order to take the lure, otherwise she would sense his deception. At the same time he evaluated Emilen's sincerity, he didn't want to lose Avanda. It would be a narrow path to walk until he could find the time alone with Avanda to discuss his plans.

"Oh," Emilen said, slightly sad at the news. "I was hoping that he had survived."

"As I. Perhaps we'll find out for sure some day. But at the time, we had to move on. In our attempt to save Ambrosius' son, Ericc, from being captured and sacrificed by Darkmere, Granna Gluic's soul was captured. We obtained the book, Vesik, to find a spell to release her essence. However, the components needed were inside of Ergrauthian Valley. That is when we were apprehended by the Delz. The only opportunity we had to release Gluic was just prior to the city falling apart on itself. Well, actually, releasing her caused the destruction of the city."

Emilen was following the story for the most part. "That doesn't explain why she was turned into a bird."

"It was the only thing available at the time," Avanda said to defend her actions.

"Oh, I see. *You* performed the spell that released her soul into that winged thing."

"Yes, but-"

"No need to explain," Emilen said, cutting her off. "Just knowing that you were involved explains everything."

The bitter sting of her words slapped Avanda hard. "You're lucky I don't have Ralph attack you right now."

"Pheosco," Pheosco said in a dry tone.

Pulling back the twine restraint, Avanda acted as though she was holding the dragon back from an attack. "Heel, Ralph!"

"Pheosco," he said, gasping slightly for air.

Emilen giggled at the sight. "He's as harmless as a sleeping Fesh'Unday."

Pheosco's head turned abruptly. His gums raised, showing his teeth as he began to growl at Emilen. The spikes on the back of his neck slowly raised and his claws extended from his fingers. "What did you call me?" he asked through closed teeth.

Emilen and Thorik instinctively scooted back on the bench as the green dragon leaned forward toward them, hunched over as he prepared to strike. "It's just an expression," Thorik said. "She didn't mean it."

The dragon placed a paw on the bench and dug his claws into the wood to show their sharpness.

"Yes. Just an expression," Emilen said. "No offense."

The dragon arched his neck and leaned close to her face. "Next time you mean not to offend someone, do it with your mouth closed." A deep exhale blew hot foul smelling air into her face, before opening his mouth to show the jagged sharp teeth within.

"That's enough." Avanda pulled the twine back, causing him to lurch backward, landing at Avanda's feet.

Never taking his eyes off of Emilen, he regained his footing. "I don't like her," he said to Avanda.

A slight grin emerged on her face. "I think you and I are going to get along just fine, Ralph."

"Pheosco."

## Chapter 3
# Ergrauthian Lake

The Ergrauthian Lake was vast in size, and the recent interval of nearly dead calm waters refused to assist Thorik and his companions in their efforts to make their way across the open waters to the northern shores. The boat felt anchored when Thorik stopped rowing for the night as well as when he took periodic breaks to rest his back and arms throughout the following day.

It was during one of these breaks that Thorik opened his weather-worn ripped backpack and removed a flat wooden coffer. Opening it, he flipped through the various papers inside until he found the one he was looking for; a partially drawn map of the eastern lands.

Emilen had been silently watching Avanda and the green dragon converse, wondering why a Num would have any interest in making friends with such a beast. But the rustling of papers caught her attention as Thorik pulled out his map from the coffer and began drawing. "Maps? You're still making maps? Why?"

"I don't know. I guess it relaxes me. It reminds me of all of my past adventures."

"Do you still keep your logs?" Emilen, reached down to open the coffer, but was stopped by Thorik's hand blocking the clasp. "What's the matter?" she asked.

Thorik had never let anyone open his coffer and look inside. It was like allowing someone to open his mind and heart to see his thoughts and feelings. "I…um…There are a lot of private thoughts in there."

Placing her hand on his, she giggled slightly. "I've seen you at your best and worst, Thorik Dain of Farbank. There's nothing in there that I haven't seen in real life. Besides, I just want to see the maps you made, not your notes." Softly pulling his hand away from the clasp, she then opened up the coffer.

He didn't understand why, but somehow he felt uneasy and almost violated as she filed through the papers inside to find what she was looking for. Any sounds she made, such as a slight scoff or snicker caused waves of emotions through his body as though she was making a personal attack on him. He couldn't handle the assumed ridicule any longer and wanted to reach over to shut the wooden lid. He finally did so, just as she pulled out the maps she was looking for.

"Very impressive work," she said as she studied one of the maps he had created. "It looks as though you've been in Southwind, Eastland, Pelonthal, and so many more. Tell me about Pelonthal, I've heard such wonderful things about it."

Composing himself, now that the coffer was closed and the clasp in place, he nodded. "It was a lush area with a festive city full of all species. Humans, Nums, and the Ov'Unday are all living in harmony."

"No Del'Unday? No Fesh'Unday?"

"Not from what I could see. The harsh tension of the Del'Unday species seemed to be missing, and we didn't run into any boars, rams, chuttlebeasts, or any other Fesh'Unday species in the forest…But we did run into the Myth'Unday."

"The Myth'Unday?" Emilen's voice raised with excitement. "What are they?"

They are the small creatures of the forest that we've heard legends of, such as pixies and such. We see them out of the corner of our eyes but can't turn quick enough to see them straight on. They cannot be seen unless they wish you to see them. And if they wish to be seen, you are in grave danger."

"Why?"

"They only allow you to see them if they plan to play with you."

"That doesn't sound so bad."

"Their games are played at high stakes and usually cost you your life. I was very fortunate and won my game against Mr. Hempton. Well, I didn't exactly win, but I did make an ally." Thorik thought about the past for a moment as he smiled. "I would like to see him again someday."

"They sound devious and dangerous."

"Oh, they are that."

"Do they have an army? Do you think they are a threat?"

"What? No. They live peacefully in their forest. It was our fault for entering their land. I can't see them ever attacking others outside the Mythical Forest, unless the forest itself was in danger."

Pondering while reviewing the map some more, she pointed to a few locations. "What threats did you run into here and here?"

"Threats?"

"Yes, armies or challenges. I've heard rumors that war is pending across the land and soldiers are being held captive, I have not seen this with my own eyes. Are the tales true? Is war mounting?"

He nodded. "It is true."

"How do we stand against the threats? Who is leading the forces? Are our people in danger?"

"Slow down. One question at a time." Thorik carefully removed the map from her hands and began to show her key points on the map. "The demon of the underground, Bakalor, is working with the Death Witch, Irluk, to take over the land."

Emilen's head shook slightly. "That can't be correct. Legends say that Bakalor can't live above ground in the sunlight."

"I know, but he plans to do it nonetheless. And he has called upon the demon of the land, Ergrauth, to lead this attack against the humans, Nums and Ov'Unday."

Emilen glanced up at the horizon from where they came. "If he should ever return to his namesake city, he will be most upset about its destruction. And if he finds out that you were the cause of the city's demise, he'll hunt you down and kill you."

"He'll have to get in line," Thorik chuckled.

Taken aback by the comment, a puzzled expression crossed Emilen's face. "Who would want you dead?"

"Let's see... The Matriarch of Southwind for escaping her slavery mines with Ericc; Darkmere for encasing his son, Lord Bredgin, into an enchanted wall and possibly killing him; and the demon Bakalor for a reason I know not. I would even assume the Oracles are rather displeased with me over destroying their grand coliseum in northern Woodlen and their Surod Temple, which they used to create souls for new species."

Emilen was shocked at the news. "How did you...I mean, you're just an average Num...How could you have..."

"It's a long story."

It only took moments for her expression to change from amazement to one of interest. "Thorik Dain of Farbank, you've been holding back on me," she said while placing one of her fingers on his hand and began gently tracing a line around and in between each of his fingers. "You have a wild and dangerous side of you under all of that plain exterior. I had no idea." She shifted her body closer so she was up against him on the bench.

Thorik's face became flushed with embarrassment, making him smile and look down at his feet. "There's more to me than most people may know," he boasted slightly to add to her comments. With cheeks fully red, he was feeling pretty good about himself. He never took the time to really reflect back at all he had accomplished. And why shouldn't he be proud, the only other Num who had ever made such a change to the history of the world was the Mountain King. "It's been over five thousand years since the Mountain King made his mark, it's about time another Num did."

Puffing up his chest, he raised his head from looking at the boat's floorboards and held it up with pride. However, across from him, what he saw stopped his ego from getting out of control.

"Now you're comparing yourself to the Mountain King?" Avanda said. She had a crusty look upon her face; the kind of look a mother would give her son when he tracks mud into a cleaned house. It was obvious she was not impressed with his stories or Emilen sitting so close to him.

"I…umm…should be rowing," he said with a nervous shuffle off the bench and to his feet before collecting the maps and placing them back into the coffer for protection.

Emilen was not much help in moving out of Thorik's way; in fact she almost seemed like she wanted to be in his way while he put his coffer away and made his way back onto the bench to start rowing again.

Pheosco took in the obvious tension between the two females who glared at each other behind Thorik's back.

Glancing over at the mountains, Thorik determined their heading. "It won't be long now before we reach the northern shore. We'll have Gluic fly ahead to help us find Rummon's Lair."

"Rummon's Lair?" Pheosco asked with great concern in his voice and his wings opened to intimidate. "What need do you have of Rummon's Lair?"

"Ralph! Down!" Avanda shouted, pulling back the twine around his neck.

"Pheosco," he coughed while the twine choked him slightly. "Why do you journey there?"

She relaxed the tension on the twine. "We plan to release Rummon's essence back into his body."

"You plan to revive Lord Rummon from his long sleep?"

"Yes."

"How can you do this?"

"Thorik found the Spear of Rummon which carries his essence," she said with excitement. "Once we find his body, I can use the spell book, Vesik, to give it back to him."

Pheosco's eyes tightened as he stared at Avanda. "Why? What do you ask for in return? Allegiance? Lord Rummon is no one's servant or slave. He is the lord of the skies and rules over all in his domain. He does not take orders."

She shook her head at the assumption. "No, that's not it at all. We only hope that he will help us prevent the coming war from happening."

"He doesn't honor requests either, especially from those not of the air and sky. This land war is not his concern. Ergrauth rules the land and ground dwellers like you. It is his domain."

"From what I've seen, he's your leader as well, not just for land dwellers."

Pheosco growled. "Lord Rummon has been gone for thousands of years. His absence caused the dragons to fracture into many smaller communities, which Ergrauth began killing off one by one. We had to unite to exist and we had two options, fight against Ergrauth or fight with him. The land demon had the numbers and the advantage. The choice was made by our ancient leaders to stand with a new leader while we waited for Lord Rummon to return. So, for thousands of years we have been secretly keeping his lair intact. Ergrauth would kill us if he knew we still worshipped another demon."

"It's been that long?" Thorik said with a gasp.

"Of course," Pheosco replied.

"We'll be lucky to find his bones after all that time," Thorik said softly, after pondering the ramifcations of the new information.

"No, not Lord Rummon. He stands like a statue since the moment his soul was ripped from his body."

"Really?" Avanda looked out at the distant mountains and imagined the sight for a second before realizing what he had said. "How would you know this?"

"I have visited his lair," Pheosco said very matter-of-fact.

Avanda's eyes lit up. "You know where he is? You've seen him with your own eyes?"

"Most dragon species make the pilgrimage to his den to pay their respects. I personally make this journey on the day of Reminiscence, like most of my species."

"This is wonderful!" she proclaimed. "We only hoped he was in this mountain range some place. Now we don't have to waste time searching. You can lead us right to him."

Pheosco sat back with a confident look to him. "And why would I help you?"

"What?" She was visibly surprised by the question. "Because we plan to save your leader."

"How do I know this to be true? You could be planning on destroying what's left of his den and his body. You may wish to enslave him."

"We aren't like that. We don't believe in slavery."

Pheosco reached up and tugged at the twine around his own neck. "Really?"

Avanda's soul-markings softened in color from the realization of her act. "But I only did this to keep you from leaving."

"So, it isn't slavery, it's kidnapping?"

"No, it's..." She thought about the situation only for a moment before continuing. "It's wrong. I apologize, Ralph."

"Pheosco."

Leaning forward she loosened the twine and started to pull it up off his neck, but stopped prior to his head. "I would very much like it if you didn't fly away."

"Avanda!" Emilen had noticed her actions. "Don't let that beast free. It's savage."

Emilen's words were all Avanda needed to determine it was the correct thing to do. A swift movement over the dragon's head freed the Del'Unday beast.

Pheosco's wings spread out to full width, over the sides of the rowboat while he screeched a loud deafening high pitched sound. The spikes along the back of his thin neck arched out and his claws extended from his front paws, causing all three Nums to fall backward.

Jerking his head back and forth from Num to Num, Pheosco finally leaped up in the air, gave a strong flap of his wings, and quickly became airborne. The ascent was clumsy at first, due to the ripped wing, but he managed to gain altitude away from the boat.

"Use your magic!" Emilen ordered. "He knows where Rummon is. Stop him!"

Instinctively Avanda grabbed her purse of magic but then stopped and looked up at the dragon struggling to flap away. "No, I won't enslave him to obtain what we need," she said, watching the dragon labor hard to fly to the north end of the lake. "Will he make it to shore safely, Gluic?"

"I'm sure he'll be fine," Gluic replied.

Emilen screamed from the unexpected voice behind her and launched herself forward toward Avanda.

Thorik jumped as well, but it wasn't clear if Gluic's sudden unexpected arrival caused it or if it was Emilen's outburst.

Perched on the rim of the boat, Gluic's oversized eyes rolled in separate directions; one following Thorik and the other following Emilen. After ruffling her feathers and snapping her head forward and back a few times, she addressed Avanda once again. "You just made a friend, my dear. Well done."

Confused, Avanda looked past Gluic at the distant dragon. "I don't think so. He's gone."

"Sometimes your closest friends are far away. And sometimes your deadliest enemies are close by. Which would you rather have?"

With a slight grin, Avanda replied, "To be honest, I'd like it to be the other way around."

"Would you now?" Both of her eyes finally worked together and fixated on Avanda. This would look normal for anyone or anything else, but the unblinking gaze was unnerving coming from the bird Gluic. "Don't be so sure of that."

A slight nod of the head was all that Avanda could manage. The sudden uncomfortable energy she was feeling on the boat had her at a disadvantage.

After the awkwardly long stare at Avanda, Gluic's eyes went their separate ways. "Thorik?"

Sitting up straight to respond to her, Thorik had felt the same odd feeling that Avanda did. "Yes?"

"Land is just north of here. I found a nice beach to stay the night."

"Excellent. It's starting to get dark. We'll follow your lead," he said, watching her clumsily launch herself from the boat. The tips of her wings splashed against the water several times before lifting off.

"Best to do so." Gluic's flight was as erratic as her eyes, swaying uncontrollably to the right and then left. "There are many sharp rocks to navigate prior to the beach. Follow me closely if you wish to avoid them," she shouted back.

Thorik gulped hard, thinking to himself, "Follow *that* course in a rowboat?"

## Chapter 4
# Beach Campsite

Splinters flew as the waves tossed the little rowboat against the jagged rocks in the moonlit evening darkness. The Nums flung about within the small vessel while trying to cling to anything that would prevent them from being ejected into the rough waters.

Thorik used one of his oars to push away from the rock they had just landed on. But, in doing so, the oar wedged itself into one of the many cracks and snapped in half as the boat shifted forward. Unfortunately it wasn't enough to unseat the boat from the rocky landing. They were stuck nearly forty yards from the sandy shoreline.

Pulling the second oar toward the rocky ledge, Thorik pushed with all his might, resulting in nothing more than pitching the boat to one side. He needed more leverage and he needed it before the next wave pushed them higher onto the rock outcropping.

Dropping the oar into the boat, he jumped out and landed on the rock itself. Gripping the side of the vessel, he attempted to lift the boat from the side, but the weight was still too much. His window of time had just about elapsed, for a large wave was mounting and would be on top of them at any moment.

Thorik shifted his attempts to the front of the craft, hoping that if he could at least drop the front of the boat off the rock, the back would follow in after it. Tripping on the rough black rock, he sliced his leg and fell on his side, cutting up his arm and hands. But, there was no time to worry about his pain as he watched the newly formed wave prepare to strike.

Swiveling on the coarse rock, Thorik pressed his feet against the bow of the boat, pushing the front of the boat off the rock. The bottom of the boat scraped along the outcropping, cracking floorboards as the boat turned to fall forward.

Seeing his success, Thorik leapt for the boat just as the vessel fell off the rock and back into the water. It was then that the wave struck, pushing the boat out from under Thorik's landing. Instead, he landed in the churning, bubbling, dark waters of the lake with no idea which way was up. Not that it would matter, for the wave had full control of where he was going, and all the Num could do was hold his breath until it had determined his fate.

The tiny boat quickly began to flood as it was swept swiftly toward the shore while Avanda and Emilen hung on. Avanda grabbed her book and purse of magic from the base of the boat, while Emilen snatched up Thorik's backpack, preventing the items from being soaked.

Prior to reaching the shore, the boat bottomed out on the sand below the surface and abruptly stopped as though an anchor had been dropped. The two Nums fell forward on top of each other and gave each other unpleasant looks before realizing that the boat was still taking on water.

Avanda collected everything she could before stepping out of the boat into hip-high waters and making her way to shore. The waves nearly knocked her over several times.

"What about me?" Emilen said, as though someone should help her to safety.

Avanda stormed toward shore, never looking back. "Stay in the boat for all I care!"

Emilen held onto Thorik's pack with both hands, searching for way to get to land without the risk of being knocked over by a wave. Just as she determined that the only opportunity was to follow Avanda's lead, she noticed a bright blue flaming light leaving Avanda's hands and headed straight toward Emilen's head. "Aww!" she screamed, ducking out of the flame's path.

Avanda had been on shore long enough to grab her components and preform a spell.

"You tried to kill me!" Emilen shouted. "You little witch!"

Avanda didn't reply as she concentrated on the blue light hanging over the water in the dim light of the evening. The flame continued to grow in brightness several feet above the water.

"What are you doing?" Emilen yelled over the noise of the shoreline waves. But she received no response from Avanda.

The hovering light increased again as Avanda focused her energy on her spell.

Meanwhile, Thorik tumbled toward the bottom of the water, waiting for the wave to release him. He continued to frantically look for anything that would give him some orientation of which way was up among the bubbles and sand being kicked up from the lake floor. He could only hope to hold his breath long enough to outlast the turbulence and then make his way for the surface, whichever way that might be.

He then noticed a blue light beaming through the churning water. It was his only option to determine his orientation, so he took it and swam with whatever strength he had left toward the blue light. Fighting the changing flow of the water, he pushed himself harder as the light continued to come into focus until finally he breached the surface and took in a long needed breath.

Ignoring his surroundings at first, Thorik gasped for air until he recovered from the near drowning. Once there, he saw Emilen in the rowboat and Avanda on the shore. He then quickly swam toward them.

Approaching the boat, he could see Emilen reach out toward him. Her face quickly changed to a look of panic. Turning, Thorik saw another wave approaching quickly. Swimming hard wasn't enough to outrun the wave which crashed down on top of him and propelled him quickly toward the beach.

Unfortunately, the boat was between him and the shoreline. He slammed into the rowboat, breaking several more boards from its side and knocking Thorik unconscious.

Emilen grabbed his arm before he drifted under the water and with both hands she pulled with all her strength, lifting him up high enough to rest his arms and head on the side of the boat. With the wave passed and the water temporarily low, she put Thorik's pack on her own back to keep it dry and jumped into the waist-high water. She then grabbed Thorik and dragged him to the beach before lying him down on the safe sand.

"Get your hands off of him," Avanda said. "I'll take care of him."

"I'm fully capable to taking care of him myself."

"He wouldn't be alive to take care of if it hadn't been for my spell."

"Are you blind? I just saved his life from drowning. Besides I know how to take care of him."

"Like you took care of all of us by betraying us to Darkmere?"

Emilen finally looked away from Thorik and directly into Avanda's eyes. "You couldn't possibly start to understand what I've done for our culture. I have served my life for our cause while you gallivant across the lands stirring up trouble."

"You don't understand what we've been through. You weren't there."

"I know more than you think, Avanda. I've seen the twin of Thorik's coffer and every time he adds maps and notes to it, they appear in the other. I've been reading them. I know *exactly* what you've been doing."

Avanda stepped back, feeling suddenly vulnerable knowing that her travels and feelings for Thorik have been exposed to Emilen. "You've been watching us all along and then feeding this information to the evil Dark Lord, Darkmere."

"Absolutely. And Darkmere was the name given to him decades ago by the Oracle, Deleth. He's changed since then. He is now the Terra King and is the rebirth of our Mountain King. He will help our culture. Or at least those who support him."

"You fool!" Avanda shouted. "He's launching a war. The Mountain King would never get us into another war, especially one to destroy another civilization."

"The war is to remove those who don't believe. It is for the best if those opposed to our ways are not around to cause disharmony."

"I can't believe this. You have undermined everything we have been working to accomplish. Thorik and I have been trying so hard to stop Darkmere. The two of us will never allow him to succeed."

"The two of you? *You* have no place with Thorik. He is mine and will always be mine. I've read his notes. I know he still dreams about me. He always will."

Avanda's soul-markings flushed with a dark red color after hearing Emilen's last statement. "He may have once, but he is over you now."

"Have you read any of his notes?" she asked, taking the coffer out of the pack. "Would you like to look for yourself to find out if your assumption is correct?"

Tempted, she was torn between proving her wrong and fearing that Emilen could be correct. "We have fallen in love since you've been gone. I can tell he loves me and is completely over you. I don't need to invade his privacy by reading his notes. He doesn't hide anything from me."

"Really?" A devilish grin crossed Emilen's face. "No secrets? So he's told you about the time we went swimming together in Kingsfoot Lake?"

Avanda shrugged her shoulders. "I would assume lots of people go swimming in the lake."

"Naked?" Emilen added and then waited for Avanda's face to turn sour before continuing. "Yes, just the two of us went swimming in the lake and then we cuddled our naked bodies up against each other as we rested from our strenuous exercise."

Avanda's eyes shifted away, unable to make eye contact with her. "It's a lie."

"No, it's not," she said as she held the coffer out for Avanda to take. "Take a look for yourself. Or ask him after he wakes. It's one of his fondest memories and mine as well."

Avanda snatched the coffer from her and grabbed the clasp, but hesitated before opening it.

Emilen smiled, and returned her free hand to Thorik's head. "But I'm sure you've been intimate with him as well, seeing that you two are in love, correct?"

"That's none of your business."

"Although I find it odd that he hasn't ever logged anything about such romantic encounters. Why do you suppose that is?" Emilen waited for an answer but didn't receive one. "Perhaps there hasn't been any because he is still in love with me."

The clasp flipped off and the lid opened as Avanda had heard enough. She was eager to prove Emilen wrong. Thumbing through the stack of papers, she finally found a few toward the bottom and pulled them out. They were the logs of when they first left Farbank and traveled to Kingsfoot.

Avanda scanned Thorik's notes until she froze in horror. Emilen had been correct. Thorik had made reference to the love and peacefulness of the swim as well as the cuddling naked on the tail of the dolphin statue.

Her eyes became red and tears flowed down her face. She was crushed and didn't know how to react. "How could he do this to me?" she said softly. The words struggled to get out and were barely understandable from her shaking lips.

Being propped up by Emilen, Thorik began to wake from his unconscious state, only to see Avanda holding papers from his open coffer. "What are you doing?" he coughed out as he quickly regained his thoughts.

Avanda didn't know how to react. In some way she didn't care that she had violated his trust by opening his coffer after what she had learned, and then in other ways she felt she was now just as guilty as Emilen for betraying him.

Dropping the coffer and papers, she stood up and ran from him, her hands covering her eyes and face. Running several yards down the beach, she finally came to a stop and sat on a large dry rock that had washed up on shore. She simply couldn't face Thorik now.

"What's going on?" Thorik asked, sitting up slowly. His eyes began to clear but his head was still fuzzy from a headache.

Emilen assisted him up with a slight push to his back. "She looks older than I recall, but she still has the emotions of a child. She can't seem to forgive me for my past with Darkmere, even when I could do nothing to prevent his powerful charm spells. I simply wasn't in control of my life at the time."

"Why was she going through my logs and notes?"

"I asked her the same question. Apparently she does that often. She must have trust issues with you, Thorik. She checks to see what you write in order to see how you really feel about her. She seems very fragile. We should be careful with her and not take too much of what she says to heart."

"That doesn't sound like Avanda."

"I know. I'm disappointed in her as well. But it was just a matter of time before she would get caught. I'm sorry she has violated your trust, Thorik. Thank the King that I was here to save you while she worried about her magic."

"What do you mean?"

"When our boat was sinking and you were drowning, I stayed in the boat to search for you in order to rescue you. Avanda, abandoned the boat to save her magical items. It's no business of mine, but she seems obsessed with magic, especially that book. Even the great Ambrosius warned us of the dangers of using magic and how it was extremely precarious in the hands of the undisciplined user."

Thorik looked across the beach at Avanda, who had her back to him. She had stopped crying and had opened her book of magic, Vesik, to read. "It's frustrating. I have had concerns about her becoming too involved in magic," he said. "In fact, I once received a warning from a spirit about her and Vesik."

"Yes, I know."

The statement struck him odd. "Em, how would you know about the spirit I met, and the warning it gave me?"

Emilen laughed nervously. "No, I meant that I know you struggle to do the right thing and it can be frustrating."

In spite of several cuts on his arms, hands and forehead, he began to stand up. "I should go talk to her to make sure she is fine. Distancing myself from her will only add to her desire for magic more than that of people. She needs my help." As true as the statement was, this was also the first opportunity he would have alone with Avanda to explain how he wished to test Emilen's trust.

Emilen stood up as well, but blocked his path. "Thorik," she said, placing one hand in his and her other on his shoulder. "Let her think about what she did wrong for a little while longer. It's best to allow her the opportunity to apologize to you. Besides, I need your help with my leg. It still hurts from the attack by the eel."

Thorik's attention lowered to her leg. He could see that it was swollen from the injury, perhaps even infected with some type of poison. But even with her obvious need, he still wished to pull away and tend to Avanda first. His relationship with her was too important to ignore her odd behavior during recent events.

Glancing up and over at Avanda for several moments, Thorik watched as Gluic recklessly approached and then landed gently next to her, giving him a bit of comfort. He figured that Gluic would help set Avanda on the right path. Eventually, he allowed Emilen to lead him back down to the ground in order to heal her.

"I hurt," she said, pulling his hand down to the red inflamed skin of her leg.

"Your leg is not well," he said, glancing over his shoulder at Avanda while touching Emilen's skin.

"Ouch! Not so hard."

Thorik refocused onto the leg he was holding. "I'm barely touching you. It couldn't be that bad." But the slightest movement of his hand caused her to flinch from the pain. "That's not good. Lie down and I'll grab my runestones."

"Please hurry, Thorik. The pain continues to grow."

He smiled and shook his head. "Lie down on your back so I can get started."

"What's so funny," she asked, wincing from his touch.

"You're such a girl."

"What's that supposed to mean?"

"Nothing. I'm just so used to Avanda. She would have to be dying before she would ask for help or flinch from an injury. She's pretty tough for a Num."

Emilen scowled for a moment at the comment before quickly changing her attitude. "Yes, Thorik. You are correct. I'm not rough like Avanda. I'm soft and loving like a proper lady. I'm the kind of Num that a man can snuggle with by the campfire and raise children with, a female who will always be there for her man. Avanda is much more of a loner and not much of the loving mother type."

Her words rolled around in Thorik's head, repeating themselves over and over again. They seemed wrong and yet he couldn't define why. He had never thought of Avanda as a mother figure or even the type who would be good at raising children. She was an adventurer at heart and loved living life on the edge with excitement around every corner. Again, what kind of mother would that make?

Thorik placed his runestones around her body while his mind was churning on Emilen's words. Once complete, he looked the stones over to make sure they were in the correct place, the way his grandmother had taught him. Adjusting a few, he placed the runestone of health on her forehead and held it tightly.

Closing his eyes, he allowed his thoughts to drift away, becoming open to whatever the runestone would give him. Within seconds, the gem in the center of the hexagon runestone began to glow.

"Thorik, I can feel a tingling in my head. Is that normal?" Her voice had traces of doubt and concern. "Shouldn't we focus on my leg? That's where the pain is."

Thorik slowly moved his hands off the runestone and to her ears, tracing them several times to the lobes. Each time he shook his fingers as though he was trying to get something off them. "Interesting. You seem to have a lot of negative energy festering just below the skin."

"Thorik!" she announced. "My leg. Get to my leg."

He nodded and methodically hovered his hands down over her face, past her torso and then down to her injured leg, as though he was pushing the energy down her body and into her leg.

Emilen began to squirm. "It's starting to hurt more! Are you sure you're doing it right?"

"Yes, this is normal, from what I can recall when Granna performed this." He continued to push the energy down her leg, but he seemed to be getting resistance, forcing him to work harder to push his hands farther. "Hang on. We're almost there!"

"Awwww!" Her scream could be heard for a mile as the pain gathered in her foot. "Thorik! Stop! I can't take it any longer!"

Thorik ignored her pleas and pushed his hands even harder down her calf and to her ankle. The area he had passed over looked natural again. However, her skin near her foot was bright red as it bulged and bubbled with black pus bursting from pinprick holes in her skin. "I can't push it any farther. Why isn't this working?" he asked himself.

"You forgot to have her remove her shoes," Gluic said, standing behind him, looking over his shoulder like a teacher watching over her student at his test paper.

The sudden startle of her comment nearly caused him to lose control of what he was doing. It took everything he had to regain it.

Emilen continued to scream, but was now thrashing about in her attempt to stop Thorik from what he was doing to her. But before she could do so, Gluic flew over and landed near her feet before reaching over with her beak and snatching her shoe off, sending Thorik's hands down past Emilen's feet along with the pain. Instantly, the pain was gone and her skin stretched back into its normal shape.

Both, Thorik and Emilen, were breathing deeply, from the healing event. It had taken just about everything out of them. Crying, Emilen sat up and wrapped her arms around him, burying her head into his neck and chest.

"It's okay. It's over now," he told her, before giving Gluic a confused expression. "Why did her shoe stop the bad energy from being released?"

Gluic's eyes rolled in different directions until one stopped and focused on him. "Because you thought it would."

"I did?"

Puffing out the feathers on her face, she replied. "Energy flows through anything except what you believe it won't."

Blinking his eyes a few times he thought about what she said while patting Emilen on the back. "You're going to be fine. It's over now. I'm sorry I hurt you."

A clearing of the throat was heard from behind Thorik. Thinking it was Gluic, he didn't turn around. But he heard it again and this time he noticed that Gluic was off to his side. It was Avanda making the noise, and she was standing behind him as he sat on the beach holding onto Emilen. Thorik immediately felt guilty.

Springing to his feet, he popped out of Emilen's grip as though her hands were on fire. Turning his back to her, he stood facing Avanda. "Avanda!" he said, feeling uncomfortable being seen in Emilen's arms. Recent tensions between them had prevented him from having time to show his affection for Avanda, and the unexpected arrival of Emilen after the destruction of Ergrauth had made it even worse. Thorik's chest tightened at Avanda's gaze. "I was trying to heal her, and-"

"Thorik," she interrupted unemotionally. "You need to know that Emilen is working with Darkmere. She told me herself that they have been watching us all this time. She is a spy."

"That's a lie!" Emilen shouted. "I never said that. Where is your proof?"

Avanda didn't allow Emilen to get under her skin, keeping her soft controlled tone when addressing Thorik. "Believe who you want. She's right about one thing. I have no proof but my own ears that she confessed. You have to trust your heart."

Thorik was shocked by the unexpected conversation and couldn't find the words before Avanda continued.

"I understand, Thorik. I'm not your keeper. I love you far too much to keep you from becoming happy, but just watch your back with her." Avanda grabbed his wrist and opened his hand, placing a blue crystal inside it before closing his fingers around it. "You are free."

Thorik opened his hand and looked at the crystal in his palm. It was more than just a stone. It was a symbol of their faith in one another. They had given it to each other when the other needed support the most. It was a symbol of their love.

Opening his mouth to protest, Avanda placed a finger on his lips. "This is not a request for your support. This is to end what we had so you won't feel guilty about getting what you want, what you've always wanted."

Thorik was crushed and didn't know how to respond. Tears formed in his eyes while staring at Avanda while she stepped back away.

Emilen watched the two gazing at each other a few seconds before she turned and rifled through her own gear. Grabbing an item, she delicately stood up on her recently healed leg. In doing so, she accidently bumped against Thorik, causing him to finally blink, as well as breathe.

"Look, Thorik!" Emilen said, holding up a runestone of her own in front of his face. It looked just as old and well-crafted as his own set of runestones. "It's the runestone of Enjoyment."

"Not now, Em," he said as his heart broke.

Not giving up on her attempt to distract him, Emilen continued. "Thorik, this is the very one you lost. The only one you are missing from your collection." She knew it was a weak bid to get his attention, but she tried it anyway.

"It can't be," he said softly, still fixating on Avanda's eyes as she continued to distance herself from him. "I traded it to a merchant in Woodlen for some food, years ago." His mind really wasn't interested on the stone.

"I know," Emilen said. Her coy smile came across in her speech. "I tracked down the merchant and purchased it back for you. You can defeat Darkmere now that you have the full set again."

"What?" Thorik was sure he heard her wrong. It was enough for him to break his thoughts of Avanda. Glancing to see her straight on, he asked, "Em, are you sure that this is the very stone we used to purchase food?"

"Yes, Thorik. I'm absolutely sure." Her smile was contagious and carried the short distance to Thorik's face.

"You don't know how many times I wished I had never given it up," he whispered. "Avanda, do you see this?" he asked, turning to see her expression, only to find her back to him as she slowly walked away. "Avanda!" he called out, but was ignored. He cursed himself under his breath. He had been excited about the runestone and because of his momentary lapse in judgment he ended up pushing Avanda away. He needed to fix his relationship with her before he lost her completely. Emilen and Vesik were pulling Avanda farther away from him.

Grabbing his arm to prevent him from leaving her, Emilen moved in front of him again. "It's late, Thorik, and everyone is tired. We still need to make a fire before it gets much cooler. Let's wait until morning and then the two of you can talk this over."

Thorik struggled with the idea, staring at Avanda's back. He wondered how far would he take this to see if Emilen was trustworthy? Was he willing to risk his future with the young Num he fell in love with, in order to stop Darkmere and conceivably win the war? He needed to find some time with her, away from Emilen and Vesik.

Thorik stepped forward toward Avanda, but was followed by a limping Emilen who hung on him for balance. He stopped and sighed, realizing he wasn't going to get any private time with Avanda without causing any conflict or question of trust. Eventually he gave in and left both Nums in order to gather branches for their fire.

## Chapter 5
# Natives

A small campfire was started on the sandy beach, halfway between the lake shore and the thick brush which lined the area as far as they could see. The dead underbrush snapped easily and made for good kindling, but had to be handled carefully for all of the plants were filled with sharp thorns.

Avanda had returned to the camp without saying a word. She quickly grabbed a blanket and snuggled near the fire next to Gluic, who had been staring into the cloud-free night sky and saying, "Yes, yes, I know. We're on our way," to unseen spirits. This was nothing out of the ordinary for Gluic. She had been doing that since they all left Farbank.

Pulling out Thorik's blanket from his pack, Emilen curled up in it and waited for Thorik as he carried another load of branches to the fire. She was exhausted, but refused to fall asleep until after Avanda had. Reality was, it wasn't long before both women were in a deep sleep.

Thorik finished stoking the fire and then gazed at the stars and moon while contemplating his journey. "What am I doing, Granna? Why am I trying to revive the killer of the Mountain King?" he asked her softly. "Who do I think I am, trying to stop a war? I'm just a Num. I'm not a king or a general of an army. I don't have the training or resources to affect the outcome of these events."

"You are who you decide to be," Gluic said with her beak still in the air while one eye flopped down to look at Thorik.

"Granna, let's be honest, I've made a mess of things and been lucky to survive."

"Luck is nothing more than the prepared mind seeing opportunities that are always around us, my grandson." Her beak rotated a few times but continued to stay up as one eye watched the stars. "You are lucky because you make the most of what is before you instead of letting it slow you down, or stop you in your tracks. Luck is a choice." she squawked.

Thorik snapped another handful of thorny twigs and dropped them into his fire. "But my luck can only carry me so far. It can't stop a war with armies led by demons. Granted, we've had this talk before, and I've overcome obstacles, but none were this grand. It is not realistic to assume a Num, a Num without his soul-markings mind you, can do such a thing."

"That's right, dear. You can't stop a war by yourself." Sharply jerking her head from right to left she kept her focus on the skies as they talked.

Thorik was dumbfounded. "Granna, you're not supposed to tell me that. You're supposed to give me advice and motivate me, not agree that I will fail in my attempt."

"Oh, sorry about that, dear. I didn't know there were rules to our relationship."

"Yes, there is. You're here to help guide me."

Dropping her beak and both eyes down to Thorik, she looked confused. "Really? I wasn't aware that was my charter in life. And here I thought I had other destinies. I don't recall you being born with instructions in your hand for me to follow."

"Of course not. I just meant that I rely on you to help guide me and motivate me."

"And there lies the problem." Her head snapped back up with both eyes scanning the stars.

Thorik waited for more details, but none followed. "What problem, Granna?"

"You. You are your biggest problem."

Slightly crushed from the statement, he didn't know how to respond. "I'm my own problem?"

"Yes, and that is why your soul-markings haven't grown in. Most Nums are honest with themselves at a much earlier age." She paused as she whipped her head to the right to look at another star. "You, on the other hand, use people as a crutch, my dear."

"A crutch?"

"You are always looking for the approval or motivation of others to make up your mind. You question everything you stand for and seek approval before you make your opinion known. You will not be you until you do what you believe is right. Therefore your soul-markings won't grow in."

"But…" Thorik shook his head at the comment. "Are you saying I should be opinionated and short sighted to other options?"

One of Gluic's bird eyes flopped down to stare at him again. "No, my dear grandson. I'm saying stand up for what you believe without prior approval or badgering from your Uncle Brimmelle. You can still be open minded to new ideas." Her eye shot back up to the sky.

Thorik was flustered and was getting tired of her staring at the sky so he peered up to see what she was looking at. "So, I don't have my soul-markings because I don't trust myself?"

"There it is."

"Okay, I think I'm understanding."

"No, dear," she said. "There it is. Just what I was looking for."

Thorik gazed at the night sky, looking for something to reveal itself. Nothing did. "What do you see?"

"Sometimes it's what we can't see." Gluic ruffled her orange feathers on the back of her neck. "What's missing?"

Thorik scanned the sky for another few moments before he noticed what was odd. "Where is the moon? Where did it go?"

"Ah!" squawked Gluic as she laughed with delight. "Isn't it amazing?"

The moon had disappeared and the stars surrounding it were also missing as though a nothingness had swallowed the entire region of the sky and was expanding. Star by star disappeared from their view as Thorik watched in disbelief.

"What's happening, Granna? What could eat the moon and the stars?"

"Only your imagination could do such a thing, dear."

"You mean I'm causing this to happen?"

Gluic laughed. "I said you should have more faith in yourself, not delusions of power. What you see is not always what is happening."

Thorik watched as several more stars were eaten by the dark void. "It's growing faster."

"No. They are growing closer."

"They?"

"Yes. They are blocking our view of the stars and the moon as they approach."

"Who are they?" Thorik asked in a slightly higher pitched tone.

"The followers of Rummon. We are outsiders in their territory. It will be interesting to see if they will allow us to explain our reason for trespassing or if they will just attack and rip us apart for invading their sacred land. The suspense of finding out is marvelous."

Thorik could start making out the flapping of dragon wings on the outer edges of the darkness. At first he feared there were dozens of them until he realized that there were hundreds. His heart sank. "*Marvelous* is not the word I would use," he said, watching the dark outlines of the dragons descend on their uncovered position on the beach. "Wake up!" he screamed to Avanda and Emilen. "We're under attack!"

"We are?" Gluic asked, dropping her beak horizontal and glancing down the beach each way for invaders.

Thorik grabbed his pack. "Run for the brush! We'll hide in there."

Avanda jumped from her sleep and immediately opened her purse of magical components. "What's attacking us? What kind of spell do I need?"

"No time!" replied Thorik, helping Emilen up to her feet. "Make your way to cover."

Still half asleep, Emilen latched on to Thorik's arm. "What is it?" she asked scanning the beach for intruders. "Who's attacking?"

Attempting to push Emilen toward the brush so he could turn and do the same to Avanda, Thorik was unable to remove Emilen's tight hold on him. "Avanda, put those components away and get to safety," he said, as he was pulled toward the brush by Emilen.

Avanda did nothing of the sort. She stayed her ground. Grabbing several key components, she made a few gestures while repeating a few phrases her magic master, Bryus Grum, had taught her. Once completed, a glowing blue ball of light erupted in her hands. It was the same spell she had used earlier to guide Thorik out of the water.

Tossing the ball up in the air, it took on energy of its own as it continued to lift a dozen yards before stopping and floating in one place. It then intensified in brightness, providing Avanda with adequate light to see what was approaching.

Swirling overhead, the Nums could see hundreds of various dragon species, each with their own unique colors and markings. Some wore headdresses or garments with symbols on them, others wore none. Most dragons ranged from the size of an infant Num to a tall human, although there were also some smaller than a sand-rat and a few as large as a chuttlebeast. The scales covering their bodies differed in shape, texture, and reflectiveness. Some had no scales, but leather or fur instead. Some had two legs with arms grown into their wings, while others had four legs as well as wings. No two dragons were the same.

Avanda stood and gazed upward. "Amazing!" she said with a smile as her arms fanned out to welcome them. "How beautiful they are."

Reaching the brush with Emilen in tow, Thorik turned back to the campsite. "Avanda! Get out of there."

She didn't respond to his calls. Instead she enjoyed the view of the dragons flying in a circle around the glowing blue ball, which she was controlling.

Thorik freed his arm from Emilen and handed her his pack and items. "Hide! I'll be right back." He then sprinted for the camp to save his companion.

As he approached, several Num-sized dragons broke away from the rest, diving down toward Thorik at great speeds. He couldn't run faster than they could fly, but he was nimble and clever as he jumped and rolled to one side or another just prior to any dragon claws latching on to his head or shoulders.

Several attack passes were made at Thorik, but each time he rolled out of the way and landed back on his feet heading toward the uninterrupted Avanda. None of the dragons had tried to attack her.

Finally, with only a few yards to go, Thorik reached out to grab her to pull her to safety. Unfortunately he was a few yards too short. One of the dragons landed square on his back, knocking him down onto the sandy beach. A second one landed quickly and helped hold his head down against the cool sand.

Thorik attempted to push himself up, lifting his head and shoulders off the beach, in spite of the two dragons on top of him. However, it was at this point that a much larger dragon landed with a thud before placing a foot on Thorik's back, pushing him back down to the sand.

Thorik was trapped. He couldn't see his companions or what was happening above them. He was at their mercy and would have to wait to see what they planned to do with them.

The sounds of flapping wings grew louder as more approached, though Thorik couldn't see anything more than a few feet in front of him where several dragons had landed and blocked his view. Visually blocked from the events, he could tell that dozens of dragons had landed on the beach and were moving about, kicking up sand as they walked.

A scream was then heard, sounding more like Emilen than of Avanda. It continued but began fading off as if she had left the campsite. "Run to safety!" Thorik shouted before her voice went silent.

"What do you want with us?" Thorik asked, hoping to engage in a conversation where he wasn't being pressed into the sand by a large powerful leg. "Let me free so we can discuss your terms."

He received no answer to his requests. However, one by one, Thorik started hearing the dragons take flight. Eventually, he was able to see from his awkward vantage point that the beach was nearly abandoned, including his companions.

It was then that the heavy weight of the dragon's paw lifted from his back, allowing him to breathe easier and roll slightly to his side. But before he got a good look around, the large brown four-legged dragon, which had been holding him down, grabbed the Num with its front two claws and launched them up in the air. Wings, easily four times Thorik's height, fanned out and began to beat hard to carry their weight high into the air.

Arms locked at his sides by the massive claws, Thorik looked back down at the empty beach. They had been the last to leave the small camp. Avanda and Emilen were nowhere to be seen, at least until he gave up on the campsite and looked forward.

Before him were dragons as far as his powerful Num eyes could see in the moonlit night. They were traveling north over the black stained mountains.

"Where are you taking me?" he yelled out to the dragon carrying him.

The creature ignored the Num and continued to follow the rest. His brown scales appeared dirty and many of them were missing. He was also the largest in weight of all the dragons in the group, but it was the smell of the creature that bothered Thorik the most. It was a dirty sweaty smell that covered the underbody mixed with a bad breath that rolled out of the dragon's open mouth as its tongue hung out to the side. Slobber rolled down the thick tongue and periodically splatted on Thorik's head.

Wiping the drenching from his face onto the side of brown dragon's front leg, Thorik began looking for his friends within the claws of other dragons. "Avanda?! Emilen?! Are you out there?"

"They're doing just fine, dear," Gluic said, flying just behind him and off to the side. Her flight path was much more erratic than the dragon's but she was able to keep up. "They are up front."

Thorik was so relieved to hear her voice that the shock of her being there never materialized. "Where are they taking us?"

"To their den, I believe."

"To see Rummon so we can set him free?" he asked, hopeful of her answer.

"That, or perhaps to sacrifice you to Rummon for invading his lands." Flapping harder to gain speed, she began to lunge forward toward the front of the pack. "I do so enjoy being able to fly. I can't thank you enough, my dear." With that, she haphazardly flew away from him into the moonlit night.

A large glob of dragon saliva splattered on Thorik's head, rolling down his neck and under his shirt. The dragon's claws, which held him tight, prevented him from using his arms to wipe his face clean, so he shook his head in order to clear the thick liquid from his eyes and lips. The small amount that entered his mouth tasted like stomach acid with a sandy grit mixed within.

Thorik spit the syrupy slobber from his mouth but couldn't remove the vile taste from within it. He eventually rubbed his face against the dragon's legs in an attempt to clean his face. With only partial success, he was able to see fairly well again.

They continued to fly along high into the mountains and, thanks to the help of the moon, he was able to see the various mountains they flew over. Many had snowcapped peaks, while others were black as ash. A few showed signs of heat, as red glowing magma churned to the surface. Unfortunately the direction they headed led to a large cluster of these forbidding looking mountains.

"At least it will be warmer there," he said to himself, knowing the dragon wasn't going to reply. "It's freezing up here." With adrenaline waning, his body was beginning to shake from the cold of the brisk night air. The more he thought about it, the colder he became. He could feel the once warm dragon saliva starting to cool and then start to ice up on his skin. The wind on his face made it worse. The Num began to panic as he felt his exposed skin freezing up like the great King's River in the dead of winter.

"Help!" he cried out to the dragon carrying him. "I'm freezing to death!"

To his surprise, the dragon tilted his head down to look at the Num. And with a gurgle in his throat, the dragon caughed up a large glob of phlegm which poured over Thorik's head and down his body.

As disgusting as the putrid liquid was, it was very warm, providing him with a liquid blanket against the harsh cold air. Thorik shook enough off his face to breathe and use his eyes again. The rest he allowed to stay on for the remainder of the airborne journey.

## Chapter 6
# Dragon's Den

Their flight eventually began to descend toward a dark mountain where dried lava flows coated its sides between ridges. Towers of sharp crystalized black points angled in every direction along the dead mountain landscape. The smell of sulfur filled Thorik's nose and rolled down his throat. Cracks in the erratic land exposed flowing magma just below the surface which heated the air within which they traveled.

A red glow from the lava reflected off the dragons in front of Thorik, allowing him to see them better. The entire group lined up and lowered themselves toward the ground, swooshing around sharp rocks and tight bends as they continued to descend.

Thorik watched the procession disappear to the right and then to the left, banking hard and just missing the jagged rocks. Eventually they disappeared inside a tunnel of absolute darkness. But somehow, Thorik's dragon knew when to turn, pitch and lower in order to avoid crashing into a wall as the passageway snaked its way into the dark mountains.

Without warning, the tunnel opened up into an enormous cavern lit with room-sized vats roaring with fire. Terraced on every wall, Thorik immediately recognized that this was no random cavern. It had been carved out specifically for the gathering of dragons with places to perch in every conceivable location. And in fact, most of the sites were either occupied or becoming filled by the dragons that had been flying in with Thorik.

Dumped on the floor in the center of the cavern, Thorik tumbled to his knees. Thick, grainy saliva gave the landing a splat sound and slowly ran down his body when he stood up. Before him were dragons in every direction. Spinning slowly to take it all in, he saw the other Nums.

"Avanda! Emilen!" he cried out, running to greet them.

Emilen did the same, running to meet him halfway, but stopped when she noticed the ooze running down his body. "What happened to you?"

"The dragon coated me with his spit to keep me warm." He had assumed the other dragons had done the same to her. "How were you able to keep warm?" he said as she handed him his backpack.

"I was tucked up under the dragon's breast plate. I wasn't able to see anything but its body heat was more than enough."

"I wonder why my dragon didn't do that," Thorik asked, glancing back at the dragon that had carried him.

The large frumpy brown dragon sat on the ground like a dog waiting for a treat; his tail wagging and drool running out of his mouth and down his neck. A momentary shaking of his head sent spittle in every direction.

Thorik needed no additional explanation to his special treatment. Collecting handfuls of the heavy liquid, he began to scrape his body clean, while Avanda approached the other Nums.

"What do you suppose they want?" Avanda asked, scoping out the audience of creatures watching from their perches. One such creature seemed out of place. It was more of a bird than a dragon. "Gluic?" she said softly to herself.

Overhearing her comment, Thorik followed Avanda's gaze to a colorful bird roosting on a ledge alongside the dragons. Its beak shifted back and forth and up and down while its eyes surveyed the cavern in different directions.

"Yes, it's her," Thorik said, relieved that she was still with them. Placing his pack on, he gave a grin to his grandmother.

The mood quickly returned to concern as all of the dragons on the main floor backed away from the Nums, except for three human-sized ones. Flapping their wings, they gracefully descended to the center of the cavern near the Nums before the lead dragon spoke in a regal tone. "I am the Grand Watcher." His head and long neck were decorated with ornate gems and finely crafted gold lace. A symbol of a dragon's eye was etched into golden plates hanging from several chains around the gray and black scales of his neck. "You, little critters who have infected our land with your filth, profess the power to revive our Lord Rummon?" The condescending manner was intentional.

The Nums exchanged glances at how he could have known what they had intended to do. "Did you say something? Who told them? I didn't tell them." they said softly over each other.

Clearing his throat, the Grand Watcher stifled the Nums from whispering to one another. "Stop murmuring about! Speak one at a time, in a nature worth me listening."

Thorik stepped forward. "I am Thorik Dain of Farbank."

"I didn't ask for your name," the dragon replied.

"Oh, sorry."

The Grand Watcher shook his head at the little Num with displeasure.

"We have come to give Rummon-"

"*Lord* Rummon," the dragon quickly corrected before Thorik could continue.

"Yes, we have come to give Lord Rummon's soul, his very essence, back to his body."

The crowd of dragons along the terraced sides erupted in hissing, screams and yelling. Even the overweight dragon, that carried Thorik into the cavern, joined in the yelling before exploding a dark vapor out of his backside and then turned to sniff it.

After a moment of watching, Gluic winked at the dragon next to her and then joined in with her own hissing. Her head snapped back and forth from right to left. Each time a dragon on either side of her screamed out, she followed suit with the same comment, eager to be a part of the excitement.

Raising his head and snapping his wings out to his sides, the Grand Watcher caused the crowd to immediately cease their uproar; all except the brightly colored bird which got in one last jab at the Nums.

The lead dragon then stepped closer and looked down at Thorik, making his height obvious and intimidating. "We have been waiting for generations to revive our Lord Rummon. His loyal servants, those of the air, have searched from the skies and land for a way to bring him back. Why would we believe that a land creature, such as yourself, has been successful in finding what we could not?"

"I looked where those of the air did not. I looked *under* the land, in the heart of Carrion Mire." Thorik said, reaching back and pulling his spear forward from his pack.

Jerking away, the Grand Watcher showed his teeth at what he perceived to be Thorik's aggressive grab for a weapon. The two other dragons with him, jumped in front to protect their leader and showed their claws and spread their wings before pouncing on Thorik and stripping him of the weapon.

The crowd growled and hissed at the Nums, including the bird, who found the entire event entertaining.

"No!" Thorik cried out over the intense noise. "That is the Spear of Rummon, the very weapon that was used on him in order to remove his soul. We have returned it here to give it back."

Releasing the Num, one of the guards stepped back and held the spear out for the Grand Watcher to examine.

Thorik stood back up, keeping a keen eye on the spear. He needed it back to complete his mission.

"See, Grand Watcher, what I told you was the truth," came a smaller voice from behind the three dragons standing before the Nums. As the perceived threat from Thorik was now removed, the two guard dragons backed off. Once they moved to the sides, the Nums could see where the smaller voice came from. Standing next to the Grand Watcher was a small green dragon.

"Ralph!" Avanda said with delight.

"Pheosco," he replied dryly.

"Thank you for having your friends bring us here so we can revive Rummon."

"*Lord* Rummon," the Grand Watcher sternly insisted.

"And," Pheosco added, "These are not my friends. They are the followers of Lord Rummon, those of the air. Your pleasure of being here may be short lived."

"I'm confused," Avanda said. "This is a time to celebrate the rebirth of your leader."

Pheosco bowed to the Grand Watcher for permission to step before him and he received the acceptable nod of approval. "It is still in question whether we shall allow you to attempt such an act."

"Why?" asked Thorik and Avanda at the same time.

Pheosco ignored Thorik and continued to speak to Avanda. "There are several reasons. For one, you may be deceitful in your quest and actually wish to harm him."

"We would never do such a thing."

"Yes, I noticed how kindhearted you were to the City of Ergrauth as it now lies in ruins."

Avanda glanced at Thorik but didn't wait for him to step in. "But we didn't-"

Pheosco stopped her with a jerking of his head up. "It matters not. The demon, Ergrauth, has ruled over us far too long as it is. This may be good for our species to come back to our own roots."

Thorik watched the guard inspect the Spear of Rummon. "How can we gain your trust so we can perform the needed spell and revive Lord Rummon?"

Again, Pheosco kept his attention on Avanda. "Even if we trusted you, there are many who do not wish this to happen."

Lowering herself onto one knee, Avanda looked at him at his eye level. "Why wouldn't they want such a thing?"

"We have followed the philosophy of Lord Rummon for generation after generation. We have built our lives and beliefs on them. These thoughts are who we are and what we stand for. They are our very foundation and dictate every decision we make."

Avanda nodded. "I don't see the conflict."

"What if we misunderstood him before his soul was stolen, or perhaps if the stories have been changed over time? What if the ancient writings on his statements were not true or were interpreted wrong? What if the ideas we believe and the morals we share aren't correct? If Lord Rummon is revived and says something different, how do we go on knowing that we have wasted our lives on false beliefs?"

All three Nums stood motionless, pondering this new perspective. They had never considered such an issue.

Pheosco squinted his eyes and lowered his voice a bit. "What if Lord Rummon awakes and is angry with us for living against his wishes? His wrath could kill us all. How do we make such a decision with these unanswered questions?"

"So you don't want him revived?" Avanda asked Pheosco as well as the Grand Watcher who stood behind the smaller dragon.

"Of course we do," Pheosco replied. All creatures of the air wish this. But if he is different than what we have been taught, then who is to say the correct soul has been placed within him. What proof do you have that the essence within that spear is truly his. Right now, our faith in our beliefs keeps us unified. Lord Rummon's return could divide us between those who question whose essence possesses our Lord's body and those trusting that it is truly him."

Thorik looked around at the cavern filled with every dragon type imaginable. "Have you never thought this day would come?"

"We've been waiting for it our entire lives," Pheosco said.

"Then why have these questions not been resolved?"

"Time has created just the opposite effect. The issue has grown more intense over the years, polarizing those of the air into two factions. It is more volatile now than ever before."

"We sure have perfect timing," Emilen said to Thorik. "Perhaps we should leave and let them fight it out amongst themselves."

Pheosco overheard her comment. "You cannot leave. No outsiders can ever leave without permission from Lord Rummon himself."

The Nums looked at each other before Thorik spoke up. "But he can't give permission unless we release his soul back into his body."

"Correct."

"But if you don't allow us to revive him, we can't leave? We surely can't live here."

"Correct, again," Pheosco said. "If the answer is no, then you will be eaten. This is sacred land and you are trespassers. Trespassers are not welcome here."

## Chapter 7
# Prisoners

Pheosco and two large gray dragons escorted Thorik, Avanda and Emilen out of the main cavern, through various tunnels and into a small room. Random intervals of blue light were given off by dripping oil from the cavern's ceiling into small shallow pools in the floor, which had been lit on fire. On occasion, a flame would work its way up an elongated drip from above causing a thin vertical thread of fire for a moment, causing a flash of light within the cave. The burning of these oils gave off a thin gray smoke which hung in the deep caves, irritating the Num's eyes and throats.

After the two dragon escorts stopped at the open entrance to the Num's waiting room, Pheosco entered with Thorik and company. "You will remain here until the Grand Watcher has determined whether you can attempt to transfer the soul of Lord Rummon or be eaten and the spear destroyed."

"I want my spear back," Thorik said firmly, without receiving any acknowledgement from Pheosco.

Avanda looked around at the small cavernous room with smooth walls, ceiling, and floor. It looked uncomfortable and cold. Clearing the smoke from her throat she asked, "How long will we be here, Ralph?"

"Pheosco," he corrected before answering. "It could be hours or weeks. It is not my place to determine the will of the Grand Watcher. He has the right to avoid making any decision if he so pleases."

"We can't survive down here," Emilen spoke up with a cough. "You have to help us escape."

Keeping his eyes on Avanda, the small green dragon replied, "I don't have to help you do anything. I will, however, have some food and skins brought to you to keep you warm for your stay."

Wiping his eyes free of the smoke ash, Thorik had noticed that Pheosco always addressed Avanda when he spoke. "Are you in some type of debt to Avanda?"

"She freely released me from slavery, even though it was her that put me into it."

Avanda was surprised by his choice of words. "Slavery? I simply placed a twine around your neck to keep you from leaving."

Nodding, the dragon agreed. "You had me under your control. We call this slavery. But you allowed me to leave by your own volition. Per Lord Rummon's words, I am now bound to you." He turned and began leaving the room.

"You mean you'll do whatever I say?" she announced with pleasure, before coughing. "Then free us and help us escape."

Stopping between the two large mean-looking dragons guarding the room, he turned and looked back at Avanda. "I said I am bound to you. I didn't say I am your slave again. There is a difference. I will do what I can, when I can, to help you. But I will not jeopardize my good standing in our order, nor will I tarnish my faith, just to appease your needs for a whimsical command you haven't fully thought through." With that, he left from their view.

The Nums were uncomfortable and tired. They hadn't slept and the danger before them kept their minds racing on ways to solve their dilemma. Leaning up against the walls, they all sat quiet for a time, covering their nose and mouth with cloths, wondering what would happen next, as the smoke from the burning oil wafted into the room.

Bored, Thorik pulled out his sack of runestones in order to find out what secrets they held. His Uncle Brimmelle had always discouraged him from tapping into the runestone powers. In his uncle's eyes, such powers should only be obtained by the ancient Mountain King himself and using them was seen as a violation to the King.

Seeing that his uncle was not with them, and there was simply nothing else to do, Thorik grabbed one for testing while Emilen looked on with curiosity. "Let's try the Runestone of Pride," he said to Emilen. Flat and hexagon in shape with a large crystal in the center, just like the rest of the runestones, this one had four tan smaller outer gems with the large center one of green. Each runestone had a unique raised pattern on top and many shared similar outer gems. It was easy to mistake one from another. However, Thorik had them memorized by touch alone on the raised ridges.

Thorik adjusted the runestone in his hands, placing three of its smaller gems in one hand and the fourth gem on the opposite side in his other before closing his eyes. There was always some anxiety with the first time he tried to meditate with a new runestone, causing the effects to be uncontrolled and thankfully less powerful than what they could be. In addition, the smoke in the room continued to fill his lungs, making it that much more difficult to relax for the task at hand.

Sensations of electricity raced up his arm, through his body, and back down his other arm. Holding his breath, he felt his body fill with air. Squinting, he checked to see if the massive air bubble in his lungs was causing his chest to expand. It felt as if it had increased tenfold in size, however it had only lifted slightly.

Anticipating something to happen, he glanced around the room waiting for the floor to sink in, or the ceiling to collapse, or the air to change color. Anything was possible.

Nothing was happening, other than the strained feeling from his chest being filled with air.

Emilen searched for some type of event to take place as well. "Well, do you see anything?"

He shook his head and released his breath in a slow sigh of relief that no damage had been done. In doing so, a wave of fresh air sprang forth from the runestone, clearing the oil's gray smoke in the room and then down the hall as far as they could see. There had been no gust of wind pushing the smoke away. Instead, the air had simply been purified.

Emilen breathed in deeply and smiled. "That went well. Try another."

Thorik released the runestone, ending the cleansing, and tossed it back into the sack. But before he could grab another one, Emilen had already done so, and handed it to him.

"Try the Runestone of Love," she said with a wink.

"Sure, why not?" he replied in a dry tone. He had learned that the name of the runestone rarely had anything to do with the power it possessed. However, he doubted that she realized this.

Avanda rolled her eyes at the obvious flirting by Emilen.

Holding onto the hexagonal stone with both hands, Thorik closed his eyes and allowed the energy from within the stone and the crystal in the center to travel up one arm, across his chest, and then back down the other, allowing the runestone to release its powers. He was very excited about the possibilities after the success of the last one. Perhaps he could still save them from their situation.

Sitting cross-legged and smiling uncontrollably, he quickly felt his body begin to sink. The stone wall and floor near him had turned into mud. Thick glops of mud slid down the wall and slapped onto Thorik's back, while his legs sank into the liquefied floor.

Avanda chuckled at the sight. "That should come in handy," she said, opening up Vesik to study spells that could actually benefit them.

Thorik was embarrassed. Just when he felt slightly cocky about his ability to impress the other Nums, something always seemed to go wrong.

Even Emilen sat back and laughed at the sight of the now muddy mess of a Num, before she finally helped him out and then helped clean off the majority of his clothes.

Once that was completed, they all decided to get some rest until they found out the decision on Rummon's fate, as well as their own. The air was now fresh and resting was more comfortable, but the endless waiting was driving them crazy.

It was hours before any movement in the hallway could be seen. So, it was a pleasant sight to spot the approach of the oversized brown dragon which had carried Thorik from the beach.

Slowly waddling back and forth as he walked on all four legs, the brown dragon approached the opening.

"What do you got there, Chug?" one of the guards asked.

Lifting his head, Chug showed the mouthful of white and fury skins wrapped around a slab of meat for the Nums. His long tongue hung off to the side and drool dripped from the end.

"Yeah, I see it. Drop your load off before you make a mess on the floor," said the guard, watching the pool of saliva form on the floor.

Chug nodded and straightened his overly thick neck before squeezing into the passageway to the room.

"So, your name is Chug?" Thorik asked.

Hearing the Num say his name, Chug nodded and his eyes opened wide. He smiled the best he could with a mouthful and then placed his head down against Thorik's side as though he wanted to be petted.

Cautiously, Thorik lifted a hand and gently placed it on the wide snout of the dragon.

Chug's tail began flailing about, slapping the dragon guards outside the room.

Realizing it was safe, Thorik began to pet Chug on top of his head and then behind his ears, causing the dragon's eyes to roll back in their sockets with pleasure.

Sighing with delight from the relaxation of Thorik's touch, a gurgling noise could be heard from Chug's stomach. It was quickly followed by a loud blast of brown vapors exploding from beneath his tail, which was now straight back and up at an angle.

The fumes filled the hall, causing the guards to gasp for air.

"Chug! Get out of here!" one guard yelled as they both began kicking the larger dragon's backside. "Drop your load and leave!"

Chug smiled and gave Thorik a wink after hearing the comment.

Thorik's eyes grew large as he watched the dragon squint his eyes and groan. "Chug? You're not going to-"

Before he could finish the sentence, a loud splat hit the hallway floor. Chug had dropped his load.

Once complete. Chug's eyes opened wide and he dropped the supplies on the room's floor before slapping his tongue upside Thorik's body, knocking the Num over.

Screams and yelling could be heard from the guards as Thorik regained his legs. "Thanks, Chug. We could really use the skins to keep warm."

"They're all wet!" Emilen said, grabbing the end of one and showing Thorik how Chug's drool had soaked into the cloth.

Chug nudged open the rest of the skins with his snout. Once the slab of meat was exposed, they could see that it was half of a recently killed wild boar. The back half had already been eaten, most likely by Chug, and the rest of this fresh meat was for the Nums.

Emilen recoiled from the sight, while the other two were only startled. The blue light from the burning oil, dripping from the ceiling, flickered against the boar's face and open eyes, giving all of the Nums a sense that death was too near for all of them.

"We can't eat this raw!" Emilen reprimanded Chug, causing his face to look sad.

But before they could get any more out of the beast, he began to move backward. The guards had cleaned up his mess, and were dragging him backward out of the room.

Once fully in the hallway, they scolded him again for his misdeeds and sent him on his way before returning to their post just outside the Num's room. A dark soiled spot remained in the middle of the hallway between the guards who continued to complain about Chug's actions.

The lingering stench wafted into the room, causing the Nums to find dry parts of the fury skins in which to hide their nose. It was a most unpleasant smell.

Eventually the unpleasant odor faded and Thorik decided to clean up the other smelly mess by using the bottom of his boot to roll the boar head over near the room's entrance. The Nums were not starving enough to try their hand at eating raw pork.

Emilen had found a dry skin and was waiting for Thorik to settle in next to her. She innocently gazed at him and smiled warmly each time he gave her a look.

Removing her book of magic from her pack, Avanda opened Vesik and began to read while sitting on the opposite side of the room from Emilen. She gave no glances or interest in Thorik's doings as he tidied up the room.

Thorik tended to pace and straighten up a room when he was nervous or unsure of his next action. Pacing was a last resort when he couldn't keep his hands busy. "How can we help influence the decision when we aren't even part of the discussion?" he asked himself.

"We had a chance to speak before we were removed," Emilen replied. "Hopefully that was enough."

"No, we were escorted from their chamber before I had a chance to convince them of what needs to be done." His anxiety was up and he was flustered about the situation he had put them all in.

Emilen reached over, opened Thorik's pack and pulled out his coffer. "We could ask for help."

He stopped in his tracks. "What do you mean?"

"Thorik, I know what this is. It's a prattle box. Everything you write on paper and set inside appears on the paper in the twin prattle box."

Thorik was stunned at her knowledge of such things. Even Avanda looked up from Vesik and glared at Emilen.

"Em, how could you know of such things?" he asked.

"Darkmere told me about it. He said that both he and his twin brother, Ambrosius, received them as gifts when they were children. Ambrosius still has his, and now you have Darkmere's. He complained that this is how Ambrosius was always able to keep one step ahead of him."

"Are you sure Darkmere didn't have the twin?"

"I'm sure. He was eager to collect yours."

Taking the old wooden coffer from her, Thorik held it out to inspect it again, as though it would give him clues to the truth he had never seen before.

"She's a liar, Thorik," Avanda said. "How can you possibly listen to anything that comes out of her mouth? She spews more poison than a serpent."

Biting her lip at the verbal stab, Emilen composed herself and returned her efforts to Thorik. Standing up and approaching him, she tapped her finger against the wooden box. "Who gave you this coffer?"

Thorik took in a deep breath. "A traveler named Su'I Sorat." Flipping the coffer over, he pointed at the base of the box. "He carved his name onto the bottom so I wouldn't forget his kindness."

Still, gawking over the top of her book, Avanda smirked at Emilen. "See. It belonged to someone else."

Emilen smiled back. "Thorik, what's Ambrosius' brother's name? Before the Oracle Deleth gave him the name Darkmere? What was his birth name?"

Thorik thought for a moment. "The Dovenar King's sons were born Ambrosius and Tarosius."

Glaring an evil grin toward Avanda, Emilen asked the last question along these lines. "Can you read Su'I Sorat's name backward for me?"

"Taros I'Us...Tarosius! Em, you're right! This is the twin to Ambrosius' prattle box!" He began dancing in place with excitement before grabbing her in a tight hug, which she eagerly returned.

Ever since he had learned of his coffer's powers he had always wondered who had the twin and who was reading all of his notes. "I had only wished for Ambrosius to be reading my travels. But not knowing for sure, I had to be careful as to what I wrote down. Now I can let him know exactly what is going on and that I know he is reading them. This way he will feel open to writing me back with advice."

"Not so fast, Thorik." Avanda closed her book, tucked it under her arm, stood up and walked over to him. "We don't know who has the other prattle box. This could be a trap, or at the very least a misunderstanding."

"Avanda, Look!" Releasing Emilen, he displayed the carved name in the base of the box. "It's his name spelled backwards. This is Darkmere's prattle box. There is no misunderstanding."

Stepping back away from the box being placed so near her face, she sighed and regrouped. "Fine, think whatever you want. You obviously want to embrace Emilen's ideas. Her words are golden and mine are stupid or childish."

"I didn't say that." He pointed at the carved letters on the base again. "But the facts are there before our eyes. It just makes sense."

"You know what doesn't make sense, Thorik?" she shouted, being pushed past the point of disappointment to anger. Racing up her neck, her interlacing soul-markings flushed red. "What doesn't make sense is that Emilen used us for Darkmere's gain. She left us for him and has been working for him ever since. And now, in the far reaches of our land, she shows up with treasures from your past. A runestone which you had always wished you hadn't given away. Knowledge of the prattle box you had desired to have. On top of all that, she is giving you her body and obedience which you have lusted for since the day you met her!"

Thorik was shocked at the tirade. "Avanda, what has gotten into you?"

"Me? You're the one that has changed. Your love for her has made you blind, when you are normally so observant."

"Love for her?"

To Thorik's horror, she snatched the prattle box from him, flipped the clasp, and swung the lid open. But before he could stop her, she reached toward the bottom and pulled out several papers. Rifling through them, she pulled out one and pushed it toward his face, dropping the rest on the ground. "I know about your swim with Emilen. I know what you did and how important it is to you! I know that I can never live up to this image you have of her. But I can't stand watching her take you down this path again. Even if you're no longer in love with me, I still love you too much to see you destroy your life!"

Embarrassed about what he wrote on the paper, Thorik became defensive. "Avanda, this is not the right time for this!" he shouted back. "We're about to be eaten for trespassing!"

"Not the right time? When is the *right* time? When the Del'Unday are chasing us out of the City of Ergrauth, when the Guardian insects are attacking us, when the demon Bakalor has captured us in Della Estovia, or when waves are crashing us up on rocks and sinking our boat? There is *never* a good time for you to talk about these things!" Her tight fists shook at the bottom of her straightened arms near her sides. She was furious and fit to be tied.

"You had no right to go through my things," Thorik said, defending himself. "These are my private thoughts and memories. How could you break my trust by doing this?"

"Break your trust?" she said before stepping up to him and placing her face nearly against his. "Break *your* trust? I can't believe you have the nerve to say such a thing after your escapades with Em."

"This isn't fair. You broke into my private notes and are mad at me for something I did a very long time ago. At the time, my relationship with you was as a teacher to a student. I didn't have any romantic feelings for you back then. So I wasn't doing anything wrong by being with Emilen."

Like a slap of a wet rag across her face, she stood there in silence, stunned by his words. Eventually, she slowly, calmly, began to talk again. "I guess that's where we differ, Thorik. I've *always* had feelings for you."

Turning her back to him, she began to walk back to her corner of the room.

"Avanda..." Thorik said, realizing what he had said hurt her, but it was the truth. He had fallen in love with Avanda after Emilen had left his life. To crucify him for his acts prior to that was unfair. "Avanda, I'm not done talking about this."

His words had no effect on her and, as expected, she sat down and buried her head in the book of magic, shutting off all interaction with him.

Emilen struggled to hold in her obvious pleasure over the fight. The more the two distanced themselves, the more likely Thorik would support her needs. Tossing her curly, golden and red hair over her shoulder, she moved closer and whispered into his ear. "How ungrateful she is, after everything you've done for her."

Her words made his blood pulse faster through his body. He felt betrayed and unjustly convicted by Avanda. "Avanda, I'm talking to you!"

Lifting the book higher, Avanda used Vesik to block him from her view.

"Magic," Emilen said softly. "You were right, Thorik. She only seems to care about her magic. The more she knows, the more distant she becomes, and the more dangerous she is."

Thorik nodded in agreement. "Avanda, put Vesik down." He only waited a few seconds before continuing. "You can't solve your problems with magic. It's unsafe and unstable, and you seem to become more and more reliant on it."

Avanda's muffled voice finally floated out from behind the book. "I don't know. Looks like I can solve just about anything with what's written in these pages."

"No, you can't," he replied back.

Avanda's eyes peered slightly above the ridge of the book as one eyebrow raised in a very devious manner. "Want to test that?"

Thorik had seen enough of her magic to know two truths. First, she was fully capable of casting spells. Second, her spells often had much worse effects than even she had planned.

Backing off slightly, he allowed her to have her space. He would address his concerns with her obsession with magic in a less confined location.

## Chapter 8
# Escaping Judgement

Thorik's Log: October 3rd of the 650<sup>th</sup> year.

*It's been at least a day since Avanda, Emilen and I have been taken prisoner by Rummon's followers, as they determine whether or not we will be allowed to attempt the rebirth of Rummon or be murdered for perceived crimes against him. If we are fortunate enough to be allowed to try the soul transfer from the spear back into his body, we could still be murdered if it is unsuccessful. Our only chance is to be allowed to cast the spell and be effective in doing so.*

Silence filled the cavern hallway, aside from the soft sound of crackling from the blue flames within the pools of oil. The stagnant air hung on the Nums while they waited for some answer as to their fate. The smell of the raw meat from the half boar continued to become more pungent with each hour. Time seemed to move slowly.

Avanda repositioned herself every few minutes, sometimes with her head hanging like a branch with a far too heavy apple hanging from the end. Other times she would lie on her back with her legs and feet straight up the wall. And other times she would make her arms or legs into knots as she tried to make sense of the magical book of spells.

Once in a while she would let out a gasp or a sigh when she finally figured out another glyph or symbol on a page. "It's as much of a puzzle as it is a spell book," she muttered to herself.

Thorik had finally collapsed from fatigue and boredom as they waited for a response to their request to save Rummon.

Once he was sound asleep, Emilen quietly moved from his side. She kept a keen eye on Avanda while moving toward Thorik's coffer. Opening it with a delicate finesse, she slipped in a piece of paper before closing the clasp and placing it back where Thorik had left it. Before anyone had noticed, she had moved up against Thorik's back to keep herself warm.

Nevertheless, even with the soft long fur skins, she struggled to fall asleep on the hard floor. She tried propping her head up with an extra skin, before trying her arms, and then Thorik's pouch full of runestones. Nothing seemed to work.

Sitting up from her uncomfortable sleeping arrangements, she sniffed the air. It still had the foul air from the fresh half boar that bled in the corner. "Better you than me. I plan to make it out of here in one piece," she said under her breath to the dead Fesh'Unday, before trying to relax once again, snuggling up to Thorik. It wasn't easy but eventually exhaustion took over.

After drifting off to sleep, a rumbling began. It started off as a low, distant vibration and quickly became clearer as pounding feet could be heard. The entire room started to shake, causing even Avanda to look up from Vesik.

Thorik finally jolted awake and sprang to his feet. Unaware of what was happening and still half asleep, he peered down the hallway as the pools of oil were stomped out one after another while moving toward the little room. Following the series of extinguishing flames, something was racing down the hall toward their room. The veil of smoke prevented the vision needed to see who it was.

The guards out front stood their ground, waiting for whatever it was to get close enough to know what they were up against. By the time they realized what the shadowy figure was, it was too late to stop it. One of the guards cried out before being slammed against the wall from the speeding mass. "Chug!"

Barreling up to the room's entrance, the large brown dragon followed a small green dragon at an uncontrollable speed. Pheosco sailed into the room before extending his wings like a parachute to catch him, while Chug body-blocked the second guard into the wall. With both guards knocked out, Chug stuck his thick neck and wide smiling snout into the room before dropping the Spear of Rummon out of his mouth and then knocking Thorik over with a slap of his tongue.

"Drop your clothes!" Pheosco yelled to the Nums, who were obviously stunned by the entire situation, let alone his request. Snatching an extra shirt from a pack, the dragon began shredding it apart. "Chug, grab the Fesh!"

Carrying out the small green dragon's orders, Chug picked up the boar in his mouth and squeezed it tight, his teeth easily ripping through layers of flesh and bones. Then, like a dog after getting wet,

Chug shook his head and neck, spraying the room with blood and peeled off bits of meat.

The Nums shielded their faces from the splattering of skin and internal organs. Avanda covered Vesik in her own clothes to protect it before covering her own head. Unsure what was happening, Thorik instinctively collected the spear and his pack.

"Hurry, if you wish to stay alive!" Pheosco yelled, ripping off a large chunk of Thorik's shirt before slicing it up and tossing it about.

"What are you doing?" Thorik asked, trying to stop the green dragon from stripping him down naked.

"Saving you, so you can release Lord Rummon!" Grabbing Avanda's pack, he attacked it as though it was prey, ripping it into pieces and tossing them in every direction.

Soon, blood soiled walls dripped with fleshy bits and fragments of clothes from Chug and Pheosco's attack. It looked like a massacre, although none of the Nums had been hurt.

"That should do," Pheosco told the brown dragon. "Back up and let the Nums climb on." His voice showed signs of being nervous as he rushed the words.

Avanda never thought twice. Holding Vesik tight under her arm, she climbed up Chug's neck and onto his back. It was obvious that she trusted Pheosco.

"But-" Thorik didn't have time to finish his thought before Pheosco began waving Chug back out of the room and into the hall. Thorik glanced at Emilen and then back at the Avanda, who was preparing to escape their captivity with the help of the two dragons. Thorik grabbed his pack and items. "Wait for us!"

Now, fully in the hall, Chug was able to make the ninety degree turn to head further toward the center of the mountain. But even with Pheosco prompting him to start racing behind him, Chug gave Thorik an extra few seconds to climb on his back with Emilen. Once all three were on, Chug leaped forward, racing down the hall with his wings tight to his side.

The small green dragon led the way down the winding cavern. It was far less structured than a castle's hallway, and much more consistent in size than caverns the Nums had seen before. That said, it often veered to the left or right as it angled up or down.

Sitting up front, Avanda clung onto the brown dragon with one hand and protected Vesik with the other. She smiled as large as her mouth would allow. Totally exhilarated, she couldn't get enough of the swooshing around tight corners and quick drops. The closer she came to being thrown off, the more fun she had trying to retain her grasp on the brown dragon.

The other Nums hung on for dear life. Despite Chug's bulky size, he sprinted down the passageway at unbelievable speeds. Even Pheosco struggled to stay ahead of him as he flew with all his might.

Side halls and rooms became less and less frequent until they stopped completely. At that point, so did the burning pools of oil. They had departed the heavily traveled path and had entered a pitch dark cavern.

It immediately felt different. Sounds didn't bounce off the walls and the air was less fresh, carrying an unpleasant odor. The other change was in Chug's path, it was completely straight.

"Em, hold onto me," Thorik instructed. Now that they weren't being tossed from side to side, he wanted to use this opportunity to grab one of his runestones.

Emilen held onto Chug with one hand and Thorik with the other, while Thorik found the runestone he needed. Fortunately for him, his grandmother had taught him to find runestones without having to see them, simply by touching the ridges on their surface.

Pulling out the Runestone of Belief, he wrapped his arms around Avanda and Vesik until both of his hands held the runestone. He then closed his eyes and concentrated on becoming one with the stone instead of worrying about being thrown off. Energy immediately began to flow from the runestone, up one arm like a parade of electrical ants, across his chest and then back down the other arm until the circuit was complete. Once there, a bright red light emitted from the gem in the center of the runestone, providing the Nums a clear view of their surroundings.

Pheosco was leading Chug through an enormous cave, perhaps a mile in width and several miles long. Within this volcanic vent shaft was a clear path in which they traveled, lined with unlit basins that were once filled with oil. Beyond the basins were hundreds of thousands of bones strewn out across the ground. Piles of dragon skulls and leg bones and ribcages were as far as the light would allow them to see.

"It's a graveyard," Thorik said in awe, racing past a few monuments and statues within the bone-created dune waves. The eerie sight ran tingles down his spine. He felt they were breaching sacred ground and disturbing things that should not be meddled with. "We have invaded their private cemetery."

Beyond the reach of Thorik's runestone light, a red glow could be seen in the distance before them. With the light that was provided, the cavern seemed to have no end and the ceiling slanted up and out of reach the closer they moved toward the red glow.

Soon, the runestone light wasn't needed. Thorik broke the connection with one hand, causing it to softly extinguish, before he placed it back in his pouch with the rest of the runestones. Glancing up, he could see stars. The cavern had opened up and they were able to look directly up and out of an ancient volcano. But his enjoyment of seeing the night sky again was short lived. They quickly approached the source of the red glow.

## Chapter 9
# Rummon's Lair

Surrounded in every direction by piles of dragon bones for as far as the eye could see, a red glow emanated from a half-sphere dome nearly fifty feet high. Its surface swirled with shades of reds as sparks of yellow flared out at random intervals, some of which were powerful enough to rupture the dome's liquid-like surface allowing a quick view inside.

Encircling the dome were a dozen dragons dressed from head to tail in symbol-laden clothes and jewelry. Rummon's eye was the primary symbol on the necklaces, earrings, and headgear, while sewn writings coated their robes and jewelry on their lower and back half. Their wings were straight out to their sides, in spite of the incredible amount of gold and metal attached to them. Thick rings, piercings, and embedded metals in the dragons' fleshy wings weighed them down from being useful to fly. In fact, it took an enormous amount of strength just to keep them open and off their body. Regardless of the hardship, they all kept their wings fanned out to feel Lord Rummon's pain in order to honor him.

Chanting in low tones, the dragons followed each other in an endless procession around the giant red glowing dome. The words may not have been understandable to the Nums but it was apparent that there were many sequences of some scripture vocalized prior to repeating them all over again.

Pheosco fanned out his wings as they approached, causing Chug to slow down as well. With the lack of speed and the close proximity to the dome, the Nums began to notice the non-visual changes.

The smell of rotting flesh penetrated the bug-infested air surrounding the dome and the nearby vicinity. Bitter gaseous acids burned the insides of the Nums' nose while a heavy green mist clung to the floor, seeping out of the dome's base. Clumps of thick clouds rolled out the electrically sparked yellow ruptures near the base of the dome, which quickly dispersed on the outside of the dome.

Thorik kept his voice down in order not to disturb the dragons parading around in a circle. "Pheosco, what happened back there? Why did you free us? What's going on?"

Slowing Chug to a walk, Pheosco continued to lead the group closer to the dome without looking back at Thorik. "The Grand Watcher presented his case to the dragon council."

"Ah," Thorik sighed with relief. "So he won and you were ordered to take us here to free Rummon. But that doesn't explain the tearing up of our clothes and spraying of the boar's blood."

"Yes, the Grand Watcher won. However, he sided against you and has ordered your death."

All three Nums were struck by his words before Thorik responded. "Then why have you risked your life to save us?"

"You have no idea what you've started here. We of the air are now at war against one another. We have chosen sides and will battle to the death. Chug and I chose the side to revive Lord Rummon. Sneaking away from the discussion, we came to free you before others arrived for your murder. Our deception to make it look as though you have already been eaten may not buy us much time, so we must hurry. It won't be long before both sides rush in here to Lord Rummon's side to battle for his fate."

A long yellow electrical flash raced across the dome, opening several small ruptures in the shield, revealing a large, red-scaled body beyond it. The sparks quickly faded and the openings closed behind them.

"Is there a lightning storm happening under that dome, Ralph?" Avanda asked.

"Pheosco," he replied in a dry tone. "The storm you see is only the shield itself, conjured by the Sentinels of Rummon, keepers of the shield, and protectors of Lord Rummon. Without their prayers the dome would begin to fade away."

Thorik watched the ceremony continue around in a circle within a wide channel in the floor, which appeared to have been worn away by constant use for an unimaginable number of years. "They have been protecting him for a long time."

"Yes," Pheosco replied to Avanda as they all slowly approached the last dozen yards. "Time has been his primary enemy. Lord Rummon's body would have decayed and turned to dust a thousand years ago if not for the constant and relentless prayers to keep him safe. Generation after generation has stepped in to assist in shielding the outside from our Lord. Some journey here to become new Sentinels, others arrive to worship and pray for his return, while others bring food and supplies to those who do the prior."

Chug stopped near the Sentinels, allowing the Nums to climb off him while he panted from the long run. His tongue flopped out and slapped on the ground just prior to him pushing his thick legs out from under him, causing his body to crash down onto the cavern floor with his mouth still smiling as he gathered his breath.

The Sentinels appeared to be in a deep trance, completely ignoring the Nums. They often walked for weeks without rest before being relieved by other Sentinels. The only way to survive such enduring tasks was to focus so tightly on their prayers that they would forget time and events around them.

"Will they allow us to touch the dome?" Avanda said.

Pheosco nodded. "Of course. These are dragons of worship, not guards. But you must be respectful, and not break their concentration. Without it, the dome could collapse and Rummon would be vulnerable. In fact, time itself could rush in and destroy him." Pheosco glanced back the way they had come, to see if any more dragons were on their way. "You must proceed with Lord Rummon's transfer. I don't know how much time we have."

Avanda waited until the next Sentinel walked peacefully by, chanting his words, before she quickly approached the shield. The surface felt like a thick gas cloud, so thick that she couldn't push through it. Swirling, darker red clouds appeared and spun around her hand, pushing it back out of the vaporish shield. "How do we get in?"

Pheosco's neck went rigid, squinting his eyes back across the dragon graveyard. "No one ever has. That's the point of the shield." Popping his head back, he shot a look at Avanda. "You're on your own! Hurry up and get in there." Flapping his wings he lifted off. "Chug! We have company. Prepare for battle."

Thorik ran over to the shield and began to help Avanda look for a way inside. Putrid smelling green mist continued to roll out from random small electrical fractures and over the Nums' feet. None of these temporary cracks were large enough to even place in an arm.

In the distance, flames could be seen as the warring dragons battled to be the first to reach Lord Rummon. Hundreds were becoming visible while tenfold more followed closely behind in the dark.

Pheosco prepared himself to fight against the first of the Grand Watcher's followers who were planning to stop the Nums. "I don't know how many we have on our side. A thousand would give us a fighting chance to give you enough time to free Lord Rummon. Five thousand would give us even odds."

"You don't know how many are backing your cause?" Emilen scolded the green dragon. "What have you gotten us into?"

Hovering a few dozen yards over her head, he assessed the battling dragons as they approached. "I didn't have time to take a vote!" he spat back. "Don't you understand what you've done? You've ended thousands of years of peace among the dragons. War is upon us! They are coming for you."

Emilen was obviously surprised at his response. "I had nothing to do with it. It was those two who wanted to free Rummon, not I."

Screams and roars from the approaching dragons began to fill the air. Diving and clawing at one another, they still raced toward the shield that protected Lord Rummon. Some dragons teamed up to break the neck of an opponent while another landed upon an enemy of his beliefs before taking his claws and shredding up his wings. Creatures were flying in every direction, many were tumbling to the ground and landing on piles of bones, while a few crashed into statues of important dragons of their past. Nothing was sacred at the moment. It was all about the Nums reaching Lord Rummon.

Avanda tried several times to push her way through the gaseous shield before stepping back and began looking for ways to use her magic. "Vesik can do anything," she said to herself, opening the book of magic and searching the pages within.

Thorik had only attempted to force his way through twice before realizing that it was a waste of time. Stepping back, he watched the swirling clouds and periodic spikes of yellow lightning flash across the barrier. "Come quick! I think I know a way in!"

Emilen watched as the gigantic cavern filled with flying beasts, fighting back and forth. One broke away and dived down at the Num, preparing to grab her waist with its strong jaws and sharp teeth. She froze with fear; running wouldn't do her any good.

Opening its mouth, the dragon prepared to strike with an obvious desire to snap her in half. But as he focused on the Num, he failed to notice the brown dragon above her. Dropping like a bolder after folding up his wings, Chug crashed down on the attacking dragon's head seconds prior to Emilen's pending death.

Chug and his victim bounced on the ground and then off the shield before rolling back away from it. They had nearly landed on Thorik and Chug's tail had lightly slapped Avanda out of her trance in finding a spell within Vesik.

"Hurry!" Thorik yelled. By the time the other Nums had reached him, he had another one of his runestones out and was concentrating on it without activating it.

"What's the plan, Thorik?" Emilen said as she pulled in close to him for protection from the dragons.

Without losing his concentration, he instructed them carefully. "Stay very close to me. Do not leave my side for any reason." He then went back to focusing on the runestone and the shield just inches in front of him.

His words were sound, but there was a war happening behind his back. Emilen clutched onto Thorik's arm and buried her head into it, while Avanda pressed her back against Thorik's so he knew she was there while protecting them from oncoming attacks.

War continued amongst the dragons. Fire, hail, acid, and lightning shot out of the mouths of various dragons. Claws ripped away at wings and tore scales from their skin. Blood poured from their mouths as well from their necks, sides, legs and tails. Those who could no longer fly continued their battle on the ground, spraying graveyard bones up in the air as they tossed each other back and forth by their tails or necks.

Chug used his weight to slam into the sides of others, knocking the wind out of them or snapping their wings. He looked invincible until four other dragons worked together against him and started ripping at his sides.

Pheosco wasn't doing much better. He had used his agility to avoid being attacked while blinding his opponents, but all it took was one good swipe of a large claw to send him flying to the ground and smashing into a graveyard stone monument, knocking him out.

Chug and Pheosco were now unable to help the Nums. They were on their own.

"Thorik," Avanda said, her voice now cracked with concern. "Let me use a spell. Vesik will help us!"

"No, we're almost there." His voice was calm and distant, unwilling to take his mind too far off of his plans.

Avanda watched as a dark red dragon, the size of Chug, broke free of his enemy and landed before her. They were in the open and vulnerable up against the glowing shield. Holding back the urge to seek shelter, she screamed at Thorik. "You better do it now or we will never have the chance!"

The dark red dragon roared at the Nums, sending their hair flying back toward the shield.

"Thorik! Now!"

Before he could confirm anything, the dark red dragon sucked in a gasp of air and blew out a ball of flaming gas. Rolling out of his mouth, the flame shot directly toward the Nums. There was no time to escape or to shield themselves before being engulfed by the inferno.

Emilen turned at the last moment to see the rolling flames engulfing them. But to her surprise, the motion of the flames stopped in midair, as though time had stopped.

"It's time to go!" Avanda called to Emilen, snapping her out of her stunned state. "Thorik's runestone has stopped time long enough for us to get beyond the shield."

Turning, Emilen could see that a long horizontal yellow streak of lightning had sparked its way past their point on the shield, opening up a hole for them to see through. Much like the dragon's flame, the lightning was frozen in time. This was true for all things outside of a small area around the three Nums. Dragons hung in the air without flapping, battles in midstride were held motionless, and the sound of dragon roars remained silent.

Thorik focused on his runestone while giving instructions. "The open area inside the shield is frozen in time as well. Toss our items to the other side along the sides of the fracture in the shield so we don't land on them."

Avanda grabbed his pack and spear and heaved it into the opening caused by the yellow lightning. Even though she gave it a mighty push, the items slowed once they passed the runestone's power boundary. Dangling in the air, just inside the shield, the items waited for time to resume.

"Now, jump in!" Thorik said. He was having difficulty holding the time from starting up again. This became apparent from the slow swirling of the clouds on the shield and the heat starting to be felt from the dragon's breath.

Emilen didn't wait a moment before leaping into the open fracture. Halfway through, Avanda could see Emilen starting to slow down on the inside of the shield. Unfortunately her feet never made it through before her body came to a complete stop.

Avanda moved over and tried to give the feet a push, but wasn't able to budge them. "I don't know what you see in her," she told Thorik. "She's nothing but trouble for us."

"Get in!" Thorik ordered as the heat from the dragon fire was starting to break through.

Giving up on Emilen's feet, Avanda clutched Vesik and her purse of magical components tight before making her own leap beyond the shield. Coiling up her legs behind her, she was fully inside the opening before she floated between Emilen and their gear. All hung silently in suspended time.

Thorik opened one eye to survey the shield, the opening within it, and the Nums who hovered on the far side. He didn't want to crash into them while making his own leap. While planning his jump, he lost a moment of control of the runestone, shifting the holes created by the yellow lightning and allowing a portion of the dragon's hot flame to burst into his area.

There was no time to think. He leaped into the nearest hole, breaking his concentration on the runestone and ending its power.

All three Nums and their gear splashed to the soggy ground inside of the shield, followed by a small portion of the dragon's fiery attack. Thorik's shirt and the soles of Emilen's boots instantly caught on fire.

Thorik had expected it and quickly began rolling on the ground to suffocate the flames.

Emilen was taken by surprise and screamed in horror before waving her feet about in the air. "Help! I'm on fire!"

Irritated at her incompetence, Avanda grabbed Emilen's lower legs and placed them firmly on the wet floor, immediately putting out the flame. "I'm not your babysitter," she said, making sure Emilen knew she didn't take pleasure in helping her.

Breathing hard from the frightful idea of being burned alive, Emilen quickly noticed that she was lying on a soft muddy floor hidden below a layer of thick green vapors which clung to the ground within the entire dome area. Bugs flew around her head in a mad frenzy and gathered in groups hanging in the air throughout the entire dome.

"We have to hurry," Thorik said, gathering the spear and his gear.

"I think we're too late," Avanda replied, staring up at the mighty red dragon before them. Its size was more vast than they had imagined, easily the weight of a dozen chuttlebeasts at a length of over sixty yards long from nose to tip of its coiled up tail.

Amazed by the creature's size, Thorik knew that this specific attribute wasn't what she was referring to. It was his state of preservation. Over the thousand years of stasis, the shield hadn't fully protected Rummon from the ravages of time or insects.

Large sections of Rummon's body had been eaten away. His ribs were exposed on one side, half his snout, portions of his tail, and hind legs as well. Even those solid areas of flesh were not in good shape as rot and decay had taken their hold. Scales were missing and many clung on by thin strings of skin and muscle.

Lord Rummon looked more dead than he did preserved.

The three Nums stood without words as they stared at the carcass of the once proud lord of the dragons. They wondered what to do now.

Crash! The loud noise echoed within the dome as one of the dragons smashed its body against the shield. It was quickly followed by a second and then third one. They were trying to break into the domed area.

The Sentinels had been stopped from their endless walk and prayers. Held back by several dragons under the orders of the Grand Watcher, it was just a matter of time for the entire dome to dissolve away.

Emilen waved her arms to shoo away the bugs while searching for some place to hide, but the green mist along the ground and the giant dragon, Rummon, were the only options to choose from. "We need to escape before they break in."

Ignoring her, Thorik grabbed his spear with both hands, looking for an answer from Rummon to set them on the right path. "What now?" he asked the spear.

After receiving no answer, he gave Avanda a puzzled look as more loud crashes on the shield echoed inside the dome.

Wasting no time, Avanda opened Vesik and began searching for a spell. "I'll see if I can stop the dragons, should they break in."

"No." Thorik realized that the magic of Vesik was strong but Avanda couldn't use it to keep the dragons off them forever. They needed a better plan. "Does Vesik have a spell for animating the dead or allowing the dead to live?"

"Yes, but it doesn't work unless we also have a spell to control his movements. Even if I could make Rummon live, he has no conscience."

Lifting his spear up into the air, he showed her his plan. "If we release his essence, he will die from his poorly kept body. However, if we animate his body first, then release his essence into it, he may survive the transfer."

"But he'll still be dead. He'll keep crumbling apart until there is nothing left of him. Once the shield is down, it may happen instantly."

"It may, but it may not. We have to take the chance. What other options do we have?"

Avanda nodded and turned the pages of Vesik until she found the right spell. "We'll need sand, one of Rummon's bones, and his heart to perform the first spell."

Stretching his neck, Thorik searched for access to Rummon's heart. It was visible between his exposed ribcage, but the heart weighed much more that all three Nums together and it was lodged between other organs. Cutting it out and bringing it down was not an option. "Start climbing. I'll find a bone to bring up."

Emilen didn't understand what was happening. "What are you doing? We need to escape before the dragons figure out how to breach the shield."

Thorik ran over to one of Rummon's massive feet. "Escape is not our plan. We're climbing up inside Rummon to cast the spells from within him. You better start on your way."

Shaking her head, Emilen stood silent as she watched Avanda begin her climb.

The ascent was slow, but Avanda quickly picked up the pace. Large chunks of flesh ripped off his body where scales had already exposed the skin. "Use the scales to climb up. Most of them seem to be stable."

Taking out his hunting knife, Thorik reached down into the eaten-away section of Rummon's claw and cut out the remaining flesh holding one of his toe bones in place. Once it was free, he headed up the same path as Avanda, toward the wagon-sized heart.

Emilen gasped at the idea. "Thorik! Get back down here! Are you insane? You're going to place the soul of Rummon into a revived corpse?"

"Yes," he shouted over the thunderous banging against the shield. "Care to join us?" he said sarcastically.

"No!" she shouted back. But her stubbornness was short-lived.

Yellow lightning flashed more frequently in the red clouds of the shield. The openings began to become larger, making the visibility of what was happening on the far side more clear.

The Grand Watcher could be seen standing just outside the shield, waiting for it to fall apart now that the prayers to keep it strong have stopped.

Seeing this sight, Emilen changed her attitude and began climbing up Rummon's body. Hand over hand, she pulled herself up, grabbing onto scales and reaching into Rummon's open wounds for support. At one point her hand landed in pile of maggots, causing her to scream and lose her balance while larva wormed their way between her fingers and down her wrist. Shaking them off, shivers ran up her spine just at the thought of them. Even after wiping off the last few maggots against Rummon's scales, the sensation of the small infant insects crawling between her fingers gave her the shakes.

By the time she reached the opening in Rummon's chest, Avanda was already casting the spell to reanimate the dragon's body.

Thorik and Avanda were crammed inside Rummon's ribcage, pressing their backs against various organs to provide enough room for Vesik to be open and useful. Thorik held a runestone over the open book to provide plenty of light for Avanda to read.

Opening her purse of magical components, Avanda emptied grains of sand from a small tan leather sack into her palm. "Sands from the white dunes of the Ergrauthian Desert," she said while rubbing the sand into the moist and fleshy end of the bone Thorik provided.

"Why do you have sand from the Ergrauthian Desert?" he asked.

"I needed it to keep my Govi Glade beetles alive," she replied, watching several dead beetles fall from the sack. "I guess I forgot to feed them."

Thorik nodded. "Apparently. So, what's next?"

Pressing the sandy end of the bone against the side of Rummon's heart, Avanda read the magic words from Vesik and performed the physical gestures required. Nearly complete, additional words appeared on the pages, allowing her to finish.

Vesik's energy traveled through Avanda as she stated the final phrase. This was followed by a moment of silence and then a loud thumping of the heart, which nearly caused the Nums for go deaf.

Clasping their hands over their ears, they began to escape the chest cavity, only to see beyond the ribcage that the dome shield was quickly falling apart.

Dragons continued to fight in the air and on the ground as the Grand Watcher ordered his followers to crash into the shield in order to break through and stop the Nums. The holes created by the lightning continued to increase in size but none of the dragons were quick enough to burst through before it closed. That said, it wouldn't be long before they did.

"You did it!" Thorik yelled over the loud heartbeat. He grabbed the Spear of Rummon and prepared to stab it into the remaining muscle and tissue around them. "Now cast the other spell to release his essence!"

Flipping through the pages, she found the spell she performed once before. "Hopefully this works out better than it did on Gluic," she mumbled, prepping her components.

The shield finally gave off a series of bright yellow electrical sparks and flashes and then ended completely. There was now nothing between the Nums and the Grand Watcher's followers. The dragons attacked.

"Hurry!" Thorik yelled, causing the light on his runestone to dim.

Emilen screamed at the sight of the attacking dragons before crawling her way farther into Rummon's chest, over the top of Thorik, Avanda and Vesik.

"Get out of my way!" Avanda scolded her, pulling her components back together.

But before she could grab the vial with red and black grains in it, Rummon's body began to shift and sway. His legs began to buckle and his weight transferred, causing the Nums to begin to roll around inside him.

Jumping for the vial before it rolled out of his chest, Avanda snatched up the spell compound. In doing so, she wasn't able to stop the momentum of her body from rolling out of Rummon's chest. Her free hand grabbed wildly in the air to prevent her fall until she latched onto something firm. Hanging by one hand from one of Rummon's ribs, she sighed with relief until she noticed several dragons coming for her.

Thorik grabbed her arm and pulled her back inside the ribcage for safety.

Rummon's body swung back the other way, blocking the attack from the dragons against the Nums.

"Is Rummon alive?" Thorik asked.

"Yes and no. He has no conscience or thoughts yet, but his body lives." Pouring out the red and black granular powder, she began mixing the components as quickly as possible without dumping them due to her environment shifting directions.

"I thought Bryus Grum always told you not to mix them too fast," Thorik warned, just as a large dragon made an unsuccessful attempt to bite the Nums through Rummon's ribs and into the open wound.

"Are you sure you want me to take his advice?"

A second snap of sharp teeth from the dragon cleared Thorik's thinking. "No! Get it done now!"

And with that, in the center of Rummon's body, while a dragon attempted to tear them out and rip them apart, Avanda performed the spell as Thorik drove the Spear of Rummon into the ancient thick flesh of the internal organs. It was now time to find out if all of their efforts were worth it or if they were in vain.

Standing tall, Rummon swayed one last time before gravity wielded its power and pulled the mightiest of all dragons down to the cavern floor with a crash that shook the entire mountain. Rummon had fallen.

Chapter 10
# Reunion

---

Silence followed the moment of Rummon's collapse. All fighting had ceased by the dragons on both sides as they looked upon Lord Rummon with their own eyes for the first time. He was larger than life, but to see him lie motionless with gaping wounds throughout his body was more disheartening than they could have expected.

Dragons in the air flapped their wings softly as they slowly approached. Bones snapped and tumbled out of the way as those on the ground walked, limped, or dragged their injured bodies toward Lord Rummon.

The violence was over. The war had come to a temporary truce while the dragons of Terra Australis showed their respect to the fallen lord of the air.

Stepping closer than the rest, the Grand Watcher surveyed Rummon's body and shook his head with disappointment. After a solemn moment, he turned his back to Rummon and addressed the thousands of dragons who were in shock from the situation. "This is what happens when my words are not adhered to!" he shouted. "Lord Rummon has been ravaged by a few outsiders and the unfaithful dragons that followed them. Those who have supported this loathsome act must be punished. Rummon must be revenged!" With his wings spread out to his sides, he fanned them with quick vibrations. "Those who oppose my words must die!"

And with that, the truce was over and the war of the dragons continued.

Unaware of the events happening around them, the Nums were trying to escape their captivity. Once Rummon fell, their exit had been blocked and the open cavity, where they sat, squished into tight and dark confines.

"Where's Vesik?" Avanda asked, her body contorted and pressed against the other Nums in the inner walls of Rummon's chest. She could barely move her head and one hand. The rest of her limbs were jammed into place.

"I think it's pressing against my back," Thorik replied, unable to do much more than the others.

"That's better than this spear up against my face," Emilen complained.

Continuing in their attempt to escape their prison of organs and bones, movement was very slow with few successes. A hand here and a foot there were freed, followed by an elbow finally able to move and then an arm. Piece by piece they worked to escape their confinement.

But before they were able to escape the dead dragon body, the heart of Rummon let out a loud beat. With only a moment delay, a second one followed and then a third. The heart was active once again.

"Did it work?" Emilen asked.

Neither of the other Nums knew the answer and remained quiet to see if the answer would arrive on its own.

The heartbeat strengthened and became consistent in its rhythm. Lungs could be heard filling with air as the chest cavity changed shapes and moved about. The whoosh of air leaving the lungs caused the cavity to reshape again. Slowly in and out, the lungs began to create their own tempo, much slower than the heart.

Muscles began to flex in Rummon's body, first a twitch and then a controlled stretch. One eye opened and then the other. A back leg straightened and a claw curled up tight before it extended with sharp talons. Finally, his neck slowly lifted from the ground, raising his head up to look upon the war raging all around him. The mightiest of dragons was alive, and yet no one but the Nums had noticed.

Slowly lifting his massive body up on his legs, Rummon stretched out his neck and tail before opening his enormous wings. The cavity within his chest had opened up from his repositioning and the Nums were able to see the battle as well as one of Rummon's wings.

"Incredible," Thorik said. "His wings must span the length of the entire village of Farbank."

Avanda nodded. "Isn't he amazing?"

Scanning the ground, which now was much farther away than when they first climbed into the dragon, Emilen looked for a way down. "We need to get out of here before he takes flight."

"Why?" Avanda scanned the skies. "I feel safer in here than out there."

The three Nums looked on as dragons continued their fight. Battle cries and screams filled the air as the biting and clawing continued. Bodies crashing against bone-covered cavern floors, knocking over temples, and deep angry roars came from every direction. The noise was tremendously loud.

"QUIET!" yelled Rummon. His voice was so powerful that it literally knocked over dragons nearby, including the Grand Watcher who had his back to Rummon. The thunderous shout caused the cavern to rumble and shake, rocks to fall from the ceiling and stone monuments to topple over. To say it was a powerful yell would be misleading; an explosion of energy would be more accurate.

Once again the battle came to a stop with all dragons mesmerized at the sight of Lord Rummon standing up with wings spread wide. The fact that he was truly revived was simply amazing and something they had all wished to see during their lifetime. But seeing him stand there with gaping holes in his body and clumps of his flesh slowly tearing off due to the pull of gravity was not expected or foretold by anyone. The dragons had no idea how to react.

The Grand Watcher shook off the effects of the sound blast and stood back up. Gazing up at the ill-fated body of their lord, he could not foresee how he could ever worship such a hideous abomination. "You are not our Lord!" he claimed. "You are the soul of an outsider who has violated Rummon's body. His scales and muscles are obviously rejecting your attack from within as they fall off your bones." His persecution was loud for all to hear. "You aren't the Lord Rummon who we have waited for and I refuse to bow to your desires!"

"I didn't ask you to bow before me," Rummon said in a low echoing voice with no emotion. Pulling one of thick massive legs up in the air, he stomped it back down to the ground, right on top of the Grand Watcher, crushing the smaller dragon with ease. "I told you to be quiet."

The sight of the Grand Watcher's immediate death struck the warring parties with awe. The Grand Watcher was the only spiritual leader most of them had ever seen, and to see his life snuffed out in an instant, by the enormous claw of Lord Rummon, put all dragons on notice. Fear spread faster than a virus.

After scraping the Grand Watcher off the bottom of his foot, Rummon glanced around at the thousands of onlookers, all of them silent, all of them showing hesitation. All accept one.

Flying around the stationary dragons and toward Rummon, a colorful crazy-eyed bird approached the giant dragon's muzzle. Its course was erratic as it finally stopped just feet in front of Rummon's snout.

"Welcome back, my dear," Gluic said, in a soft grandmotherly voice.

Rummon nodded at the bird. "Hello, Gluic. I see you received my message."

"Oh yes, dear. The spirits informed me of your request. We're here to help."

"We?" Rummon gazed out at the dragons.

Gluic's neck snapped to the side and her eyes unscrambled for a moment, long enough to look down at the gaping hole in the dragon's chest.

Arching his long neck back around toward his own body, he placed one of his enormous eyes up near his exposed ribcage and looked inside the open cavity. There sat three Nums among his internal organs.

Thorik was the first to speak to the greenish yellow eyeball which blocked the entire entrance. "I am-"

"Thorik Dain of Farbank," Rummon said, before Thorik could finish introducing himself. "Yes, I know. You've always been so proud of your name."

Avanda and Emilen stared at Thorik, curious as to how Rummon would know such things.

"Ah, I see Avanda is with you as well," Rummon said.

Thorik and Emilen moved their gaze to Avanda with intrigue. It would appear that Rummon was truly a lord with knowledge of all things.

Emilen then turned and looked at the mighty eye. "And I am…" she waited for Rummon to interrupt by saying her name, but he did not. "I'm Emilen."

The giant eye blinked. "Good for you." His lack of interest was not disguised in his voice.

Pulling his eye away from the gaping wound in his side, he looked his body over. "It appears that I have not been preserved well."

Still surrounding him, the Sentinels all bowed to Rummon for forgiveness for their inability to keep him in better shape. This was followed by a shout from one of the dragons flying above, blaming other dragons for purposely allowing this to happen in order to keep the Grand Watcher in control. This statement fueled the anger of both sides. It was only a matter of moments before the two groups began fighting once again, filling the volcanic cavern with the sounds of battle.

Rummon squeezed his eyes shut. "I don't like the noise."

"Then perhaps we should be on our way," Gluic said, fluttering her wings while making a landing on his head between two rows of large horns. She then secured herself in a decayed gap between a cluster of smaller horns alongside the large ones. Squatting, she looked as though she was nesting for the winter. Only the top of her back along with her neck and head could be seen.

"Agreed," Rummon grumbled. He then crouched his legs before leaping straight up in the air, bolting his way out of the top of the volcano and into the morning sunrise, leaving the dragons behind to finish the battle without him.

The incredible force from the launch caused the Nums to flatten against the backside of the internal cavity. Bits of flesh from the opposite wall broke free, landing near or on top of the Nums. A clump of dead muscle slapped against Thorik's arm, a splattering of liquids sprayed against Avanda's legs, and a mound of maggots broke free, landing on Emilen's neck. It wasn't a pleasant experience for any of them.

It wasn't until Rummon finished gaining altitude before the Nums were freed from the heavy pressure on their bodies. Once unrestricted, they all quickly began scooping debris off them, none faster than Emilen.

"This is awful! Could it get any worse?" Emilen's body shivered from the encounter with the fly larvae, even after she had brushed them all away from her. "I can still feel them all over my body," she complained, scratching at the skin around her neck and shoulders. "How does Rummon know your names and not mine?" she asked Thorik with obvious jealousy.

Shaking his head, he grabbed a handful of loosened flesh and tossed it off to the side. "Nothing surprises me anymore."

"Well, I don't like it. We're in a demon, Thorik. The very demon that killed our Mountain King. Doesn't it bother you that we're in the stomach of this same dragon?"

"We're not in the stomach. We're next to his heart."

"We're still inside of him. He might as well have already eaten us. What are we going to do?"

Thorik finished cleaning up his own space of extra globs of flesh and the stray maggot. "Rest up and enjoy the ride," he said, with a shrug of his shoulders. Sniffing the air, he coughed and slightly gagged from the smell of rotting meat. The previous turmoil of returning Rummon to his body had prevented him from noticing it before. "I don't know what else we can do."

Flustered and speechless, Emilen found a few more maggots in her hair and frantically tended to them before responding to Thorik.

Avanda ignored the conversation and gazed out past the large ribcage at the sun rising over the snowcapped mountains. It was beautiful and romantic, enticing her to consider shoving Emilen out of Rummon so that she could share the scene with Thorik. She smiled at the tantalizing thought, knowing she could never really do such a thing. After basking in the silly idea for a moment, she reminded herself that she was on her own. She had lost him to Emilen. Pulling Vesik tight against her chest, she closed her eyes and whispered to the book, "I don't need anyone as long as I have you."

Emilen finished removing the last maggot from her hair. "We're stuck in this demon's body with no way of knowing where we're heading."

Thorik leaned up against a fleshy wall and tried to relax. "Hopefully Gluic can guide him."

"You mean that bird which you keep referring to as your grandmother? Are you insane? She can't fly a straight line, let alone guide someone."

Thorik sighed, knowing that there was more truth to her words than he wanted to admit. "Well, if we can't stop the war in time, I hope Santorray and Asentar are able to."

## Chapter 11
# Er'Que Dooma Badlands

S antorray led Asentar west of the destroyed Ergrauth City, across the desert, past the white sand dunes, and into the rocky Er'Que Dooma Badlands. This was a trek that few could survive without an escort of support, but to attempt it with no supplies was suicide. No rivers and few plants existed in this region for as far as the eye could see. Their view was limited as they traveled in the basins between the flat topped mounds and buttes.

Fortunately Santorray was much more than the average Del'Unday. He was the exiled son of the great demon, Ergrauth. He also once held the rank of the General of the Elite. He had been trained to deal with pain his entire life and the blood that coursed through his veins was partially his immortal father's. Santorray was a half-demon Blothrud.

Between the mesa tops, sparsely lined with dead shrubs, Santorray focused on the distant mountain with trained eyes, never allowing his shoulders to slump or his head to droop from exhaustion. His half dragon and half hairless wolf-like neck and face tightened as he growled to block out his pain. His red muscle-bound human torso anchored onto large wolf legs. "Hurry or I will leave you behind."

Asentar, the last knight of the Dovenar Kingdom, struggled to keep up. His physique was also very impressive with thick muscular arms, chest and legs. He easily stood a head taller than most other humans, and he was a force to be reckoned with. Yet he was shorter, by several hand lengths, compared to the Blothrud he followed. "I will need a break soon. Just to catch my breath." In spite of the great shape he was in, he simply couldn't keep up with the lesser-demon.

Santorray growled. "We stop. We die."

Head slumped forward and shoulders uncharacteristically drooping, Asentar shook his head. "Just for a few minutes. I need to tend to cuts."

The two had been on a run since they battled their way out of the City of Ergrauth just as it had collapsed. There had been no time to mend wounds or sleep. The pace had slowed to a jog, and water had been pulled from containers made of faralope skins. However, those skins were now empty and a trail of blood was starting to be seen in Asentar's footprints.

"I must bind my wounds!" he insisted, stopping in his tracks.

"What good are bound limbs if you are going to die?" Santorray continued on without him.

Asentar sat on a rock and removed his boot, exposing a foot leaking critical bodily fluids from dry cracks on overworked feet. Without a complaint, he ripped off some fabric from his tunic and wrapped up his foot before placing it back into his blood soaked boot. The second foot was in even worse shape. "Looks like I may lose a few toes from this one," he said to the Blothrud who had slowed to a walk.

Grudgingly, Santorray finally stopped and turned around. "You humans are always worried about the wrong issues!" he growled as he started back toward him. "Your concern over your own wellbeing shows your selfishness and arrogance."

"It is not selfish to ensure one is healthy enough to survive," he said while wrapping up his foot.

"It is when you put the lives of others at risk!"

"How am I doing that?" Asentar asked, pulling his boot back on. He then began to check on his battle wounds.

He was stopped by Santorray, who grabbed the large man with one hand and lifted him into the air, up to eye level with himself. The Blothrud's solid red eyes glared at the man, inches from the end of his muzzle. He breathed heavy hot air out his nostrils, into the Asentar's face. "Not only are you putting both of our lives at risk, but by doing so, you won't be able to warn your army of Ergrauth's attack on your kingdom."

Hanging from the large hand of the Blothrud, Asentar composed himself the best he could. "And what's in it for you? Why do you care about us humans?"

"Who says that I do?" Santorray's skin raised and quivered on one side of his snout, exposing his teeth and gums. His growling became more intense.

"I seriously doubt that you are completely selfless in your acts to help me for the good of mankind. What is your motive in helping me get past these badlands and over the Lower Canine Mountains so I can warn my people? What *selfish* act are you doing?"

The spikes across Santorray's shoulder blades and from the back side of his wrists began to fan out. Squinting his eyes, he bit his lip, allowing the blood to be obvious as it ran down his skin before dripping to the desert floor. "I don't have to explain myself to anyone!" He shouted, pulling back his other arm with a fist so tight that the red from his skin faded around the knuckles. Without hesitation, he swung his fist toward Asentar's exposed face.

Both warriors froze just prior to the deadly punch. Asentar had fully expected it, but had hoped to prevent it. Fortunately for him, he had been successful. From his dangling hands, he had grabbed his own sword and placed the tip of the sharp metal firmly against the front of Santorray's neck at the last second. It was a gamble that paid off.

The blade glistened in the hot sun, pressing the skin inward. The slightest slicing motion could kill the Blothrud. "You are playing a dangerous game, human."

"The game of survival always is."

Slowly retracting his fist, he waited for the sword to pull back before tossing Asentar back to the ground. "I'm leaving, with or without you."

Asentar stood back up and returned his sword to its scabbard. "You can't very well succeed in your *noble* quest without me." Lifting his shirt, he inspected the cuts to determine how severe they were. "I will only require a few moments to tend to these."

Santorray raised his muzzle, sniffed the air, and then growled. "It's too late,"

"And why is that?"

Santorray pulled out his two sabers from his back sheaths and scanned the tops of the flat basins. "We have been found."

"By who?"

"The Kewtall. Cover your wounds, it makes us look hurt and weak."

"We are hurt," Asentar said, covering up his wounds. "What is a Kewtall?"

Santorray finished his scan of the hilltops before answering. "They are the wild Del'Undays. They are mutated creatures, living out here away from the cities."

Asentar pulled his sword back out and stood back to back with the Blothrud, allowing them to see in every direction. "Why do they live away from the cities?"

"They are without order or laws. Living within our cities requires commitments."

"You mean obedience. I know that your society must follow Ergrauth or pay the penalty with their life. Your people live in fear, not commitment."

Snarling, he turned his thick neck to peer down at Asentar. "Don't start with me, human. I'd rather strike you down and take on a tribe of Kewtalls by myself before I allow you to disrespect my ways."

"Yes," he said with a nod, "I believe you would."

The two continued to shuffle their feet, moving around in a circle, while back to back. Neither could see any sign of danger.

"Are you sure there is something out there?" Asentar asked.

Without warning, a large wooden spear flew from the top of a mesa directly toward Asentar, landing near his feet.

"Hold your ground," Santorray said. "They are testing you to see if you'll jump away. They will attempt to separate us, and if they succeed, you will stand no chance."

"I appreciate the words of encouragement. What makes you think I'm the weaker of us? You haven't had water for two days and you refused to take any of mine."

Heads began peering over the mesa tops, staring down at the two warriors. There was easily a few dozen Del'Undays.

"Like most humans, you didn't exactly offer to share it." He watched the various Altered Creatures begin making their way down the cliffs. "Besides, one swipe from a Kewtall and your body will burst from all that water you've had."

"You're as stubborn as a chuttlebeast. I offered you a drink, but you refused."

Cautiously, the Kewtalls made their way to the bottom of the various mesas. The creatures were different than the normal Del'Unday. They were hybrids of various species mixed together after generations of cross-species relations. The mutations had made for some hideous looking forms with anywhere from six or less legs and eyes, jagged teeth extending far outside of their usefulness of their mouths, and extra claws and spikes on skin ranging from thick hide to dragon scales.

"Refused?" Santorray coughed at Asentar's words. "You shook your skin of water toward me, once. And that was only after you placed your lips all over the end of it, tainting the water with your human spit."

Circling the two, the Kewtalls drooled at the feast before them. There was no need to hesitate, for they had them outnumbered twenty to two. The obvious choice was to take Asentar out first, seeing that he was over a head shorter. Leaping forward, two Kewtalls attacked Asentar.

Surprisingly light on his feet for a man so muscular and tall, the Dovenar Knight had been trained by the best and had quickly exceeded his teacher's ability. Spinning to his right he swiped his sword across the neck of the first creature, opening up a large deadly gash. Within the same swing of the weapon, he stabbed the second attacker in the side, deep into his chest, puncturing his heart. "So, you refused to drink from the same water skin as a human?" he asked the Blothrud. "You Fesh!"

"What?" Santorray bellowed, launching with his own attack on the mob of creatures, going after the closest ones first. His sabers made quick work of the several small Kewtalls before putting his sights on the largest one of the pack. "I've killed others for calling me less!"

"Well I'm right here when you're ready." Asentar spun his sword in his hand, gripped it in the opposite direction, and then used it like an ax to cut into an oncoming cat-like beast. "I'm not afraid of you!"

"If you were smart, you would be!" Santorray charged the largest Kewtall. It stood taller than the Blothrud, but not as wide. Instead it had four long muscular tentacle-like appendages with thick and heavy spikes on the end, growing out of his sides. The first attack missed Santorray, but the second one crushed his side, knocking his sabers from his hands and his body to the ground.

Asentar pulled his sword out of the cat-like beast and tossed it into the open mouth of an oncoming attacker. "So, now I'm not as intelligent as you either? You really are a Fesh!"

Grabbing the side where he had just been attacked, Santorray could see how the spikes from the tall Kewtalls tentacles had ripped through his skin. "That's it! Once I get done here, I'm coming for you!" Rolling out of the way, he dodged another tentacle attack before getting back on his feet and jumping directly at the large beast. Using his spiked shoulder, Santorray plowed into the creature, causing them both to fall over with the beast under him.

"I'm ready when you are!" Asentar yelled, pulling out two long daggers and swirling them in his palms while planning his next move. "Once you get done playing with your friend, I should have all of his companions taken care of." Twirling his body, he fell to one knee with one dagger out in front of him and the other out to the side, both hitting their targets and both creatures falling to the ground.

"You should already be done, seeing that I gave you all the easy ones." Santorray straddled the large beast and pounded his fist into the thick hide of his chest. The blades on the back of the Blothrud's hands struggled to cut deep enough to open the creature up, and before he could, all four heavy spiked balls from the ends of the tentacles smashed into the Blothrud's sides.

"Easy?" pulling his daggers out of his enemies, Asentar jumped over them to gain a better vantage point for his next attack. "I'm fighting several at a time. You only have to worry about one."

Santorray's breath had been knocked out of him, causing him to gasp for air. While doing so, one of the muscular appendages swung again, knocking hard against the Santorray's snout, spraying blood across the sand. "It's a big one!" he coughed out once he got a breath. "With tentacles!"

Asentar flung both of his daggers at the same time, nailing two different attackers in their heads. "I'm fighting creatures with teeth and claws. How bad could tentacles be?"

Another crushing blow hit Santorray's side from one of the spiked balls. "Bad!" Pushing the pain out of his mind, Santorray dodged another powerful blow, grabbed his sabers from the desert floor and leaped back on the creature before it could get back up. Swiping down both sides of the creature's body, he cut off all four of the powerful tentacles.

"I think you're over exaggerating," Asentar said. "I could have used a real warrior to help me clean up this mess." Pulling his sword out of the body of a prior victim, he swung at the next Kewtall heading his way. Unfortunately there were four such beasts jumping on him all at the same time. This time his abilities only allowed for stopping one of them. The remaining three began to claw and bite at the knight, knocking him to the ground.

Asentar's sword had lodged itself in his last target, making it unusable to defend himself as he lay on the hard dirt ground while being assaulted by the Kewtall. Grabbing a spare short dagger, he was able to stab one of the beasts in the heart. Then, to his amazement, the other two creatures stopped their attack.

One of the creatures quickly disappeared from sight, giving Asentar enough view to see what was happening. There before him, Santorray was swinging one of the large tentacles as a weapon. The heavy spiked ball on the end slammed into the second creature on Asentar, just as it had the prior one, and knocked the creature several yards away, leaving a gash in its side.

"What do you mean, 'How bad could it be?'" Santorray shouted at Asentar, preparing his next swing to be at the human.

All of the Kewtalls had fallen, leaving the two warriors. Even the large beast had been slaughtered once it lost its limbs.

Santorray swung the tentacle over his head like a hammer, straight at Asentar.

Rolling to the side, he barely escaped the attack as the spiked ball smashed into the ground where he was just lying. "What is your problem?"

"Fesh! No one calls me a Fesh and gets away with it!" Pulling the spike out of the ground, Santorray prepared for a second attack.

"You're awfully sensitive about that. Did you have a Fesh encounter you'd rather forget?" Asentar dodged the next attack from the swinging appendage. "You seem to have a lot of pent-up anger. You should seek help."

Santorray tossed the tentacle aside. "I find the only thing that helps me is some physical exercise." Leaning forward, the Blothrud charged at the human and then jumped at him with his arms wide to his sides.

Asentar leapt out of the way before Santorray could land on him, but the Blothrud's spikes caught the back of his clothes, dragging him backward and to the ground. They both rolled in a tangled mess of swinging arms and legs until Asentar landed on top, holding Santorray's arms down to his sides.

Pulsing, muscles flexed and strained as the two fought for control. The size of Asentar's arms were enormous and perhaps larger than any human's arms had ever been, but they were no match for the Blothrud, especially a son of the demon Ergrauth. Asentar's arms began to shake as he held the beast down.

Santorray grinned at the effort Asentar was giving. Allowing the Dovenar Knight time to see his expression, Santorray calmly lifted his arms up from his sides, pressing the man up above him. "You have no idea who you're messing with," he said with in a dry tone.

Dropping Asentar off to one side, back to the ground, the Blothrud gathered his footing, but not before Asentar did the same. Standing among the dead bodies around them, the warriors were ready to strike each other. Continuing to breathe heavily from exhaustion, they were both injured and bleeding.

"We could call it a draw," Asentar said.

Santorray shook his head. "You could never defeat me, even on your best day and my worst."

Looking at the damage around them, Asentar's diplomacy training kicked in. "We could resolve this later, and in the meantime we can rest and drink. Several of the Kewtall had water rations. Surely, you'll honor me this one last request before you end my life."

Glancing from side to side, he did his best to prevent his body from divulging its need for rest and water. He eventually nodded. "I could use a victory drink before I defeat you."

## Chapter 12
# Well Needed Rest

The Er'Que Dooma Badlands stretched out in every direction with tan mesa tops separated by shallow weatherworn valleys. Streaks of rust-colored minerals mixed with veins of yellows and deep reds along the sides of the mesa walls. Scattered brush trimmed many of the mesa tops with a crown of sun-bleached grey limbs that only sprung leaves during the monsoon season.

Using the vantage point of a mesa top, Santorray and Asentar watched for potential attackers while enjoying some overdue water and rest. Both of the warriors had collected a few skins of water. It wouldn't be enough to reach the distant mountains, but it would help them get another few days through the desert.

The Blothrud, Santorray, opened his mouth wide and poured the water in with obvious pleasure.

"I don't understand you." Utilizing the down time, the Dovenar Knight tended to his wounds, replacing coverings and wraps. "You won't drink from a water skin of mine, but you'll gladly use one from a Kewtall. At least you know my water is fresh, we have no idea where they gathered theirs from."

"It is our custom to drink from unblemished vessels."

"Unblemished?" the man asked before beginning another sip of water.

"Untouched by the lips of others. We pour our water into our mouth, we do not treat it like an infant treats its mother's breasts."

Stopping his motion, Asentar slowly removed the water skin from his lips as he began to chuckle. "Perhaps we aren't as good of an aim as the Del'Unday."

"Perhaps," the Blothrud said, sniffing the air for any sign of approaching Kewtalls. "We are superior in many ways to humans."

"Apparently," the knight chuckled before noticing the Blothrud's hands. "When we escaped the City of Ergrauth, the skin on your fists were raw from your battle there. I swear that I could see the bones on your fingers. But in the short time we've traveled, your skin has regrown, and not only on your hands, but your other injuries have healed as well. How can this be?"

"The saliva of Blothruds have healing powers." Santorray spit in his hand and wiped it on a fresh cut he had received during his battle with the Kewtall. The liquid began to bubble as it reacted to the wound.

"I've heard of this, yet I have never heard of such rapid repair of skin."

A slight grin crept into one side of Santorray's mouth. "There are a few benefits to having an immortal as one of my parents." Returning his attention to the horizon, he was always uneasy about others sneaking up on him. "All Blothruds have this same ability. However, it would take months for most of them to heal what I can in a few days."

"Odd," Asentar said to himself, continuing to watch the saliva's react to the wound.

"Perhaps, but your entire culture has many oddities of its own."

"As does the Del'Unday and the Ov'Unday. All societies have its benefits and challenges."

"At least the Del'Unday rules are precise and well understood. We are very clear of what is expected and what the punishment is for not following them. The same crime in your kingdom could have different results pending what province or city you are in or even by the local law official."

Asentar gave a slight nod. "There is some truth to your words. But it is the price we pay for allowing free thinking instead of absolute control."

"Your people lack the leadership needed to survive."

"The Dovenar Kingdom has stood strong enough to hold off the Del'Unday for over six-hundred years. I would say we have had a long list of great Kings and Queens," Asentar said with pride.

"Perhaps," Santorray grumbled. "But you have been leaderless ever since the civil war, ending the royal line. The royal twins, Ambrosius and Darkmere, were removed from power after the war and now your provinces must fend for themself. Unless there is an unexposed bloodline to the throne, your people are without a leader. The Dovenar provinces will never reunite without a king. My father, Ergrauth, and the demon Bakalor know this and will use this to their advantage against your kingdom in this new war."

Asentar took his words and gave them deep consideration. "If Ambrosius returned, he could reunite our people."

"No, there is too much history there. Plus, Darkmere has poisoned his brother's name even further while in the disguise of the Terra King, spreading the word of the Mountain King's rebirth and preaching the evils of Ambrosius' actions."

He stopped to pour a little water on his dry throat before continuing. "No, I see no hope for your civilization. There is too much stacked against them and they will scatter like sandrats into the distant caves and forest. The time of your kingdom has ended."

For the first time since Santorray had met the man, Asentar's shoulders drooped with a show of defeat as he gazed into his dirty hands.

"Then," the Dovenar Knight eventually said. "Why are you fighting to help us?"

The Blothrud took his time to finish another scan for danger before answering. "I don't run from a fight if it's something I believe in, regardless if I believe success is possible. I have given my word to Ambrosius himself to help him in these times of need. Only a coward would back out when times became bleak."

Asentar's shoulder's rolled back into place, giving him his normal proud bearing. "You, my Blothrud friend, are correct. We must continue, in spite of the odds." He then poured water into his mouth without his lips touching the skin. "But you are wrong about one thing."

"And what might that be, *friend*?" He emphasized the last would slightly, mocking the knight's use of the word.

"There is another heir to the Dovenar Kingdom."

"And who might that be? You?" Santorray laughed at the idea.

A grin crept into Asentar's lips as an eyebrow raised.

Santorray shook his head. "You can't simply appoint yourself this title. It is a birthright."

"I'm well aware of the process. Ambrosius' father married into the throne. But his mother, who was next in line for the throne, had a younger brother who was pushed out of the view of the public. Few knew that the brother married and had a child. A son. A son who one day would become the leader of the Dovenar Knights."

Santorray tightened his eyes while skeptically listening. "Nice story. Regardless if I believe it or not, I don't think you'll be able to convince the likes of Ambrosius and the province leaders."

"Ambrosius already knows. He was the one that confirmed my identity. As for the province leaders, I have been working with them to unite against the coming war without having to tell them about my bloodline. I need them to follow me for who I am and what I believe in, not because of who my parents or grandparents were."

Squinting his eyes to look for any deception in Asentar's face, Santorray spit in his hand and rubbed it against another wound. "Even if you are who you say, what good is it if you don't know your enemy and their plans?"

"I have been traveling for the past many years gathering information. I know that the demons plan to attack the Dovenar Kingdom in Doven, near Rivers Edge. Ergrauth brings his Del'Unday army and the children of Rummon, while it is believed that Bakalor has found a way to come above ground in the light of day."

Asentar continued, peering out across the landscape for Kewtalls. "The Dovenar armies may have a chance to hold them off if they were prepared. However, that is not the case. Darkmere, disguised as the Terra King, has convinced the local leaders to move all of their troops to the north side of Woodlen, on the opposite side of where the attack really will happen. I need to reach our troops and lead them south, prior to Ergrauth's attack."

"Don't be naïve. Ergrauth is not your only enemy and his attack on Doven is not the only battle you must win."

"Yes, I know. Forces in Corrock will be heading to Trewek to slaughter the Ov'Unday. Afterward, they will attack the men of Eastland before joining Ergrauth at Doven. On top of all of this, the Matriarch of Southwind has made a deal with Darkmere to take over Pelonthal and Greenbrook before assisting him at RiversEdge."

Santorray sniffed the air again before continuing. "The battle at RiversEdge appears to be the final main thrust to break the kingdom's strength. Once inside Doven's walls there will be no stopping them."

"You are correct. We must move all of our allies to this location without the enemy knowing we are on to them."

"This information will do you no good if we die here in the desert. Even with this newfound water, we must find more to cross the western mountains." Santorray sniffed the air from a new direction. "More Kewtalls are on their way. We need to get moving."

## Chapter 13
# Santorray's Act

After several more hot and dry days of non-stop traveling in Er'Que Dooma Badlands, Santorray climbed to the top of another desert mesa and looked out over a large flat valley filled with green vegetation surrounding a sky-blue colored lake. Sprawled out over the majority of the valley were groupings of huts made of sticks and mud blocks. Larger collections of structures were near the center, next to the lake.

Santorray reached down with a hand to help Asentar up the last few feet. "We will wait here until nightfall. Then we will search for some water in the outer part of the village." He then braced his hands on his knees with straight arms and a bent back. It had been a long trek in the desert heat. He was exhausted, and he could no longer hide it.

Asentar fell to his knees after reaching the top. Watching the distant villagers go about their lives, he wiped his dry and cracked lips free of sand from the climb. "There must be a thousand of them. If we get caught, I'm not going to cover for you again, like last time," he said with half-hearted laugh and cough.

"No problem," the Blothrud replied, panting from the rough day of desert hiking and scaling of cliffs. "This time I'll let you have the big ones."

Crawling to get under the minimal shadow cast from one of the dried out desert bushes, Asentar attempted to shade his body from the strong sun. "We'll have to use the cover of darkness to approach the lake and fill our skins."

"We'll use the cover of darkness, but lakes in the badlands are poisonous if not purified properly. We'll have to take some that has already been through the process."

Asentar nodded. "Night it is. Wake me when you're ready."

Instinctively, Santorray wanted to reach over and smack the knight for expecting him to stay awake to protect them, but he was too tired to start another physical match. Instead, he sat down on the edge of the mesa with his legs hanging over the ledge. Ripping brush up from their roots, He placed them in front of him in order to hide himself from those below.

Resting his head on his arm, while watching the activities down in the village, Asentar cleared his dry throat. "Would you mind if I ask you a question?"

Santorray delayed his answer. He hated conversations that started off with such questions. "Depends on the question."

"I understand the offensive nature of calling someone a Fesh, especially with Del'Undays. But why are you so very sensitive about it. You're obviously a master fighter. Such things are so absurd that you couldn't possibly take them seriously. Such a word would make the presenter of it look foolish if it were not in jest."

Another long delay followed as the Blothrud unconsciously gave a low growl from distant thoughts. Slowly recovering from his personal journey into the past, he finally answered. "Normally I don't care to talk of such things. However, seeing that you will most likely die from this desert, or at the hands of the Kewtall, or by my own hands if you call me that name once more, I have no concern of my answer being used against me."

The knight raised an eyebrow. "So much for being optimistic of our fates."

"Oh, I'm sure I'll survive. It's your frail human body that I doubt."

"Thanks for the words of confidence." Asentar waited a few moments before prodding him. "Fesh."

"What?" Santorray's teeth were instantly exposed as his head shifted toward the man.

"The word 'Fesh.' You were going to tell me about why that word affects you so."

"You are playing a dangerous game."

"Yes, I realize that, but if I am soon to die by this desert, the Kewtall or even your hands, then I might as well feel free to live as though there is no tomorrow." Picking up his head, he looked directly at Santorray and smiled with sand-covered bleeding lips.

A low grunt was all he received back from the Blothrud, which Asentar welcomed, considering his audience.

Silence followed.

"F-"

"Say that word again and I'll drag you down to that village right now and help them serve you up for their next meal."

Asentar kept his eyes on the Blothrud, waiting for him to start his answer.

Even though Santorray had turned back to the villagers in order to make sure they hadn't been spotted, he could feel Asentar's eyes upon him. "If I tell you, will you stop staring at me like some chuttlebeast in heat?"

"Absolutely."

Santorray shifted his position. He was uncomfortable discussing the subject. "I was traveling through the Lakewood Forest when I came across a lost human child. She was injured and was hiding up in a tree from a sounder of boar; eight in all. It is the law of nature that the strong shall survive. So, it was my fault."

"You let her die?"

"No, in spite of common Del'Unday logic, I saved her life. That was my undoing. I fought off the wild boars before reaching for her. She seemed more scared of me than of the boars."

Asentar smirked. "I can see that."

"Do you want me to tell this or not?" Santorray said through tight teeth.

"Go on. I'm captivated by your story."

Stretching his neck to one side and then back, he continued. "I finally broke off the limb she clung to, in order to get her down to the ground. I shook it several times before she fell like an apple from a limb."

"You do have a way with people."

Santorray ignored the side comment and continued with his story. "After chasing her down-"

"You chased her?"

"She screamed and ran from me. Injured and bleeding, she would have died out there if I hadn't stopped her. She would have bled to death or the boars would have been back for a feast." His voice was now raised, defending his actions.

"Understood," Asentar replied, trying to calm down the Blothrud. "It now makes sense why you were chasing a little helpless girl through the woods as she screamed in terror. Please go on."

"You make it sound as though I'm the one who's at fault!"

"No. Not at all. Please continue. I'm intrigued to find out how this ends."

"By the time I caught up to her, she had jumped into the nearby river. Not strong in the water, I knew my best chance of saving her was to give her something to grab on to. So I picked up the end of a large fallen dead tree trunk and slapped it quickly into the water near her position."

Asentar nodded. "Let me guess. Instead of being thankful and grabbing on, she undoubtedly screamed as though you were trying to crush her with a large log."

"I can't figure out humans. I slapped that log a dozen times within arm's length of her so she could grab it. Eventually, she finally did and I pulled her to the shore. Exhausted, she made no more attempts to leave as I bound her wounds. By the time I had finished, she had fallen asleep."

Santorray returned his attention to the Kewtall village before continuing his story in a solemn voice. "She was cold from the night air against her wet clothes and needed my body heat. I am not one to share my space while sleeping, but I felt compelled to ensure she was safe and warm. Without blankets or shelter, my body was needed to wrap around hers in order to protect her from the night air."

The mood had changed and Asentar was now truly riveted by the tale.

"I don't recall the last time I slept so sound, so comfortable in my mind. Perhaps that was the closest I ever felt to being content. However, the next morning we were woken up by a crowd of angry men with bows and spears."

"Her father?" Asentar asked.

"Yes, along with family and friends. They showed up and surrounded us. By the time I was fully awake they were on the attack. An arrow in the leg and another in the shoulder caused me to jump up and prepare for a battle, dropping the little girl to the forest floor. They grabbed her from me and pulled her from my protection before her father began scolding her for running away from home. He then slapped her across the face, knocking her to the ground."

Without realizing it, Asentar was leaning forward to hear how it would end.

"Fighting off the spears and arrows was one thing, but to see this father continue to mistreat his child, was more than I could take. I began tossing men out of my way as I charged for the father while hearing his question to her. 'If you didn't run away, than how did you get out here?' he asked her. I could see the panic in her eyes, fearing another beating from him, before she pointed at me and said, 'The Fesh took me from our home to eat me.' I stopped and stared at her with disbelief while the humans chanted, 'Kill the Fesh!'"

Asentar stayed silent. He hadn't expected the story to end with such a twist.

"Several nets were tossed over me while I stood there motionless. I had lost the desire to fight. After my capture, they placed me in a wagon to be sold into slavery. However, I saw the girl one last time before being taken away. I asked her a simple question of, 'Why?' She replied, 'You would be gone the next day. I have to live with him.' And even though her age was that of an innocent, she was correct in her thinking."

"What happened to you afterward?" Asentar asked.

"I was sold into the gladiator games, where I was treated as a Fesh in a cage, fed like a savage, starved when I wasn't vicious enough, and branded with a hot iron as their property. They referred to me as Fesh, and for all intense purposes, I was. My birth name was never used."

"And that is why you do not like to be called such."

"Yes."

"I can respect that and I will hold my tongue from uttering such a word around you."

Santorray gave a deep growl. "I do not need your sympathy."

"Nor do you have it. It is respect for your actions that I do."

"I let my guard down and was captured, only to become a slave. There is no respect to be had."

"We will have to agree to disagree on this one, my friend." Asentar put his head back down, waiting for the sun to set so they could go to the village and gather some water.

Chapter 14
# Kewtall Village

Night fell on the desert mesas and the open flat terrain they surrounded. The cliffs facing the central lake gave off a slight glow from the campfires of the Kewtall tribal village, which had transformed from a calm environment during the day to a tribal festival after dark.

Drums and metal clanging instruments were played with great enthusiasm near the center of the community, while the residents danced around the large roaring fires. A feast gathering was a time to rejoice for the odd-looking creatures.

After generations of inbreeding and cross-breeding, these Altered Creatures were a mix of every known Del'Unday and Ov'Unday that existed. Shunned by both cultures, they had survived in bands throughout the Er'Que Dooma Badlands, preying off of those who traveled through it. Tonight's feast appeared to be a small herd of chuttlebeast that had strayed into the region. All tribal members would eat well tonight.

Santorray waved Asentar closer. They had reached the outskirts of the village without being detected and needed to quickly find some food and water. "I'll enter the huts while you keep watch."

Asentar nodded, turning his back to the structure's entrance before scanning the area.

Cautiously, the Blothrud sniffed the air before poking his head inside the stick and mud hut. The single room was filled with skins for bedding and tools for working. The smell of body odor was pungent, causing him to forcefully hold off a sneeze. "Unclean savages," he mumbled to himself, pulling at hides to see if vessels of waters were hidden underneath, but none were found.

Exiting the hut he took in a deep breath of fresh air. "Nothing of use."

"Everyone seems to be near the lake," Asentar said.

"Unfortunately, I think that is where they store all of the food and water. Meals might be a community based ritual for this village. This is not uncommon for those living in areas of such few means."

"You mean we're not going to find any water or food?"

Santorray investigated the next hut over to see if his assumption was true. "No, we'll find some. We'll just have to move to where it's located."

"There could be a thousand of these creatures surrounding the food and water, how do you propose we get to it?"

"Getting to it is easy. Escaping with our lives will be the challenge." Santorray glared at the flames reaching over the tops of the huts from the distant celebration.

Asentar searched for options. "Are you suggesting a disguise? Many of the Kewtalls are covered with skins. Perhaps we could cover ourselves with some to cloak our identity enough to skirt through the back of the crowds in order to reach the supplies."

"I would rather meet them head on instead of hiding behind some deception."

"What good would that do? You couldn't possibly take them all on."

"I'd only need to defeat their leader. Perhaps a fight to the death. It has to be enough to strike fear into the rest so they don't challenge me. Such an act should grant me food and water and the right to leave."

Asentar sighed. "One of these days you'll have to learn that you can't *always* use violence to solve your problems. Physical negotiations will only get you so far."

"One of these days you'll have to learn that you have to use more than just words to negotiate with some factions. Many use words as a veil to hide the truth."

Shaking his head at the aggressive thoughts, the knight recapped the plan. "So, instead of going down to try to reason them, you are suggesting to walk right into their celebration and request a battle in order to acquire sanctuary for us?"

"No, they would never grant it for both of us. Being Del'Unday, I would be the only one they would consider this for. You would be attacked and placed on a skewer next to the chuttlebeasts before the first words left your mouth."

"So, I'm on my own."

"No. If I challenge the leader, all eyes will be on me. This will be your chance to obtain the supplies you need for your escape across the mountains and back into your valley."

"What if you don't win, or if they don't accept your terms? They may not play such a noble game as you are assuming."

"This will still provide you with the time you need to gather and escape."

"I'm not leaving without you."

Santorray turned, grabbed Asentar by the shirt and pulled him up toward his growling muzzle. "Listen to me clearly, human. If you are truly the heir to the Dovenar Kingdom, then your people are relying on you to save them. And if Ambrosius has placed his trust in you, then he has most likely made some sacrifices to ensure you succeed. Do not allow those efforts to die here today. You are needed by the people of your kingdom. I cannot save them, only you can do this."

Knowing the Blothrud's words were valid, he pulled away and straightened his shirt. "And what becomes of you?"

"I am the son of the demon Ergrauth and I once held the title of Elite General before my father and I parted ways. I have survived much more than the Kewtalls."

"Are you immortal, such as your father?"

"I do not know, but I may find out tonight."

"Then I shall wait for you on the far mesa."

"No, you shall head towards your homeland. Soon after I am exposed, they will start a search for any companions. You will have very little time to gather and leave. Do not turn back. Do not second guess these actions."

Asentar shook his head. "We will continue on together. There will be another waterhole along the way." His suggestion fell on deaf ears as Santorray proudly walked straight toward the center of the village.

There was no stopping the Blothrud. The Dovenar Knight's words became a mumble in his ears while he focused on his venture forward. Eventually, Asentar's voice faded off just before Santorray reached the exterior of the crowd.

Shoulders back and snout up, he proudly walked through the Kewtall toward the center as the villagers reacted with hisses, growls, and barks. The festive environment changed to one of hostility, and yet none had launched an attack on the muscle-bound Blothrud who towered over most of them.

Flames lapped in the air from two enormous blazing fires near the center of the village. Between them crackled a third smaller fire, which roasted one of the many chuttlebeasts, the reason for the festival. Resting behind the roasted beast, a wide stage held the leaders of the community. They were a variety of cross-breeds ranging from the very large down to the size of a sandrat. A Num-sized insect lifted its front pinchers at the sight of Santorray, while a petite white-skinned attractive female, of human-Blothrud mix with solid red eyes, smiled as she rested against the largest of the Kewtalls.

The largest of the wild Del'Unday mutations was a creature that stood eye to eye with Santorray. Feline in body structure, its neck held a skull-looking head wrapped with a thin layer of skin and muscles. Two distorted faces had grown together, each sharing one eye in between them. Above all three eyes were thick ridges on its forehead which tapered back into one ear on its left and two on its right. A layer of glossy scales coated the creature's body, as they shifted colors in the reflection of the flames. At times, the creature was difficult to see as it blended into the background.

Santorray stepped up in front of the large dangerous feline Kewtall and staked his claim. "I am Santorray, Son of the almighty Ergrauth, the rightful leader of all those who live on the land. I demand to partake of food and water for my journey across my lands."

Scales of the giant cat-like creature changed various shades before settling on a dark brown. Stretching its neck out toward Santorray, both mouths opened as it roared in anger from the intrusion. Its massive claws dug into the stage as it prepared to leap forward and attack the Blothrud.

"Who has brought me this gorgeous dessert for our grand meal?" the white-skinned female said.

Santorray was confused. Surely the largest and strongest beast must rule. Could this Del'Unday logic be wrong?

The petite female smiled to her followers as though she expected an answer. She patted the side of the roaring feline beast beside her, calming it enough to prevent it from leaping upon the newcomer.

Howling and roars filled the small flat valley in response to her question. An interruption such as this, just before a substantial meal, was unacceptable.

Confused, Santorray's eyes darted back and forth between the female and the feline. It seemed only logical that the strongest would be the leader, and yet he quickly realized he was in error.

Hissing through their teeth, the villagers slowly lowered their complaints about the Blothrud.

"Welcome Santorray. I am Ahzvietaweh, or Ahz to my friends. Your father, Ergrauth, who is not my friend, has no power here in my village. Therefore, you have none." Standing up, her playful voice was loud enough for all to hear without being forced. "Purebloods exiled us many generations ago. We have no loyalty to your father or your kind. If anything, we seek vengeance for your father's acts against us. He nearly exterminated us on more than one occasion."

Santorray nodded. "This is true. But if it had not been for him, all Altered Creatures, including the Ov'Unday and Kewtalls, would still be slaves to the Notarians. You owe him your lives."

"Oh, yes, we do." Her tone was still one of amusement with a hint of sarcasm. She set her long-bladed spear down and stepped up close to him. "I would suggest we travel to his namesake city and bestow gifts to him, showing our allegiance."

Standing firm, facing the raised stage, only his eyes followed the white-skinned Blothrud toward his side. "That is unnecessary. Providing me with food, water, and safe passage will be enough to show your support."

Rounding his side, Ahz reached out and dragged her fingers over his red skin and across his back, feeling the ridges of hundreds of scars. "Oh, but I insist. How often do we get an ambassador of goodwill dropping by?"

"Ergrauth does not appreciate…" he thought a moment for the right word, "…outsiders dropping by unannounced."

"I believe the word you were looking for was 'Aberrations.' That was the word he used to use when talking about us." Completing the circle, she stood before him and looked eye level into his broad chest before running her hands up his chest and then back down across his tight abdominal muscles. "At least that is what I heard him call us in public."

Santorray never moved from her touch. Instead he kept his focus forward. Knowing that Ergrauth referred to the Kewtall as aberrations, he could only assume that most others knew this as well. "You have never met him. If so, he would had sliced you down before a conversation could take place. He has no tolerance for the Kewtall."

"No tolerance, you say?" Ahz laughed, turning her back and leaning up against him, running her hands up the sides of his legs. "It is because of his obsession with us that I am even here."

Confused, the Blothrud dropped his muzzle down to glare at the female leader leaning against him. "Obsession?"

"Yes. The females of your lands no longer hold interest for him. Perhaps they bore him in their attempt to please him, or perhaps he fears that they may kill him if they get too close. Either way, he comes here and to other Kewtall settlements to have his way with our young females. He knows we live in fear of him and he prefers rape instead of obedience from his home city." Turning around to face him, Ahz lifted her head and stroked a hand against the side of the Blothrud's face. "Do you prefer obedience…" she said, before slapping him hard across the snout, "…or rape?"

Santorray growled from the sting of the slap, but held himself back from retaliating. "Neither. Nor do I believe that he has any interaction with the Kewtall aside from slaughtering them."

"Oh, but both are true." Backing up, Ahz leaned against the large scaled feline. "Many of us are outcomes of his seeding. Some recent, while others, such as myself, happened many generations ago. He lives a dual life. He arrives and ravages our young in a chaotic frenzy of lust and destruction, while ruling the rest of you with a firm grip of control."

"He does *not* control me," Santorray said before thinking.

Intrigued, she leaned forward. "Really? And what would make the son of such an evil ruler say such a thing?"

Growling at his lack of restraint from speaking, he realized he had started down a path by doing so. However, staying the course by forcing Ergrauth's name was obviously not working. He needed to try a new tactic. "I was once the general of the Elite, Ergrauth's primary force to wipe out those who questioned his authority. At least until I also questioned his authority. We have since parted ways."

She laughed at his last statement. "I doubt it was that easy. Disagreeing with Ergrauth is high treason. He would have killed you for such disrespect."

Santorray lowered his brow and glared at her. "And so he tried. But I survived and have returned to face him."

"But he has led his army past the Guardians to the western valley," she said, watching a hint of surprise cross Santorray's face. "What? Do you not think we watch all that happens in these lands? We know you were taken by his troops to the City of Ergrauth along with several others. A giant and several Polenums accompanied you. Where are your companions now?" She glanced off to the mesas surrounding the valley.

"I am alone on this quest to end my dispute with my father."

"We will find out soon enough if that is true." She then nodded to a few villagers standing near the side of the stage. They sped off, gathering others to join them as they left the center of the village. "I'll have my spotters see if any have unfortunately followed you here."

Santorray grinned on one side of his mouth, hoping he had given Asentar enough time to make his heist of supplies before escaping the area. "I have left them in order to stop my father from launching an attack on the humans. He will do to them as he has done to you. Surely, you can see why it makes sense to provide me food and water in order to be on my way."

Laughing at the idea, she allowed other villagers to join in at the humor. "You are quite the specimen, Santorray. But, there is only one way you could be anything more than amusement and our next meal."

The scaled feline gave a low growl and recoiled its body in anticipation of leaping forward to pounce on the outsider.

By this point, Santorray's grin was gone. Instead, he flexed his muscles as he stared at the large scaled feline, waiting for the show of strength to begin. He had competed in many battles to the death, this would just be another few more scars on his tortured skin. "And what might that be?" Growling at the feline, he scratched his own left shoulder, causing is to bleed, showing he had no fear of pain.

Amused by the action, Ahz smirked while patting the enormous feline to keep it calm and prevent it from attacking Santorray. "A battle to the death normally resolves this issue."

"Agreed," Santorray said quickly, before stepping back and bending his knees slightly in his preparation for the battle.

"But in this case, because you are the son of the demon who terrorizes us, I think we should do something else."

Santorray glanced around for additional opponents. "How many? Two, Three?" With arms out to his side, his hands were open and ready to grab the first Kewtall who came close to him and rip him in two. Roaring to intimidate any challengers, he spun his head back and forth to prevent any rear attacks. "What will it take to prove to you that I am on a mission to kill the one you hate, freeing you of fear and bringing you peace?"

Her one word answer was short and clear. "Love."

"Love?"

"Yes, to prove to me that you are not like your father, instead of a fight to the death, you must make love to me. If I should feel in any way that you are violent or controlling, you shall be our next meal. But if I should feel genuinely loved by you, you shall have my support."

Santorray couldn't comprehend what she was saying. He understood the words, but he simply refused to want to grasp the meaning. "Three? Or is it four? How many must I kill before I earn your trust?"

Shaking her head slightly, it was now Ahz's turn to grin. "Fighting to the death is Ergrauth's way of determining one's fate, and would surely put us at a disadvantage, seeing that you are his son. I think we need to test your word of truth in another way."

"And what if I refuse?"

"Then you must defeat the entire village in your escape."

Standing tall, the Blothrud glanced at the crowd of growling villagers.

"Well?" Ahz asked, smiling from the knowledge that she had the upper hand with such a great warrior as the son of Ergrauth.

Glaring through thinned eyes, he mumbled to himself, "How did I let Thorik and Grewen get me into this?"

## Chapter 15
# Perspective

"We're almost there. You really need to have some faith," Grewen said in his normal deep calm tone, while walking through the difficult mountain terrain. His wide twelve-foot tall body lumbered back and forth while navigating his way from one boulder to the next. He had been walking for days since they left Thorik at the city of Ergrauth in order to warn the Ov'Unday of the coming war. Exhausted, he talked to his companion to take his mind off of how tired, hungry, and thirsty he really was.

"Need some faith?" the stout Num shouted. "I am Fir Brimmelle Riddlewood the Seventh, spiritual leader of Farbank. I teach faith, as did six generations before me." A thick soul-marking ran down each arm from what once were very elegant clothes. Now dirty and torn, his attire was far beneath what he liked it to be.

"You read it and preach it, but I'm not sure you teach it or have it." Lifting his leg up to the next boulder, he spanned a crevasse hundreds of feet deep.

Brimmelle was appalled at the statement, causing him to nearly fall out of the giant's open palm. He had been carried across the desert and up the mountainside by the Mognin, citing his short legs as making the trip impossible for him. Sitting in the giant's hand seemed much more logical to the Num. "I know every word on the Mountain King Scrolls. Every evening I've read them out loud from memory ever since Thorik allowed a Thrasher to destroy my original scrolls. How dare you have the audacity to suggest that I do not have faith!"

Rocking back and forth over the crevasse to gain enough momentum to make a final push across, Grewen remained calm like usual. "Reading about a belief or reading a belief out loud is not the same thing as having faith." Making a final rocking motion, he swung the second leg over to the new side, but nearly fell anyway. A quick grab to a rock knocked the Num over within the giant's palm and narrowly saved them from plummeting to their death.

"Hey, be careful!" Brimmelle shouted, sitting back up and straightening his shirt before returning to the conversation at hand. "You're talking nonsense. How can you have faith without reading it or having someone read it to you? Of course I read it. I've read the words since I was eleven, when my father passed away."

Scaling the side of the mountain with nothing more than a thin ledge for Grewen's enormous feet, the Mognin took his time to respond. "Having faith is more than knowing the words. It's about taking a risk to believe in something."

"There is no risk involved in having faith in the Mountain King."

Grewen grinned at the Num's response. "Actually it's just the opposite. Having faith is taking a risk in something that you could not possibly know is true."

"Are you suggesting that the Mountain King's words are false?"

"Not at all. I'm saying that we have no evidence and we weren't there to witness it, so you will have to have faith in the writings and stories of old."

"And I *do* have faith in these, because it did really happen. So, I've proved you wrong. I do have faith."

"Don't confuse faith and acceptance. You know and accept the Mountain King's scrolls but you don't follow them or live them out. Instead of living to the words you read from your memory, you use them as tools to get others to do what you want. I've seen you use them to coax your nephew into making decisions in your favor."

"Leave Thorik out of this. He is one that lacks faith and spirituality. I've worked with him for years, appointed him my Sec to serve me in spreading the word, and yet he doesn't memorize them."

"And yet," Grewen said with a grin, "He lives to the words and concepts of your Mountain King far more than any other Num I've met." Holding Brimmelle off to the side in his wide hand with thumbs on both sides, he continued to shuffle his wide feet across the ledge to a safe landing. "As far as spirituality goes, people don't need to be faithful to be spiritual. These are two things that can work together and work apart."

Brimmelle had heard enough. "I don't think you know what you're talking about. I should be the one teaching you about these concepts. I've spent my life teaching our king's words."

"And it is a shame you never stopped long enough to listen to the meaning of what he was trying to say."

"I don't have to tolerate this persecution of my character any longer!"

Resting for a moment on the landing, near the edge of the crevasse, Grewen opened his fingers and thumbs wide, making it easy for the Num to jump out. "You're not my prisoner. You can leave any time you want."

Brimmelle eased his head over the side of the palm he sat in. The deep canyon below made his stomach churn and his legs begin to tingle and become limp. His fear of heights caused him to nearly pass out from the view. "No," he said, pulling his head in and rolling onto his back in order to collect his bearings. "I see no point of going at it alone. Four feet on this steep terrain doubles our odds of falling versus just your two feet."

Nodding at the attempt on logic, the giant smiled. "I see. So your decision to not climb this passage is solely based on increasing the odds for both of us to survive."

Brimmelle liked the sound of that. "Yes, that's correct." He then clasped his hands behind his head, pulled his legs in, and rested while he waited for Grewen to finish the journey through the mountains.

"Didn't you recite one of the Mountain King's passages a few days ago about the need for all members of a community to lend a hand to help each other?"

"I did."

Grewen waited a minute to see if the Num would understand his purpose for bringing it up, but if he had, he didn't let on. "So, what part of lending a hand applies to you?"

"I've given you these valuable words of wisdom. That is the part I play and that is how I help my community."

Chuckling at the denial within the Num, Grewen analyzed the terrain to determine the safest path down the south side of the mountains. "Well, I suppose I need to do my part and lead us to Trewek." Leaving the safety of the ledge, he slowly proceeded forward.

Continuing down the south side of the Ossuary Range, the landscape was filled with loose rocks and sand, making each placement of the Mognin's foot critical to staying safe. It didn't help much that one of his hands was holding Brimmelle instead of being used for balance.

"You know what I don't understand?" the Num asked.

"Do tell." Grewen cautiously took another step forward on the mountain ledge.

"I don't understand why so many don't follow what's right. It's just common sense."

Grewen paused from walking long enough to use his free hand to pull up a few desert plants from the mountainside and toss them in his mouth. "Common sense is based on your own perception of what is right," he said while chewing.

"But there are some facts that we all know, such as the Mountain King freed us from the Notarians and then wrote the words of wisdom to live by. Why doesn't everyone just follow them?"

"Not everyone believes that he did these things."

"Well then, they are just idiots."

"Interesting. So anyone who has different beliefs is wrong?"

"We've seen the Mountain King Statue and the scrolls with his words on it. We know this to be true. So, yes, if they refuse to accept these facts then they are wrong."

"Did the Mountain King create the statue of himself or carve out the stone monoliths of the scrolls with his own hands?"

"No, of course not."

"Then others did this to honor him, correct?"

"Yes. What's your point?"

"Isn't it possible that what was written was the best interpretation of what the Mountain King stood for instead of his exact words?"

"No. Those were his words." Brimmelle's own words were sharp and clear. He was making a firm point.

"So, are you saying that all those who follow his words are correct in their beliefs?"

"Following his words will lead you to a happy life."

"Do you follow his words?"

"Of course, I do!"

"Are you leading a happy life?"

"Not since I left Farbank."

"How can that be, if you follow the King's words."

"Don't you turn my words around on me. My life was just as I wanted it prior to Ambrosius showing up and leading Thorik on a mission of disaster."

"So, it's Ambrosius' fault that you are unhappy, not your own."

"No, I blame Thorik for leading us away from our village and for the death of my mother, as well as having to team up with an Altered who talks too much!" Brimmelle complained, poking at Grewen's large nose to strengthen his point.

Pulling his head back from the Num's finger, the ground slipped out from under one of Grewen's massive feet, causing him to shuffle to a more stable location on the mountainside. Once stable, he responded to the comment. "I find it interesting that you don't take any responsibility for your own fate. You complain constantly about how terrible you have it. Reality is, you are exactly where you have put yourself. Your fate is in your hands."

"What? Just how can I be blamed for being in the mountains with an Altered? I left Farbank to protect my mother."

"You may have excellent reasoning as to why you are where you are, but these are still due to choices you have made. You didn't have to follow Gluic out of your village."

"Are you suggesting that I just let her leave, unprotected?"

"No, I'm not saying that at all. Life is full of choices, and even if you elect to make difficult ones which put you in difficult positions, they are still your choices."

"How did we get from following the Mountain King's words to you telling me that I make bad choices?"

"I think it started with you asking about common sense."

"Yes, that's correct. If everyone would follow the words of wisdom, civilizations would live in peace. We wouldn't have all of these battles and wars to worry about."

"Really?" Grewen reached for another plant, this time on an upper ledge just out of his reach.

"Really."

"If that is true, than the followers of the Terra King we met in Woodlen would be on our side."

"That's not fair. The Terra King is Darkmere in disguise who proclaims that he is the rebirth of the great Mountain King. They are being misled for his own desires."

"But he is using the words of the Mountain King."

"True, but only the parts of his choosing to get others to do his bidding. I don't understand why people believe him. The original King was a Polenum and he never foretold of his own rebirth."

"He brings them hope, and that is a strong emotion. It can capture a person's thoughts and allow them to forgive pieces that don't fit. All societies need hope, and the Dovenar Kingdom has been without it for some time now. Darkmere understands this well. He inspires their emotions on the back of an already established belief, such as yours, and then fills their minds with his own desires between his teachings."

"Why would anyone tolerate it?"

"What's their other option? If they don't follow him, they are considered an outcast for being a non-believer. If they join but then wish to leave, they are shunned by the believers and criticized by those who never believed for being gullible."

"Can't they unite up against him?"

"Again, why would they. They have hope that he will unify their broken kingdom. Even if they doubted his story of rebirth, they still wish for a better life than what they have now."

"Why hasn't he tried to sway your culture? Do the Ov'Unday have no hope?"

Grewen smiled. "We have great hope. In fact, perhaps more than most cultures. We hope for peace even in spite of the deadliest enemies."

"Do they hold too much hope? Is our journey to Trewek in vain?"

"I'm optimistic. The city leaders asked for proof of a pending war prior to them being willing to join others in stopping the evils who wish to take over our land."

Brimmelle scoffed. "We have the proof. But I'm skeptical that this will be enough to cause them to join the fight."

"You may be correct. But this is a choice they must make."

Shaking his head, Brimmelle muttered, "You and your kind are a waste of time. You don't use common sense."

Working his way across a sandy slope, the earth under Grewen's feet gave way again, this time causing him to slip and fall. Tossing the Num off to the side, the Mognin slid down the mountainside followed by an avalanche of rocks and sand, heading for the edge of a cliff.

Brimmelle rolled to a stop before looking down at the out of control giant. "Grewen!"

Using his wide feet and hands, Grewen attempted to slow himself down. The ground simply moved with him, preventing his efforts, as the edge of the cliff was approaching quickly.

Helplessly watching, Brimmelle took a step on the loose ground and nearly followed in Grewen's path. Fortunately, he was able to step back in time to see the Mognin plant one of his large heels deep into the moving mountainside.

The action started to slow Grewen's descent, but it wasn't until the final few yards that his heel hit upon a solid stone, causing him to jar forward from the abrupt stop. He was safe at the edge of the cliff. At least for a few seconds.

Watching in disbelief, Brimmelle saw the landslide of rocks and sand finally catch up to the Mognin, swallowing his giant body.

Sand sprayed off the cliff across the ledge except for the portion where Grewen still hung on. Instead, the sand gushed passed him on either side and showered the air above him from the force of hitting his body and bouncing off.

The stream of sand and rock hitting the Mognin was all that was visible by Brimmelle, who watched with concern for Grewen.

Shocked, he watched the flume of sand near the Mognin's head disappear along with the rest of the gushing around his body. There was no longer anything holding back the landslide because Grewen was no longer standing there. He had been swept over the ledge.

## Chapter 16
# Faith

---

For the first time in Brimmelle's life, he was alone for as far as the eye could see. This was emphasized by the fact that he stood on the mountainside with a view over the valley below and the peaks along the range. The grandness of the scene triggered feelings of being small and vulnerable.

He stood silent, not sure what to do. His companion had been swept over the cliff by a landslide; the very same companion he had complained about since the day he met him. Brimmelle's fear of heights prevented him from chasing after the giant to see if he was still alive, which in turn caused him to become angry with himself for his weakness.

"Clumsy Altered Creature." Complaining tamed his self-persecution by blaming Grewen. "I finally have need of his services and he goes and does something stupid."

He puffed up his chest and glared down at the edge of the cliff. "I suppose I will have to save him from himself." Taking a few strong steps forward, he slipped and began to tumble down the very hill Grewen had slid down.

Rolling, he attempted to grab onto anything that would stop his fate of rolling off the edge to his death. Unfortunately, everything he latched onto fell with him. Brimmelle began to panic. His arms flailed and his legs kicked at the ground as he tried to stop himself prior to the ledge.

"Help!" he screamed out of instinct. However, this time there would be no one to hear his cries for assistance.

Dirt and small rocks filled his shirt sleeves and pant legs. His once fine clothes were beginning to rip apart under the friction of his slide down the hill. A layer of dust coated his body and face and inadvertently was inhaled and swallowed, causing him to choke and cough. With his eyes shut, he prayed to the Mountain King to save him from certain death.

The only thing working in his favor was that the hillside had been swept clean of the majority of loose gravel by Grewen, lessening the ramifications for Brimmelle who slid to a halt at the edge of the cliff.

Face down, Brimmelle clung to the edge with all his might, fearing that he would start to slide again. Eventually he slowly opened one eye to check out his surroundings, realizing that he had stopped inches from the ledge. "Thank you," he said to the Mountain King.

Grasping the earth, like an infant clutching their mother for safety, he opened both eyes and cautiously leaned his head over to see the bottom of the ravine. Even though his body was stable and flat against the ground, he felt his legs and ankles ache and begin to weaken from the view. His stomach churned and his head began to spin as he stretched his neck out mere inches to take a look.

Fifty feet below was the top of a pile of freshly fallen rocks and sand which had landed on prior piles, all of which encroached onto a small stream, forcing it into a shallow pond before changing course to go around it.

Lining the waterway were plants and trees, a welcome site from the dry mountains. The various shades of green made for a nice contrast to the browns and grays as of late.

Brimmelle sighed at the sight, missing the greens of Farbank. The lush environment of his village was filled with rich colors year-round. Bright flowers painted the landscape in the spring with color and fragrances, a summer rainbow of greens and browns from the forest gave the villagers a sense of energy, and the colored leaves of the fall brought joy and excitement that the Harvest Festival would soon be there.

It had been years since he actually thought about the virtues of the village's terrain and climate. The last time he actually even paid attention to them was when he was eleven years of age. In fact, he even recalled the day and what he was doing at the time.

It was on a spring morning, his birthday to be exact, after climbing on the lower branches of Old Man Sammal's oak tree with his friend. Well, Olena was more than a friend. She was very special to him. He had grown up with her and had planned to spend his entire life with her.

That morning, Olena had asked him what his favorite food was and he had told her that it was freshly picked Sundle Mushrooms fried in hog fat. It was a delicacy that only took place once a year due to the mushroom's growing season. Unfortunately, they hadn't started growing yet in the village, but they had up on the mountainsides.

Later on, young Brimmelle relaxed the day away on the dock, wading his feet in the river, while taking in the smell of the nearby lilacs, the songs of the birds, and the colors of the enchanting valley. The sound of a fish popping up to the surface broke his concentration and allowed him to hear Olena's younger brother, Delanno, calling his name while running toward him. Olena had gone to the mountainside to collect some fresh Sundle Mushrooms and had fallen. Delanno had seen her on a ledge screaming for help and he believed her leg was broken.

Racing to his father, the spiritual leader of Farbank at the time, Brimmelle alerted him of Olena's distress. He, his father, and Delanno ran to help her.

Telling his son to stay below where it was safe, Brimmelle's father climbed up the mountainside to pull Olena from the ledge she had fallen to.

It was up on that cliff on that very day that Brimmelle's life changed forever; for once his father reached Olena he saw that her leg wasn't broke, but was instead being held by a cat-like creature with the ability to blend into its environment. Olena was bait for the Altered Creature's trap.

Changing from a nearly transparent set of colors, the cat's scaly body turned tan before attacking Brimmelle's father and girlfriend, as Brimmelle watched in horror. There was no time to save them and no time to obtain help. Their deaths were quick before the Altered Creature dragged their bodies up the mountainside and away forever.

The vision engrained itself in Brimmelle's mind, playing it back time and time again. He would never forgive himself for telling Olena he wanted those mushrooms, or leading his father into a trap. He would live with that guilt for the rest of his life. He would also live with the hatred of Altered Creatures and the fear of the land outside of the safety of his own village. This one event changed his life forever.

Appointed as the new Fir, spiritual leader of the Farbank, he replaced his father. Brimmelle's childhood playfulness was over, along with the joys of seeing the various shades of green.

Snapping out of his memory, he began to weep from the thoughts of that dreadful day. Normally he would have avoided thinking about it completely, but the times were different now. Dehydration and lack of food had begun to affect his judgment. Muscles cramped across his broad Polenum body and his wide soul-markings had diminished from a dark shade to one only a few tones darker than his normal skin. To add to all of this, the fear of lying on the edge of the ravine had paralyzed his body from making any movements to escape the situation.

"I'm alone, lost, and stuck," he said, sobbing slightly through his words. "How could this happen to me? I praise the words of the Mountain King every day. Should I not be protected from such misfortune for doing so?"

He pulled his view from the plants along the shoreline below and closed his eyes to avoid seeing the sight of the long fall before him. "Where are you, you stupid Altered?" Half crying, anger crept into his voice. "How dare you put me in this situation, alone in these infernal mountains with no chance of escaping." Blaming Grewen reduced his self-pity and began to dry up his tears. His voice became louder as his frustration grew. "Damn you, Grewen. You should have been more careful!"

The echo of his raised voice bounced back and forth across canyon, loosening up sand and a few rocks that slid down to Brimmelle. He immediately clutched onto the ledge even tighter as the small wave of pebbles stacked up against him and then rolled over his body and down the ravine.

After it stopped, he was half buried on the ledge looking down to the stream and his doom. "Why does this always happen to me. I follow the rules. I should be granted happiness for doing so. But instead, I have seen far too much death of my loved ones and have been placed in harm's way more often than a dozen lifetimes should hold. Why has the King abandoned me?"

A small section of the ledge broke free, causing one of his legs to swing down below the ridge. Loose rocks tumbled down off his body, down past his hanging leg. Brimmelle's body went rigid again as he held his breath and his eyes closed tight, waiting for the rest of the ledge to give way.

"I'm sorry," he said softly. "I don't blame you, my King. I just don't understand why I am being tested so hard? I've spread your word to everyone I meet. What else would you have me do?"

He waited for a response even though he knew he wouldn't actually get one.

The Mountain King had died long ago, but in some way Brimmelle had hoped the spirit of the King still followed him and was proud of what he was doing. He had missed the feeling of a proud father figure ever since his father had been killed. There really had never been anyone to praise him and lift him up when he was down. Even his mother, Gluic, gave praise sparingly, and when she did he always felt she was trying to tell him something different than what he wanted to hear.

Brimmelle had been the Fir since he was eleven years old and his responsibilities were too important to allow his followers to see that he had need for praise. That would show he had a weakness. For them to trust him, he couldn't permit them to see his times of sadness or in need. All he asked from the Mountain King in return was to be free of fear; fear from injury and death, fear from Altered Creatures, fear from dangerous height, and fear from the unknown. Was this too much to ask? "I've memorized every one of your writings and have learned everything I need to know. I held up my end of the bargain. Hold up yours and keep me safe."

The entire section of the ledge that he clutched onto broke free and slid thirty feet down before being stopped by an outcropping. The rock Brimmelle rode on slammed onto an already cracked boulder before it teetered back and forth. Sand from above rushed down on top of the Num, changing the balance of the rock from side to side.

"I'm sorry," he softly said again. "Perhaps there is still more I can learn." He searched his thoughts for some weakness in his character, but struggled to find any.

The outcropping cracked again from the recent arrival of Brimmelle, causing his teetering rock to shift dangerously close to falling off. "I'm *sure* there is something else I need to learn." He searched his thoughts beyond himself and to what Grewen had said. "Perhaps knowing the words isn't enough. I must do better at living them out as well."

He waited for an answer. "Give me a sign if this is what I must do?"

The outcropping broke free, sending the Num off his rock and into the air. He flew toward the rock pile below, waving his arms and legs in a state of panic while yelling for help at the top of his lungs. Unfortunately, there was no one there to help him.

## Chapter 17
# The Robe

What seemed like a long aerial flight down into the depths of Della Estovia, was only the remaining twenty feet to the top of the rock pile. But even a twenty foot fall onto rocks could kill Brimmelle or at the very least break several bones, if it hadn't been for a Mognin catching him.

Covered up to his waist, Grewen had been busy clearing rocks from around him, while Brimmelle had been clinging to the ledge above. His own fall onto the pile of rocks had completely, but only temporarily, buried the Mognin. The thick brown hide covering his body had protected him from fire, arrows, and now a fifty foot drop. Then again a fifty-foot drop for a five foot Num was considerably more dangerous than for a twelve foot tall Mognin.

"Hello," Grewen said to the Num he had caught.

Collapsing from the fall, Brimmelle had assumed he had crushed against the rocks. The sight of Grewen's smirk took him a few seconds to realize that he was not dead. "Grewen? Is that really you?"

"How many handsome Mognins do you think roam these mountains," he chuckled.

"Oh, Grewen. I am so thankful to see you." Jumping down from the Mognin's dual thumbed hand, he turned around on the pile of rocks and hugged Grewen's exposed torso.

Surprised by the reaction, Grewen had to comment on it. "Now that I've established who I am, who are you and what have you done with Brimmelle?"

Stepping back, the Num realized what he was doing. It was not like him to show emotions such as these, especially to an Altered Creature. Clearing his throat, he straightened up his soiled shirt. "I'm just glad that you are alive and well…for Thorik's sake. The boy thinks very highly of you and would miss you greatly if something should happen to you."

"I'm glad to hear that. Do you suppose he thinks highly enough of me for you to help free me from this pile before the next landslide covers me up again?"

Brimmelle glanced up at the ledge he fell from. "Yes, of course. I would be willing to help you so we can leave this place…for Thorik."

Grewen grinned at the game. "Excellent. Please pass on my appreciation to him next time you see him." Taking his overly large hands, he calmly removed shovels of rocks and sand from his sides and front, while Brimmelle worked on removing what he could from behind the giant.

Periodically more sand and pebbles rolled off the cliff ledge and down on top of them, but nothing that would be more than a reminder of the potential danger they were in by staying there. It also put Brimmelle back into a grumpy mood as the majority of sand seemed to fall on him regardless how many times he shifted his standing location. This little dance with the falling cliff debris prevented his ability to be effective in helping dig the giant out. In addition, he complained about the strain on his back and arms each time he moved a rock from behind the Mognin's back.

It wasn't long before Grewen had removed enough rock and earth to break himself free. Pulling one thick leg out at a time, he rolled to his side and then onto his knees and then feet before they made their way down the pile of rubble to the shallow pond area of the stream in order to take a drink.

Brimmelle had reached the water moments prior and began to have his fill of the cool liquid, but he stopped when he looked upstream at the Mognin reaching his lips down to suck from the stream. The idea of drinking the water downstream of the giant caused him to stop.

"What's the matter?" Grewen asked.

Brimmelle struggled with the answer. A few hours ago he would have had no reservations about telling him the problem. He was not going to drink downstream from an Altered Creature.

Looking back up at the ledge he recalled his discussion with the Mountain King before looking back at Grewen. "Nothing. Nothing is wrong," he said, reaching back down into the water to scoop up some water. Holding it, he looked at it a little longer. It looked fine. He smelled it. It smelled fine. He finally sipped a small bit from his palm. It tasted fine.

Grewen drank some more, watching Brimmelle out of the corner of his eye as the Num began to drink from the stream.

Brimmelle eventually closed his eyes and placed his entire face into the water to clean it off. It felt fresh and cool as he scrubbed his hands across his forehead and cheeks. He was proud of himself for getting past the fear of using water downstream from an Altered.

Taking a quick breath, the Num then dunked his whole head into water to wash his hair, scrubbing the dirt out with both hands. It felt wonderful to get clean again. He had felt filthy for so long that he wasn't sure how much effort it would take to tidy himself up.

Pulling his head back out of the stream, he was amazed at the amount of dirt that was now in the once clear stream. The entire area around him was saturated in mud. He waited for the stream to clear itself, only to find the new water was just as bad. The water he was washing his hair with had already been muddied.

Glancing upstream, the Num was appalled at the sight. Grewen had disrobed and was lying on his front in the pond area with his head on its side so he could breathe. A swirl of brown dirt and body oils filled the entire pond before traveling downstream. Brimmelle placed a hand in the air to cover the sight of Grewen's wide naked rear extending from the pond. It was a sight he had wished he had never seen and one that he, unfortunately, would never forget. "What are you doing?"

"Enjoying the little things in life. Jump in, it feels great."

Looking back at the murky and oily water, his answer was quickly made. "I was washing my face with that water!"

"It felt wonderful, didn't it?" Grewen reached over to the side of the pond and grabbed a handful of plants and began eating them.

Backing away from the water, Brimmelle stood up. "It did until I realized it was your filth I was washing it with."

Grewen picked up his head a bit and looked at the water around him. "Oh, sorry about that," he said with a grin. "I guess I was dirtier that I had thought."

Marching over to the edge of the pond, the Num was disgusted in what he saw. "This is not right. Put your robe on. Have some decency."

"We're out of harm's way and need to take a rest anyway. I'm going to enjoy this stream for a few minutes before we start up again. Care to join me?"

"What? Get in the stream with you? Are you insane?"

"Well, if you're not going to relax, could you help me out and scratch an itch I have on my shoulder blade?"

"No! I'm not getting in there to scratch your back. Even if I normally would, which I wouldn't, I especially would not while you're naked."

"Odd. Why is that?"

"Because you're naked!"

"What does that have to do with anything? Does my body offend you in some way?"

Brimmelle looked over the giant's wide body before placing his hand back up to block the sight of his rear cheeks extending upward. "Yes it does. I don't want to see anyone's naked body, especially yours."

"What are you afraid of?"

"I'm not afraid of anything," Brimmelle responded, glancing back up at the cliff and recalling the conversation he had while awaiting his death.

"Then stop being so timid and get in." Grewen swiped his arm across the pond, creating a wave of water which knocked Brimmelle over and into the pond.

Gasping, as though he had been drowning at sea, the Num began standing back up. All of his clothes were drenched and the water dripping off was thick with brown dirt. "I can't believe you did that."

"Then you won't believe this either," the Mognin laughed, spraying the Num with another wave of water.

Splashing back down into the stream, he popped his head out. "Why are you doing this? This is foolishness."

"Yes. It's important to have a little foolishness from time to time."

Still on his hands and knees in the stream, the Num gathered his breath. "And why is that?"

"Because if you don't, you'll remember your journey of life as all hardships." He took another bite of the local weeds from the shore. "Take this stream for example. If we simply took a sip and moved on, you wouldn't recall it. The only thing you would remember is falling down that cliff. However, by taking a few minutes out to enjoy such a stream, we will recall this as a pleasant memory."

Brimmelle took the opportunity to leap out of the water and onto dry land.

Grewen grinned, as he did so often. "You don't think I'll spray you with water up on dry land?"

Jumping out of the way of the next wave from the Mognin, Brimmelle chuckled at his accomplishment.

"Oh, you think you're quick?" Grewen sat up with crossed legs and scooped water from both sides of him with his wide hands out toward the Num.

Brimmelle was going to get pounded by the water from one side or the other. Looking for protection, he grabbed Grewen's robe, which had been lying on the ground, and used it as a shield while both waves smacked up against him.

Slapping his hands in the water one after another, the giant continued to scoop up handfuls of water and send them toward the Num.

Brimmelle labored to stand up with the Mognin's robe over his own head and body. It was heavy to begin with, but now with the added weight of the water soaking into it and the splashes hitting him, it was getting harder by the moment.

Knowing he couldn't stand there and take it forever, Brimmelle attempted to run with the robe covering his body. The dampness started bringing out the smells of the long used robe, causing him to gag and cough. It was a short escape as he tripped and fell into the stream, while Grewen continued to splash him.

Rolling the robe off him, he pulled his head up for air as he sat on the bottom of the stream. Without realizing it, he was laughing. The entire ordeal of him trying to run in a wet stinky robe that was twice his own height suddenly seemed stupidly funny.

"Brimmelle?" Grewen said.

"It's alright." Brimmelle laughed so hard that he nearly lost his breath. "I can't recall the last time I've had a good snigger."

"But, Brimmelle-"

"I know, I know. I need to take it easy so I don't hurt myself." He laughed some more at the idiotic sight of Grewen splashing him while he ran with the robe over his head and body. "This is your fault. I haven't laughed in years. It feels…" He thought about it a moment. "…good."

"I'm glad to hear that. I really am," Grewen said. "But my robe has now been taken by the stream and is now out of my view."

"What?" Brimmelle's laugh stopped as he turned to see the stream lead around a bend. The robe was no longer visible. "Grewen, I'm sorry!"

"Don't be sorry. It was worth it to finally see you enjoy yourself. But now I need to get my robe back."

The two hopped up and ran downstream to catch the robe.

Mognins are clumsy runners as they sway back and forth from their enormous size. Grewen was no different. His long steps helped, but they were not quick or frequent enough to make any serious headway on the speed of the stream.

As a Num, Brimmelle was smaller but quicker. Unfortunately, he was not much of a runner and he soon began to tire out from the race with the water. Turning at the bend, he could see the robe floating on the surface, spanning most of the stream's width.

There were two reasons Brimmelle didn't look back prior to making the bend himself. First, he didn't want to slow down, seeing that he was struggling to keep up his momentum as it was. Second, he had no desire to see a naked Mognin running toward him. One glance and he would always curse himself for imbedding such a vision in his memory.

Snagged by the brush on the stream's banks, the robe stopped. Brimmelle couldn't believe his luck. Huffing and puffing while running toward it, his fortune had finally turned for the better.

Narrowing the gap, he slowed to catch his breath. Hands at his hips he gasped for air in the high altitude of the mountains. He finally stopped, just feet from it. "Okay, enough fun. Time to get back on your owner, so I don't have to veer my eyes from his private regions."

Pushing the brush out of his way to enter the stream, the robe broke free just as he reached for it. "No!" he called, as though it had a mind of its own to purposely tease him by leaving.

Flowing down the stream again, the robe turned and shifted from one side of the stream to the other, all along being chased by the out-of-breath Brimmelle.

Turning around a second bend, the stream merged with another larger stream, increasing its width and depth. Large boulders rose above the water's surface, most likely after they had rolled down from the cliffs above. There was very little shoreline before the vertical rock face of the canyon walls.

Brimmelle was now nervous. It was no longer a few steps into the stream in order to grab the robe, it was now potentially a swim. Panting, he leaned forward and rested in order to catch his breath.

"Did you find it?" Grewen yelled from the first bend.

Shutting his eyes as he turned his head back to the Mognin, he shouted, "I can see it!" He then made the turn, out of Grewen's view, and ran along the thin shore of the joined streams. Ignoring his aching body and pounding chest, he ran in front of the slow moving robe so that he could have time to move out into the stream and let the robe float to him.

The plan was sound, if it wasn't for what lay ahead. The stream led to a cavern, taking the water beneath the desert mountain's surface.

With his heart racing faster than he could ever recall, Brimmelle trudged his way out into the stream. Ankle depth soon became knee, knee depth soon became waist, and the next thing he knew he was swimming.

Stroke after stroke, he moved out toward the middle. The current was much more difficult than he had imagined. At any moment he could easily be swept away underground. Nearing his planned location to grab the garment, he swam against the current of the stream in order to hold his position. With his legs and arms burning from overuse and his lungs hurting to take another breath, he waited for the robe to get close enough to grab.

Finally within reach, the robe opened up and surrounded the Num's body, wrapping itself around his legs, body and arms. Kicking and trying to swim only tangled his body up more in the enormous cloth. Brimmelle quickly went from trying to save the robe to trying to save himself from the robe.

The current carried him downstream and into deeper waters. The stream narrowed prior to going into the cavern and underground, causing the depth and speed to increase.

Freeing one arm from the heavy wet cloth, he reached out and grabbed onto one of the many boulders extending from the surface. It wasn't much, but he hoped it would keep him from being washed away while he tried to free up his other arm.

The rushing water caused the thick robe to rap itself around the Num like a jellyfish, pulling him downstream like a sail on a ship. For a moment he considered letting go. The task was too much for him. But then the sight of the naked Mognin approaching him gave him strength to hang on. It wasn't a view he ever thought he'd want to see, but under the circumstances it was well received.

Wading into the water, Grewen allowed the water to push him down the stream toward Brimmelle. The water quickly moved up his body until it was past his waist and then up to his chest. "Hold on!" he called to the Num.

Brimmelle watched his companion approach. The water moved him quickly, giving the Num a sigh of relief that it soon would be over and they would be safe. It was then that he realized that Grewen was no longer under control of his own speed. The water grabbed the giant and pushed him directly toward him.

Barreling toward the Num, Grewen reached out to stop himself by grabbing the boulder which Brimmelle was holding onto. The successful grab with his hands and one foot stopped the Mognin from squishing the Num into the boulder, but in doing so, it dislodged the boulder from the base of waterway, moving it a foot from where it had been.

"What are you doing out here?" Grewen asked.

"I was saving your robe!" he yelled back.

"Why would anyone risk their life for a robe?"

Brimmelle open his mouth to reply but realized that he didn't have a logical answer. "I don't know," he answered honestly, still out of breath. "Get me off of this rock and to a safe place."

The boulder shifted again from the Mognin's weight. "I don't think we're going to have a choice about getting off this rock. Sometimes in life the safe place is the unknown. Hopefully that is true this time. Hang on!"

Shifting once again, the boulder fell backward, allowing Grewen and Brimmelle to pass over it.

With the robe still wrapped around his legs, Brimmelle grabbed around Grewen's large neck from behind. He then rode on the back of the Mognin into the shadows of the cave. There was no stopping them.

Chapter 18

# Arrival

Darkness engulfed Grewen and Brimmelle as the mountain's waterway launched them into a cave and under the ground. The current was too strong for swimming to the side or navigating, then again, the darkness prevented them from knowing what to navigate toward or away from.

The only thing they knew for sure was that they were both still together and that they were traveling down at a steep angle. Brimmelle clung to the back of the Mognin. The Num's feet were still wrapped up in Grewen's robes, leaving the giant naked, a sight that Brimmelle truly did not wish to see. Fortunately, due to the darkness, this wasn't an issue.

The two companions drifted down the rushing waters as it swayed to the one side and then the other. A few sudden drops nearly broke them apart, but they managed to stick together with their heads bobbing above the surface. It was a fast and wild trip that no rational being would ever do on purpose, for the risk of death could approach at any moment with nothing to warn them.

Grewen bounced off of several underwater cavern walls and slapped his legs against many submerged boulders. Unfortunately, that was not the worst part for him, Mognins tended to sink in water, so he was constantly trying to tread water in order to keep them both breathing.

The rushing waters continued. It was pointless to keep track of time as they struggled to stay alive on a moment by moment basis. The underground stream was relentless and it had taken its toll on both of them.

Exhausted and nearly depleted of energy, the waterway gave them one last surprise, dumping them out into a large open cavern after a twenty foot waterfall.

The two broke away from each other during the waterfall. The robe, finally being stripped from Brimmelle legs, floated down behind them and landed on Grewen's head. The ride was over. The water they landed in spread out and slowed down. The cave they had sprung from was one of many that led into the cavern several miles across. Light from the center of the ceiling burned against their eyes after so many hours in pitch blackness.

Eventually, the travelers worked their way to the shore and rested on the soft muddy banks. The air was moist and had a fragrance of freshly turned soil from a farm. Chimes could be heard in the distance, most with a very low tone to them; soothing and welcoming.

Brimmelle's eyes adjusted faster than Grewen's, seeing several large towers in the center of the cavern spring up and out of the top opening and into the light. It was as though giant tree trunks had rooted themselves on the islands in the center of the cavern and reached above the vine-covered ceiling for air and light.

"We made it," Brimmelle said. "We've arrived in the city of Trewek."

Arriving through one of the many underground waterways into the giant sinkhole below the desert floor, the two were grateful to be alive, let alone end up in the location they had planned to reach. Still in the outer regions of the sinkhole, the cavern was shaped much like the inside of a pumpkin with the top cut open in a circle. Instead of the fruit's internal ligaments, vines hung from the cavern walls and beautiful city towers rose from the center.

Surrounding the core towers, the city of Trewek was filled with buildings and homes resting on the various islands connected by bridges designed to look like roots from the tree trunk towers. Past the internal city was the farmland, fed by the waterways and the sun which was given to them through mirrors high in the towers, allowing crops to be grown nearly all the way back to the cavern walls where Brimmelle and Grewen rested.

"That worked out well," Grewen said sarcastically, feeling the pain in every part of his body from the long water ride. "As the saying goes, 'By land, air, or water, there's more than one way to travel to Trewek.'"

"Put your robe on," Brimmelle coughed out, lying on the dry ground.

Grewen looked down at himself and then at the soaked robe next to him. "Oh, I suppose that would be wise prior to talking to the elders."

"I know I would appreciate it."

Grewen donned his robe and waited for them to rest long enough to have the strength to walk into the city. Once there, they asked for an audience with the elders.

Knowing that they would have some time prior to their reply, they were provided assistants to escort them to their own rooms in order to freshen up.

Brimmelle asked his assistant for some food and water before cleaning himself up the best he could. Standing before a tall mirror in his room, he shook his head at the sight before him. His once fine clothes were ripped and soiled beyond repair. His appearance had always been very important to him, but he was starting to learn throughout his adventures that it was what is inside that counted, not the clothes he chose to wear.

Missing several buttons on his shirt, he used the ones remaining. One sleeve was nearly gone, while the other had large frayed sections. After combing his hair, he put his boots back on. The leather sole in one had worn through and both had been cut and worn beyond repair. He was just thankful that he wasn't being seen in his village of Farbank. Thankfully he was in Trewek, a city of Altered Creatures who did not care about such things.

Recalling the memory of Grewen splashing him in the mountain stream brought on a slight smile. It had felt good to not have to always be so formal and in control. "I have learned something new," he said to the Mountain King in a soft voice. "We must not allow our lives to become so tense that we miss out on the small joys in life." He scanned his dirty, ripped and soiled clothes one last time in the mirror and smiled at the ridiculous sight. "Who would have ever envisioned that I, the Fir of Farbank, would be seen in public like this?" A sigh of relaxation was release as he heard someone approach his room.

"Are you ready, Brimmelle? We only have a few minutes before we are to speak to the elders." Grewen's deep baritone voice was calm, as always.

"Yes, I'm coming." Brimmelle took one last swipe at his hair with no success in making himself look well groomed. He chuckled at his reflection. "Anything will look good compared to Grewen and that filthy robe."

Stepping out of the temporary quarters that the city had provided, Brimmelle brushed off a few more pieces of debris from his clothes, prior to gazing at Grewen. "What in the world?"

Grewen stood tall and straight in a new decorative royal green robe lined with golden stitching of various famous phrases by Trewek, the city's namesake. The glamorous ankle-length robe was open in the front, revealing a glimmering silk gown cut off just below the knees. On his feet he wore thick leather sandals made from the finest craftsmanship, and his normal body odor had been replaced with a sweet fragrance of honey.

A concerned eye fell upon Grewen's face. "Is that the best you can do when meeting our city elders?"

Brimmelle was visibly upset and his hands began to shake from the comment. "How did you get those clothes?"

"Didn't the elders provide you with an assistant to ask you what you needed?"

"Yes, but I thought they were just asking for what I needed to eat. I had no idea I could ask for new clothing!"

Grewen shook his head at the Num's appearance. "Well, it's too late now. We need to leave this very moment. Try to comb your hair or something. It is important that we make a good impression."

Frazzled, Brimmelle ran his fingers back through his hair and then vigorously wiped down his outer jacket, only to accidently tear it a few more times as they walked to the base of the largest tower.

Guarding the double doors, two large Mognins stood with no weapons. They were there to control the traffic more than to protect the elders. No one had ever attempted an attack on the city or had broken their way into the elder's chamber, so there was no need.

Grewen approached. "We are scheduled to speak with the elders."

One of the guards turned and entered the tower to obtain permission, while the other studied the clothing of the Num next to Grewen.

Feeling very embarrassed about his attire, Brimmelle kept his eyes down. Shuffling his feet, he stepped behind Grewen while waiting for their time to enter.

The door finally opened by the guard who had left them. "Your audience with the elders is now granted and awaiting the two of you," he said to Grewen, before looking down for the Num who had disappeared. "Wasn't there a second requestor?"

"Yes," Grewen said looking down next to him and finding nothing. He then turned farther to find Brimmelle hiding behind him, tucking in his shirt one more time. "There you are. You're awfully fidgety today. Are you up for this?"

"Yes. Yes, I'm fine." Straightening his sleeves, he nodded to Grewen.

"Follow me," the guard said, leading them into the main hall.

Once in the main chamber, the elders sat quietly as they watched Grewen and Brimmelle approach.

"Truth be said," the leader of the elders said.

"Truth be heard," Grewen replied.

"I am Bevex"

"And I am Grewen"

"You have returned with evidence of a pending war?"

Grewen stepped closer. "We have proof that the Winds of Conquest have been released from their prison and the children of the great dragon Rummon are now back in our skies. Ergrauth now has them at his command. He has used the Winds of Conquest to defeat the Guardians and pass over into our lands. We have seen this with our own eyes."

"Your eyes may tell the truth, but they can also be fooled. Your tongue may be honest, but it also can be misled. What proof have you brought us?"

Reaching into his new robes, he pulled out a pouch, which he had removed from his old robe. Opening it, he removed several pieces from a vase. They had received it in the city of Ergrauth in a few large pieces, but now it was in many smaller ones. "Broken now, this once was the magical prison of the Winds of Conquest." He set the pieces in order so the elders could review them.

Carvings on the vase showed views of battles and lightning and storms. Magical symbols and ancient writings lined the upper and lowers parts.

"These markings look correct, and if they are, the Winds of Conquest have truly been released."

Grewen nodded. "Then the Ov'Unday of Trewek will join the fight against Ergrauth?"

"What is your proof that Ergrauth has the Winds of War under his command? And if he does, what proof do you have that he plans to use them against us?"

"What? You can't be serious!" Brimmelle stated without thinking. "We've risked our lives to bring this to you in order to save your city, and this is the response we receive?" His shyness from his appearance had quickly vanished and his years as a village leader had kicked in.

"Brimmelle," Grewen said, shaking his head with displeasure at the outburst.

"Oh, no you don't. I didn't want to go on this search for your proof in the first place. We witnessed Ergrauth's army firsthand and were nearly killed by the Del'Unday and all the other Altereds out there. I was attacked by bugs, I almost starved to death, I nearly drowned, and I had to see Grewen naked, all to prove to you that you are in danger. This is unacceptable. By you asking for more, you're saying what we did was a waste of time!"

"Grewen, is this high-tempered Polenum a companion of yours?"

Grewen watched as Brimmelle's soul-markings turned a deep black from his frustration. "He is. He is part of my family pod and a dear friend. I trust him with my life."

Even in Brimmelle's agitated state, the Mognin's words hit him by surprise.

Bevex nodded. "If he is of your family pod, his voice speaks for you. Truth be heard?"

Grewen glanced down at Brimmelle who was still furious at the elders. "Truth be said. I share his thoughts. We have done what we can to prove our case in order to save the namesake city of Trewek. We can do no more. It is now up to you to determine if you will prepare defenses to save your own city and the Ov'Unday who live here, as well as if you will join with the humans against the forces of the Ergrauth."

The elder nodded back. "Truth be said."

"Truth be heard," Grewen replied. Turning, he moved to leave the room.

Brimmelle did not. He had more to say. "I was once like you. I had my paradise in Farbank. And when I was warned of an unseen threat, I ignored it. Fortunately, my nephew was willing to take it seriously. He saved us. This isn't my city or my people, but I would hate to see Grewen's culture die without even attempting to save it. Ignoring the outside world doesn't mean it will ignore you. War is coming. I've seen the demon that drives this. He will not propose a plan to this elder council. You will not have time to deliberate on an agreement for peace. They come to rule you or kill you. There is no other option."

The elders stayed quiet as the Num eventually shook his head, turned and then walked out, followed by Grewen.

The two exited the tower without speaking until Brimmelle reached the first Bridge. "I'm ready to go home, Grewen. I'm ready to work with my people in Farbank and give them the knowledge I've learned out here."

"Have you given up on our cause?" Grewen asked as they crossed the bridge.

"No, but these are not my people. I can't influence them. This is a waste of my time."

"My people are a waste of your time?"

"Don't play games with my words. You know that I don't belong here. My place is in Farbank."

Reaching the far side of the bridge Grewen motioned for the Num to have a seat in a small open social sitting area, where wood-carved benches and seats faced each other. "Will you need help returning home?"

Brimmelle leaned back in the smoothly carved wooden seat. He just wanted it to be over, as he looked up at the clear sky through the opening in the top of the cavern. "I want to be able to feel safe."

"Feeling safe is a state of mind. You can do that just about anywhere."

"No, I don't think I can."

Grewen was intrigued. "Do you feel safe here?"

"No."

Grewen looked around at the soft roaming water that separated the lush green islands where beautifully carved bridges spanned. Soft chimes could be heard in the background as the Ov'Unday went about their business in a calm manner. "Why do you not feel safe here, of all places?"

"Because of that," Brimmelle said, pointing up at the opening above them.

Two hundred feet above them, surrounding the rim of cavern, various creatures were looking down from above. Many were starting to lower ropes, while others were tossing grips onto the high towers. The invasion of the Del'Unday no longer needed proof, it was here.

Chapter 19
# Ov'Unday Elders

Thorik's Log: October 9th of the 650th year
*We are able to fly great distances in a short amount of time with Rummon. Never in my wildest dreams would I have expected to ride on a dragon, let alone inside one. We've stopped a few times to rest and eat. Watching Rummon eat is an experience I will never forget. I thought Grewen ate a lot. We camped next to Govi Glade for several days while Gluic retreated to be by herself and Rummon spent the time getting used to his old body. I took a chance and suggested we return Vesik into the magical spheres within the glade, now that we don't require its powers any longer. Not only did I lose that battle, but I'm afraid it only pushed Avanda further from me by even suggesting such an act. I am very concerned about her dependence on her book of magic.*

R ummon, the mighty lord of all dragons, ruled the skies once again after being held in magical stasis for thousands of years. He had been protected from his perceived enemies by those of the air, only to recently fall victim to an insect who accidently flew its way into his protective dome. This one small insignificant creature had nested in Rummon's well-preserved flesh and then bore offspring, which led to future generations of insects. The infestation soon ate gaping holes in Rummon's once magnificent body.

Now revived from his stasis by the Nums and the spell book Vesik, Lord Rummon took flight over Terra Australis in spite of the damage done to his body. Magic kept him alive, but his mind and body were under his own bidding. Although the bird Gluic, tucked behind his ear in an open wound to his head, influenced his flight path.

Nestled in a large open cavity, protected by Rummon's ribcage, three Nums rested against various organs. The area changed size when Rummon's lungs filled with air, pressing the Nums toward one another. Strong consistent beats of the wagon-sized heart rung in the ears of all three passengers who had grown accustomed to its deep percussion beat as they waited to see where they would land next.

"I see smoke," Avanda said. Her soul-makings had flourished over the past year with intricate designs around her neck and down onto her wrists and hands. She had been reading from the spell book, Vesik, on new spells which had previously been blank pages. Over time, the book had slowly provided her with more to learn as it trusted her with its powers.

Thorik was in a dazed state of having nothing to do in the cramped quarters. He had been staring at Avanda for hours, pondering what he needed to do in order to get her back into his life. Memories flooded his mind of her touch against his skin and her drive to overcome anything that threatened them. Her fanciful soul-markings had blossomed over the years and he had begun to yearn to trace them with his fingers and kiss her upon her lips. She may not have been the most sensual and seductive female he had known, but he could trust her with his life and she had become his very best friend. No, more than just a friend. A partner for life.

Even though they sat a few feet apart, Thorik missed Avanda dearly and oddly enough felt threatened by her new love, Vesik. "Smoke?" he eventually said, snapping out of distant thoughts.

Leaning against one of the dragon's large ribs, Avanda hung her head out of Rummon's body to get a better look.

Following the wide Volney River, the land had changed from the sandy brown terrain of the Kiri Desert to the grasslands and then the heavy foliage of the forest, just prior to great Luthalum Tunia Lake. Smoke billowed up from the forest in an arc across the green landscape as though a wave of fire was pushing north, leaving a trail of ashes in its wake.

"The Mythical Forest," Thorik said, staring in disbelief. "The Myth'Unday are in danger. Their land will be destroyed from the south. Southwind must be making their move north. Therefore, the Matriarch is joining the war and has chosen Darkmere as her ally." Standing on the organs and flesh which Avanda sat on, he grabbed onto Rummon's ribs and leaned out over Avanda's head to obtain a better view of the scene. "Mr. Hempton," he said, wondering how his friend of games was faring. Unintentionally, he leaned against Avanda. Once he realized it, he waited for her to pull away, but she didn't. The lack of movement on her part caused him to sigh in relief as maybe she still cared for him.

"Mr. Hempton?" Emilen asked, causing the other two Nums to tighten their shoulders and pull slightly away from one another. "Who is Mr. Hempton?"

Thorik took one more gander at the tall flames coming from the line of fire before turning to her. "He is a friend…sort of."

"Sort of?" she questioned, pulling herself upright by pressing her hands against the dragon's organs on either side of her. It was difficult to stand on soft fleshy organs while Rummon shifted his body to new directions.

"Mr. Hempton is a Myth'Unday who gives visitors to his land a chance to pass unharmed if they can win a game." Saying that, Thorik could tell that Rummon had started to descend toward the forest. Turning back around, the Num gazed out between the ribs to see where they were approaching.

"He lets you pass if you can beat him in a game?" Emilen asked.

Thorik answered without looking back into Rummon's open cavity. "Yes, well, no. He doesn't play against you. You have to play against yourself. If you can face and overcome your own fears, then you've won your passage."

"And if you don't win? How will he stop you from passing?"

"If you lose, you'll be taken by the Myth'Unday, never to see the outside world again. I'm not sure if they let you go mad from your own fears or if they serve you up as their next meal. I didn't really want to know the details."

Thorik and Avanda kept their heads out of the side of the dragon's chest as Rummon lowered them into a clearing on the north side of the fire line. It was a small green meadow surrounded by the lush forest.

Landing with a jolt, Thorik turned back toward Emilen to see if she was ready to depart. To his surprise, he saw her toss a small piece of paper into his wooden coffer and quickly close the lid and lock the clasps.

"What are you doing?" Thorik asked at the scene.

Emilen's eyebrows narrowed. "What do you mean?"

"What did you put in my coffer?"

"Your notes," she said with innocence in her demeanor. "You left it open when you rushed over to see the forest fire and then Rummon's rough landing caused your papers to fall out." She gave

Thorik a concerning look. "Thorik Dain, are you accusing me of something after I just tried to clean up your mess?"

Thorik was torn. He couldn't recall if he had closed his coffer prior to his daydreaming of Avanda and her soul-markings. "No. It just surprised me to see you with it."

Avanda rolled her eyes and pushed him out of her way in order to grab her gear. "You might as well be blind, Thorik, if you can't trust what you see with your own eyes." Pushing him out of the way a second time, she exited the open cavity through the dragon's ribs.

Thorik stood there, crouched over in the hole, surrounded by flesh and large organs, unsure what to say.

"Why do you put up with her?" Emilen said. "She pushes you around and never shows you any respect. I, on the other hand, support your endeavors and respect you for the mighty leader you've become."

"Leader?" Thorik scoffed at her choice of word. "What kind of Num leader doesn't have his soul-markings? This is a common passage from childhood into adulthood. One that I have obviously yet to take."

Emilen set the coffer down and placed both hands on his shoulders. "Listen to me, Thorik Dain of Farbank. You have accomplished more than any Num since the great Mountain King himself. You have stopped the most powerful E'rudite of all time, Darkmere, from accomplishing his plans on several occasions. Who would have guessed that the Dark Lord would have a Num as his nemesis?"

"Nemesis? I'm no one's rival. I'm just trying to do what's right."

"Of course, you are. And by doing what you believe is right, you have foiled Darkmere's plans time and time again. He is always one step behind you."

Coughing out a laugh, Thorik struggled to accept the comment. "I think it's been the other way around. It seems as though he knows my plans well before I carry them out."

"If that were true, then how have you constantly defeated him?"

"I think by pure luck."

Emilen straightened up his shoulders. "Don't sell yourself short, Thorik. You are very smart and clever. The only way he could ever win against you would be to know your every move." She stopped and glanced out of the open cavity for Avanda. She wasn't within their view. "Can we trust Avanda?"

"What? Of course. She's been with me from the start of this quest."

"Exactly. She has known your plans. She has influenced your decisions."

"No," he said clearly with vigor. "I can't go down this path. She has stood behind me on everything I've done. Plus, she has no ability to contact Darkmere even if she wanted."

"Really? How about Vesik? She clings to that book of magic."

"Avanda wouldn't betray me."

Emilen gave him a few seconds to calm down and lower his shoulders. "Perhaps you're right. Perhaps she is not even aware that she is helping Darkmere. Vesik could be pulling her thoughts from her without her even knowing. That book of magic is evil, Thorik, and you know it as well. I've seen it in your eyes when you talk about it with her. She's been enamored by Vesik."

Thorik's thoughts raced at the idea. "I was warned in the Govi Glade about her having the book."

"Yes. See, you know that it's wrong for her to have it."

Thorik nodded. "I do, but that doesn't mean that Vesik is a portal of information to Darkmere."

"True, we don't know if it is or isn't, but why take the chance? Removing it from her will relieve you of the warning you were given in the Govi Glade. If this allows you to potentially stop Darkmere from knowing your plans, then all the better. Yes?"

Taking in a deep breath, Thorik nodded again before grabbing his pack. "First things first. I want to see why Rummon has landed here at the Mythical Forest."

Once all three Nums had exited Rummon's body and stretched their legs, which were cramped after being in small quarters for so long, they sized up the mighty red dragon in the daylight. Larger than any creature they had ever seen, it was terrifying to see the massive strength in his common movements. A simple step forward for balance was deadly to anything that happened to be in the path. A swipe of his tail knocked over trees when in the way.

Rummon paid no mind to his surroundings as he stretched his appendages from the long flight after countless centuries of being frozen in a single position.

Gluic had left her perch in the hole in Rummon's skull, and flew down to meet the Nums. "Hello dears, how was your flight? Were you able to catch up on some sleep?" Her colorful head snapped back and forth while her eyes moved independently from one another as she looked around the open grassy plain.

"Granna," Thorik said. "Are you able to control Rummon?"

"Control? I don't control him. He is an old friend who is kind enough to listen."

"Old friend? There is no way you could have met him. You couldn't be *old* friends."

"Perhaps 'friends' is a strong word. He's known me much longer than I have known him. He's been nagging me for so long to free him, it's just nice to have him out of my head." Her long neck extended and both of her eyes fixated on Thorik. "I suppose you could now say that I've been inside of his." She squawked at her own joke as her eyes began to roll around again.

"Granna, why are we here? We need to help Brimmelle and Grewen warn the elders of Trewek of the pending war."

"That would be nice dear, but they have their task to perform and you have yours."

"I do?"

"Why yes, dear. Didn't your mother ever tell you that things happen for a reason?"

"Yes, she did. What does that have to do with-" Thorik was cut off before he could finish.

"The tables have turned. The game has changed. It's time to... Oh my, here they are now."

"Who?" Thorik asked, turning away from his grandmother who haphazardly launched herself into the air.

Moving out of the edge of the forest, small shadows could be seen moving the knee-high tall grass. Dozens of paths could be seen moving toward the Nums as whispering voices were heard over Rummon's movements.

The sight struck the Nums with fear. "At least we have Rummon this time," Thorik said to Gluic, who had just landed back in the hole behind Rummon's ear.

"Good luck, my dear. Allow your love to conquer your enemies. Rummon and I have other tasks to complete," Gluic said before whispering in the red dragon's ear.

The Nums' turned from the approaching Myth'Unday to see Rummon's wings open and lift the giant red dragon from the ground.

"Granna!" Thorik yelled in disbelief.

But she either didn't hear him or chose not to respond. Either way, the Nums were now standing alone in the small clearing as shadowy figures made their way toward them through the grass.

## Chapter 20
# Myth'Unday

Racing toward the three Nums through the knee-high grass, the small creatures could be heard in whispers ranging from high-pitched squeals to low rumbles of an oak tree yawning from heavy winds.

They approached from the south, where the line of fire had vanquished them from their natural forest habitat. Thorik had no idea if they were running from the fire or running toward their next meal. He was hoping for the prior.

Within seconds, the Myth'Unday had surrounded the three Nums, who were now back to back.

"Get away!" Emilen shouted to the unseen creatures lurking in the grass before her.

"No. It's okay," Avanda said. Her curiosity with the Myth'Unday had always swayed her to believe they were friendly. "They won't harm you." Bending down, she reached out an open hand for one of the Myth'Unday to land on.

Thorik turned. "Avanda, no! Once they allow you to see them, then you're theirs."

It was too late. A small faerie leaped from the grass into her hand. Skin of green flower stalks covered with silk, tree bark for hair, and maple leafs for wings, she was nearly weightless in Avanda's palm as she smiled at the Num.

Avanda smiled back.

The small faerie then gave a whistle, alerting the rest of the Myth'Undays to come out of hiding.

Various creatures sprang up from the grass. Some with and some without wings, appearing in colors and shapes of the forest leafs, butterflies, and beetles. Some had eight legs, others with two. Silk, flower petals, twigs and stalks replaced skin, while tree bark, nuts, and grass their coated heads. Each Myth'Unday was unique.

"Hello there," Avanda said with excitement. She had always wanted to see and play with the Myth'Unday.

"You are not afraid of us?" said the small frail creature standing in Avanda's palm.

"No. Not at all. Why should I be?"

The petite creature casually flew up near her face and shouted. "Because you have burned down our forest and destroyed our homes!" Her size immediately doubled and then doubled again and again, until she was twice the height of Avanda. The texture of the Faerie's skin had also turned into a dark brown tree bark with short broken limbs out of her head.

"But I didn't-"

"You and your kind have waged war against us, and we shall fight you to the ends of the earth!" The faerie grabbed Avanda, before she could run, and lifted her high into the air. "One by one, we will take our revenge."

Emilen screamed while being grabbed by several of the creatures at once. Pulling her hair, they quickly dragged her to the ground.

Thorik grabbed for his pouch of runestones, only to have a thick root reach out of the ground and snatch it from him before lifting it high into the air. The Num then jumped up onto the vertical root and began climbing. Hand over hand he climbed the root while it reversed direction and began sinking into the ground at the same speed. His quick efforts to ascend gained him no distance from the ground, but he was closing in on his runestones.

A Myth'Unday creature, standing behind Thorik, laughed at the Num as it controlled its rooted leg. Seconds later, dozens of other Myth'Unday showed up and pulled Thorik off the vertical root by his feet.

Avanda broke free from the giant faerie long enough to grab Vesik and open it up. However, once she started reading the spell out loud, the monstrous creature ripped the spell book out of her hands and tossed it off to the side.

"Vile creatures you are," the faerie complained, shrinking down to her normal size. She was quickly joined by dozens of her kind, all agitated about the situation, wanting some revenge. Flying up to eye level of Avanda, she pointed her needle-like fingers toward the Num's nose. "You burn our home. We burn you."

A small group of cheering Myth'Unday danced at the idea, waving their arms and yelling with delight. Those not participating in the merrymaking had started creating cages out of sticks and tightly wrapped weeds. They moved quickly and nimbly, working together better than fingers from the same hand, stringing lines around stiff sticks and tying them tight. Within minutes two cages were built, each ready to hold a single Num.

Collectively, the Myth'Unday pushed Thorik into one and Avanda into the other before tying off the cage doors and hoisting both of them up into the air. Hanging from two separate trees, the two Nums had to shout over the noise coming from below in order to hear each other.

Emilen continued screaming while the Myth'Unday tied her to a wooden spit in order to roast her first. Faeries, pixies, brownies, and the like cursed at the Nums and poked their sharp nails and sticks at their prisoners.

"Stop this!" Thorik shouted. "We came to help you."

The response was an eruption of Myth'Unday flying or jumping up onto his cage, reaching between the cage openings and trying to scratch through his cloth at his skin. The sudden attack caused the cage to swing violently and send Thorik to one side where he was clawed and scratched by tiny little hands.

"I'm a friend of Mr. Hempton!" Thorik yelled. "Theodore J. Hempton!" Pulling forward, as the cage swung back the other way, he pulled a few of the little winged creatures off his neck and set them in the base of the cage. "I am not your enemy." His voice was still agitated from the hundreds of tiny little pokes he had received in his back.

"You're out of luck! Hempton isn't here to verify your claim," one of the little creatures said with a laugh."

The unpleasant news didn't derail Thorik from his goal. "That doesn't matter. What matters is that I can help you defeat your real enemy, the Matriarch and her Southwind Army. They are burning down your forest and we need to stop them."

"Big words from someone who can't even defend himself from a few of us."

"That's because I'm not trying to defend myself. I'm trying to help save you."

"How do we know this isn't a trap? You could be a master of disguise, pretending to be Thorik Dain of Farbank."

Thorik's expression shifted after hearing his full name. He hadn't spoken it since they had met the Myth'Unday. "True, but for all I know, you could be Mr. Hempton in disguise, testing my observational skills."

Laughing at the comment, the winged faery shifted its shape into a large frog with a nut for a cap. "Brilliant, lad. You're still good at the games, I see. Figured that you'd be in too much of a panic by your capture to catch me this time around."

"Mr. Hempton, your forest is burning. Can't you stop it?"

"We would if we could, but we can't so we shan't."

"Shan't?"

"Be flexible to break the rules and improvise, my boy. You can communicate in more ways than just by the limited words we've been taught. You understood what I meant, did you not?"

"Yes, of course."

"Then what's the issue?"

Thorik blinked a few times, trying to get his thoughts back to the real issue at hand. "There is a forest fire working its way toward us. Is there any way to put it out?"

"Oh, yes. We've extinguished many a great fires in my time." Mr. Hempton drifted off, thinking of the many times they had battled the blazing heat to save their land.

Thorik interrupted Mr. Hempton's daydream. "Then do it again! This fire is out of control and heading this way."

"Normally we would, but the Southwind Army is fanning this one, driving us north. Each time we start to put the fires out, their men light the fires again."

"I figured the Southwind Army is behind this."

"The Matriarch is behind this. The army is just at her disposal."

"Why does she wish to destroy the Myth'Unday?"

"Darkmere has promised her all the land south of Rivers Edge. That includes us. She's just taking what she believes is hers. She's quite mad, you know."

A loud snapping of trees was heard to their north, followed by the voices of many men.

"It would appear that they've been playing a game of their own," Mr. Hempton said. "They've used the fire to drive us into a trap. Very clever, for humans." He started to leave.

"Wait! Free us before you run for safety!"

Theodore smiled at Thorik. "Surely you know me better than that. No one gets free without playing a game."

Armed with nets, soldiers rushed out of the forest and across the open field toward the exposed Myth'Unday.

Thorik turned back to Mr. Hempton. "But I've already beat your game."

Hesitating, the frog waffled on the idea of freeing him.

Screams from the Myth'Unday in the open field could now be heard while they scattered in every direction to avoid being captured. Cries of panic were heard from Emilen and Avanda still held captive; Avanda sealed in a tiny cage and Emilen tied on a spit.

Thorik's voice was now quick and ridged. "I can help you defeat the Southwind army."

"Now who is playing a game with whom?"

"Please, Mr. Hempton. If I am caught, we will have no more games to play. Are you willing to risk the end to all games?"

The comment was enough to push him past the breaking point. "Alright. Let's have a wee look at that cage," he said, raising one eyebrow and snapping his fingers.

The cage around Thorik instantly crumbled, dropping the Num to the ground at the base of the tree.

Once he recovered from the fall, he rolled onto his knees and turned toward Avanda and Emilen. Soldiers were already nearing them. "How are we going to save them?"

"We aren't, lad." Mr. Hempton shot a look behind them and then directly back into Thorik's eyes. "Stay perfectly still if you value your life." The serious tone of his voice commanded attention.

Thorik did as he was told, and instantly felt his body change in shape. The next thing he knew, he was a large tree stump next to the tree he fell from. Hr. Hempton hopped up on top of the newly made stump and acted more like a frog than Thorik could ever recall.

It was unclear to the Num why Mr. Hempton had done such a thing. Perhaps it was another one of his games. And even without eyes, Thorik could somehow see beyond his bark form in every direction. Avanda and Emilen were being removed from their Myth'Unday confinements and then captured by the Southwind men. Mr. Hempton had saved Thorik from the soldiers who were paying the tree trunk no mind.

From the opposite direction of the soldiers' invasion, the forest fire could be seen moving toward the open field. However, one area of the fire line began quickly dying off. The trees near this area quickly turned a shade of gray and every leaf on those trees suddenly dried up and fell to the ground.

Stepping through the area was a young baldheaded man with thick tattoo designs running from his forehead, behind his ears, and down past his neckline. The end of his quarterstaff shined with a narrow focus like a lighthouse, but changed direction and intensity at the owner's will.

A dark haze surrounding his body turned all color into shades of gray. Everything that came in contact with the darkness immediately lost its energy and life. Grass turned brittle and light brown, while trees became weak causing heavy limbs to fall from their own weight. Even the firewall suffocated from his presence from the lack of fuel to sustain it. Nothing could survive once it was near this mysterious man.

Walking toward the center of the field, he calmly strolled past Thorik and Mr. Hempton, calculating each step and movement he made.

Even though Thorik was outside the young man's gray perimeter, he could feel his body become weak and fragile. Dizziness and nausea began to take effect in the few seconds it took the young man to pass by.

Moving out toward the open field, the man of shadows stopped. Below him, the grass died and the rich dark brown soil and red clay turned a light gray with no moisture remaining. Looking at the chaos of the soldiers trying to capture the Myth'Unday and the little creatures fighting back, he swung his quarterstaff out in front of him. The beacon light on the end intensified to a power greater than sunlight, blinding and stunning all in his view.

Flying faeries and other creatures from the Mythical Forest fell out of the air, while soldiers collapsed onto their knees. All fighting was temporarily stopped.

To ensure that the Myth'Unday wouldn't regain their strength too quickly, the young bald man raised his other arm and expanded his sphere of gray shades out over the open area for a few seconds. It was enough to drain all within the area of enough life to prevent any Myth'unday from escaping.

Once completed, a second wave of Southwind soldiers rushed in from the trees and into the opening, picking up the Myth'Unday and placing them in sacks.

Thorik did everything in his power to stay silent. Fear was causing him to breathe hard and his body to shake. He wanted to flee from the young man who controlled darkness and light.

Mr. Hempton stomped his foot onto the stump, knocking Thorik in the head in an attempt to keep him silent and motionless.

Snapping his head around, the baldheaded young man glared toward Thorik, viewing the short stump with a large frog on top. Eyeing the frog, he squinted and waited to see anything out of the ordinary.

Mr. Hempton glared back at the newcomer. Upholding his vow to make those who spotted him play a deadly game, he hesitated from the feeling of dread and lifelessness surrounding the man. Never before had he felt such gloom emanating from a life form. This was a game he did not feel he wanted to play. Gulping, Mr. Hempton lowered his eyes. He then waited until the man's attention had returned to the capturing of prisoners before taking his next breath.

Wagons arrived and were quickly loaded. Emilen and Avanda were taken away along with everyone else. Within minutes, the open field was empty.

Thorik felt his body return to normal and he wiggled his fingers to make sure everything was back in working order. Crunched down on the balls of his feet, he had been on his knees and elbows during his transformation.

"What in blazes was that?" Mr. Hempton asked, still sitting on Thorik's back.

"Lord Bredgin," Thorik said. Shivers ran through his body as he said the name. "He is Darkmere's son." Brushing himself off, he slowly stood up while Mr. Hempton moved onto the Num's shoulder. I thought I had killed him."

"You? Surely you jest. I think we would need Ovlan herself to hold back such powers."

An aftershock of shivers ran the course down Thorik's back while he looked upon the dead path Lord Bredgin had walked. "We have to do something to save Avanda and Emilen. Can you convince Olvan to help us?"

"No, lad. She does not interfere with the outcomes of wars. She only provides guidance."

Disappointed in the answer, he asked, "She is the greatest of Oracles, why wouldn't she help save this land?" Thorik walked over and picked up Avanda's fallen pack as well as his own.

"She is only an observer in this great experiment. To interfere would contaminate the outcome." The frog looked up at the Num's sad face. "However, she has been known to add some stimuli to see how it affects the outcome."

Thorik nodden. "I'll take whatever I can get."

"No doubt, lad. But it's my understanding that she has already added it. She wouldn't tell me what it was. However, Ovlan did say you had been given the tools you needed to succeed and now it would be up to you to use them." Mr. Hempton stretched his legs and back. "Do you know what she's referr'n to?"

"I...I think I do."

Chapter 21
# Aftermath

Del'Unday from the city of Corrock had taken siege upon the nonviolent Ov'Unday city of Trewek and raped the fertile land of its innocence. They had attacked from ropes dropped from the cave entrance above as well as the ramp which led down to the base. Terror had reached peaceful lands.

The Ov'Unday never resisted, hoping to show their invaders that there was no need for violence, but violence came anyway. It came with claws and swords and axes. It came upon adults and children alike. It came to those who stood proudly in defiance and it came to those who fled in fear.

The mission of the Del'Unday had been misunderstood by the residents of Trewek. The Del'Unday did not come to take them over or to enslave them. They came to eliminate them and take the supplies they needed before destroying Eastland on their way to Ergrauth's final battle for world domination.

Brimmelle strained as he pushed the wooden debris off his body. The building he was in had collapsed during the siege by the Del'Unday and had buried him alive.

Tossing the last piece of ceiling off to the side, he stood up and paused to take a breath. What he saw caused him to wonder if his eyes had been damaged from the attack.

A gray hue coated the city and cavern with ash from the burning within the sinkhole. Smoke billowed from homes and buildings, rising and clogging the opening of the sinkhole. Random flames lapped up in the air, snapping sparks and sending burning ashes on erratic voyages across the city.

A single tower remained standing, high in the air, penetrating the thick cloud of smoke above and reaching the desert floor. The other towers had fallen, crashing down onto the city itself.

The Ov'Unday's had attempted to move the ramp from the entrance above but had failed to do so prior to the Delz locking it in place from the surface.

Brimmelle stood in awe at the devastation around him. The towers were destroyed, buildings were on fire, and bodies were scattered about. Arms and legs were seen extending out from under the fallen structures. Others lay dead from bloody attacks by the weapons of the Del'Unday when they attacked and killed every Ov'Unday they could find. There was no discrimination on their part. All live Ov'Unday were to be destroyed, regardless of their age, species, or gender.

He stood in disbelief. "They chose not to fight, and yet they were still attacked," he said to himself. "They ran for cover, only to be attacked from behind. They wished no one harm, and yet harm came to them. This could have been my villagers at Farbank. It still might be if something isn't done to prevent it."

The eerie calm sound of crackling fires was interrupted by the sound of a door slamming shut behind him.

Startled, he spun around and watched as one of the large doors into the only remaining standing tower crept back open after being slammed shut. It was the doorway he had entered to gain access to speak to the Ov'Unday Elders.

A shiver ran down his spine at the sight. He immediately assumed it was a Del'Unday soldier making sure that all in the city had been killed. His fear of the idea caused him to step backward before he once again caught the vision of the dead bodies scattered about. Many had been running in fear when slain. It was this sight that caused his soul-markings to turn a dark tone and his back to straighten up with confidence. "You have done enough damage on this day, Del. I will run no longer."

Making his way across the open foyer, he reached the half-open door, which had made the earlier noise. His heart began to pound so hard that he thought for sure it would break through his chest. In spite of his instincts to hide, he quietly leaned around the door to see what species of Del'Unday was inside.

A haze of smoke filled the room before him as a few small oil vats still hung on the wall for light. It was strangely quiet and still, smelling of burnt flesh combined with the normal incense of the room.

Unable to see anything, Brimmelle made his way in, avoiding making any door movement, which could alert the intruder of the Num's location. Once inside, he made his way toward where the council held their sessions.

There, on the far end, were the elders, lying lifeless as their bodies dripped blood on the floor. A few limbs had been severed, but most appeared to have been stabbed in the chest or had their necks slashed. Many of the weapons used were still lodged into their victims. The leader of the Elders had been burned to death. None appeared to have been attacked from behind, nor was there any obvious evidence of a struggle by the Elders or the other Ov'Unday that had been in the hall at the time of the massacre.

The hinge of a side door gave a slight squeak, causing Brimmelle to jump. His body froze with fear at the sight of the door opening. He simply couldn't make his body run for cover as the outline of the massive creature stepped out of the side room through the smoky air. It carried a club of some type, wielding it in both hands such as one would carry a long sword.

It was time for Brimmelle to prove to himself that he was not a coward, and no longer was hiding behind the words of the Mountain King. He was Fir Brimmelle Riddlewood the Seventh, spiritual leader of Farbank. Pulling a broadsword from the chest of a Gathler, he raised the heavy weapon up over his head. "In the name of the Mountain King, I forbid you to harm any more of these Ov'Undays!" he shouted, trying to stabilize the weapon overhead. Struggling to keep it from falling to his side, he had no idea it would be so heavy.

"I think it's a little late for heroism," a baritone voice responded from the creature coming out of the side room. After a few more steps, it became obvious who had replied. Grewen nodded at the Num. "But it is good to see you have it in you."

Brimmelle dropped the heavy sword with delight before running the few steps over to his giant companion and clutching his new robes which now were dirty. "Grewen, they're all dead. The entire city has been wiped out."

"No. Not all." Grewen's voice was soft and tender, unlike his normal causal and jovial candor. "We have lost many, but Trewek's words will live on." The giant Mognin motioned to the long item he was carrying. Nearly as long as Brimmelle was tall, the hollow wooden tube was carved with various markings.

The Num stepped back to have a look at the item he carried. "What is it?"

"It is the words of Trewek. The words we live by."

The Num nodded. "I understand. You keep your scrolls of his speeches rolled up inside."

"No." Grewen's voice was still soft, and tears dripping down his face were now visible to Brimmelle. "His words."

Stepping over to the Ov'Unday Elders, Grewen sat down cross-legged in front of them as he placed the long wooden item before him on one foot.

Quietly watching, Brimmelle was unclear of Grewen's answer but felt uncomfortable asking anything more while his friend appeared to be preparing to say goodbye to his culture's leaders.

Grewen set the wooden tube in front of him. Within the carvings, there were random holes throughout the length of it. Unseen to Brimmelle until now, were hundreds of thin strings which spanned over one or more of the holes. Some strings extended the length of the entire tube while others were only a finger in length. Raised above the surface by small wooden supports, prior to each hole, the strings were kept taut such as a musical instrument would be.

With the base of the tube resting on the top of his foot, he placed one of his thick thumbs over the top of the wide opening. He then strummed the strings with his other hand, releasing his thumb from the top at various levels to control the sound given from the device.

Expecting to hear some beautiful music worthy of the Ov'Unday Elders to the great Ov'Unday species, Brimmelle was astonished by what he heard instead.

Words were spoken from the instrument, to which the Num could only assume were in the voice of Trewek himself. Each string plucked was a different word and Grewen's control of what was released out the top affected the tone of the word to make the sentence sound correct.

Instead of learning songs to play on this instrument, the Ov'Unday had passed down the beliefs of Trewek by learning how to play them generation after generation. When played correctly, they could hear it in Trewek's own voice, even though he had passed many ages ago.

Brimmelle was amazed at how clear the words and sentences were. Moving closer, he could see that the carvings along the side were actually instructions on the various speeches to play. The current one was of the respect of the dead who died while honoring their beliefs.

Trewek's voice sounded like that of a Mognin, but more relaxing and gentle than Grewen's. "To live a life of truth is to be willing to die to uphold it as well. For your success is not to be measured by the numbers of our following, but the improvement of the lives it has touched. At your end, reach out once more with open hands to spread the culture of peace. Recognize those who wish to not accept it with kindness, and embrace your enemies to ensure they understand you mean them no harm or ill will." Trewek continued as Grewen played the instrument before his dead leaders.

Fir Brimmelle placed a hand on Grewen's side, watching the giant perform with tears of honor and sadness run down his face. He had never seen the Mognin in such a state. Somehow he never thought of him as anything but a big Altered Creature, having no depth of emotions.

Allowing Grewen to complete his performance of respect to his leaders, Brimmelle eventually spoke up. "I think we need to leave here. This city is now a graveyard."

Grewen stood back up and straightened his back. "Yes, we need to gather all those who have survived and head west."

"West? Toward the war?"

Grewen began walking toward the doors to leave the tower. "Yes, we need to be a part of the solution instead of hiding in this hole."

Brimmelle was more than a little surprised at his friend's words. "Perhaps you should think about this for a while. We don't want to be hasty on such a decision. The Delz have weapons and have been trained how to fight. The Ov'Unday have not. You'll be slaughtered."

Opening the large door he stepped out into the devastated city. "We will spread the word of peace and embrace all those who accept it or deny it. We will no longer hide and avoid the outside world."

Following the giant across the open foyer, the Num had to jog to keep up with Grewen's long strides. "What has gotten into you? I know your leaders have been murdered, but you are becoming someone you normally would not like. Don't lead the remainder of your people to their deaths just to take revenge for their attack on your people. Now, more than ever, you should hide until this blows over."

Reaching one of the city's enormous gongs, Grewen set the Trewek instrument down and picked up a long handled mallet and pulled it high into the air. With a mighty swing of his arms, he hit the gong with the mallet.

The low gong sound resonated across the city, vibrating everything within the city and outer farm land. Within seconds, heads could be seen pulling up from hiding places for as far as the eye could see. The signal of safety had been rung and those still able would begin their trek into the center of the city.

Grinning, Grewen looked down at the Num. "It's okay, Brimmelle. This is not an act of revenge. I have a plan."

The facial expression on the giant looked very familiar to Brimmelle, providing him with a sense of comfort that the giant hadn't gone crazy, as well as a sense of concern that he had a plan that would put them on another dangerous venture. "I suppose this is going to delay my return trip to Farbank."

Grewen's grin grew. "Yes, it will."

## Chapter 22
# Lu'Tythis Tower

Eating through rock and stone, living spherical beasts of crusted-over molten lava tunneled its way under the Lu'Tythis Tower. Alone it would take years to topple the two-mile high tall structure, but with a half dozen siblings, born from the demon Bakalor, they could quickly create major destruction to the mile wide foundation.

Yard-wide tunnels now snaked their ways back and forth under the tower, remnants of the lesser demons devouring everything in their paths.

Rolling out of a freshly formed tunnel, a lesser demon fell into a large cavern near the center of the tower's base, landing a few yards from the feet of a tall thin man with mahogany hair and well-trimmed beard. Clothed in a light gray tunic and cloak, he held out a long wooden staff in one hand, the other was out in front of him in a blocking position.

"Be gone!" Ambrosius commanded. "The damage you do will destroy all of us if unchecked."

The crust of the beast cracked open to reveal a mouth filled with liquid rock, glowing and churning with the heat of the surface of the sun. Sweltering fumes exploded out of the creature toward the man, impacting him in the chest and knocking him off his feet.

The creature attacked, rolling its sphere of a body toward its prey.

Still on his back, Ambrosius used his E'rudite powers to hold off the advancement. The heat roared against the invisible shield, spilling around the sides, causing the fine hairs on his head and face to coil and char. Struggling to increase the width of the barrier without weakening it, he concentrated on his powers instead of the creature.

The heat intensified, forcing its way through the shield and burning the hands of Ambrosius as the vile fumes from inside the beast made its way to his lungs.

Knowing his time was limited, Ambrosius released the barrier and immediately focused on pushing himself away from danger.

The flames burst forward, lighting his cloak and lower pants on fire.

Ignoring his own jeopardy, he turned and reached out with both hands, creating an intense pressure on the beast from all directions.

Shaking from the force, the lesser demon struggled to escape.

Pressing harder, the molten sphere began to shrink, but increased in heat. The pressure was far too much for the creature to control. A burst of E'rudite energy was released and the lesser demon was crushed down into a rock the size of a fist. This caused a massive light to radiate from it, blinding Ambrosius before the now dense rock exploded into thousands of small pieces, which carried their own light within them. The cave filled with debris and the blast extinguished the flames on Ambrosius' clothes.

It became as dark as a moonless night, as the small pieces of glowing hot rocks slowly faded as though a slight cloud cover blocked the stars in the sky.

Ambrosius coughed from the fumes and fell to one knee from exhaustion before creating a light at the end of his staff. He could hear something else coming through the tunnels. It was a familiar sound.

Racing into the cavern was a reflective scaled dragon, who was obviously in search of Ambrosius.

"Draq! You've missed the excitement." He coughed a few more times before continuing. "One more has been destroyed. Where is Ericc?"

The dragon circled once before landing. "We've destroyed another one, ourselves. Ericc should be here soon. As long as we can fight these one at a time, we should be able to defeat them before they topple the tower."

"Agreed," Ambrosius coughed out, hearing an approaching rumble.

The cavern wall in front of him turned red and melted away, exposing a pulsing sphere of crusted over molten lava. It was another lesser demon. But before they could react, a second one arrived from their right and a third from their left. When the fourth arrived from behind him, Ambrosius' expectation of surviving the encounter vanished.

Out of nowhere, a young man appeared next to Ambrosius. "Father?" he asked, just as the lesser demons began their attack.

"Ericc! Get us out of here!" Ambrosius yelled.

Without thinking twice, Ericc touched his father and Draq. All three vanished from the room, leaving the demons to crash into one another in their absence.

Materializing in a different cave, free of the lesser demons, Ambrosius cleared his lungs of the harsh fumes given off by the vile creatures. "Thanks," is all he could say between coughs.

"This is why you hid me away all those years?" Ericc said.

His father took a moment to take in several breaths of clean air before relying. "There was no sign that you would have inherited any of my E'rudite powers. Without them you would have been killed within a week for existing. My brother would have never allowed you to live. He fears the prophecy of you killing his son."

"These creatures work for Darkmere?"

"No, they are the offspring of Bakalor, Demon of the underground. However, Darkmere and Bakalor are allies."

"Why are they here?"

"To destroy this tower we stand under," Ambrosius said, looking up at the surface of the cave's ceiling they stood under. "If they can topple this tower, they will destroy life as we know it."

Ericc appeared confused. "The Lu'Tythis Tower is several thousand feet high and its base fans out at least two. It would take a lifetime to dig out enough ground to cause it to fall."

"Not if you eat rock at the pace those lesser demons do."

"Even so, what possible purpose does it serve to knock over this tower?"

Ambrosius sat down to regain his strength. "Lu'Tythis Tower was built by the Notarians in order to house the crystal in the top of this tower. This crystal was embedded with powers for purposes that few know about. The first was to keep the weather in our land stable. Without the crystal, severe storms would lash out at us and destroy our lands with tornados, floods, and extreme winds. The sky would turn black like the dead of night with no end in sight. Freedom from the sun could allow Bakalor to return to the surface."

Clearing his throat, he continued. "The second purpose is even less known. The crystal was designed to push on the inside of the Weirfortus dam in order to give it the strength it needs to keep the ocean on the other side from flooding our lands with two thousand feet of water. The crystal has gravitational powers that push against the dam to our west as well as several mountains to the north, east, and south. The one to the north is the White Summit, a volcanic mountain that could erupt if such a gravitational shift occurs, burning everything in King's Valley with hot waves of lava."

Ericc's eyes looked off to the side for a moment before returning to his fathers. "I understand the issue with the flood, but not the one of Kings Valley. The Haplorhini Mountain range will prevent it from spilling into the Dovenar Kingdom."

"True, but the magma will race down the valley, killing everyone that lives in Longfield and Farbank. The Polenums won't have time to react."

## Chapter 23
# City of Veil

Standing behind the tower's battlement, General Lund took time from his daily troop inspections to casually search the eastern desert horizon for movement. He stood confident that nothing would arise, even during these uneasy days. Not only was it well known by the kingdom that the Del'Unday were heading to the north with plans to attack the Woodlen Province, but it was simply foolish for the creatures to think about an attack on his tower or any walls along the Doven boarders.

Over six-hundred years ago, the Doven Province was the first to have the walls and towers to prevent the Altered Creatures from attacking the humans. Victor Dovenar, himself, led the building of the structures that had since protected them. It was the beginning of the age of humans that eventually led to expanding the kingdom into seven provinces and the walling off the Del'Undays' access to Luthralum Lake. This specific section of wall was the strongest of all the provinces and the pride of the Dovenar Kingdom. Tall and thick, it was also well-armed with long range weapons which would cause massive damage to any approaching armies. There was little concern of it ever being attacked.

Turning from the desert, he rested against the battlement wall and looked over the city to the west toward the lake at what did concern him; the weather. Not just any weather. A dark storm could be seen swirling over the Lu'Tythis Tower. Lightning raced out in all directions from that central area, reaching out to the tops of distant mountain peaks. The weather had been changing and becoming more severe as of late, but this current storm was like nothing he had ever seen before.

A tugging could be felt on the general's chest, followed by a push. This soft pulling to the east and then the west had been going on for days without explanation. At first it was assumed to be the wind, but when the effect continued behind closed doors, the breeze was ruled out. Several of the general's men were out sick due to this oddity, many of which had a history of motion sickness when on ships. The constant soft pushing and pulling could easily be missed until the soldiers were relaxed. It was then that the rocking motion was felt across their entire body.

Once again, the general shook off the odd feeling and glanced out to the eastern desert before looking back at the storm. He believed this storm and the tugging feeling had some relationship, seeing that they had started about the same time.

From his vantage point he could also look upon the city of Veil below him on the west side of the tower. It was an old city rooted in traditions and culture established hundreds of years ago. Little had changed as people lived their lives in the same small homes and cramped neighborhoods that their ancestors did, as multiple generations of family lived under the same roof. "It is a fine place to live," the general thought out loud.

Turning south, the Volney River meandered westward tightly up against the south side of his tower. Once the location of the beautiful Rivers Edge Province, the vast majority of the land within its walls was now under water. It had been this way since the end of the civil war, when a wave rushed across the province and wiped out both military sides during the final key battle. Since then, structures such as homes and buildings could still be seen rising up from the water. Even the occasional apex of a bridge could be seen when the river was low.

The final battle of the civil war was fought between Ambrosius' and Darkmere's armies. The two brothers commanded mighty forces to fight for the rights to the Kingdom. However, the brothers escaped when the flood swept in from Lake Luthralum and killed all the troops. Perhaps killing isn't the correct term. Darkmere's army had previously been enchanted to prevent their deaths, so even though they were destroyed, they remained alive under the water as undead, forever to haunt the submerged province.

General Lund smirked about the idea of being attacked from the south. The undead would drag the Del'Unday down to the depths of the muddy waterway long before the general and his men would get a chance to participate in the battle. He had heard the moans of the undead during his younger years when guarding the tower and walls overnight. He had also seen boats capsized and taken down under the thick brown water. The dangers within were all too real.

"Only a fool would sail upon those waters," he said to himself as he spotted a ship sailing down the river toward the Doven province. "Fortune is on their side to have survived this far without being attacked."

The general watched with great curiosity at the approaching vessel. Eventually he was able to spot the crew. Most of them were leaning over the sides of the ship swinging oars at the semi-flesh covered skeletal remains of Darkmere's army. The tower's location, up against the river, loomed over the long abandoned docks where the ship was heading. He continued to gaze from thirty feet above the outsiders with growing interest.

From every part of the ship, the Rivers Edge undead attempted to climb aboard. Crewmen could be heard screaming from the attacks and being pulled overboard. There was no shortage of undead while the crew continued to dwindle in numbers.

Standing on the high deck were two figures. The one at the helm barked orders and turned the wheel in an attempt to make a landing in the abandoned docks. Shirtless, his large gut hung over his red pants and black belt. Bald on top, he made up for it with a hairy chest and arms. This man was without a doubt in charge as he raised a large Fesh'Unday leg bone in the air and yelled at his men for not fighting off the undead.

The person standing next to the heavy man wore a hooded cloak which was open enough to make it obvious that she was a female. Aside from the cleavage between two large breasts, General Lund could see the slim woman had all the right curves.

"General Lund, sir," a guard said after stopping at attention.

"Yes, what is it?" he responded, keeping his eyes on the woman approaching in the ship. Her face being hidden by her hood added another level of interest.

"I believe we have movement in the desert."

"Really?" Raising an eyebrow and a giving a smirk, the general turned to the eastern side of the tower. "What is it that you see?"

The young guard pointed into the distant northeast at a dust cloud spanning several miles across and a few hundred feet in height as it rolled toward them.

"Son, you have a lot to learn. It is far too wide to be an army in order to kick up that much sand. Only a dust storm could span that much of the desert. Besides there is nothing in front of the cloud that could have stirred it up. You've been through a few before. Alert the others, and cover the equipment. The weather will be our largest threat on this day."

"Meanwhile..." The general turned back to the ship approaching the dock near the base of the tower. "I think I will greet our new guests and see why anyone would take such a risk sailing through Rivers Edge with such a beautiful gem on board." He then made his way down the tower and out of the front gates to welcome the newcomers.

Following the general's orders, the young man raced down the tower and alerted others of the general's orders, which spread quickly down the length of the wall. Equipment and weapons were placed inside or covered up to prevent any damage or clogging of gears or straps with a thick layer of dirt. They had become very effective at wrapping up their equipment to prevent damage from even the worst sand storms. They would make sure there wasn't a loose strap or knot in the entire area.

Meanwhile, General Lund had exited the main gates and made it to the Rivers Edge wall, which held back the water from flooding more of the desert. Taking every other step up the wooden staircase, made for guards to access the top of the Rivers Edge wall, the general heard a crash from the far side.

Racing over, he saw the ship perched up onto the docks. The captain had rammed the ship up onto the dock in order to knock off a half-dozen undead. Many of his own men went flying off as well. But the other obvious reason for the hard landing was to make an easy escape for the captain and the woman who accompanied him.

General Lund watched the rest of the crew fight for their lives as the captain and his companion ignored the issue at hand. In fact, it appeared to the general that they were too busy arguing to even notice the attack by the undead.

"Shut yur hole," the captain yelled, before taking a swig from a bottle. "I didn't hav'ta bring ya. If it was up ta me, I would'a rather been bending a rod and put'n some blood on the deck than haul'n ya here. But I got ya 'ere didn't I?"

"Out of pure luck, you stupid lush. I should have poisoned that bottle to prevent you from getting drunk when we needed you the most."

"Poison me mistress?" Covering his bottle to protect it from her, he collected a second bottle prior to departing the ship onto the dock. "How dare ya even think of do'n such'a thing to me Nectar of Irr?"

The female followed him off the ship, while the crew fought off the undead from reaching the upper deck where they had been standing. "That Nectar will be your undoing one of these days." She then made her way up the steps to the top of the wall.

"Nonsense," the captain said. Handing his two bottles to her, he stepped back onto the vessel to collect his yard-long Fesh'Unday leg bone.

His timing couldn't have been worse, for one of the undead climbed up onto his deck and lunged for him. The captain's instincts kicked in and he swung the thick bone, knocking the undead off the top deck and back to the lower deck, landing on a closed crate.

The act seemed to have caused the captain to snap. His eyes went large and suddenly charged into battle, jumping off the high deck and landing on several undead as well as his own crew. Rolling to his feet, he began swinging the bone club around, knocking over anything within range.

Charging forward, the captain ripped off the side of the closed crate, sending wooden splinters in every direction. Inside of the now destroyed box were three more bottles of Nectar of Irr.

It was at that point when the captain realized the severity of his situation. The last few of his crew now stood around him, facing the oncoming undead who were launching their final attack. Each of his men were quickly grabbed by one or more of partially flesh-wearing skeletons. The captain had to make a quick decision before he was totally on his own, and so he did. Leaning into the crate, he grabbed the last few bottles of Nectar of Irr. "They weren't much of a crew anyway," he mumbled while pulling himself up, protecting the bottles.

The captain now stood in the center of his ship with no crew protecting him from the army of walking dead. Moving all three bottles into one arm, he raised his bone club in preparation for his fight. "Ya aint gonna be want'n to mess with me if ya make me drop one of 'ere bottles," he said to the undead before noticing his companion had reached the safety at the top of the wall. "Okay, Grum, I got ya 'ere safe. Help me outta 'ere!"

"Grum?" General Lund said, while extending a hand to the woman to help her up the final few steps onto the top of the wall.

The gorgeous lady stepped up and tossed her hood off her head. But instead of seeing a marvel of a beautiful female face which would finish the perfect body, her face was one of an old skinny man. "Bryus Grum," she said in an unexpected man's voice. "Perhaps you've heard of me?"

The general was horrified at the sight of the old man's face on the gorgeous body, but was unable to reply or express his dismay while he continued to stare at the female body and then the geriatric man's face.

"Bryus!" the captain yelled, swinging his club at the approaching undead. "We had a deal!"

Bryus looked away from the shocked general and back down at the man swinging the giant leg bone. "Captain Dare, you are an inebriated narcissistic flatulent idiot. Your deal was with Ambrosius, not me." Lifting up one of the bottles Dare had handed to him earlier, Bryus smashed it against the stone wall, pouring the liquid down the side.

"AH!" Dare screamed at the sight. "I've killed men for less!" His temper exploded and his club began knocking undead out of his path as he eyed his new target, Bryus Grum.

Bryus grabbed the second bottle of Irr and held it ready to smash. Stopping for a moment, he grinned at the still shell-shocked general. "Would you like to have the honor of smashing the second one?" Bryus said with a wink.

General Lund snapped out of his trance and unpleasantly shivered at the wink given to him by Bryus. "No," he coughed out.

"To each his own," Bryus said before smashing it against the wall.

"AHH!" Captain Dare screamed as though the damage was being inflicted upon his own body. By now he was in a state of rage, knocking over undead left and right as he made his way up to the top deck and then off onto the dock platform, where the undead stopped their chase.

Running up the stairs, Captain Dare was completely out of breath and was using his Fesh'Unday leg-bone as a cane to keep him upright. "I be kill'n ya for yur misdeads," he said between breaths.

"Good lord, man. It was only a trick. A bit of magic and sleight of hand. Your bottles are safe," Bryus said, lifting his cloak to show the two bottles filled with Nectar of Irr.

In a moment of relief, Dare reached out for the bottles, dropping his bone cane as well as the contents in his other arm.

There was a moment of silence as the three bottles of Nectar of Irr fell from Captain Dare's arm and crashed against the stone floor.

With his bald head still down, watching the liquid run down the side of the wall, he spoke very humbly. "Bryus, tell me that this be a trick as well."

Bryus shook his head. "No," he said very straight forward. "You just destroyed three of your last five bottles of Irr. Nice move."

Captain Dare picked up his club and pulled it over head as though he was about to strike Bryus.

Without thinking, General Lund jumped in between them. "Sir, put that weapon down. You will not strike a lady in my presence."

"Lady? Who ya be call'n a lady?" Dare's arm relaxed slightly.

Bryus answered for the general. "I'm guessing he's calling you one? Your man-breasts are nearly as large as mine."

"I be big boned!"

"You're a big bone-head, is what you are."

Once again, Captain Dare prepared to strike at Bryus. "I'll be show'n ya what this bone feels like against yur head!"

General Lund raised his hands. "Gentlemen! Or man and... whatever you are. Stop this arguing. You've just lost your ship and entire crew."

Dare glanced back down at the empty ship perched up on the dock. "Well, she ain't really me ship and the crew really weren't that good," he said with a shrug of his shoulders while protecting his last two bottles. "But me Nectar of Irr, she be safe and that's worth celebrating."

"You're wasting your time," Bryus scoffed. "We'll be here all day if you are going to try to reason with this overweight hairy seafaring slob."

The general straightened his shoulders in an attempt to get back to business. "We don't have all day." He then pointed to the sand storm heading their way. "We need to take shelter immediately."

Bryus squinted his eyes. "Ah, we made it just in time. Here they come." Bryus started digging through his purse of magical items.

"They?" the general asked.

"The Winds of Conquest be com'n," replied Dare before popping the cork and taking a swig from one of his bottles.

General Lund looked back and forth for a more clear definition. "The what?"

Dare rolled his eyes toward Bryus. "And you be call'n me stupid?"

Casting a spell with his magical components, a blue ball of light shot from his hands up hundreds of feet into the air, where it hovered and pulsed brightly. "Let's get beyond those walls. We can explain inside," Bryus said with some urgency to the general.

Confused about nearly everything that had happened in that prior few minutes, the general gave a good look one last time at Bryus' pale wrinkled face before comparing it to the young and bodacious chest and slender female body.

"Excuse me," Bryus said, interrupting the general's gaze. "Are you staring at my wife's body?"

"What? No!"

"He was. I seen 'em," Dare chimed in.

Pulling his shoulders back and puffing out his chest, General Lund tried again to regroup. "What exactly are you? Are you a man or a woman?"

Bryus shook his head in disappointment. "You're asking the wrong questions. You should be more concerned about what's headed this way." Pointing toward the sandstorm, he could see the general was still concerned about his body. "Let it go. I'm simply borrowing my wife's body. Surely you borrow things from your wife from time to time."

General Lund opened his mouth to answer but, before he could speak, he was quickly cut off when Dare's bone cane jabbed him in his side.

"I doesn't think he really wants an answer, mate," Dare said plainly before taking another sip from his bottle.

"What is going on here?" the general said in a powerful tone in an attempt to gain control of the situation.

Bryus and Dare began escorting the general back to the gate while explaining.

"Ambrosius has sent us here to help fend off the Del'Unday attack." Bryus looked over his shoulder at the wave of sand closing in on them. "Being without transportation or a body at the time, I have placed my wife and child in hiding while the captain here provided passage for me to arrive prior to the battle."

"Your wife's body?" the general asked while entering the gate.

"You really need to get past this point. As the former high-wizard of EverSpring, I've mastered many types of magic and I've worn many hats, and many bodies as well." He laughed at his own joke while Dare shook his head. "I've been through more limbs than you have of swords," he said while looking at his current arms. He then smirked. "Actually, one time it was an actual limb from a tree."

Once inside the Kingdom's walls, the large gates closed and were locked by the guards on duty.

The general's head spun with confusion. "I don't have time for this." He shook the chaos of the travelers out of his head. "I have duties to perform before the storm hits." He then walked away from the two and made his way to the highest tower in order to make sure all had been prepared to his approval.

Bryus and Dare were stunned by what they saw. Instead of seeing an army preparing for battle and loading catapults, they saw tarps covering every weapon they had. Thick ropes had been securely put in place as though they would all be in storage for a long time.

Street merchants were calmly closing up for the day as children still played in the streets. There was no sense of what was about to hit.

"Did I happen to mention the Del'Unday were attacking?" Bryus said in an arrogant tone.

"Aye, ya did," Dare replied. "Don't think anyone cares."

"Or they don't believe us." Bryus shook his head in disbelief. "If I were to tell me something as important as this, I would listen to me, wouldn't you?"

Dare looked him up and down and took a sip of the Irr. "Not in that outfit. Clashes with yur eyes."

Bryus ignored Dare and tossed his hood over his head and walked straight for the tower where the general had entered.

The few guards that were on duty were busy getting the last few items secured before the storm. They looked up at Bryus' wife's body and assumed the head matched as well. In doing so, they were more than cordial in opening doors and allowing her to go where Bryus pleased.

Dare followed behind, taking sips from his bottle and waving his fingers at the men overtaken by Bryus' beauty. "She's too much for ya, mate," he said to one who looked as though he was going to attempt to speak to Bryus.

Reaching the top of the tower, Bryus found the general as he gave his men orders. "There you are."

The general and his men glanced over at the hooded female body. The younger men were in a trance until the hood was removed. Then their faces turned sour. One man actually vomited over the side of the wall while two others covered their mouths as bile regurgitated into their mouths.

"What now?" the general asked in an authoritative voice.

Bryus flung his arms around in disgust. "Why have you stored your equipment for winter when you should be preparing for their attack?"

"Ma'am, sir, whatever you are, you need to vacate this tower immediately. We are about to be hit by a very powerful sandstorm."

"No, you're about to get hit by an attack of the Del'Unday. The children of Rummon have been released from captivity. They are flying in front of the army and are stirring up the sand you see in order to prevent you from viewing them."

The wall of sand was nearing them as the wind raced west toward the general's face. "It's nothing more than a sandstorm." Turning around, away from the desert, he watched the storm darken high in the skies above LuTythis Tower. "I'm more concerned with the odd weather than your stories of Rummon's children," he said before heading down inside the tower for protection. "Take cover!"

Closing the hatch after everyone was one floor below the top of the tower, General Lund stood silent with a few of his men, Bryus, and the now drunk Captain Dare, waiting for the storm to hit.

As expected, the wind picked up and sand began blowing through any cracks in the walls, ceiling and openings in the door and window sills. The only thing to do was plug the holes until the storm passed.

Unexpectedly, a loud thud was heard and felt as the entire tower shook. Something large had hit the side of the wall. "What was that?" the general asked.

"I can't imagine," Bryus said sarcastically.

"I'll check, sir," a young guard said, racing up the ladder and opening up the trap door.

Wind ripped the door from his hand and flung it off its hinges, allowing sand to whip into the room from above.

Covering his eyes, the young man climbed up anyway to determine what the loud bang had been.

General Lung watched the soldier climb the rest of the way up the ladder before his feet lifted up as though he had flown straight up into the air.

Bryus glared at the General. "If only someone had warned you."

Glossy-eyed, Dare squinted at Bryus before whispering, "I thought we did."

"What in the world is going on here!" the general yelled, making his own way up the ladder to understand the situation. Firmly grasping the ladder, he powered his way up against the sand and wind blowing at him. Resistant to the elements, he reached the top of the tower, and made his way to the eastern side. Holding on for balance against the rough winds, he attempted to see where his young soldier went, as well as what the thud against the wall was.

As quickly as the sandstorm had started, it ended, freeing up visibility for the general to see.

Tens of thousands of Del'Unday creatures were now at his doorstep, covering the east to the first desert ridge. They were armed with catapults, giant slings, and other missile weapons to destroy the wall he stood on. A second such attack came in the form of a large boulder slamming up against the side of the wall, shaking it and cracking its foundation.

Turning to see the storm which had passed, he could see two dragons flying eastward, pushing the sandstorm forward across the city. They had successfully provided a cover for the oncoming army, just as Bryus had suggested. One of the dragons held a young man in his claws, but dropped him to his death once they ended the storm and returned to the battle at the wall.

"Load everything we have and start firing! We're under attack!" the general screamed to his men.

Soldiers fled their protective rooms from the sandstorm in order to carry out the general's orders. Unfortunately, all of the military equipment had been covered and tied down. Not only were they unprepared, but they were at the disadvantage of having to remove the ropes and tarps. They had fallen for the Del'Unday trap.

General Lund watched as the two dragons made their way down into the city to feast upon anything alive they could get their claws into. Turning his back to them, he tried to quickly assess the enemy below to the east. He could see the Del'Unday forces approaching with ladders and hand to hand weapons, while missile weapons were being locked down and prepared for firing.

What concerned him the most was the Blothrud who stood in the middle of the army, giving orders. At first the general thought he was standing on something to gain his height, but he quickly realized that he didn't need to. Legs of a wolf, arms and chest of a human, and head of a dragon, the red muscle-bound creature put fear into the hearts of all who looked upon him.

"What in the King's name is that?" the general asked himself.

Bryus had walked up behind him to see the oncoming army. "That is the one and only demon of our land, Ergrauth. He'll rip your people apart just for existing." Touching his neck where his old head attached to his wife's young body, he added, "I know that from experience."

"ATTACK!" the general yelled to his men, but no weapons were prepared to attack. They were defenseless aside from arrows and spears.

The mighty Ergrauth glanced up to see if the Winds of Conquest sibling dragons were returning to the siege. In doing so, he noticed the human general, on the tower, yelling for his men to fight. A devilish smile crossed the demon's long snout. "This is a good day to reclaim my land." Reaching to his side, he selected the appropriate weapon to start the attack.

Among many sturdy spears, swords and maces, the demon grabbed an ancient, thick-handled, metal-trimmed hardwood war-hammer with the word "Quake" engraved on it. Normally a two-handed weapon, Ergrauth's size allowed him to pick it up and over his head with one, before swinging it forward and releasing it. Sailing amazingly far through the air, the wide hammer eventually struck the side of the Doven Wall with a thunderous rumble, violently shaking the entire area, followed by his armies racing forward.

As the two armies launched themselves into battle, a swirling mass of ashes and burnt debris hovered above the high tower. The gray and black fragments churned around in a small tornado, revealing a woman's face and body. Her cloak and long hair waved in the air from unfelt wind. Her skin formed, cracked, and then blew away in the constant spinning air. The Death Witch, Irluk, had arrived to collect the souls of the dead, and today there would be more available to her than she could possibly desire.

## Chapter 24
# Ergrauth's War

The Winds of Conquest flew across the battling landscape. These two dragons were the siblings of none other than Rummon himself. Together, they could control the skies over the battle and turn the tide of victory. In this case, forcing a sandstorm in front of the Del'Unday, they had allowed Ergrauth's army to approach undetected.

Battlements began to crumble as catapults and counterweight trebuchets hurled heavy loads against Doven's walls and towers. It was a relentless attack on the unprepared humans who struggled to uncover their weapons and prepare for battle.

Aerial missile weapons were quickly defeated by the Winds of Conquest, as they knocked projectiles from the air and then swooped down to crush the Doven giant crossbows and the like. Their weapons were destroyed faster than they could load them for a second attack.

The air now belonged to Ergrauth, while his army's siege towers and ladder climbers were starting to take control of the once impenetrable Doven Wall.

Bryus Grum stood on the high tower casting various spells toward the invading army. He caused whirlpools of sand which sucked many creatures underneath the desert floor. Another spell sprayed streams of acid from his hands which ate away at ladders and those climbing them. He then created an illusion of the Dovenar Wall falling over on top of the enemy, causing many Del'Unday to run for cover.

Swaying from the alcohol, Captain Dare assessed the damage and pointed to the next group that needed Bryus' attention. "Yur pulling to the right too much. Keep them spells focused better. Here comes a batch to ya left. Keep yur eyes open!"

"Perhaps if you pulled that paunch out of my way, I could see better!" Bryus then turned his back to Dare in order to prevent another ladder attack from becoming successful.

"Make'n fun of me appearance now? I can't just steal a new body once mine displeases me," he argued before taking another drink from his bottle. Spying the perfect curves on the female body before him, his eyes glazed over from the alcohol. "And a fine body it is," he mumbled, grabbing a handful of the female buttocks.

Bryus' acid spell sprayed across the top of the Doven Wall as a result of the unexpected grab from behind. Stopping the spell he spun around in anger toward the drunken man. "Did you just grab my wife's buttocks?"

Squinting one eye, Captain Dare took a quick sip before answering. "Aye, I did. And a fine backside she has. Whatever possessed her to waste such a body on an old wrinkly sour-attitude man such as yourself?"

"Yes, I'm sure she would much rather have a flatulent obese drunk with leftovers from the prior two meals still clinging to his chest hair, than a powerful wizard who was once the leader of EverSpring."

The captain smiled at the thought. "Give 'er a chance and I'll charm the clothes right off a 'er."

"Listen you sick-minded chuttlebeast-smelling fesh, I'm a little busy to be arguing with you over my wife's choice of men. I'm trying to stop this invasion. Now get out of my way," he said, trying to push him to the side.

Captain Dare laughed and belched at the same time from the weak push against his heavy body. To show him how it's done, he grabbed his companion's thin body and tossed it over to the west side of the tower. "Bryus Grum, you only be one wizard. It be take'n more than that to fight off Ergrauth's army. We be needing a plan and more reinforcements. Stay'n 'ear to fight on our own is a death sentence."

Bryus pulled his frail body up off the tower floor and looked west, out across the city. He could see the remaining residents running for their lives while the dwindling number of soldiers continued to race toward the battle. "You're right," he said to the captain. Standing up, he could hear a sound coming from deeper in the city; a sound he hadn't heard in years. "But one wizard can lend a powerful hand to those forces who can win a war." Turning, he raced back over to the east side and grabbed Captain Dare by his shoulders. "I did it, you fat puke! They saw my signal!" He then looked straight overhead at the spell he had created earlier.

Captain Dare tilted his head back to look up at the blue glowing ball still pulsing several hundred feet above them. "Aye, ya did that."

Placing the cork on his bottle he took a moment to try to shake the cobwebs out of his skull. "Ambrosius told me he be needing us to do one last chore for him after I got ya here. It's time for me to be off. I'll meet you there. Don't be late, mate, or we'll be see'n each other in Della Estovia," he said with a slur while spinning around and heading towards the stairs that lead to the lower levels of the wall.

Ignoring the drunken captain, Bryus began collecting components for his next spell.

Meanwhile, General Lund had given the order for all citizens to evacuate the city and hide in the hills. There was no stopping the demon's forces. He only hoped that his men could hold the Del'Unday off long enough for his people to flee to a safety.

A loud crash rumbled through the area as the main gate into the Doven Province collapsed from another missile attack, crumbling inward toward the city. For the first time in over six-hundred years, there was no barrier stopping the Del'Unday from entering the Dovenar Kingdom.

General Lund quickly pulled his men together at the gate's entrance for one final stand. He looked up onto the wall and watched his men being attacked and defeated with ease. "We no longer fight to defend!" he yelled out to his men. "We fight to kill as many Delz as we can in order to save our families!"

With that, he charged the front gate with several dozen men at his side, all yelling war cries.

Racing through the gate they took the Del'Unday on in hand-to-hand combat. It took the Altered Creatures by surprise and quickly carved a hole through their front line, only to be filled in behind them. Quickly surrounded on all sides by the Del'Unday, they stopped for a moment to regroup.

The circle of the enemy closed in step by step, enjoying the sight of fear in the eyes of the humans. It was over for the Doven Province army and, once inside the wall, there was no stopping the Del'Unday attacks.

Ergrauth approached the circle of remaining humans. He then spotted the general and gave him a smirk before speaking one simple word. "Goodbye."

Upon the Demon's words, the human army disappeared, literally vanishing from the sight of the Del'Undays. The scene caused the creatures to pause from their forward movement in an effort to understand what just happened.

Ergrauth raised his muzzle and sniffed the air. "I still smell them. They are still in front of us! Attack!"

A barrage of arrows suddenly flew out of the empty area, piercing the chest of many of the Altered Creatures.

Unknown to anyone in the battle, Bryus had cast a spell, causing everyone inside the perimeter of his illusion to become invisible to anyone outside of the spell. Fortunately for the humans inside the spell boundary, they could still see everyone outside of the border, giving them the advantage to start firing off rounds of arrows.

Keeping his focus on the center of the humans, Bryus could only hope it gave the Doven army the time they needed.

A second round of arrows shot out of the invisible barrier; two of which embedded in Ergrauth. One landed in his leg and the other in his shoulder.

Ergrauth roared with anger. "Attack!" he ordered, before pulling the arrows out of his skin as though they were nothing more than thorns from a bristle bush.

The Del'Unday attacked. Once inside the spell's border they disappeared from Ergrauth's sight, but those individuals could now see the humans. The help from the spell was over.

Savage cries resonated from the attack. It was indistinguishable which side they came from as Bryus Grum's spell ended, revealing the humans once again. However, the war cries quickly came from a new location, this time they were from within the Dovan Walls.

A large muscular man riding a two-legged faralope raced from the city, out through the gate and into the battlefront. He was accompanied by a legion of men riding their own Fesh'Undays.

The beasts they rode were strong-legged and thick-necked creatures of various shades of gray with thick coarse hair thinned out and patchy around the ankles and back of the neck. They could outrun most creatures and had a kick that could stop a chuttlebeast in its tracks, if hit in the right spot.

In front of the army of riding warriors was Asentar, dressed in his Dovenar Knight blue robes and full battle gear. Asentar had made it across the desert to Woodlen and had led the kingdom's troops south to the real location of the battle. He and those who followed him were ready for the battle that Ergrauth had started.

A flood of riders followed the knight out of the gate and into the battle. They were skilled warriors with sharp weapons and the eye of a hunting party. They wanted blood and they were excited to see some spill. The Del'Unday had terrorized the Dovenar Kingdom for too many generations and it was time to end it once and for all.

The new force of men pushed the Del'Unday back a hundred yards from the gate with their initial attack. They had the upper hand of surprise and excitement. Scattering, the Del'Unday attempted to defend their ground with little success.

Ergrauth was outraged at the performance of his army. "Stand your ground!" he demanded, but his warriors were being beaten back by the riding warriors.

A flood of Dovenar riders continued to race out of the gates and into the battle, pushing the battlefront back east and then to the south toward Rivers Edge. The humans cheered with excitement, entering the conflict with a desire to win this war and defeat all the Del'Unday.

Asentar coordinated the efforts in order to maximize their forces against the creatures before them. He knew they were still outnumbered five to one, but he had skilled fighters who had a desire to protect their land and family. The Dovenar Knight hoped that this and his own strategic battle skills would be enough to defeat creatures fighting out of fear from Ergrauth.

One of Asentar's men waved various flags to convey the Knight's orders to the rest of the troops. Each move was well planned out and allowed the Dovenar army to eventually regain control of the Doven Wall and the north side of the battle.

Ergrauth's army had been pushed up against the Rivers Edge wall with the east still open for escape if needed. However, escape was not even contemplated by the demon. "Darkmere has failed us!" he roared. "He was to have the human armies in northern Woodlen."

Stepping forward to the front line, he yelled to his troops, "Step back!" the demon's roar was powerful enough for all to hear, even in the heat of battle.

The Del'Unday had been trained their entire life to obey Ergrauth's every command, and immediately ended their attacks. They then moved confidently back in line behind Ergrauth, causing an empty path between the two armies.

Standing in front of his warriors, he called out to the other side. "Who among you, speaks for your kingdom?"

Both sides stood exhausted, waiting for someone to step forward.

It was only a matter of seconds before General Lund pushed his way through his men and stepped out in front. His head was bleeding, coating his right eye and side of his face with blood. The man's limp gave away his leg wound and his torn shirt exposed a serious gash to his side. The general could barely stand.

Ergrauth laughed at the sight. "Surely you can do better than this." His deep voice resonated across the entire battlefield.

"We can," said Asentar, riding his Faralope down the open path between the two armies. He sat confident with his shoulders back and a long glistening blade in one hand. "Step back, General. You have done your part in protecting your people. It is now my time."

General Lund stepped back into line, quickly to be held up by a fellow comrade. His body was giving out on him, but he refused to give the Del'Unday the benefit of seeing him suffer or fall.

Asentar rode his faralope right up in front of Ergrauth. "Your war against us is over. We have alerted the other provinces and more of our people will continue to flood into the conflict. We eventually will outnumber you and defeat you."

The demon squinted his eyes at the Dovenar Knight. "Even though your entrance took my army by surprise, we still outnumber your forces right now. It could be days before the rest of your kinsmen arrive. By then you will all be wiped from this land."

"Greensbrook and Southwind will be arriving from the south while our well-equipped Eastland army will be arriving very shortly from the east. We now stand at your west and north. All paths will be blocked. Staying to fight only serves as a death sentence to the Del'Unday. Leave now and cross the eastern mountains back to your valley. Return to what you had or you will lose everything on this ground we stand on."

Ergrauth gave a low growl, staring into Asentar's eyes for deception. "You are a fool to assume you can defeat me. I have waited far too long for this battle, and today is my day of victory. Your threats of additional forces are foolhardy. There is no one coming to save you or your people."

As he finished his sentence, a rumbling became apparent from the east. It was an army, rising over the eastern sand dune. Support had arrived.

An army, half the size of Ergrauth's own, rose over the eastern dune and down toward the rest of the humans and Del'Unday. These reinforcements would easily change the tide of the battle. Unfortunately, it was in Ergrauth's favor. Corrock's army had arrived after defeating the Ov'Unday at Trewek and then wiping out the mighty Eastland army. They were proven in battle and ready to demonstrate to Ergrauth that they were worthy of his leadership. This was important to them, for they had lived in disgrace for so many years after their leaders had disobeyed Ergrauth's orders. It was now time to for them to justify their return under his leadership.

The demon grinned at the Dovenar Knight. "Darkmere has ensured that the Matriarch of Southwind has taken over the southern armies for which she will be granted ruler of the southern lands. Eastland has been defeated by the Corrockian army, so they will not be joining us either. There is no one coming to save you. This war has been playing out for years, right under your nose. You've only joined it in the final battle. It is over. I have already won. The deaths here today are only the final pieces on a much larger game in which you've lost.

The Corrockian army charged the battlefield, disrupting the temporary ceasefire.

"Attack!" yelled Ergrauth with obvious enjoyment.

## Chapter 25
# Below The Tower

Four children of the demon, Bakalor, continued to carve yard-wide tunnels underneath the Lu'Tythis Tower, leaving chaotic paths similar to wormholes but on a much larger scale.

Back and forth, the lesser demons ate their way through the solid rock which had held the mountain-sized tower for thousands of years. It would have lasted tens of thousands more, if its foundation hadn't been compromised by the attack of these creatures.

All of Bakalor's children looked about the same. They had an internal fiery center with a crusted over surface. When needed, arms and legs would grow out of the rock sphere, however, no eyes existed. These creatures relied on their keen sense of touch to feel movement on the ground to determine where their opponents were.

One of the creatures stopped in its path to assess the damage to determine where to focus its attack. At rest, it felt the slight tremors in the ground from the tower's weight pressing on the compromised rock foundation. The lesser demon could also feel the direction of where the stress was the greatest. Once determined, the creature moved forward, carving a new path in an attempt to perform more damage in the area of higher stress.

Tunneling forward, the lesser demon found its way to a large open area, carved out by two of its siblings. The cavern ranged from ten to sixty feet deep and over a hundred feet wide. Within it, two lesser demons continued to expand the size while eating away at the walls and floor.

A sudden quake rocked the cavern, cracking the ceiling in several lightning bolt patterns. The weight from the tower was pressing so hard on the roof that it had begun to buckle and bulge downward. It was just a matter of time.

The two lesser demons would work on expanding the cavern until the tower completely toppled under its own weight. The new arrival to the cavern joined in to help make the tower's foundation less stable.

The more they ate, the more frequent the rocks above cracked and shuddered under the pressure.

Stepping out of one of the few naturally made tunnels and into the cavern, Ambrosius led his son, Ericc, and his silver-dragon friend, Draq, toward their final battle to save Lu'Tythis Tower.

"We're too late," Ericc said, scanning the shifting ceiling for movement as it dropped rock fragments onto the floor below. "We've lost this battle."

"Your father doesn't understand the nature of giving up," Draq replied to the young man. His eyes thinned while watching the three lesser demons etch out the cavern even wider. "He has saved me from worse fates than this."

Ambrosius ignored the discussion behind him. "Ericc, are you ready to put your E'rudite powers to the test?"

"Name your need," he replied.

"How much can you carry with you when you spatial jump?"

"I don't know. I've jumped with two other people before. I've never tested it to see how much I can carry. Why?"

"I need you to bring in some stone columns to hold this ceiling from collapsing."

Ericc watched as the roof of the cave cracked again, shifting a large section downward by several feet. "Stone columns? I've never attempted such a thing."

Ambrosius turned and looked his son square in the eyes. "It can be done. You just have to trust that you have the power. You are only limited by your own perception of yourself."

"Shouldn't we focus on destroying Bakalor's children?"

"I will, once you get started on moving some columns in here." Another loud crack from the ceiling prompted him to add haste to his words. "Go now! We haven't much time."

Confused, Ericc's eyes darted back and forth, attempting to think of a location with columns. "Where would I collect such a thing?"

Ambrosius turned back to the open cavern and raised his open palms forward, allowing him to sense the stress in the rock overhead. "There are strong well-built columns in Pwellus Dementa' as well as in the Woodlen Coliseum." Rotating his body, he was able to sense where the largest stress pockets were and the locations they needed to place the columns.

"I've never been to those places. I can't jump to points I've never been."

After finding a critical weak spot, Ambrosius used his E'rudite powers to crush the rocks on the ground into a flat surface several feet in diameter. "Place one of the columns there," he said in an urgent voice, pointing at the flat landing he had just provided. "You've been to the Coliseum. I took you there when you were younger."

"I was only an infant at the time!"

Another loud crack came from the ceiling, while additional fissures opened above them.

"Then find someplace else!"

"But-"

"There's no time for this conversation." Ambrosius' voice was sharp and filled with authority. "Find something to hold this ceiling up!"

The direct order from his father caused his face to flush and anger to seep into his expression. Without a word, Ericc vanished into thin air.

Draq remained quiet, keeping his eyes peeled for any attacks coming from the busy lesser demons.

Ambrosius created a second flat surface after discovering another weak spot. "I know I missed most of his life as a child, but I need him to be a man right now." He returned to sensing the next weak point. "Do you think I'm expecting too much from him?"

Growling, Draq focused on a section of wall as it started to turn red. "I would expect more out of him. He won't achieve his potential if not pushed and challenged." The red glowing on the wall increased. "The fourth and last of Bakalor's children has arrived."

Glancing over his shoulder, Ambrosius could see the red wall break away and melt. "Watch my back. I need to find and prepare a few more locations for Ericc's columns."

"I've always had your back," Draq said with a snarl, watching the last lesser demon enter the cavern from his newly created tunnel.

Once the new creature entered, it stopped to feel the ground and sense who was in the room. It immediately picked up the dragon's footfalls and headed toward Draq.

"I can keep this one busy for a while." Leaping into the air, he watched the lesser demon stop in order to feel Draq's movement.

However, with the dragon in the air, there was none to follow, until it could sense the heartbeat of Ambrosius through his boots and ground. Although it was extremely faint, the creature turned and headed for the man.

Draq quickly responded, landing hard in the opposite direction of Ambrosius. "Get over here you stupid piece of rock," he said, stomping heavy on the ground to get attention.

It worked. The creature's rolling mass curved to the right and back toward the noisy dragon.

Draq lifted off the cavern floor prior to it reaching him, and then landed hard in a new location to keep the focus on himself and acquire more time for his companion.

Ambrosius identified another key location and again used his powers to clear off a base for the soon to arrive column. "Hurry, Ericc," he thought to himself, being very careful not to make any noise that the lesser demon could pick up.

While Draq's game of deception was going well, large rocks began falling from the ceiling. Several hit him across his wings and then one in the head, knocking the dragon to the ground, as many more tumbled down upon his right wing. He was trapped. The rocks were too heavy to pull his wing free.

Bakalor's child rolled toward the fallen red-tipped silver dragon, turning a bright glowing red while it prepared for its attack.

Even before the creature touched him, Draq could feel the immense furnace of heat radiating from it. Dragon scales would protect against a great many things, but molten lava was not one of them.

The lesser demon attacked, charring Draq's leg instantly upon its touch while it made its rolling assault upon his body.

Draq screamed in pain from the melting of his own skin. His leg was now in flames and the lesser demon was just getting started.

Moving up to Draq's hip, the creature unexpectedly flew through the air and crashed into the far wall. This event was quickly followed by the rocks on Draq's wing suddenly rising and pelting the lesser demon.

Standing a few yards away, Ambrosius continued to use his E'rudite powers to push and pull objects of his choosing. "Can you move?"

"Yes," Draq said, flapping his injured wing and attempting to stand on his damaged leg. "My wing will cause us problems, but my leg is useless," he growled, falling back down after trying to put his weight on it. "Did you get all of the locations ready for Ericc?"

A series of cracks in the ceiling showered the two with more rocks.

"All but one. But it will have to do."

A new fissure snapped open across the center of the cavern, allowing half the ceiling to sag down several feet.

Ambrosius moved underneath it and raised his hands upward, using his powers to push the ceiling, preventing it from falling any further. This was no small task even for the likes of him. The tower and its foundation were pressing against him. The question wasn't about who would win this, it was how long could Ambrosius last before being crushed.

Hopping on one leg and unable to fly, Draq yelled out to his companion, "Watch your back!"

Taking the slightest possible moment to glance behind him, Ambrosius could see the lesser demon rolling straight at him.

 Heading directly toward his enemy, the creature's heat increased, thinning the dark crust on its surface. It zipped across the cavern floor, leaving a trail of scorched rock.

Feeling the heat, the hairs on his exposed arms started melting off even prior to being hit. Ambrosius pulled one arm down from above and used it, and his powers, to hold off the attacker. However, his powers were already being taxed and the lesser demon was not pushed away, nor was it even stopped. It was only slowed down.

Inch by inch, it moved closer to Ambrosius, scalding his hand and the clothes closest to the beast.

Ambrosius would have to use all of his efforts to destroy the creature, but by doing so he would most likely die from the ceiling caving down on him.

His entire body shook from his efforts to do both at the same time. The strain was beyond comparison and his arms felt as though they would snap off his body from the weight. More and more pressure built until he began to black out.

It was at this point that a silvery flash washed past Ambrosius' view, taking the lesser demon with it.

Between hopping on one leg and nearly flying with an injured wing, Draq had obtained enough momentum to plow his entire body against the molten rock creature.

The attack allowed Ambrosius a reprieve from fighting two fronts, as Draq and the lesser demon tumbled off to the side.

Draq was now badly injured. Most of his body was now charred, broken, or in flames. Lying on his back, he struggled in his attempt to roll onto his side in his effort to continue the fight. His mind was still in it. However, his body was not. His left claw had been completely melted off from the lava. The ceiling was now too low to fly, and he was unable to walk. His fight was over.

Rolling to a stop, the lesser demon felt the massive power being released by Ambrosius and headed toward the E'rudite again.

Watching the rolling, glowing red rock heading toward him, Ambrosius knew he didn't have it in him to fend the creature away. He took a deep breath and braced himself for the impact.

His vision was suddenly cut short. Instead of seeing the creature roll up onto him, he was staring at a large metal door. This was followed by a loud crash from the other side, where the demon had run into it.

The thick door was nearly the height of the ceiling and had several locks along one side of it. Half of the hinges were missing from the other side.

Ambrosius blinked at the sight before seeing Ericc standing next to it.

"This isn't a column," Ambrosius said in an exhausted voice.

"I know. These are the strongest things I could think of on such short notice. This is one of the doors to the Southwind prison mines." His paused ever so slightly before continuing with a devilish grin. "I hope no one escapes."

"Are there more?" Ambrosius asked, lowering the weight of the ceiling on the metal door.

"Yes."

Moving his powers to a new area of the ceiling, he braced his legs while pushing upward. "Get them! Quickly."

He nodded back at his father.

"Ericc," Ambrosius said before the young man disappeared. "Good thinking," he said with a proud nod.

A smile appeared on Ericc's face just as he vanished from sight.

The ceiling cracked again and more rocks continued to fall around the E'rudite. "Hold strong, Draq. I'll get you out of here."

"It's been an honor to fight by your side," the dragon replied in a muffled voice.

"Don't talk like that. We have many more battles in our future."

More rocks rained down upon them prior to another major fissure in the ceiling. In addition, the lesser demon had gained its bearings and started to roll toward the two.

Ambrosius kept one hand up toward the ceiling and dropped the other toward the approaching lesser demon with the other. "I promise you, my dear friend, the world will not see the end of us on this day." Taking a deep breath, he pushed with his E'rudite powers to hold all at bay.

## Chapter 26
# More Arrive

General Lund had been taken to the high tower so he could oversee the battle. His body was failing him, but he wished to watch his people's final defense from his favorite vantage point before he passed away.

His soldiers gently leaned him against the west side battlement, near Bryus Grum.

The wizard never gave him a second look while casting spell after spell onto the enemy below. "I don't have time to heal the wounded," Bryus said to the soldiers.

The general leaned against the stone blocks that had protected his people for generations and gazed over the scene below. "I ask for no healing, simply one last look at our progress."

"Have you been drinking Dare's nectar? We're losing! We had a slim chance against Ergrauth's army, but the Corrockian army has made this a slaughter of Dovenar soldiers."

That now familiar tug was felt again on the General's body, just as he had been feeling on and off for days, but this one was stronger. Turning, he looked upon the circling dark storm over Lu'Tythis Tower while lighting raced from the center every second or two. "The storm is coming, Bryus. Do you feel it tugging on your body?"

Bryus tried to ignore him so he could focus on saving lives. "I don't need your overly dramatic report on the meteorological conditions, I need reinforcements! The Dovenar Kingdom is being slaughtered!"

Swiveling his head back to the east to view the devastation, General Lund watched the outnumbered humans being knocked off of their faralopes and tackled to the ground. Sand-eels leapt from the desert sand and wrapped themselves around necks and faces before extending hundreds of painful needles into their victims. Giant frog-like creatures shot their tongues out into the chest of humans, filled their reptile neck air sacks, and then blew through their hollow tongue, causing the victim to explode from the sudden pressure.

The scene was one of carnage. The humans were falling quickly. The Death Witch could be seen as a swirling of debris leading the vapors of fallen souls in an endless parade from the battlefield.

"In the name of the King, no more," mumbled the general, pointing toward the eastern dune before he passed away from his injuries and the sight of certain doom. The sight of yet another Altered Creature army arriving had been just too much for him to endure.

Rising from the east, a new line of creatures arrived. Varying in sizes and shapes in a line spanned across the horizon, they were consistent and unified in their calm movement toward the battle. They were also less than a fourth of the size of the current Del'Unday army, and unexpected by Ergrauth and his forces.

"I thought the Ov'Unday were taken care of," the demon said to the leader of the Corrockian army.

"They are of no concern to you, my lord. A small portion of the Corrockian forces will quickly wipe them out and rejoin your battlefront before you know it." He then proceeded to take his lead fighters to the east.

Brimmelle and Grewen stood in the center of the Ov'Unday's from Trewek, watching as the Corrockian leader collected forces to protect their backs. It was a small group compared to the number of Ov'Unday standing on the ridge.

Grewen's twelve-foot tall Mognin body stood firm, allowing the Del army to come to them. "Creating two battle fronts for the Del'Unday should give the Dovenar Kingdom a fighting chance."

Brimmelle grimaced. "Yes, but what are you going to do when they get here if you have still chosen not to fight?" He appeared very tiny among the row of Mognins, even though he was tall for a Num.

"We will not change our beliefs, but we can still assist in the campaign of this battle."

The Num watched the Del'Unday coordinate their efforts and then begin racing up the slope toward the top of the dune. "Here they come. Prepare to do nothing and be slaughtered," he said sarcastically.

Grewen grinned at the nervous Num. "We do outnumber them."

Fir Brimmelle puffed out his chest and criticized the Mognin. "How does that help if we don't fight back?"

"It may appear that the minority has the strength because they make the most noise, but real power is in the masses if they can unite and stand firm on their convictions."

"Are you suggesting that they will eventually get tired of killing the idle Ov'Unday and will finally give up and go home?"

"We believe engaging fighters with fighting will only escalade the conflict. But we never planned on standing idle while being attacked. We will overpower them with our conviction to peace..." Grewen watched as the first Del fighters arrived and attacked, "...and the strength to work together to stop those who wish to do us harm."

The Mognins in the front of the Ov'Unday stepped forward and collectively grabbed the Del attackers. At a ratio of three Ov'Unday to every one Del, they quickly captured their enemy and tied them up with nets and ropes, setting their captives behind their battle front.

The only one to escape was the Corrockian leader, who charged toward the line of Ov'Unday several times in an effort to make them move back in fear. However, he received no such pleasure as the Ov'Unday stood strong and calm.

After a few more attempts to strike fear into the Ov'Unday, he finally returned down the dune to gather more forces. This time he began pulling all of the Corrockian troops together in order to ensure they had the odds against the Ov'Unday. In doing so, he released the pressure the Del'Unday were putting on the Dovenar armies.

Grewen nodded. "The plan has worked. The Dovenar army now has a fighting chance to defend itself from Ergrauth's army."

"That's wonderful," Brimmelle said, watching the Corrockian army establish a battle line to rush the dune. "They had better take advantage of it before we are removed from this situation."

"Agreed," Grewen said thoughtfully.

## Chapter 27
# The Matriarch

After destroying a major part of the Mythical Forest and chasing the remaining Myth'Unday out, the Southwind army arrived on the north end of the forest, near Rivers Edge. The wall which held back the flooded province was within sight. Beyond the wall was a river with the tops of various structures peeking out of the water's surface. The once thriving city of Maegoth had been underwater for thirty years, haunted by the undead from the final battle of the civil war.

On the other side of the river was a similar wall and then a desert. Normally quiet and peaceful, the sand wasteland was currently full of disarray as humans and Altered Creatures fought near the Doven Wall, just west of the battlefield.

The Matriarch was carried on a pillow-covered bed by a dozen men to the front of the Southwind military line in order to view the distant battle.

"How will we get across the river to help?" one of her advisers asked.

She smirked at the idea. "We will not. Our task was to destroy all of our enemies south of Rivers Edge. Northern territories will not be ours, so we care not."

"Understood," the man said with a bow of his head.

"Have we completely captured or destroyed all of the Myth'Unday on the east side of the Pelonthal's wall?"

"Yes, my Matriarch."

"Excellent." Turning west, she viewed the wall running south from Rivers Edge. "Then we shall enter the wall and start pushing whatever life inside it out into Lake Luthralum. I want all of those pesky Myth'Undays either destroyed or bowing to my every command."

"And the cities within? Pelonthal and Thasque? They are filled with Ov'Unday."

"They are pacifists and will not put up a fight. They are also very talented artists and musicians. I look forward to hearing their praises of me."

"We are not to kill them?"

"Of course, you will. At least enough of them to make the rest understand who is in charge." After cutting a piece of cheese with a short dagger and tasting its sharp flavor, she took a deep breath at the view of the distant battle before commenting to herself, "As we agreed, the north is all yours, Darkmere, and the south is all mine."

Smiling at the thought of total power, her mouth changed to a frown upon a disheartening sight. There, in the tall grass between her and Rivers Edge, she could see movement. Hundreds of Myth'Unday were flying in and out of the thick grassland.

"Pilwa," she said to one of her other advisors. "Did you hear Mikar tell me that all of the Myth'Unday had been destroyed?"

"Yes, my Matriarch," he replied.

"And are those Myth'Unday in the grass before us?"

"It appears so, my Matriarch."

"That is what I thought." The Matriarch turned to the adviser Mikar. "You lied to me."

Panic rushed across his face. "No, not with intent. I was told by the commander of your army that they had all been killed."

"So you passed on a lie to me. You know how I feel about lying."

"Please, my Matriarch, I beg your forgiveness."

"Oh, I forgive you, but this will not happen again."

"Thank you, my Matriarch, it will never happen again."

"Pilwa, kill Mikar to ensure this doesn't happen again," she said with a cold and detached voice.

Mikar's eyes widen, while Pilwa nodded to the Matriarch. Soldiers grabbed Mikar to prevent his escape, as Pilwa pulled out a knife with no emotion and slit the other man's throat, causing his body to fall to the ground.

"The deed is done, my Matriarch."

"I don't like it when people lie to me."

"Yes, my Matriarch."

"You would never lie to me, would you, Pilwa?"

"No, my Matriarch."

"Good. Now tell the commander to surround these grasslands so we can trap these creatures against the Rivers Edge Wall. I want to be up front to see them scream for mercy before we kill them."

"Do you think they saw us yet?" Thorik asked Mr. Hempton. He had been crouched down out of sight in the tall grass.

"Don't know how to be more bloody obvious without blowing horns and waving flags." Mr. Hempton nodded to the Faeries and Pixies to keep jumping into view. "The question to you, lad, are you sure this plan will work?"

"No, but I'm willing to gamble on it. Are you?" Thorik tossed back.

The frog's eyes opened up wide. "Never been known to turn down a game of chance."

"Good. Have everyone start moving to the wall."

"Already done, but the Myth'Unday I've rounded up won't be lasting long against all them soldiers. Are the odds in our favor?"

"Yes," Thorik said with confidence.

"So you've done this before, lad?"

"Well, no, but my grandmother told me I could defeat my enemies with love and that is exactly what we're going to do."

Mr. Hempton nodded. "Ah. So, she has performed this before."

"No, but she's usually right about these things."

The frog adjusted his nut of a cap and crossed his arms. "Usually? We're betting the lives of my fellow Myth's on a 'usually'? I'd prefer to be a wee bit more confident."

Thorik grabbed his and Avanda's packs to move toward the wall. Winking at the frog he said, "Why Mr. Hempton, I thought you liked games of life and death."

The frog watched the Num turn and crawl away, keeping his head down below the height of the grass. "I do when *I* get to make up the game."

Both of them made their way toward the wall when they heard a horn sound off from the Southwind army. Immediately following it, the sound of feet from three sides started to close in on them. The soldiers were squeezing in on them.

"Hurry," Thorik announced. "Up against the wall!"

A flurry of movement could be seen in the grass as all of the Myth'Unday raced to the center against the wall, while the Southwind army steadily moved toward them from the sides and front. The Matriarch herself led the way in the center of the half-circle, enjoying the sight of the fleeing little creatures.

Closer and closer the army gathered to the center until all of the small creatures had been cornered in a grassy area less than a dozen yards across. It was at this point they stopped.

"Surrender and we will let you live," the Matriarch announced with a laugh.

Thorik stood up from the center of the grass, his back nearly flat against the wall.

Shocked, the Matriarch was momentarily confused. "You aren't a Myth'Unday."

"No, I am not. But they are my friends and I cannot allow you to harm them."

"And who are you to tell me what I can and can't do?"

"I am Thorik Dain of Farbank."

She glanced over at her adviser. "Pilwa, didn't we send assassins out to kill a Thorik Dain of Farbank?"

The adviser nodded. "Yes, my Matriarch."

Smiling, the Matriarch turned back to the Num. "What a pleasant surprise, we will be killing you along with your friends today. What a fine way to end a day of battle."

"Matriarch," Thorik said over the laughter of the Southwind soldiers. "I prefer not to harm you and your troops, if there is a way to talk things out."

"I'm sure you rather that be the case, seeing that you are in my trap."

"I'm only going to ask you once. Leave this land, release your prisoners, and return to Southwind. If you do not comply, I will have to go to battle with you."

"Very courageous, but foolish," she replied. Tossing a carefree hand toward the Num, she announced, "Move in and kill Thorik Dain of Farbank along with all of his friends."

The half-circle of soldiers moved forward toward the Num.

"Tree Faeries!" Thorik yelled, pulling out the Runestone of Love and placing it against the wall while activating its powers.

Dozens of tree faeries with seed-looking bodies had been hiding behind the soldiers and upon Thorik's order they buried themselves into the ground around the perimeter. Within seconds they began to grow into various types of trees at an incredible speed, launching themselves up into the air, towering over the Southwind army. Branches and exposed roots from the various trees intertwined, making it impossible for any soldiers to escape.

As this was happening, Thorik focused on his now glowing runestone. This was the same runestone he had used in Rummon's Lair when he accidently turned the cave walls into mud. However, this time it would be no accident. A three yard section of the wall before him began turning from hard block stones to a soft mud, crumbling and collapsing under its own weight. Falling in toward the Num, he deactivated the runestone and jumped out of the way.

Myth'Unday flew in every direction to escape the falling wall before attacking the soldiers head on. Several others grabbed onto Thorik and lifted him up to the top of the wall, near the recently damaged section.

Even with the sudden feeling of chaos, the Matriarch was far from shaken. "If a fence of trees and muddy wall is all you have, this will be a short fight."

Thorik turned his back to her, and toward the river. "As Gluic had told you I would," he yelled out to the river. "I am here to free you!"

The last half-dozen feet of the wall finally turned to mud and the river broke through, filling the grassy area nearly four feet high.

The trees had continued to tightly intertwine their roots and lower branches, creating a barrier for the water to stay in.

The soldiers began to panic.

"It's only water, you fools!" The Matriarch yelled at her men to gather their senses. "The Myth'Unday drown just as easy as we do. Grab them out of the air and hold them under the water. And shoot that Num down off that wall!"

The battle continued with her army swatting the little flying creatures out of the air while the Myth'Unday fought back by poking and scratching their victims. Even with that, the soldiers had the upper hand.

"Hang on!" Thorik shouted down from the wall, keeping himself out of view of the archers. "Here they come."

The Matriarch swatted another Myth'Unday away before looking through the broken area of the wall. Unsure at first as to what she saw, she could make out what appeared to be heads floating on the water's surface as they moved toward them. It wasn't until they reached the wall opening that they stood up.

The undead of Rivers Edge were entering the battle. Thin layers of skin hung onto their bones as they moved south of the home they had been trapped in for over thirty years. Many of them still had military outfits clinging to their body.

Droves of undead moved into the submerged grassy area and began attacking the Southwind army.

Some soldiers raced for the trees, only to be stopped by branches swinging out and knocking them back into the water.

One after another, soldiers were being pulled down under the water by unseen hands. Men swung their swords and pressed their spears into the muddy water to fend off these new attackers.

Pulling his spear back up, one soldier found an undead stuck onto the end of the weapon. Before he could react, the Rivers Edge walking corpse slid itself along the spear up to the soldier and attacked him.

The Matriarch watched in horror as the undead continued to attack her men. "Fight them! Cut their heads off!" she screamed. "They are mindless inferior beasts. We are superior in body and mind, so start using them, you fools!"

One of the servants carrying her platform began to struggle, kicking at something under the water. Within seconds he was grabbed and pulled down. Grabbing onto the rod he had used to hold the platform up, he now used it to keep his head above water. In doing so, the platform tilted and several decorative pillows fell off while the rest of the servants worked harder to hold it up.

The platform jolted as the man hung on for his life while screaming for help. The Matriarch reached over and snapped his hands with the blade she used for cutting cheese. "Let go you idiot! You'll knock me into the water if you're not careful!"

The man finally let go after the third snap on the hands from her blade. But the rocking of the platform did not stop. A second man was pulled down, and then a third. It wasn't long before all of the men holding up her traveling bed had been compromised and pulled under.

Clutching the last ornate pillow, the Matriarch yelled in anger at her men. "Idiots! Cowards! What have you done!" Floating on her platform turned raft, she watched as the last few soldiers were pulled under.

Silence followed, an eerie calm that spooked even her heartless soul.

"Do you surrender?" a voice said.

Whipping her head around, she could see Mr. Hempton behind her on the raft. To her, he appeared as a pointy noised and eared little goblin with saliva dripping from his fangs. "You wicked little monster. I will hunt you and your kind down until everyone of you have been wiped off this land."

Mr. Hempton nodded. "I'll take that as a no." He then was gone in a blink of an eye.

The silence that followed was short lived and was interrupted by a hand slapping up onto the raft. Half of the bones on it were exposed and it was difficult to know what was skin and what was mud.

A second hand slapped up onto the floating bed from the other side. More continued until some of the fleshy skeletons began emerging from the muddy water, lifting themselves up on to the platform.

She began kicking and swinging her short blade. "Get your filthy hands off me!" she ordered. "Let go of me at once!"

For the first time in many years, her orders were not being obeyed.

The platform began to slowly sink under the water due to the strength of the undead. Grabbing the dagger from her hand, they reached out and grabbed her, pulling the Matriarch off her pillows and down under the murky depths.

Thorik watched from the top of the wall as she disappeared from sight. The water rippled and then a large bubble rose to the surface, followed by her blood staining the hue of the muddy water. He could only assume it was her last dying order to leave her alone.

"Well played, lad," Mr. Hempton said to Thorik.

"Our game isn't over yet. We still need to free Avanda and Emilen."

## Chapter 28
# Dragons of War

Displeased with the progress in the battle, Ergrauth called the Winds of Conquest back from their assaults on the far side of the wall. Historically, victory had always been achieved to all armies who had the Winds of Conquest on their side. The son and daughter of Lord Rummon prevented any aerial attacks and allowed for strikes behind the enemy's frontline.

Pulling a horn from his side, the demon blew into it. The long-lasting high pitched screech hurt the ears of many on both sides of the battle. But the horn was not a weapon, nor was it painful enough to cause soldiers to stop fighting. It simply called the Winds of Conquest dragons back to him.

The unique sound caused the dragons to snap their heads in the direction it came from. It was only a few seconds of the long screech of the horn before they both launched themselves from their locations and into the air to fly back over the Dovenar Wall toward Ergrauth.

The demon blew the horn until he saw the dragons sail over the wall and spot him standing near the Rivers Edge wall and river. "Attack the wall! Knock it down!" Ergrauth commanded once they were within earshot.

Skimming just over the heads of the battling troops, the two dragons split and banked their flight path back to the wall.

Arrows flew at the dragons as they made their approach toward the thick stone structure, but the Dovenar archers couldn't penetrate their strong scales.

Racing toward the wall, the two dragons moved in toward one another until their wings nearly touched. The white dragon pulled out front and opened its mouth, spraying a mist of subfreezing fumes across the front of the thick stone wall. The dragon's weapon had flash frozen an area over a dozen feet wide and nearly a foot deep. It was quickly followed by a blast of lighting from the blue sibling. The first foot of the now frozen fragile stones burst out from the shock of the lightning.

Shards of stone showered the backs of the Dovenar army while holding their ground against the Del'Undays. The battle to defend the wall was looking bleak as it was, but now the Winds of Conquest were blasting a hole in the wall. The strategy of lowering the gates for their last line of defense would no longer be available.

The twin dragons went separate ways in wide sweeps above the wall and back up over the battlefield before coming together for their next run toward the wall.

Another barrage of arrows and thrown spears were sent from the Dovenar soldiers. Again, none had any effect on the dragons.

The Winds of Conquest struck the wall again in the same location as the first time, etching out another foot of stone blocks before flying up and over the wall as they prepared for their next pass.

The Dovenar wall was the strongest of all walls, but even it couldn't withstand the constant attacks of the Winds of Conquest. After six hundred years, the wall was going to be breached.

A series of deep freezing blasts and heated lightning rapidly shattered another layer of stones from the wall, making easy work of the stronghold which had withstood countless attacks from the Del'Unday.

Banking in the air, the two dragons went opposite ways again only to reconnect over the battle field for their next run. They had gathered their rhythm and each pass had improved their timing to join together faster and with less thought. It was becoming a routine that was effectively drilling a massive hole into the Dovenar Wall.

Another layer of stone exploded away from the structure as the synchronized attacks continued. All was going as planned until they raced over the wall in the normal pattern to separate. However, this time something was different.

Rising from the far side of the wall, a massive red-dragon appeared and reached out toward the unsuspecting sibling dragons. Dwarfing the size of the Winds of Conquest dragons, this dragon had chunks of flesh missing with exposed muscle and bones, making the already ferocious creature appear demonic as well. Their father, Lord Rummon, had arrived.

Both of the siblings were taken off guard and spun out of control in an attempt to evade being captured by the jaws of their father. The blue dragon tumbled down into the buildings of Veil, crushing roofs and caving in walls before coming to a stop. The white dragon arched backward, plummeting onto the wall's walkway.

Neither of the smaller dragons noticed the odd colorful bird that had been tucked away behind the red dragon's ear. "There they are, just like I promised," Gluic said as she spread her wings and began to fly off. "Don't forget your commitment."

Rummon let out a roar so powerful, it shook everyone on the battlefield as well as the desert floor itself. Fighters who turned to gaze upon the sight of the great Rummon standing on the Dovenar Wall were awestruck by the surreal scene. A scene that became their last to behold, for others who were able to keep their focus on the battle at hand took advantage of the distraction to slay their enemy.

Even Ergrauth was enthralled by the spectacle. "How did you escape after all these centuries?" he muttered in a gruff, irritated voice. Standing tall with his shoulders back and chest out, he stood in defiance to the new arrival to his battle. Raising the Winds of Conquest horn up to his mouth, he blew hard into the instrument.

Reaching out for the white dragon before it had time to roll off the top of the wall, Rummon slapped his mighty paw down on his daughter's tail prior to her escaping. "Not so fast, Wintercrauf." The wall's walkway cracked under the the weight he placed on her tail. "You and your brother helped plot my captivity. You must learn your place."

Unable to escape her father's grasp, Wintercrauf turned and looked at her father. She immediately saw his decay and gaping holes. "Your reign is over. It is now our time to rule the skies."

Reaching for her with his other claw, Rummon was not ready to hand over this power without a fight. However, before he grabbed her, a bolt of lightning raced up his legs and across the red dragon's back. It had been spit out by the blue dragon who was returning from his tumble into the homes below.

"Your days have passed!" yelled the blue dragon, flying up out of the wreckage below. "We are the rightful heirs to the air. You are a flying corpse."

A quick backhand swatted the blue dragon out of the air and back down into the buildings below. Unfortunately, the act caused him to accidently release Wintercrauf. "Fulgura, my son, your self-love has always been your greatest flaw," Rummon roared from the top of the wall.

Whitercrauf sped out from her father's grasp, causing the mighty Lord Rummon to launch himself into the air in chase, only to be followed by Fulgura once he regained his bearings.

Lightning shot from Fulgura's mouth, shocking every nerve-ending on Rummon's body for a moment, causing the massive red dragon to arch and slow his chase.

Taking advantage of the opportunity, Wintercrauf turned for her own attack. Deep freezing liquid sprayed from her mouth, causing parts of the red dragon's side to crack and break off once hit by another of her brother's blasts.

Working in tandem, they blasted their father time and time again. Frozen chunks of flesh and bone shattered from the heat of the lightning strikes, blowing holes in his wings, legs and chest.

Even with the constant attacks from his children, Rummon fought back with his massive size and a blast of fire that could melt the hardest of metals. In addition, each slap of the red dragon's tail sent the dragons tumbling, and strong swipes of his claws easily cut through their normally resilient scales. In full strength, Rummon would have easily overpowered the two offspring, but with the damage of time to his body, it was taking a lot of effort to control them, but he did so all the same.

All three dragons continued to fight in the air, often crashing into the Dovenar Wall and knocking large sections out of it or striking the ground and crushing soldiers under their massive bodies. They tumbled and clawed and propelled destructive assaults from their mouths in their rage to win and defeat the other.

The battle in the air had begun over the warring armies below. Each demon led their own battle with a strong upper hand; Rummon with his sheer size and strength, and Ergrauth with his large and powerful army. The air was still Rummon's and the land was still Ergrauth's, just as had been several thousand years ago.

Thorik and Mr. Hempton had just finished watching the defeat of the Matriarch when they turned to see the battle of dragons begin.

"Rummon seems to be holding his own," Thorik said, watching the battle from the wall on the far side of Rivers Edge.

"Not easily." Mr. Hempton. "Do ya care to wager a bet, lad?"

Thorik shook his head while watching the dragons tumbling across the sky. "This is nothing I wish to profit from. Although I do believe he is still strong enough to win this battle."

"Perhaps now, but he may soon be outnumbered." Mr. Hempton pointed in the sky beyond the local battlefield.

From the northeast, a large dark mass moved in the air toward the battleground. It appeared to grow in size as it moved closer. Widening, it thinned in denseness. Movement within the mass could eventually be seen and the flapping of wings was the first sign of what it was. It wasn't long before the outlines of dragons could be fully recognized. There were nearly a thousand of them heading toward one central point; Rummon.

Thorik squinted his eyes to see the approaching legion. "They've come from Rummon's lair!"

Mr. Hempton pondered, "Do they come here to help protect him or to tear their master apart?"

"I don't know. It all depends on who won the battle in the mountain." Thorik hoped that the winners of the dragon war were those who wanted to see Rummon alive. However, he feared that the approaching winged army would be the followers of the late Grand Watcher.

"I do love a good bit of mystery," the frog said with a smile.

Rummon blasted his way over the battlefield, knocking over any war equipment in his path taller than a few yards high. Chasing Fulgura, Rummon grasped his son's tail in his mouth and began dragging him along the desert floor. He then slapped him hard against the mighty Dovenar Wall, sending stone blocks in every direction.

Wintercrauf lurched at her father as the red dragon breached the wall's height. Using her back claws around his neck, she squeezed as tight as she could. Her front claws grabbed his muzzle and held it shut while spraying freezing liquid across his face and eyes.

Breaking free, Rummon was temporarily blinded. Swinging out at her, without any success, he pushed away and flew up in the air to gather some distance from her until he could regain his vision.

Fulgura pulled himself away from the broken stones at the base of the wall and shook his head, trying to gather his wits. Wounded with torn wings and broken bones, he could see that Rummon was blinded and retreating. Knowing this would be his only chance at ending the demon's life, he leaped into the air and flew toward the red dragon for his final attack.

Both of Rummon's children raced toward him, clawing and biting him once they arrived, cutting into his wings and ripping flesh and scales from his body. Their attack was relentless.

With his massive claws, Rummon eventually grabbed the two dragons by their necks and squeezed hard enough to prevent additional spray attacks, but not enough to kill them. The tide of their fight had suddenly changed. "You are my children and I refuse to kill my own. But you must be punished for what you have done."

"We will kill you the moment you free us," Fulgara coughed out before swinging his claws at his father and grabbing large chunks out of his body.

Wintercrauf followed her brothers lead and did the same from Rummon's other side.

Rummon roared in pain.

The incoming dragons raced to the battlefield with exceptional speed. As soon as they arrived they swarmed Lord Rummon in midair causing the massive ball of fighting dragons to plunge to the ground, wiping out siege equipment and warriors in their wake.

"No!" cried out Thorik, still watching the attack from a distance.

An occasional arm, wing, or tail of Rummon's could be seen through the assortment of different dragons attacking him and ripping chunks of flesh from an already decaying body. This large ball of creatures rolled about the battlefield randomly destroying everything in its path. More dragons arrived faster than those who fell to the side after breaking their legs, wings, and necks under the massive ball of dragons.

Several dragons lay dead from the rolling mass of winged creature, including Wintercrauf and Fulgara. Both had been crushed under the pile when it first plummeted to the desert floor. Their necks, wings and legs were twisted and contorted in ways that meant only one thing, the Wings of Conquest had been defeated.

The situation looked bleak. The Del'Unday were winning the battle upon the land, and the dragons had taken Rummon out of the sky and possibly out of existence.

Thorik began searching through his pouch of runestones, looking for anything he could use to help the situation. Knowing that none of his runestones had the range to affect anything on the other side of the nearly mile-wide river, he became frustrated. "There must be a way to get to the other side."

"No problem, just ask the locals to carry you across," Mr. Hempton said sarcastically.

Thorik looked at the water and the sight of various undead moving within the muddy waves. "I'll bet I could do just that," he said softly to himself.

Mr. Hempton perked up at the idea. "You're on, my friend. We finally have ourselves a bit of a game!" Mr. Hempton, leaped up onto Thorik's shoulder. "This should be good. Are you going to order them to take you across, use some fear tactic, or plead with them? What will it be?"

"I'm going to let them die."

"Brilliant! Why didn't I think of that?" he said, mocking the Num.

Thorik shouted over the river while digging into Avanda's sack. "Great warriors of Rivers Edge! You have suffered enough. The spell you were put under at the battle of Maegoth has caused you to endure endless pain without being able to die from your wounds." He pulled out a jar from Avanda's bag. It was filled with red and black grains. "This is Ergrauthian Spice!"

Mr. Hempton was amazed. "Have a wee look at that. There's only one place you could have found such spice?"

"We gathered it at the Guardian's desert passage. It can unravel any spell that has been casted upon you. And it is now yours."

A gathering of undead moved toward the wall, near Thorik. Open hands and arms reached from the muddy water toward him.

"All I ask is that you bring me, and my companion, safely to the far side of the river."

More undead approached.

"I hope they believe me," Thorik said, his voice trembling at the idea of them tearing him apart once he reached the water.

Mr. Hempton smiled. "What an exciting game! Life or death hangs in the balance. You surely know how to play."

Thorik began making his way down the wall toward them.

Waiting until the Num was halfway down, Mr. Hempton asked, "How do they know if the spice you have is real? They don't know if you're duping them."

Stopping his descent, the Num's nerves became more intense. "Would you stop that? You're making me very edgy."

"Well, I would be a bit too, if I was about tp step into a known death trap."

Cautiously lowering himself to within a yard from the water, Thorik opened the jar and poured a few of the grains in his hands. He then tossed them into the water. "Here! This is to prove what I say is true. Once I'm across, I will give you the rest."

Several undead screamed in pain and then floated to the top of the water before drifting away.

Mr. Hempton hopped down next to Thorik. "Was that the reaction you were looking for, lad?" The frog's voice was very excited about the stress Thorik was under.

"Yes," Thorik said softly, truly not knowing. He gulped and waited for the possibility of the undead soldiers to jump out of the river and attack him.

After a few more moments, the Matriarch's platform rose to the surface of the water near Thorik's feet. Partially skinned bony hands held onto the sides all the way around the platform.

Thorik took a deep breath. "I hope this is a good sign."

Mr. Hempton couldn't stand the excitement. "What a game! What a game!"

## Chapter 29
# More Altered Creatures

From the northeast Kiri Desert a new force emerged and headed toward the great battle. It was not of humans, Nums, or Ov'Unday. Instead, it was a vast legion from Ergrauth Valley, one comparable to the size of the one from Corrock. They approached from behind the Ov'Unday and could easily move north to flank the human's northern lines.

"Another wave of attack?" Asentar said under his breath, disheartened at this turn of events.

There was no ignoring it. They had yet another front to fight, thinning the forces that he felt were already spread far too lean in order to maintain their current defenses. But he had no choice. War was upon them and they would have to do with less along their lines.

"First through fourth battalions, follow me!" Asentar ordered, leading them to the north before the newcomers could attack them from behind.

Charging forward, they raced around the north side of the battle in an effort to prevent the Del'Unday from boxing in his troops. To their surprise, this new campaign quickly took a change once Asentar realized that the newcomers were racing past the Ov'Unday and attacking Ergrauth's army.

Confused at first, the Dovenar Knight watched the new army attack their own kind until he realized that they were not Ergrauth's followers. This new army was made up of mutants.

Scanning the front line of the new military force, Asentar spotted Santorray leading the charge of Kewtalls, accompanied by the white skinned female Kewtall leader he had seen in the Ergrauthian Valley before escaping with his life. She was riding the giant two-faced feline creature.

"Santorray!" he screamed, raising his sword high into the air. It was at that point he realized that it was the Del'Unday that had been boxed in. Santorray's Kewtall attacked from the north, while the Ov'Unday's pushed from the east. Asentar pulled his forces from the north and focused on holding the Doven Wall on the west. They had the Del'Unday with their backs up against the Volney River at Rivers Edge.

Santorray pulled back, allowing the female Kewtall leader, Ahzvietaweh, to lead the charge, while he turned his own movement west to meet up with Asentar.

The Dovenar Knight swiped at another Del'Unday while moving toward the new army from the north. "Running a little late? I figured I'd have to take care of all these without your assistance."

"I decided that even if it wasn't my battle, I'd have to show up to bail you out once again." Santorray sliced his claws across the chest of a Del before landing his large fist square in the creature's face. "It appears that you have been successful in leading your people to the south from Woodlen," he yelled over the battle cries.

"Yes I was. And I see you were successful as well. How many Kewtall did you have to slay before you became their leader?" Asentar yelled back.

Santorray glanced over at the white skinned Blothrud creature. Swinging her long jagged bladed spear, her agile fighting ability showed grace and speed while she raced forward on the muscular two-faced feline, who chomped its sharp teeth into any Del'Unday crazy enough to get in its path. "Just one," Santorray said.

"One?" Asentar questioned before realizing what had taken place. "I thought all you understood was violent and physical negotiations."

"Who said it wasn't?" The Blothrud smiled out of the corner of his mouth.

Asentar gave a good look at the pure white Blothrud leading her tribe of mutated Del'Unday into battle. She was aggressive, dangerous, powerful and sexual all in one, just the type of mate Santorray needed. "Well done," he congratulated the Blothrud. "Let's hope she's as impressive in battle."

"She is," he boasted. "Make sure you stay out of her way, as well as mine. I have a family matter to take care of."

"I've already taken care of most of the big ones, it's your turn to take the rest!" the knight jested, swinging his sword to prevent another attack.

"I'll be right with you. It looks like you missed one." His voice trailed off as he ran into battle toward the largest Del'Unday in the army, Ergrauth.

"Santorray! No! You fool!"

Whether he hadn't heard the Dovenar Knight's pleas to stop, or he simply ignored them, Santorray carved his way through the Del'Unday soldiers and straight for the demon. "Father!" he screamed, knocking everything in his way to the ground.

Ergrauth heard the cry and couldn't believe his ears. "Santorray? You escaped! You show promise, my son. I knew you had my blood in your veins."

"But not your desires," he claimed upon arriving at the demon. Santorray's massive body stood over eight feet in height. However, he looked short compared to this twelve-foot tall demon.

"I have tried to beat it into your head, but you simply won't accept it," Ergrauth raised his arms at the Doven Wall before them. "All of this was once our land until it was taken from us. After all these years, we are finally taking it back. Stand with me and your people to reclaim our land. Once we have vanquished these humans, you can have the area of your choosing to rule."

"Unlike you, I have no need to rule. I only have the desire to be free and to free those from your rule. You are nothing more than a self-appointed dictator who leads through creating fear of death to any who shall disobey your orders."

Ergrauth's arms had lowered. "I have once again extended my open arms to you and you repay me with insults. If that is who you see me as, than that is who I will be to you." Reaching out with both hands, he grabbed Santorray and lifted him in the air. "Goodbye, my son."

## Chapter 30
# Undead Warriors

By the time Thorik had rode the Matriarch's platform the majority of the way across the river, the dozens of undead had grown to thousands, surrounding the Num for tens of yards in every direction. Skulls bobbed at the surface, many of them cracked and broken open, while hands missing digits reached toward Thorik for a chance to end their suffering.

"I can't imagine what these soldiers have endured over the past thirty years," Thorik said to Mr. Hempton. "To have a spell cast on them for endless life and yet no spells to prevent them from feeling pain, was a deal only Darkmere could have convinced people to take. They felt every slice of a sword and crushing blow of a mace as well as the decay of their own skin. What a horrible existence. I wouldn't wish this upon any being."

Mr. Hempton stuck his frog head out of one of Thorik's sacks. "Oh, I've seen a wee bit worse," he said before returning inside the leather sack. "Then again, I think I've caused worse," he said under his breath.

Ignoring the frog, Thorik gazed in the sky above the battlefield. "What's that?" he asked, watching a second wave of dragons show up to the battle. His heart sank at the thought and his emotions started to grow uneasy with the slow process of the trip across the river.

"Thorik, where did you get these runestones?"

He still wasn't listening. "We need to hurry up. There isn't much time. I need to reach the other side to help Rummon."

"These are bloody originals," Mr. Hempton mumbled. "Very old and powerful. Looks to be made by Wyrlyn himself." Leaning out of the bag, he spoke up. "Any chance we could play a bit of a game for a few of these? Will you share your magic?"

"What?"

"You're not willing to share your magic, eh? Mad with greed, you are!"

"No! It's not like that."

"It's because my skin is green, isn't it? That's why you're not sharing!"

"Of course not! They've been in my family for a long time. I'm not sharing with *anyone*!"

The platform stopped suddenly.

Confused, Thorik looked around for the reason. "Why did they stop?"

Smiling, the frog noted, "Crossing this river is a game, you see, and I can't let you win this easy."

"What do you mean?"

"You just told the Rivers Edge undead that you don't share your magic with anyone."

"I did not."

"Did so. And I'd say they are considering other options, seeing that you aren't sharing with *anyone*."

Thorik looked around at the change in the calmness that once was. Many of them started to rise out of the water as they started reaching for Thorik. "Mr. Hempton! Why?" the Num asked.

"Lad, it's just a game. For the right price I could help you out."

"Just a game?" Thorik shouted as the undead began climbing out of the water and reaching for the Num. "What do you want?"

"You mean the prize, dear lad? It's your runestones, of course."

Bony fingers wrapped around the Num's legs and arms as the undead attempted to pull the Num off the raft in both directions at once.

"Mr. Hempton! Help!"

"Interesting game, eh? Is your life worth more than those runestones? Only you can answer."

Tugging at Thorik, the undead pulled him back and forth as more muddy arms reached up and grabbed his torso and head.

"NO! They are only tools. They are not worth my life!"

Mr. Hempton smiled. "If that's true, lad, Give them to me and I'll free you."

Straining to move his arms, Thorik tried to reach for the pouch, however the undead prevented his ability to do so. "Okay, I promise to give you one of the runestones!" he screamed as a semi-flesh fingered hand grabbed Thorik's mouth, sticking three fingers in it.

The frog turned his back to the Num. "No, this is my game, not yours. I set the rules and I want all of them."

Thorik began to be pulled off the raft as he attempted to shout his approval to the conditions. Unfortunately, the fleshy fingers in his mouth prevented it. Instead, it came out as a mumble.

With his head nearing the murky water, he only had a few seconds left to agree to Mr. Hempton's terms. Biting down hard, he snapped off the fleshy fingers and spit them back out, before yelling, "I agree! All of the runestones if you can make them all go away!" His head then splashed down under the water, causing him to close his eyes.

After a moment of disorientation, Thorik opened his eyes to see that he was sitting up on the little raft, while the undead continued to escort him north. They were approaching the dock where Captain Dare's ship had crashed. The dock was located against the west end of the Rivers Edge Wall, where it intersected with the taller Doven Wall. A large tower marked the corner of the two walls coming together in order to spy down on those who crossed the river or used the docks.

Startled by movement next to his side, Thorik realized that it was Mr. Hempton rolling around in his sack of newly acquired runestones. After a sigh of relief, he noticed that there was no sign of muddy hand prints on the Num's body. The mud and scratches has all disappeared.

"It was an illusion," Thorik said, nodding his head. "You used my fears against me, again."

Mr. Hempton smiled. "Yes, once again. Brilliant, wasn't it? You really need to learn a wee bit more control over them."

Thorik reached out and grabbed a dock post while shaking his head at his own naïve thoughts. "I thought you were my friend, but I see now that you are only in this for yourself."

"Nay, lad. I am here to teach you. Sent by the great Oracle, Ovlan."

"To teach me how to not listen to you?" the Num said, pulling himself up onto the dock.

"No. To control your fears."

"Sometimes things need to be feared. There are dangers in life."

"True, dangers exist. But fear causes poor decision making. Understanding the dangers will help you avoid them as well as allow you to keep a level head." Mr. Hempton picked up one of the runestones and eyed it. "Unfortunately for you, you allow fear to affect your judgment."

Thorik pulled himself up to his feet and gathered his gear. "I thought I could trust you. I thought you were my friend."

"I am a friend, but you must understand that everyone has their own background with their own plans and agenda. They're rarely the same as yours, but that doesn't mean that they are cruel, just different. Don't feel slighted because they got what they wanted."

Thorik nodded. "You're right," he said while pulling the frog out of the sack before setting him on the dock. "No hard feelings." He then tied off the end of the sack of runestones and attached them to his belt before walking down the dock.

"Wait just a moment, lad. I won those fair and square."

Thorik stopped and turned around in surprise. "But you didn't fulfill your agreement."

"You have gone mad. I freed you from them undead! Them stones are now mine."

"Yes you did free me, and I do very much appreciate it, but that was not the agreement we made."

"Sure it was. You agreed to all of the runestones."

Thorik smiled. "I've learned two things from you. First, fears control people, causing them to make bad decisions."

Mr. Hempton crossed his arms and patted his webbed foot. "And the other?"

"The second thing I've learned from you is that greed is just as powerful and can cause people to hear only what they want."

"Greed?"

"Yes. If I had said that I would have given you all of the runestones if you made all of the undead go away, then you would have focused on the entire sentence. But, because I said I would only give you one of them, you ignored the rest of the sentence. Your greed caused you to only desire all of them instead of the one."

Mr. Hempton clasped his hands behind him and leaned forward. "Regardless. I still made them go away, so I still won."

"No, you didn't make them go away. They are still all around us." Thorik pointed to the water on both sides of the dock. The dirty water was crammed full of undead.

"But that's not what I meant…"

"I know, but in your greedy haste, you misspoke." Thorik smiled and turned around and faced Captain Dare's ship which had crashed upon the dock, blocking his ability to exit the dock.

Reaching into his sack, Thorik grabbed the Ergrauthian Spice and poured some into the water.

Screams from the undead faded to sighs of relief. Dozens of the ancient warriors were finally released from eternity in this Rivers Edge muck.

Thorik held up the rest of the spice. "I am ready to free the rest of you. I simply ask one last request. Can you lift this ship back off the dock and into the water?"

Waiting for an answer, the ship slowly started moving backward as hundreds of hands reached up from underneath and lifted the front of the ship off the dock and back into the water, where it belonged.

"Thank you. I hope your suffering has come to an end," Thorik said as he lifted the spice high in the air.

"Wait, lad! Think about the bloody opportunity you're going to miss out on."

"I know what you're going to say, Mr. Hempton. We have them where we want them. They could do more for us than a simple ferry across the river. We could use them to wage our battle."

"Nay. That there Ergrauthian Spice can dissolve any known magic. Do you understand the possibilities of what you could do with it? We could counter any spell ever created. Think of the games we could play."

Thorik didn't even give it a second thought. "No. A promise is a promise." He then slowly began to pour the spice as he walked up and down the dock, ending the spell that had kept them alive in pain. As those who passed on floated away, others moved in to take their fill. The spice mixed with the water and spread quickly out in every direction. It wasn't long before all that had arrived had been freed.

"Greed." Mr. Hempton grumbled. "I can't believe you trumped fear with greed."

"It was a very close call...and a very exciting game."

The frog smiled. "Ah, it was at that." He nodded his head in agreement. "Well played, lad. Well played. What's your next step?"

"You stay here." Thorik said, looking up from the base of the tower to a familiar sight. There, leaning over the edge of the battlement, was a man's head and his arms waving about as he cast spells towards the battle below. "I can't believe my eyes. That looks like Bryus Grum. How did he survive our last encounter! I need to reach him to see what we can do to help Rummon."

With the old wizard clearly in view, Thorik ran from the dock, up the stairs, across the wall, and down the other side in an effort to reunite with his friend to determine what could be done to win the war.

Mr. Hempton hopped up onto the ship and watched the Num race out of sight. Sighing, he broke a smile. "The lad is learning, Ovlan. Just like you said he would."

"What's that?" The unexpected voice came from within the ship before a trap door flung open from the deck floor. Pushing his way out, Captain Dare looked around for the source of the comment he had heard.

Because Myth'Unday appear differently to different people, Captain Dare was treated to the view of a stunning mermaid sitting upon the edge of the ship.

With long flowing locks of fiery red hair which covered her naked upper female body, and a long smooth fish tail, Mr. Hempton was ready for some excitement. "Hello there. Are you up for a game, sailor?"

Captain Dare gazed upon the amazing creature before him and puffed up his chest and attempted to suck in his hairy gut, which hung over his thick black belt. Lifting a bottle into view, he smiled. "Sorry, lassy, I've already found me love," he said before lowering the tone in his voice and raising a large Fesh'Unday leg bone in the air. "So get off me ship before I debone yur scaly bottom and serve ya up for dinner."

And with that, Mr. Hempton splashed into the river as the mermaid he had made himself appear to be.

## Chapter 31
# The Tower's Crystal

Nearly a dozen tall thick metal doors were set in place to prevent the cavern ceiling from collapsing. Most of them were already showing signs of pressure as they started bending and warping. The sound from the strained metal echoed in the cavern.

Ambrosius stood defiant, with both hands up in the air holding the ceiling up with the strength he had left. The stress had taken a toll on his body and his pale, exhausted face showed his exhaustion.

Ericc's delivery of metal doors had given Ambrosius enough time to destroy the lesser demons with only minor injuries to himself. He was covered with burns and open cuts. His only focus now was to keep the cavern from collapsing.

"I can find more someplace else," Ericc said, as he watched the doors twist from the increased pressure.

Ambrosius shifted his exhausted eyes over to Draq, who was still struggling to stand to help out in their efforts. He then looked around him as the cavern continued to shrink in height. Shaking his head, he knew they had lost the battle. "Take us out of here."

Ericc ran over and touched Draq before reaching his hand out to Ambrosius. "I need to be touching you in order for you to travel with me."

His father glanced at Ericc several yards away before looking up at the ceiling he was trying to hold up. "Take him to Kingfoot Lake. The mineral water has healing properties."

"That distance will take too long, even for me. I need to get you both out of here."

"Fine! Take him to the Doven's West shore and then come back for me."

Draq turned his long neck toward the E'rudite. "I'm not going anywhere without you."

Ericc looked into his father's eyes and upon seeing Ambrosius' slight nod, Ericc and Draq disappeared.

Draq suddenly felt himself outside. They had reappeared on an island looking out over Lake Luthalum Tunia at the magnificent Lu'Tythis Tower. The white rocks along the shoreline would normally be a pleasant venue to gaze upon the tower. However, Draq and Ericc watched in horror as they witnessed the tower start to collapse.

At first it tilted and then the weight of the top forced a series of cracks up the side, splintering the tower into several large sections.

"Father!" Ericc screamed before disappearing from Draq's view.

"No!" Draq yelled as he attempted to grab the young man. His effort to prevent Ericc from taking a spatial jump back underneath the tower had failed. Not only had he lost a close friend, but he had also lost the boy who he had helped raise for so many years.

The tower continued to buckle and split as the thousands of feet of rock came crashing down on its own island.

Residing in the very top of the tower was a glowing crystal the size of a chuttlebeast. It had controlled the weather for thousands of years and had held back the ocean waters beyond the two thousand foot high dam. Its function, from its long standing platform at the peak of the tower, was no longer. The world was about to change.

Lightning burst forth in every direction from the falling crystal. The dark clouds that had gathered and swirled due to its instability now turned black and expanded across the sky in every direction, shutting off the sun to all below.

If that hadn't been enough, the crystal's influence over gravity spun out of control. Until now, it had pressed up against several eastern mountains to offset the pressing against the western Weirfortus dam. As of late, it had been causing a pressing and pulling sensation on all things in the region, causing locals to become motion sick.

Now with the crystal falling, gravity shifts began to happen in chaotic patterns. Water surged upward and then forced back down. Loose boulders were knocked off their stable setting place and tumbled down hillsides and mountains.

Even the white summit rocked back and forth, causing the volcanic mountain to erupt, turning the glacier on its side into a wave of water. Blasts from its peak sent fire and rock though the air as the mountain came alive with a deadly vengeance to any within its vicinity. The massive flume of ash billowing miles in the air mixed with the static-charged storm clouds, creating a storm of lightning upon the volcano, blasting it with dozens of strikes per second. The glacier's ice was now a wall of mud racing down King's River Valley toward Farbank. All life in its path was about to be ended.

Cracks snapped open across the Weirfortus dam, allowing streams of ocean water through on its way to reclaim the valley below. Thousands of feet of saltwater pushed against the dam, which was no longer being held up with the crystal's power. The expanding cracks would soon completely break the stone dam and flood all life in Terra Australis. There was no stopping it now.

Nearly two thirds of the tower's structure crashed into the island and lake below. The base stayed standing, but at a tilt, while the huge crystal spun out of control in the lake's muddy base, pushing and pulling in various directions.

Lying on the white stone beach, Draq watched the scene in shock. He was unable to help. The damage had been done.

The crystal's powers were not dowsed by being submerged. A huge wave of water shot out toward Draq, flattening the dragon onto the rocky shore. A second wave raced across the lake's surface, stopping just prior to reaching the beach. Gravity shifted and the wave moved back from the way it came, dragging Draq along with it.

The contents of the beach around Draq rolled along with him on the now dry lake bottom, pulling everything out to sea until the crystal shifted and released its energy in a new direction.

Once freed from its powers, Draq slid to a stop as the lake water rushed back in to its normal levels, over his head.

Swimming back to the shore with his one good wing and leg, Draq dragged himself up onto the rocks before turning back toward the destroyed tower. Dark clouds churned and rolled from the crystal's powers. Vegetation and debris from the nearby land were being tossed about in the air, pulling one way and then the other. Waves changed direction and whirlpools spun out of control. The fluctuations increased with every minute that went by. "The world is coming to an end," he said to himself.

Chapter 32
# Southwind Camp

In a wooded area a few miles south of Rivers Edge, Southwind soldiers finished setting up tents as they prepared for a few nights rest before launching their campaign to the west in order to take over Pelonthal. Their conquest through the eastern Mythical Forest had been a success and they now waited the arrival of the Matriarch with her legion of soldiers so they could plan their final attack. They had no idea that she had been killed by the undead soldiers of Rivers Edge.

The aroma of roasted hog and various stews wafted between the tents and back to the storage bins and cages. Within several large crates, Myth'Unday banged on the magically enhanced lumber as they attempted to break out. Their capture would surely not end well. The Matriarch despised faeries, brownies, and the likes. They most likely would become servants, or toys for amusement.

Near the stacked crates, two small iron cages contained one Polenum each. Avanda was in one while Emilen was in the other. They hadn't eaten since being captured and the smell of food in the camp made their stomachs growl.

Tightening her arms across her chest, Avanda pouted about the situation. "If I had Vesik, or even my purse of magic, I would teach these soldiers a thing or two."

"But you don't. So why don't you just shut up," Emilen snapped back. Her eyes kept darting back and forth, searching for someone to talk to.

Eventually several soldiers swaggered back toward the crates and cages. Cocky from their battle victories, full from their meal, and lightheaded from their drink, the four men walked up to the Nums.

One of the men reached out and dangled a piece of bread over Avanda's cage. "Let's see you do a trick. Trick for a bite of bread?"

"They don't do tricks, you idiot," another soldier said.

"I thought all Myth'Unday do tricks."

"They do. This is a Num. They don't do tricks."

"Then what do they do?"

The second soldier thought about it for a moment. "I don't think they do anything."

"Then what good are they?"

Shaking his head, he couldn't think of an answer. "Nothing. They aren't good for anything."

Waiting for the soldier to not pay attention, Avanda reached up through the iron bars of her cage and snatched the bread from the man's hand.

"What? Did you see what the little Num did? She stole my crust," the soldier said before kicking her cage. "Who do you think you are?"

Avanda was able to get a bite in before the kicking started. After that, she held on to prevent herself from smacking her head on the inside of the cage.

"I don't like the looks of these two." The soldier kicked the cage again before kicking the other cage in frustration.

"Hey, watch it!" Emilen yelled at the man.

The other soldiers spoke up to their companion's defense. "Don't you give us orders!" one said as they gathered around the two Nums.

Taking his weapon out, one of the men lifted his sword over his head while eyeing Avanda. "You need to learn some respect, little girl." And with a swing of his sword, the lock snapped off.

Two of the men grabbed Avanda's cage and flipped it so that the door swung open and hung straight down to the ground. After some serious shaking by the men, the Num fell out and onto the flattened grass.

"Leave me alone!" she screamed.

Pulling at her arms and hair, the men quickly got her under control.

However, she was not yet done fighting. She hated the feeling of being at the mercy of others, especially when being physically restrained. With her instincts of self-survival, she began kicking, biting, and spinning out of their grasp. Within a minute, she was free and turned to make a break for it, but it simply was not meant to be. Two of the men jumped on her from behind, landing on top of her.

Avanda fell hard on her front with one man on her back and the other on her legs. She had been captured again, but this time by a man she had just given a bloody nose and another she had bit a chunk out of his arm.

One soldier grabbed her hair and pushed her face into the ground to keep her from biting again. Things were not looking good for her.

As if it wasn't bad enough, Avanda noticed a set of white leather boots walking up to her. The boots were not standard regulation for any army she had ever seen. These were expensive and elegant.

The owner of the boots walked right up next to Avanda's face before stating, "Tie her up and put her in my tent. I may have use for her later when I return from the battle."

Shifting her head, Avanda glared up at the owner of the white footwear. Towering over the Num was a thin man in white robes, with a white beard and globes of solid white for eyes. She had seen this man once before in Woodlen while in disguise as the Terra King. Darkmere had arrived.

Chapter 33
# Rise of the Demon

Thick storm clouds had emerged from over fallen Lu'Tythis Tower, bringing darkness over the battlefield and causing torches, lamps, and vats of oil to be lit in order to continue the battle. Both sides assumed the darkness had been created by some magic from the other side. Seeing that it didn't encumber their fighting, the battle continued.

The giant demon, Ergrauth, hurled Santorray through the air and into a siege tower, destroying the weapon. The two had been in a bloody battle with both of them taking on deep cuts and broken bones. It was just the kind of fighting Ergrauth enjoyed.

Breathing hard, the demon waited for his son's next attack. Blood dripped from his dragon face and down his red muscular human torso before becoming lost within the dense coarse hair on his lower body and thick wolf legs. "Come now, son. I expected more from the general of my elite forces."

Santorray was moving slowly. His body ached and his mind was foggy from the blows to his head. However, defeat was not acceptable, so he began digging his way out from under the destroyed siege tower. Timber after timber, he moved the mound of rubble off of him.

The demon began to move toward him and take advantage of his son's situation, but was cut short by a white skinned warrior mounted upon a semi-transparent giant feline.

Ahz rode in front of the demon, swinging her long jagged bladed spear across his front, spilling blood down the front of his chest. The Kewtall leader had made her first strike against the demon, a strike she had waited her entire life to make. Her attack was just as much about taking the demon down as it was giving Santorray enough time to free himself and get back on his feet.

The scales on the creature she traveled upon turned various colors until it was a solid dark green. A single neck led to the base of its two skull-like faces which blended together, sharing an eye between them, as well as one on each side. The creature opened both mouths and roared at Ergrauth before reaching out to bite at the demon's neck.

Ergrauth instinctively reached forward and grabbed the creature by its head, stopping it from chomping on his throat.

In doing so, Ahz was free to make another attack to his side. Her blade carved into his waist before she rotated the spear handle and the blade.

The demon roared from the pain. Releasing one of his hands from the feline creature's head, he grabbed the spear and jolted it out of his body. In the same motion, he used the spear to knock the white female Blothrud off her mount. He then spun the spear around in his hand before driving it into the feline creature's side.

Ahz's ride fell backward in pain, attempting to pull the spear out of its side with one of its mouths. The squeal of the creature was excruciatingly loud.

The Kewtall leader rolled to her feet after finding a broken sword on the battlefield. Charging at the demon, she jumped up and rotated her body to confuse him before swinging the blade at his throat.

The powerful arm of Ergrauth swung out at just the right time, knocking her straight up in the air, only to catch her with both hands in midair before slamming her body into the ground. "How dare you touch me, you low life aberration." Raising one of his massive wolf claws, he prepared to snap her neck with it.

Knocked out, Ahz lay motionless and unable to defend herself as her two-headed feline screeched in fear of her death.

"I am sick of your ways!" Santorray yelled from behind his father. Wielding a thick timber like a two-handed sword, he limped his way toward his father from the siege tower attack. A long metal rod was now embedded in his leg. The rod had gone all the way through his right calf and extended out both sides.

Ergrauth turned away from the unconscious Kewtall and watched the blood pour out of his son's leg wound. "You were my only hope for a warrior to take my place and rule this world. All of your sisters and brothers have failed in their attempts to destroy me and take my throne. It is now clear that I will always be unmatched and must carry on my legacy by myself."

Santorray stopped a few yards from his father, still holding the timber over his shoulder as a weapon. He was a bloody mess and was missing several teeth. One eye was nearly swollen shut and he could feel several of his ribs were broken. "Your legacy is nothing more than tyranny, and it ends here today." He then raised the timber higher as he prepared to strike.

Before another word could be said or a blow could be made, the earth trembled under a large section of the battlefield, knocking many of the fighters off their feet. The ground then bulged upward, cracking and crumbling apart as a beast from below began rising from the beneath the earth. Emerging from the desert floor was a creature of rock and mud who stood nearly that of two Mognins, towering over everyone on the dark battlefield. Within the mud, along the seams of the rocks that made up his body, an ill-colored green flame burned from oil that dripped from its body. Bakalor, demon of the underworld had arrived to take over the land.

Ergrauth was taken by surprise at the sudden appearance of the demon of the underworld. "It's true. After several millennia being underground he has finally returned." His moment of disbelief was put to an end with an attack from his son.

Santorray's timber cracked Ergrauth across his head, sending splinters in every direction. The Blothrud then used the remainder of the timber in an attempt to break his father's legs before he could recover from the first attack.

Falling to his knees, the left side of Ergrauth's face was now crushed. Shards of the timber were embedded into it, including one that went through his left eye.

Santorray limped forward and towered over his fallen father. "You are blinded and you are down. Relinquish your empire to me so I may free the Del'Unday. Do this and I will allow you to live." His words were as strong and commanding as he could make them. This was not easy, seeing that pain sparked across his chest each time he spoke and down his legs with each step he took.

"You'll have to kill me before I give you anything." Reaching out he grabbed onto the metal rod in Santorray's leg. Pulling it to the side, he caused his son to howl in pain. He then pulled the rod out and stabbed his son in the side with it.

Santorray's body shook uncontrollably as he staggered backward until he fell onto the broken siege tower. Both he and his father were now down. Neither could rise.

Bakalor stood above all on the battlefield. Oil seeped out between the rocks that made up his body. The brightness of the

burning oil changed intensity upon his choosing. A short trunk-like
nose hung over the front of his mouth which exposed large grinding
teeth. Diamonds, the size of a Num's head, were used as his eyes as
he scanned the battlefield. Chaos ruled the land, just as he had hoped.

Arrows flew at the new arrival, bouncing off of his rock body
upon impact. Spears, swords, axes and maces were used by the
Dovenar fighters against Bakalor with no effect. He calmly began
walking toward the Dovenar Wall, swatting fighters out of his way or
stepping on them if they fell before him. They were but insects to
him.

It was then that the gravity began to shift, pushing everything
and everyone in the area out toward the desert. The gravity effects of
the Lu'Tythis Tower crystal had grown in strength to reach the
battlefield.

It was as though the ground had tilted, causing the river and
everything around it to run upstream. Fighters and their weapons
rolled out toward the sand dunes and the river water backed up to the
east.

Bakalor stopped and watched the odd scene. Several soldiers
flew off the top of Dovenar Wall and into the battlefield. Dead
fighters rolled past him along with siege equipment, supply wagons,
and loose debris for several long minutes.

When it finally stopped, gravity shifted back toward the wall at
an even greater strength, launching everything in the battlefield back
toward the wall.

Fighters and weapons flew past Bakalor, who used his demon
powers to grip the stone below the sands with his feet. Faralopes,
wagons, and corpses flew past him. Confused, he watched everything
in the battlefield start stacking up against the tall Dovenar Wall.
Eventually, some started flying over the wall and out of sight.

The sand dune was not immune to the gravity shift and the
entire battlefield started to become a sandstorm, pulling tons of sand
pebbles from the desert floor. Ahz woke from being knocked
unconscious just as she was pulled away by the odd gravity, along
with many others of her village.

Santorray dug his wolf claws into the ground as he slid toward
his father. Pulling the metal rod out of his side, he let out a piercing
roar of pain.

Ergrauth fought against the gravity as well. Clinging to the ground, he waited for his son to get close enough to reach. The fight wasn't over yet.

Blood poured from Santorray's side while he was being dragged toward the wall. Dropping the rod, he applied pressure to the wound to minimize the loss of blood.

The rod rolled across the ground and into the outstretched hand of his father. "You will not outlive me," Ergrauth announced as his son slid up against him. Leaning forward with the rod to strike Santorray in the chest, one of the Del'Unday siege machines rolled over both Blothruds, taking them on an out of control dizzying roll toward the wall.

The war machine broke off pieces with each and every bounce, while Santorray and Ergrauth tumbled with it and sometimes underneath it. Neither of the warriors could escape from being smashed or tossed around.

Bakalor was the only being left standing and even he fought the gravity pull. However, when the siege weapon crashed upon the demon of the underworld, carrying the Blothruds, he became the third member of the tumbling crew.

All three spun out of control until they crashed against the mighty Dovenar Wall.

Santorray had landed off to one side, Bakalor off to the other. Between them, the siege weapon was in pieces on top of Ergrauth.

Unable to gain the strength to stand, Santorray raised his head to see his father's fate. Under the broken rubble, he was able to see Ergrauth lying face up. The rod he had taken from Santorray was now through his skull, sticking out of his forehead. His death had been immediate upon impact.

With a sigh of relief, Santorray could now rest knowing that it was finally over. In some way, he had hoped it could have ended differently, but he realized long ago that his father would fight until the end.

Bakalor stood up with his feet on the side of the wall. The gravity had completely shifted sideways and now the ground acted as a wall or a vertical cliff face with sand racing down its surface. "What has happened here?" he grumbled. "This is not the land I planned. What type of magic is this?"

Glaring out at the possibilities he noticed a Num clinging to the top of the wall. "Thorik Dain? This must be your undertaking!"

## Chapter 34
# Battle of Demons

Thorik Dain held onto the battlement at the top of the Dovenar Wall. Shifts in the gravity had caused his feet to hang in the air, pointing toward the Lu'Tythis Tower and the massive electrical storm that fanned out from that location as lightning raced across the bottom of the rolling dark clouds.

"Climb up!" the Num yelled to Bryus, pulling himself up and over the side. In doing so, he couldn't believe his eyes. The Del'Unday were still fighting against humans, Ov'Unday, and Kewtalls. However, they were now standing on the side of the mighty wall while doing so.

To add to the strangeness, more fighters were arriving every few moments, sliding across the desert floor and onto the wall along with sheets of sand and debris from the battlefield.

Reaching over the edge of the wall, he began to help up Bryus Grum, who he had just reached prior to the changing of gravity.

Bryus screamed from the tender nature of his wife's breasts dragging along the stone wall while being pulled up. "These things are nothing but a nuisance."

Thorik ignored him and continued pulling while looking at the battle of dragons still in the sky. Both sides of Rummon's dragons were fighting to the death over whether the Red Dragon had been revived with his original soul or with some other essence. "Why of all times must they fight each other, when we need them to work together against Bakalor."

"And what's with these cramps I keep getting?" The wizard tossed one leg up and over the ledge. "I better not be pregnant."

Grabbing Bryus' leg and hip, the Num pulled him the rest of the way up over the lip of the wall.

"Did you get a good enough grab on my wife's body there, Thorik?"

"Listen, Bryus, I don't even know where to start asking you about your survival from the last time I saw you, let alone the body you have attached your head to, but we have bigger issues right now than your wife. Did you happen to notice that down is now sideways and the side of this wall is now a floor?"

"Really? I hadn't observed this all-encompassing event," he said in his usual condescending tone. However, this time he said it while trying to straighten his dress and pull fabric from the crack in his rear. "This dress and corset are so damn uncomfortable. Who designed these torture devices?"

Thorik shook his head; half in frustration and half in dismay.

"What?" Bryus questioned, while adjusting his wife's breasts. "My wife asked me to take good care of her body, and I don't want to start chafing in places I don't need to know about."

Amazed that he was having this conversation in the middle of a battle, Thorik tried to shake it out of his mind and bring it back to reality. Unfortunately, at the moment reality didn't look real either. Warriors continued to stand and fight on the side of the Dovenar Wall. "I've revived Rummon. We need to help him before the dragons tear him apart!"

The Num's sharp eyes could see Santorray laying hurt, while Asentar was also injured but still swinging his long sword. Grewen was holding two Corrockian soldiers at bay while Brimmelle tossed rocks at them. All this was going on as Bakalor walked toward him. "Bakalor?" Thorik gasped silently.

He had been spotted by the demon of the underworld, who was heading straight for Thorik.

"Run!" Thorik shouted.

They both jumped to their feet and ran along the wall toward Rivers Edge, racing away from the giant as greenish flames increased over the demon's body. It was less than a minute before Bakalor caught up to Bryus.

Glancing to his side, the wizard realized that he wasn't the one being chased, so he veered off to the side and allowed Bakalor to run past him. "That was close," he said with a sigh.

Thorik continued to run across the wall, evading crushed battle equipment and fallen soldiers along the way.

The demon chasing him made no variations in his path, plowing through or stomping on anything in his way. This route allowed him to catch up to the Num in a short amount of time.

Reaching down, Bakalor plucked Thorik up with one swipe of his hand. In fact, his hand was so large, that he was able to completely close it around Thorik's body without squishing him.

Leaving a gap in the top of his fist, the demon peered in to see his captive audience.

Thorik gasped for air from the run, moving back away from the opening in the demon's fist, where a large diamond eyeball looked in at him.

"I knew it was you, Thorik Dain of Farbank. You've always caused me problems. I should have known that this tilted world had something to do with you."

"No!" Thorik shook his head, unable to understand why the demon seemed to blame the Num for his issues. "It wasn't me! If I could make this stop, I would."

"If that is true, then you serve no purpose to keep alive." Bakalor then closed his eyes and began to smile. "I've been looking forward to this for a long time."

Thorik started to feel warmth leaving his body. He had felt this before, when he traveled to Della Estovia and was captured by the demon. Bakalor was sucking out his life energy. It only took moments before his skin started to turn gray and his muscles weakened, followed by waves of pain. The Num could literally feel himself aging.

Once again the crystal stirred in the depths of Lake Luthralum and gravity shifted.

Without warning, the gravity in the battlefield returned to normal, dropping everyone on the wall back to the desert floor.

Bakalor crashed hard against the ground. However, his cargo was protected by his fist before his hand opened wide from the impact.

Thorik escaped and rolled to his feet before running toward Rivers Edge, dodging the bodies and debris raining down around him.

Piles of sand built up over ten feet high along the wall in some areas. One of these was the landing location of Bryus Grum, who slid down the wall and landed feet first, sinking in all the way to his wife's waist.

"Do something!" Thorik yelled, passing the wizard at a full run.

"I just did!" he shouted back. "You try falling thirty feet without breaking any bones." Fairly pleased with himself, he scanned to the north to see what the Num was running from. It was the giant stone creature who had been chasing him earlier. "You again?"

The demon of rock and mud lit up the dark battlefield as green flames from the oil in his joints increased in size, trailing his path while he rushed forward.

Bryus stood still, in hopes of avoiding any attention, until the massive creature raced by. But as soon as it did, Bryus began casting a spell.

Waving his arms and speaking the verbal commands needed, the desert sand before Bakalor began to swirl in a vortex, sucking down everything from the surface.

All it took was one step into the vortex for Bakalor to be trapped and pulled in. He immediately attempted to step to the far side without success. Grabbing the loose sand around the rim yielded no help either. He swung his rock arms and body back and forth, fighting the current of the sand. No matter what he tried, he could not escape.

Bryus freed himself from his own pile of sand and casually strolled over to the sinking creature. "Looks like you have met your match," he said in a cocky manner. "You're nothing but a giant cluster of lubricated pebbles scaring little folks with your size and bad personality."

Bakalor growled and turned to face Bryus as he was sinking deeper into the whirlpool of sand.

The wizard laughed. "You might be big and strong, but you haven't the intellect to tangle with me."

The growling continued until Bakalor's mouth sunk below the sand. His eyes squinted, staring at the wizard standing at the edge of the vortex.

"Have a good long look," the spell caster said with a smile.

The demon's diamond eyes sunk out of sight, followed by his rock forehead.

Ending the spell, he waved in the air with one hand, as one would wave in a parade after a major victory. "Thorik, my boy. I've once again taken care of your problem."

Thorik had stopped running and had turned to watch the end of the spell. "Are you sure?"

"He's trapped underground. What could he possibly do from under there?"

Thorik nervously stepped toward him. "Well, seeing that he is the demon of the underworld, I just assumed that being underground wouldn't bother him."

"Demon of the underworld?" Bryus' casual stance disappeared. "You mean that was Bakalor?"

"Yes, who else?"

Bryus snapped his head back and forth several times from Thorik and the sand that swallowed the demon before the wizard turned and started running from the area in horror. "You idiot! Did you think I could read your mind? How was I to know?"

Thorik also began running and quickly caught up with his friend as they both raced toward Rivers Edge. "What difference would that have made? You would have still tried to save me, wouldn't you?"

"Sure I would have," he said with a tilt to his head. "I just would have done so at a safer distance."

The two hadn't gone far before two enormous rock hands erupted from the ground, grabbing the companions.

Slowly rising from the desert floor, Bakalor lifted them above his head.

Bryus' arms were held to his sides, preventing him from using them to assist with a spell. In spite of his situation, he began muttering words to conjure magic in hopes of escaping.

Holding his two prisoners before him, the demon leaned his head back and slowly breathed in, sucking the life from Thorik and Bryus. Chills of electrical pain pulsed through their bodies with an ache which reached down to their bones.

The pain had silenced the wizard who was now struggling to gasp for air let alone say a word.

Years of life were flowing out of their bodies and there was little they could do to stop it.

Thorik's body shook. He had so little fight left within him. "Bakalor!" he screamed.

"Yes," the rock demon said, enjoying his feast of energy.

"I wish to..." the Num struggled with each and every word, "...congratulate you."

Raising his right rock eyebrow, he loosened the Num slightly to hear what he had to say. "Go on."

Thorik coughed while gaining his breath, as the soul-sucking sensation stopped.

Bryus had been given a reprieve as well. Gasping for air didn't stop him from speaking what was on his mind. "I think my breasts are starting to sag. My wife will never let me borrow her body again."

Thorik's stern gaze never left the demon. "You may have won the battle and the ability to stand upon the land," he paused, causing Bakalor to lean forward with anticipation. "However, you will still lose the war and be banished back to the underworld."

The green flames on Bakalor's face increased in strength while pulling Thorik up closer near his mouth. The heat from the flames singed the Num's face, but he stared right back at the demon.

"Thorik," Bryus quickly interrupted. "This is not a good time for you to act like a hero."

Glaring at the diamond eye before him, Thorik pulled his eyebrows together. "Go back to being the demon of an underground prison."

Blowing out heated air onto the Num, Bakalor laughed. "I am no longer the demon of the underworld, for I now rule over all life. Ergrauth is dead, so the land is mine."

Thorik glanced over the demon's shoulder and smiled. His timing had worked.

"But I still rule the air," a deep voice said from behind the demon.

Bakalor turned. Before him was a gigantic red dragon coming in for a landing. The obvious gaping holes in his sides and half of his scales missing gave clear view to the bones and muscles that held the creature together.

With the assistance of the second wave of dragons from the north to fight the first wave, the demon of the sky had been able to leave the battle long enough to take out the biggest threat on the battlefield.

Rummon landed hard against Bakalor, knocking him to the ground and freeing Bryus and Thorik, who tumbled to a stop. "Run, Thorik. It is time I pay my debt to you," Rummon said in his powerful voice. "However, all I can give you is time. It is up to you to end this."

Thorik helped Bryus up to his feet, while the dragon held Bakalor down against the ground.

Bryus stumbled as he started to gain his footing. "Rummon? That was your plan? You risked my life and my wife's perfect body on the hopes that one demon would fight the other?"

"He just saved our lives!" Helping the wizard to get moving, Thorik felt his own body ache from head to toe.

"I don't think you realize how hard it is to for a man like me to convince a woman with *this* kind of body to fall in love with him."

Now running, Thorik yelled over the loud battle sounds. "Stop complaining!"

"I'm not complaining," he yelled back, while trying to keep up. "I think you owe it to me to keep me informed. And what's this about Rummon owing you a debt? What other secrets are you hiding from me?"

Thorik glanced behind them to ensure they were pulling far enough away from the two demons. "I'm not hiding anything! I helped bring him back to life. That's all."

Lying on his back, the demon of the underworld raised his feet to kick Rummon off him. However, his feet went through the rotted flesh and into the dragon's body, becoming temporarily stuck in his ribcage.

Bryus stopped and turned back, giving the red dragon a quick scan. "You call that, 'bringing him back to life?' It looks like you just dug him up from a grave. Didn't you at least do some healing enchantment on him prior to giving his soul back?"

Thorik grabbed his friend to continue moving away from the fighting giants. "We didn't think of it at the time."

"We?"

"Avanda."

Bryus nodded at the answer while they ran for their lives. "Ah, say no more. Where is my little apprentice?"

"She's been captured along with the Myth'Unday by the Southwind Army. We need to save them."

"Save them? How about saving us first?" Struggling to run as fast as Thorik, Bryus pressed his wife's breasts firmly against his chest. "Slow down! I'm going to bruise these from all the bouncing."

Bakalor continued to punch holes into Rummon's weakened body until the dragon lifted off and smashed back down with all of his immense weight on his opponent. The impact cracked several of the rocks across Bakalor's body.

Rummon lifted off again, this time landing his full weight on Bakalor's head, driving it into the ground. The impact caused Bakalor's body to flop over, landing on his front. Rummon then lifted his massive dragon claw and hammered it into his shoulder blade with all of his strength.

Bakalor's arm split in half and crumbled into pieces. The weight of Rummon was far more than Bakalor could withstand, snapping open a fissure across his back. Sinking into the ground, the demon disappeared from underneath the desert floor and out of sight of Rummon.

Battles with mortals allowed for mending, but when demons inflicted extensive damage to other demons, they were often permanent in nature. Bakalor would never regrow the destroyed arm.

The red dragon had won this round, but the war was far from over. Several smaller dragons swooped down for their own battle upon the injured red dragon. Still believing Lord Rummon's body was being controlled by an enemy of their beliefs, they were willing to give their lives to stop him.

By this time Thorik and Bryus had reached the safety of the Rivers Edge wall and had climbed the stairs to its wide surface. On the far side of the wall, at the dock in the river, Captain Dare was preparing his ship to leave. Not a single civil war undead warrior could be seen around the ship. Thorik's agreement with them appeared to have paid off.

Glancing back over his shoulder to watch the battle, Thorik suddenly felt guilty about leaving the ancient red dragon to fight Bakalor and the other smaller dragons by himself. "We didn't have a chance without Rummon. Bakalor would have killed us for sure," Thorik said, while still panting from their escape. "We brought him back to life, and now he has saved our lives. Now we are in his debt, and we are abandoning him."

Bryus scowled. "Make up your mind, Num. Are we to save Avanda or Rummon? You can't do both at once. Besides it's not about saving Rummon. Look at him. Flesh is falling off him faster than a chuttlebeast sheds his smell. Surely he understands this is about defeating Bakalor, not his own survival. Do you?"

Blinking a few times at the sight of the decaying red dragon fighting off a few more smaller dragons, Thorik nodded. "Yes. You're right Bryus."

Tossing the last of the smaller dragons off him, Lord Rummon opened his incredibly large wings and gave them a single mighty flap in order to become airborne once again. As the lord of the air, he launched off to finally reclaim his rightful place. However, he was only able to rise a few yards before Bakalor returned.

Bursting up from the ground near Rummon's tail, Bakalor grabbed the end of the scaled appendage and sunk back under the ground. Dragging the tail underground as far as he could, he then returned to the surface, several yards away, to find Rummon stuck in the desert floor.

Rummon let out a burst of heavy fire from his mouth, surrounding Bakalor with intense heat for several moments. Once he stopped it was obvious that no damage had been done. Bakalor was still approaching.

Using one of his thick front legs, Rummon swung it through the air, knocking Bakalor off his feet and crashing down onto the desert floor with a thunderous sound.

Bakalor's face and chest had been cracked from the mighty blow. The flaming oils dripped heavy from the new cracks as well as the fissure in his back created from Rummon's prior attack. The demon attempted to push himself back up, but failed several times. Eventually, he lowered himself into the ground and out of sight.

Rummon didn't waste any time before trying to free himself. He strained while making efforts to pull his tail out from deep under the desert floor. Leaning his neck forward and down, he pushed with his back legs until the tail eventually loosened.

As it did, Bakalor's hand raised up from the desert floor, grabbed Rummon's neck, and pulled it into the ground. Rummon's neck snapped. His head lay alone on one side of where Bakalor had grabbed, his neck and body lay on the other side.

Bakalor slowly ascended from desert floor to his full height, next to his victim. He had killed Lord Rummon.

"No!" shouted Thorik at the sight before him. Bakalor had won. He had defeated Rummon and would now claim the world as his own.

More than just Thorik had noticed the demon's victory. All warriors stopped and stared at the sight as waves of gravity softly pushed and pulled at them on the battlefield. This was no temporary ceasefire; it was the end of the war. The other demons, Ergrauth and Rummon, had been killed in battle. Bakalor had won.

Standing far taller than any other creature on the battlefield, the demon assessed the situation.

Over half of the Ov'Unday had been severely injured and unable to hold off any more attacks. The Ov'Unday's tied up captives rolled in the dunes with the waves of the gravity, waiting to be saved before the dunes washed over them to never be seen again.

Ahz only had a dozen of her Kewtall village warriors remaining as she stood guard over Santorray while he attempted to bind his wounds, as he leaned up against the Dovenar Wall next to his dead father.

The humans were in just as bad a shape. Asentar had been hit and cut many times, but was still able to ride his faralope. Most of his men had fallen, but he was unable to know how many of them were dead. The number still standing was far less than he had hoped.

During this time of realization that Bakalor was now the supreme ruler of all things, the battlefield slowly migrated to one side or the other. The followers of the demon stood behind him to the north. This included the Del'Unday and most of the dragons.

The separation of two groups left a desert filled with corpses from both sides littered about the desert floor. Well over half of all that attended now lay as victims of this attempted conquest.

Irluk, the Death Witch, could be seen as a floating swirl of ash and burnt debris above the battlefield. She pulled at the souls from all those who had died in this war, as wisps of vapors rose from the fallen up into her net. The scene was nothing less than what appeared to be the end of all days. And yet the fight was not over.

Congregated along the Rivers Edge Wall were all those who still opposed Bakalor. Dragging themselves or hauling others in pain, the humans, Ov'Unday, Kewtalls, and Santorray lined up against the base of the wall. The small number of remaining dragons who supported Rummon's return roosted along the top of the wall.

Carrying Brimmelle, Grewen arrived and laid Thorik's uncle's limp body down before him. "I'm sorry Thorik," Grewen said in a soft low tone. Covered with his own bleeding cuts and stab wounds, the Mognin didn't care about his own wellbeing.

Taking his and Avanda's pack off his back and tossing them to the ground, Thorik's eyes began to weep as he placed a hand on his uncle's chest. Thankfully he was still breathing.

"He's been knocked out. I'll keep an eye on him until he awakens," Grewen ensured the Num.

In spite of the comment he tried to speak to the elder Num. "Brimmelle?" His wait for an answer was interrupted by the flapping of dragon wings.

Chug and Pheosco landed near Thorik with expressions of failure, after seeing Rummon die before their eyes.

Wiping away his own tears, Thorik stood up and scratched behind Chug's ear to make the dragon feel better, even if it would only be temporary.

Seeing Vesik in Avanda's pack, which now lay at Thorik's feet, Pheosco's brow lowered. "Where's Avanda?"

"She was captured by the Southwind soldiers, along with Emilen. Captain Dare has his ship ready to cross to the south side so we can free her."

Growling at the thought, Pheosco grabbed Avanda's pack and lifted up into the air. "How could you leave her in such peril?" he spit out before turning to fly out over the river. The weight of the pack prevented a smooth flight as he struggled with each flap of his wings.

"Pheosco! No!" Thorik reached for the pack, but was too late. "You could be flying into a trap, handing Vesik to the enemy. Stop!" he shouted, but the dragon showed no signs of changing course.

"Grewen, can you load Brimmelle onto the ship and catch up to Pheosco? We need to save Avanda, even if this battle is hopeless. Also, that book of magic in the enemy's hands could be dangerous, but in Avanda's hands it could be disastrous if she uses it in a fit of anger."

"We'll do our best, little man." Grewen lifted Thorik's uncle and carried him across the wall and down toward the dock and the ship.

Thorik followed to the edge of the wall and looked down at them. "I know you will. Please don't let anything happen to Avanda. Find her and keep her safe. Don't bring her back here. This battle is over."

The Mognin nodded.

"So, you're just going to give up," a voice said to Thorik.

Snapping his head up, he saw the odd-eyed bird with his grandmother's soul standing on Chug's back. "Granna, I'm glad you're safe, but you're too late. We've lost." He looked at the small numbers remaining to defend against Bakalor's forces. There will be another time and another day."

The bird's eyes rolled around in different directions while her head snapped back and forth and her orange feathers ruffled outward. "That's a reasonable justification to give up."

Thorik looked out across the battlefield at the slow reorganization of their troops preparing for their final strike. "Justification? It's reality."

"Dear child, one of your greatest attributes is also your greatest weakness. You know enough when to fight another day. But you need to finally pick a day and start fighting for what you want. You can't keep pushing things off forever. You use this excuse on many things when they suddenly become too difficult. You must learn to get past these points and be persistent until you finally win."

"But Granna, it's too late, for they have already won."

"Often the difference between succeeding and losing is a fraction of an idea that shines a light on how to get beyond your final barrier. The only true barrier in your path is yourself."

Thorik shook his head. "Not this time, Granna. It will take more than a gem of an idea to lighten up this bleak situation."

Gluic's head snapped toward her grandson with both eyes fixated on his face. "Exactly!" She shouted before turning away and flying down to Dare's ship and landing next to Brimmelle.

"It will take more than persistence to change the victor of this war," Thorik said to Chug, who slapped his hanging tongue up against Thorik's face. Wiping it clean with his hands, the Num glanced up at the dark storm clouds churning overhead. "That's it," he stated plainly. "What a gem of an idea!"

Looking back down over to the south side of the wall he yelled toward the ship. "Grewen! Set sail and head south to the Southwind army camp. I'll meet you there so we can save Avanda."

"No Mognin tells me when to set sail on me own vessel," Captain Dare yelled back.

Frustrated, Thorik yelled back down. "Captain, Avanda is the most important person in my life. I'm asking you to set sail to save her."

"I be in charge of me own ship and will determine when she be ready to sail!"

"Yes, Captain. You are in charge. What needs to be done to carry out your orders?"

The captain looked around to his left and then to his right before looking up and down the masts. "She all looks to be in order."

"Then do you give the order?"

Puffing out his chest, he gave the command. "Set sail, ya land-lubbers. We be in a hurry to save Avanda."

And with that, Grewen pushed off the dock as they drifted out into the water. Captain Dare immediately started shouting and complaining about his new crew who he had talked into helping sail the ship across the river.

Once underway, Thorik turned back to those still with their backs to the wall. Spotting Santorray, the Num jumped up onto Chug. "Let's go, Chug! We have one last obstacle to overcome."

Chug and Thorik flew off the wall and down near Santorray, who was being tended to by a pure white female Blothrud. "Santorray! You're alive!" Thorik yelled, with pleasure.

"Did you expect anything other than that?"

"No, I guess not. You probably fought a herd of chuttlebeast before this battle just to warm up."

Santorray grinned out of one side of his mouth and motioned toward the white Blothrud. "Thorik, meet Ahz. She is a Kewtall."

Thorik's eyebrows lowered in the center. "But I thought you said that Kewtalls were…" He stopped his sentence as the female Kewtall stepped up to Santorray and placed a soft hand around the Blothrud's back and onto his shoulder. Upon seeing this, he knew there was a relationship that he was not going to be responsible for adding friction. "It's a pleasure meeting you, Ahz."

"And I see you have a new friend," Santorray said, glancing at the brown dragon the Num was riding.

"Yes, this is Chug. He helped me escape from Rummon's Lair." Thorik patted him on the side. "I have a plan to finish this battle."

"I think it is about finished with or without your plan."

"True, so what do we have to lose?"

Santorray looked at the spark in the Num's eyes. "I'm in. What's the plan?"

## Chapter 35
# River Island

On a small island in the center of the Rivers Edge, Darkmere stood upon a flat roof of an abandoned structure. High enough to watch the events of the battle unfolding, the pale-skinned white-eyed E'rudite had kept his distance from the fighting. His thin, bony body and face stood rigid against the winds blowing from the dark storm overhead. He had left the Southwind camp in order to finish the war.

Surrounded by a pitch black barrier, a small vessel had made its way to the island, leaving a trail of dead fish and plants in its wake. A young man stepped off the boat and walked up the exterior staircase. Plants and vines that had grown along the walls and stairs instantly shriveled up and turned gray. He continued his ascent until he reached the roof and stepped next to Darkmere.

"Are we to do nothing?" young Lord Bredgin complained, while reducing the darkness surrounding his body.

"Of course not, my son. We are enjoying the fruits of our labor. For years we have worked hard to plant the seeds and feed the minds. In this one move of my plan, we have already eliminated two demons, with the third one severely injured. We have also succeeded in weakening all of the forces in the land. By the time this battle is over, we will only need to walk in and be in control of whoever survives."

"So, we just stand here?"

"Yes, and enjoy the sights. For tomorrow you and I will rule everything."

"What of Bakalor?"

"He has served his purpose. By sending his offspring to Lu'Tythis, they destroyed the tower, which in turn destroyed the crystal that controls our weather, allowing him to arrive on the surface. Once he arrived here, I knew Ergrauth and Rummon would fall. Now we simply wait for him to destroy the rest of those who strive for freedom and then we step in and take charge."

"But what if Bakalor does not wish to return to the underworld afterword?"

"Then I will send you to finish him off."

"Me?"

"He lives by the light of his flames. The powerful Notarian oils breathe life into his body of stone. However, the light of the sun overpowers this." Darkmere slowly turned from the battlefield. "What E'rudite powers have I taught you from the day you were brought before me? What have you surpassed me and become the master of?"

"How to control the power of darkness and light."

Darkmere turned back to the battlefield. "If he should stake a claim in our land, you need to show him the light and the errors of his way."

Lord Bredgin stood silent next to his father for a few moments before asking, "You have raised me to be a weapon for your return to power?"

"Yes, and a rise to your own."

"So, to you, I am just a weapon in your arsenal to obtain your victory."

"No, you are the ultimate weapon to ensure that this kingdom is never taken from our bloodline again." Darkmere's pleasant face began to sour. "My brother, Ambrosius, nearly ended our ability to be the rightful heirs to this kingdom."

"And what if he should return?"

Darkmere glanced toward the center of the storm. "If I know my brother, he fought to his death to keep that tower standing up. Seeing that he has not arrived, he most likely perished in its collapse."

"Don't be count'n him out so fast, there," Captain Dare said from behind them. After dropping Grewen and Brimmelle off on the south side of the river, he had followed Lord Bredgin and sailed his ship to the island.

Darkmere and Bredgin turned to face the shirtless fat man, wondering what he thought he could possible accomplish against two E'rudites.

"Ya been mess'n up our lands fer some time now. It's 'bout time someone be teach'n ya a lesson."

"And you believe you are the one who can do it?" Darkmere said with a grin.

"Ah, no. Not alone. Be a fool if I plan to take ya on me'self."

High above them, Draq dove down toward the island. His once reflective scales were now dim and charred from his battle with Bakalor's children. Holes still existed in his wings and he had lost one leg. He could not walk, but he could still sail the skies.

Flying down toward them at an incredible speed, Draq raced in behind the two E'rudites. Before the two could turn, Draq grabbed Darkmere from behind, pushing Bredgin tumbling forward toward Dare. The red-tipped silver dragon then held tightly onto Darkmere as he lifted back into the air.

Bredgin rolled forward toward Dare, who had pulled out his large Fesh'Unday leg bone which he used as a cane as well as a weapon. Swinging the bone, he caught Bredgin off guard and smacked him hard into the stomach.

Lord Bredgin fell to his knees in pain, gasping for breath.

"Now, I've 'eard you been caus'n some problems with me friends Thorik and Ambrosius. I don't like that."

Clearing his lungs, Bredgin still struggled. "I'm about to show you what kind of problems I can cause."

Limping to the side of the younger man, Dare swung his weapon directly at his back. To his surprise, once the Fesh'Unday bone was within a foot of Bredgin's body, the end of it turned grey, cracked, and became brittle. By the time it struck the young man's back, it was so brittle that the end simply shattered into powder-sized pieces.

Draq had raced off the side of the building carrying Darkmere up into the sky. "Can E'rudites fly?" he said with a nasty smirk.

Darkmere stayed silent.

The silver dragon shot straight up in the air, before turning and plunging his way back down, releasing his grasp of the man. However, to his disbelief, his talons were still clinging onto Darkmere. The E'rudite had somehow fused the dragon's claws onto his back, preventing him from being dropped.

"Clever," the dragon snarled. "But not clever enough." Pulling up from the dive, he headed straight back toward the rooftop where Dare and Bredgin stood. Gaining speed, Draq lowered his flight path to ensure the he would just graze the surface, causing Darkmere to crash head first against the wall.

The dark barrier around Bredgin grew as he stepped toward Captain Dare.

Dare backed up to the edge of the ledge. Poking the other end of his fesh leg bone into the dark mass surrounding Bredgin, he watched the tip of bone color turn from white to gray and then begin to crumble apart under its own weight. "What in bloody hell is this magic?"

"You're about to find out," Bredgin said with a grin.

Draq aimed Darkmere's head directly at the building's wall as he prepared for landing. The goal was to force the E'rudite off by slapping him alongside the building while he flew over it. As he approached, he felt additional weight from below and had to make adjustments. Draq raced over the ledge, striking Darkmere into the wall.

The Dark Lord had the powers to change the chemistry of all things he touched, including himself. Turning himself into a solid granite statue not only allowed him to crash through the side of the wall, but it also caught the dragon by surprise.

Released from the granite, Draq was catapulted by Darkmere's stone body slapping against the block wall. Draq toppled head over tail across the roof top and skidded to a halt near Captain Dare.

The granite statue rolled to a stop on the surface as well. Once stopped, it transformed back into skin and bones. Darkmere calmly stood up and brushed himself off. "So," he said in a condescending tone. "You are the next in line, now that Ambrosius and Ericc have been eliminated. How sad it is that they were not here to witness the final battle with their own eyes."

"I wouldn't miss it for the world," Ambrosius said, standing on the flat roof with them. Utilizing the young E'rudite's power of spatial jumping, Ericc and Ambrosius had appeared out of nowhere.

"I never seen anything like it. At least never without a bit of the Irr in me system," Dare said at the sight of them appearing out of thin air.

"Welcome, young Ericc." Darkmere nodded to the youth. "I've been waiting for you. You won't be escaping with your friends this time."

Draq rolled up onto his single leg. "This is one fight we have no plans on leaving until we are finished."

"Fools." Darkmere's tone was always calm and malevolent regardless of how he really felt. However, his confidence overshadowed any concerns he may have had as the Death Witch,

Irluk, arrived on the roof. Seeing her, a wicked smile crossed his white bony face. "You have played right into my hands, my dear brother."

Stepping toward Darkmere, Ambrosius walked with conviction in his tattered clothes. "No more games. No more hiding. No more using others to get what we want. Today, you and I, we end this once and for all!"

And with that, the battle of the E'rudites began with a spectacle of brilliant light swirling with endless darkness. Time and space changed and the forces of nature pulled and pushed at each other, ripping the very fabric of the universe.

The center of the river, surrounding the E'rudite battle, became a blur of motions and shadows to all looking in on it.

Chapter 36
# Last Chance

Flickering yellow torchlights filled both sides of the battlefield under the dark storm that raged above both armies. The flashes of lightning exposed the landscape between them to be the bloody mess of bodies and limbs as well as broken equipment and weapons. Although fresh, the battlefield appeared old due to the sands that had washed over the dead. Periodic gravity shifts continued to tug in various directions, sending the loose sand and debris across the desert floor.

Asentar stood before the enemies of Bakalor, shouting loud enough for all to hear. On one side of him was Ahz riding her two-faced scale-covered feline. On the other side was the Blothrud, Santorray. There was a unification between them that none would have ever imagined could exist, including themselves.

After several attempts to pull everyone together near the Rivers Edge Wall, Asentar was now able to speak to the masses, which included humans, Ov'Unday, the Kewtalls, and the dragons loyal to Rummon. The Dovenar Knight gazed over the crowd of various species, as one caught his eye. Riding a dragon, Thorik was flying away from the battlefield. He could only be seen during the flashes of lightning that sparked overhead from one cloud to another. It only took moments for him to be completely out of sight.

Returning to his listeners, Asentar explained the plan of attack. "We must first take out their dragons. Nothing else matters at this stage. If we only enter the battlefield a third of the way, we will have time before their foot soldiers reach us. We will use this time to have our dragons eliminate their dragons with the help of you men. Once we have their dragons out of the battle, we are at much better odds."

"That is foolhardy," shouted one man among the mumbling of the nervous crowd.

"What if we get attacked while helping with the dragons? Do you expect us to just ignore them?" shouted another.

"Do what you can, but we *must* keep their dragons on the ground. We cannot afford to have any escape and rise up into the clouds." Looking across at all the dragons who sided with him, he gave specific instructions. "Should you see any of the enemy rise to the air, you must take them before they reach the storm."

"We won't last long," someone shouted.

"This plan does not show victory for us," said another. "It only shows delay in their triumph."

"Delay, yes," Asentar announced. "We have one last chance to prevent all future generations from living under Bakalor's rule. Our sacrifice here is to provide this land with some hope. All we need to do is keep those of the air delayed long enough not to notice the storm."

Santorray took in a deep breath while he eyed the crowd before him. Most were injured and all were exhausted from the long battle. The Blothrud had his own near fatal wounds that caused him to stand before them in extreme pain. However, there was a major difference between them, Santorray still had the fight in his eyes. He could see from their expressions that they were already defeated. Despising the feeling, he yelled out, "Run! Run for safety! Flee this deathtrap of a battlefield."

The soft mumbling of the crowd suddenly stopped and an uncomfortable silence swept over the army.

"Go on! What are you waiting for?" Santorray shouted. "You've done what you can. Now you're wounded and have no more strength to give. It is time for you to give up! Run to the hills. Hide from Bakalor's new world. Leave before they attack again."

Asentar stepped in front of the Blothrud. "What are saying? Are you insane? If we do not attack, Thorik will not have a chance to reach the storm clouds before being stopped by their dragons."

"Who cares?" Santorray yelled back in his face. "What kind of land do we want to live in that we aren't willing to fight for ourselves?"

"Thorik will die, along with our last hope!"

"Most of these people don't have the desire to save him or their own freedom. They are weak!" Santorray glanced back at the crowd. "Bryus Grum, take those who wish for freedom but are not willing to sacrifice their lives to achieve it. Lead them up and out past EverSpring to the Ov'Unday city of Ovla'Mathyus. They will be safe there."

Nodding, Bryus stepped forward and waited for people to start joining him.

"Hurry, we don't have much time," Santorray shouted. "I will only take those into battle who have a pure desire for freedom. They must have a burning for what's right. Anyone can find a hundred reasons not to join us in battle. That is the easy way out. But for those who refuse to hide from injustice and are willing to do whatever it takes for freedom, you are the ones that can truly change the world. These are the only ones who need to stay."

Pausing, the Blothrud scanned the warriors. "Are you those who have wished to partake of the riches of freedom at the expense of others? If so, join Bryus now!"

Bryus stood alone. His old ugly wrinkly face scowled as he adjusted the dress on his wife's slightly aged gorgeous body. No one approached.

"Or are you among those few upon our land that will do what needs to be done for future generations, regardless of the ramifications?" Santorray shouted again.

"Yes!" the crowd shouted back in unison.

"Are you the few?!" Santorray shouted.

"Yes!"

"Will you do whatever it takes?!"

"YES!"

"Then get out there and prove it!!"

The fighters cheered and charged past Santorray and onto the battlefield.

Bryus looked back and forth before addressing Santorray. "So, does this mean I should still be on my way to Ovla'Mathyus, just in case someone changes their mind?"

"Prepare some spells, Alchemist. Your day of battle is not over yet."

After the surge of Asentar's warriors racing a third of the way onto the battlefield, the dragons under Santorray's command lifted off of the Rivers Edge Wall and joined the battle at a low altitude.

Once Bakalor's dragons reached them, the final battle began.

However, instead of fighting the opposing dragons, Santorray's dragons simply latched onto them and dragged them onto the ground, where the foot soldiers quickly jumped on and attacked, tearing their wings to prevent them from flying again.

The plan took Bakalor's dragons by surprise and nearly half of them had fallen in the first round.

Once the foot soldiers had the situation under control, Santorray's dragons lifted up for another attack. Some were successful while others struggled now that Bakalor's army knew Santorray's plan. In addition, the Del'Unday army was arriving for hand to hand combat.

The first wave of Santorray's plan had been a success, the second became difficult, the third was not looking promising.

High in the air, Thorik road Chug up toward the storm clouds. Lightning flashed in the clouds, blinding the two for several moments while the ringing in their ears from the thunder rumbled for much longer.

It was at this time that Bakalor spotted them and ordered several of his dragons to take the Num out of the air, dead or alive.

The chase was on.

Eight thin long black dragons broke away from the battle to head straight up into the air. They were all lean and quick, unlike the slow and clumsy Chug. It would be a very close race to see who reached the clouds first.

Immediately, Santorray ordered a half-dozen of his own dragons to fly up and create a blockade in order to give Thorik more time. Excitement was building on his side. There was a true feeling that they could actually win this battle.

Bakalor focused his attention back to the battlefield and specifically on its leaders. The red Blothrud seemed to be giving the most orders. A white female Blothrud was riding a two-faced scaly feline who was limping forward from a deep side wound. They fought their way forward, past the demon's front lines with very little trouble. There was also a tall human on the faralope in full blue Dovenar colors, who was coordinating strategic blows to Bakalor's west troops.

Even with the advantage of numbers, the demon's army was being pushed back. They simply didn't have the motivation that the other side possessed. Realizing this, Bakalor knew he had to take the three leaders out in order to deflate the surge from the south. One arm short, thanks to Rummon's attack, Bakalor still felt confident he could beat them in hand to hand combat.

Lowering himself into the ground, he quickly traveled to the center of the battle where Santorray was chopping his way through the troops as though they were vines in a forest.

Reaching up out of the ground, Bakalor grabbed one of the Blothrud's legs before rising out of the desert floor. Flipping Santorray upside down, while still holding onto his leg, the demon laughed at the flailing Del'Unday.

Fighting hard with his sabers, Santorray sliced and stabbed at the rock surface of the demon without inflicting any damage upon him. Bakalor was not of flesh and blood and a blade could do no damage to him.

Swinging the Blothrud up over his head, Bakalor slammed Santorray back down onto the desert floor, square on his back, knocking the wind out of him and breaking several more of his ribs.

The crash resonated across the battlefield, striking fear into Santorray's followers. If he couldn't stand up to Bakalor, then who could?

"Victory!" Yelling, to gather the view of all close enough to see, Bakalor stepped over to the fallen Blothrud for his final blow. He wanted to make sure that all understood his power.

Standing next the Santorray, Bakalor raised one of his thick rock legs over the Blothrud's head. "One quick stomp should put an end to you and a send clear message to everyone else. I am now in control."

The demon's foot swung down, but was caught by Santorray's hands just inches before crushing his face.

The two struggled. Bakalor continue to push his foot down harder while Santorray used his massive arms to push the weight of a bolder off him, but he was losing the battle as the flaming green rock foot inched closer to his face.

Without any warning, Ahz slammed into Bakalor's back with the side of her ride, knocking his foot off to the side of Santorray's face. Her giant feline changed to a bright red as she pulled him back and prepared for a second attack.

Both faces on the feline screeched at Bakalor before rising on its back legs, grabbing onto the demon's arm with its wide mouth, and clawing at his body.

Bakalor intensified his green flames, burning the inside of the creature's mouth.

The burning oils coated the creature's paws with fire which began spreading up its legs. The feline released the demon's arm and jumped back to extinguish its body. In doing so, its rider, Ahz was flung off and onto the ground.

Santorray had taken the moment to attempt to get to his feet. The effects of Bakalor's attack shot pain throughout his body as he rolled to his knees to stand up. But before he could rise, the demon's large foot kicked the Blothrud in the head, knocking him out cold.

Bakalor kneeled onto one knee and picked the Blothrud up. Lifting him from his waist with one hand, he held the mighty Santorray over his head for all to see. "This is your greatest of warrior? This is what you would challenge me with?"

Santorray hung limp in his hand. His legs dangled out one side of the demon's hand, while his chest, head and arms hung down from the other end. He appeared to be dead to the troops.

Fear filled the hearts of those who had signed up for this last battle against the demon, which was obvious as the majority of them took a defensive stance. However, they were not running or bowing to his needs. They still had hope and Bakalor didn't understand why.

Before the demon could stand up and turn around to see the entire battlefield, he was slammed from the back. Asentar had found a large war-hammer among the other scattered weapons on the battleground and, swinging it over his head with both hands, he had struck the same location on Bakalor's back where Rummon had caused a fissure. In a thunderous rumble, the crash of the hammer broke off a few pieces and widened the fracture.

Falling to his knees in pain, Bakalor dropped Santorray before leaning forward on his hand.

Stunned by the power of the massive hammer, Asentar quickly noticed the word "Quake" engraved into it. He could tell that this was no ordinary weapon. Without delay, a second swing of the mighty hammer was made by Asentar at the demon's exposed back, but this time, Bakalor lowered himself into the ground to avoid it. The hammer hit the desert floor with a masterful thud.

Ahz ran over and cradled Santorray's head to see if he was alive, while Asentar stood guard next to him with his new war-hammer.

Panning around the battle for Bakalor's return, Asentar held his hammer ready for a quick attack. "Only a demon's weapon can kill a demon. We have the right weapon to complete this. Now we need our short friend to do his part."

It wasn't long before the Blothrud opened his eyes to see the white Blothrud looking down at him. "You're still alive."

She nodded.

Asentar adjusted his grip on his weapon while searching for the demon's return. "I took on nearly the entire army, and saved the two big ones for you, and I still had to come in to help you out." Asentar said, before smirking down at Santorray.

Santorray gave a half-hearted grin at the comment while fighting through his pain. "You just say the word when you think you're man enough to take me on."

Looking at the battling around them, Ahz interrupted. "Before you two start strutting and showing off the size of your chest and war wounds, how about we finish this battle. Bakalor is still out there."

## Chapter 37
# Emilen's Victory

Tossed down into a tent, Avanda scraped her knee and elbow as
she rolled to a stop. Bound at her ankles and wrists, she
struggled to break free. She was still in the Southwind army camp a
few miles south of the battle playing out north of Rivers Edge.

"You're not so tough without your Vesik and your purse of
magic," Emilen said.

Avanda's eyes tightened. How she wished she had either of
them right now. "And what did you have to do to free yourself?"

"I simply made better friends than you did. You had your
chance to join the Terra King a long time ago, but you refused."

"You fool. Darkmere *is* the Terra King!"

"Yes, I know. And Darkmere has the Southwind army under
his power, through the support of the Matriarch, who should be
joining us soon. I think you'll get along with her just fine. Just show
her the same level of respect you give me." Emilen gave off an evil
grin at the thought of the Matriarch's short temper with people such
as Avanda.

"Darkmere is evil. He plans to destroy the kingdom and force
everyone to follow his rule."

"What some see as evil acts, others see as necessary actions to
do what's best. He has the ability to bring us all together under one
rule. This would end all fighting and create a utopia for us all. Why
are you resisting this?"

"Tell me this, Emilen. Where do people fit in this paradise if
they don't want his version of a utopia?"

Emilen shook her head. "There is no place for them."

"And if Thorik is one of those who doesn't see your way?
Could you sacrifice him as well?"

"Yes," she said plainly.

Avanda was shocked by the cavalier attitude. "But your
feelings for him-"

"My feelings for him were required to obtain what Darkmere
needed from him."

"And what would that be?"

"Darkmere wanted me to keep him informed of Thorik's whereabouts and his plans. He needed to know what runestones he had learned to control and what they did. So, I wrote notes and placed them in Thorik's coffer so Darkmere could read them."

"And what good would that do?" Avanda asked.

"He knows better than I. It was not for me to question it. However, once I told him about the Runestone of Pride and how it cleared the air, Darkmere wrote me back, instructing me to steal it from him." Pulling the runestone from her pocket, Emilen smiled and tossed it to the other Num. "We are always a step ahead of you two. We always have been."

Avanda picked up the runestone to see if it truly was one of Thorik's unique set. She had seen them enough to know that it was. "Thorik never mentioned any plans of using this runestone during the battle."

"He doesn't think that far ahead. Fortunately, Darkmere does, and he knows that if this runestone could clear the clouds over the battlefield and allow the sun to strike Bakalor, the demon would be vulnerable." Shaking her head, Emilen finished with a cold grin. "Thorik will *not* be successful in clearing the storm clouds, should he even attempt it."

## Chapter 38
# Dark Storm Clouds

Flying up toward the dark swirling clouds, Thorik rode on his overweight dragon, Chug, as quick as possible. The winds were fierce and often nearly tossed Thorik off his ride. One wrong move and Thorik could fall to his death, thousands of feet below in the battlefield.

To make matters worse, three black dragons had made it past Santorray's blockade and were on their way to catch up to Thorik. They were streamlined and shot through the air at twice the speed that Chug could. At only a third of Chug's size, they had sharp teeth and claws that could cut through dragon scales, let alone Num flesh.

Thorik turned away from the black dragons chasing them and back to where they were headed. "Hurry! We're almost there. We need to get up above the clouds."

Chug responded with a nod of his head and continued to gain altitude.

The black dragons closed in and reached Chug's location just as they entered the dense storm clouds.

Thorik couldn't see anything in the darkness. The storm's wind and rain splattered against his face and gust of freezing air caused ice to build upon his skin. He simply had one focus, and that was to hang on to the large brown dragon. His life was now in the hands of his friend.

Chug spun and dove, in his attempts to fight off the three black dragons. Each time he made progress upward, another dragon would attack from behind, clawing at him and pulling him back downward.

Thorik closed his eyes and hung on tight. He could feel claws grabbing for him and just scraping his clothes and boots. He could tell by Chug's movements that he was in a terrible battle as the dragon twisted his body, spun out of control, and then was pounded by the bodies of the enemy. The Num's frozen fingers latched on to Chug with all his might in order not to be tossed off during the battle going on around him.

The brown dragon's banking from one side to the other and up and down continued until Thorik could see the sun as they breached the upper surface of the storm clouds. They had made it. The sun was directly over them, warming the Num's cold body.

Chug was breathing hard from the flight and the fight. But in the end, he had not only survived, but he was carrying all three limp black dragons in his claws. He had won.

"Good job, Chug. I'm very proud of you." He said, patting the dragon's side.

With his tongue hanging out of one side, the dragon nodded his head with relief that the fight was over.

Thorik sat up and grabbed his sack of runestones. "Now, fly a little forward. I want the sun to be in just the right location when I open up these clouds."

Chug did as instructed.

Reaching in, he noticed the Runestone of Pride was missing. "Emilen, you've betrayed me," he said softly, with disappointment. His thoughts of their romance so long ago had finally lost whatever interest had remained. He had given her a chance, and she plotted against him. Any love he still held for her finally vanished from his heart. She had deceived him for the last time.

Chug came to a stop and looked up at Thorik with sad eyes. His strong wings flapped hard to keep them stationary, just above the clouds.

"It's alright, my friend. At least I no longer feel guilty for lying to her," he said with a sigh. "Ever since we left the city of Ergrauth, I've been telling her the wrong names of the runestones I'd been using. Hopefully her actions have given Darkmere too much confidence." He finished with a slight smile while patting the side of the brown dragon's side.

A nod of approval was returned, as slobber dripped from Chug's hanging tongue.

Collecting the Runestone of Persistence, Thorik held it out in front of him with both hands. He then grasped the real runestone that had cleaned out the air in Rummon's Liar, hoping that he could expand on its powers to open a hole in the storm clouds long enough to shine direct sunlight on Bakalor.

Tingling ran up one arm and then down the other. He knew he would have to be completely in focus to make this work, so he forgot about where he was and what needed to be done. He gave in to the runestone's powers and allowed his body be at the mercy of the stone's power.

Within seconds, the storm clouds around them quickly began to clear, evaporating into thin air in every direction. The runestone that Thorik had used in Rummon's Lair to clean out the smoky corridors was working on a much larger scale.

Crashing up through the surface of the desert floor, Bakalor knocked Asentar and Ahz to the ground away from Santorray. He had returned and his flames shot high into the air as he displayed his anger. "I've had enough of you three!" he yelled.

Asentar tried to help the white female Blothrud up, but they were both quickly captured with one swipe of the demon's hand.

Santorray rolled to a distance before rising up onto one knee in agonizing pain. He had landed several yards away from the fallen war-hammer. Reading the engraved word, "Quake," he suddenly recognized it was his father's weapon, given to him as a gift from an E'rudite many battles ago. Wielded properly, it could mean the difference between victory and death. "Let's get this over with!" he yelled at the demon.

Bakalor took a few steps forward and raised his foot to stomp on the Blothrud.

Just as he lowered his leg to crush Santorray, sparks flew from the demon's back. Bryus Grum was standing behind Bakalor, casting a spell in an attempt to break away at the fissure created by Rummon. Sand, from the desert floor, spun in a circle like a large circular saw, under the Alchemist power. The spinning sand grinded away at the demon's back, sending sparks from the friction as they cut away small fragments.

Screaming with pain, the demon swatted the spell caster with the back side of his hand, sending the lightweight old man with a female body over into a distant pile of debris.

Once his back was exposed to Santorray, the Blothrud used all of his might to grab the fallen war-hammer and leap high in the air toward the demon. The crashing blow of the ancient weapon against his back doubled the size of the fissure as rocks shot out of Bakalor's back from the impact.

Still holding onto Asentar and Ahz, Bakalor fell to one knee in pain.

With broken ribs and bones of his own, Santorray mustered everything he had to slam the war-hammer again and again at Bakalor, causing the opening to widen. He only hoped that the Blothrud's lesser demon status would be enough to keep the damage permanent.

Slapping Asentar and Ahz hard to the earth, Bakalor released them before reaching down into the desert floor with his hand. Lowering his hand under the ground, he then raised it up under Santorray's feet before pulling him down into the desert floor up past his waist.

Santorray was now struck in the ground, with the hammer in his hands, waiting for the demon to approach.

Bakalor took a moment to gain some control after the massive beating he had taken from the Blothrud. Rocks continued to fall from his back as he straightened himself up. "I will deal with you in a moment." Still on one knee, he reached back over and lifted the Dovenar Knight and the Kewtall leader for all to see. "I will crush you before your people, and then I will deal with your red friend." He then began closing his rock fist on the two captives.

It was at this moment that sunlight from above broke through the dark storm clouds and shined down on the battlefield. The contrast was so great and happened so quickly that all on the desert floor were temporarily blinded.

Thanks to Thorik and Chug, the great storm above opened in every direction and continued to grow in size, shining the light across a larger area, exposing the damage of the war. Few were left from either side.

Still half buried, Santorray's eyes adjusted before he looked upon Bakalor. The green flame that animated his body had been overpowered by the power of the sun. The demon was frozen like a statue with the two captives raised overhead.

However, the opening in the clouds had reached its apex and was now starting to shrink. Time was limited. Darkness would return.

Santorray knew that once this happened, Bakalor would come right back to life.

Using his father's war-hammer, he began pounding away at the desert floor around him.

The clouds continued to fill back in.

Again and again, the hammering continued until he finally broke up the ground enough to pull his body up and roll out of the hole. His body screamed with pain from all of his broken bones, cuts and gashes, yet he refused to allow any of these to stop him.

Jumping to his feet, He leaped toward the demon for a final blow, as the clouds closed in on themselves and the desert became dark once again.

Just as they did, Bakalor's flames exploded with energy. However, it was too late. Santorray's strike with his war-hammer crashed into the demon's back, splitting the creature in two and sending shards in every direction.

The power of the explosive blast knocked Santorray back, pelting him with fragments of rocks coated in burning oil.

Asentar and Ahz flew to the ground along with the remaining sections of the Bakalor's body, which broke up into hundreds of rocks.

"Put out the flames!" Santorray ordered, pointing at the fiery remains scattered across the desert. He then returned to extinguishing the pieces of Bakalor which had embedded into his own skin.

Soldiers quickly started stomping on the small pieces and covering the larger pieces with sand in order to douse the green flames of the oils.

The demon, Bakalor, was no more. Not only had he been defeated, but he had been eliminated. He had underestimated the likelihood that the various races and species of the world would come together in a unified effort against him.

Seeing the demon's demise, Bakalor's followers quickly fled the area to the northeast as Santorray's soldiers cheered at the hard fought victory, allowing their enemy to leave without confrontation. The battle of Australis was now over. Many had died in the fight, and would be mourned before the day was to end, but now was not the time. Celebration was the current course of action for their valor and what they had accomplished. In addition to winning, new relations had been built between the humans, Ov'Unday, and Kewtalls. This was a task even the Grand Council struggled to achieve.

Diving down below the clouds, Chug leveled off above the battlefield and dropped the injured black dragons he had been carrying.

Thorik raised one arm in the air as a signal of success while he watched the various species and races rejoicing at their victory and at the little dragon-riding Num. They had won. Finally, they had won. Thorik wasn't sure he would ever see the day that evil was finally defeated.

The excitement on the desert battlefield had caused a blind eye to the unknown E'rudite battle beyond the wall and upon an island in the center of Rivers Edge. Small in size, the battle was easily overlooked.

Raising his own hand in triumph, Santorray watched Thorik race by on Chug nodding to Thorik with respect.

Banking to his left, Thorik and Chug looped back and landed near the Blothrud.

Thorik dismounted the brown dragon and raced forward, shouting in excitement at the Blothrud, who was now accompanied by Ahz and Asentar. Leaping up, he was caught by Santorray and pulled in for a grand hug. "You did it, Santorray!" A sense of accomplishment raced through Thorik's body, making all of the pains through his travels suddenly worthwhile.

"No, my friend, *we* did it," Santorray responded, relaxing the hug of the Num. "And it is because of you that we were all here to help. You truly have become a great leader, Sec."

The words brought a smile on the Num's face and a tear to his eyes. Upon wiping them with his wrist, he noticed some dark splashes of dirt on the skin of his arms. Rubbing them off on his shirt, he could see that they didn't fade. "*Are these burn marks?*" he wondered, rubbing his thumb across the dark marking on his other wrist several times before realizing what he was looking at.

Pulling back his sleeve, he revealed that the dark patches were the ends of several lines, which spiraled up his arm. They were not streaks of mud, dirt or scorched skin. It was simply discolored skin. Sensitive in nature, the patches were a sight for his eyes and heart. He had finally received soul-markings.

Showing Santorray his arm, Thorik began to laugh and cry at the same time. "Look! Do you see what I have here?" he cried out to the Blothrud, displaying his exposed arms to all that were willing to see them. "I can't wait to show Avanda."

His own words caused the Num to freeze in fear. "Avanda? What has become of her?" Jumping out of Santorray's arms, he leaped back up onto the brown dragon's back. "We're done here,

Chug. Now we need to head across the river and save Avanda. Pheosco may already be there, so fly with haste, my friend."

## Chapter 39
# Avanda's Nightmare

Dragging Avanda out of her tent by her hair, the Southwind soldier tossed her to the ground in front of a half dozen other soldiers, all waiting for further orders.

"Let the soldiers have their way with her," Emilen said, stepping out of the tent. "Darkmere will want to see her begging for his forgiveness by the time he returns."

Avanda's eyebrows lowered and her lips pulled in tight while staring at the other Num. Her hands and ankles were still bound as well. "I'll make you pay for this," she growled through tight teeth.

"You have no magic to protect you now. And without that, you have nothing. You're fear of being vulnerable is finally going to be realized. You have no power to stop us from doing whatever we want to you." Emilen smirked at the defenseless Num on the ground. "Power is in knowing which side to be on and befriending those who can get you what you want. The Terra King is our future, whether you like it or not. He is your new master."

"I'd die before I followed him!"

"You just very well might." Emilen looked up at the soldiers. "Gentlemen, here is your entertainment for the evening. Enjoy yourself for as long as she lasts, or until she has a change of heart."

Avanda tried to break free with no success. "I'll never change my mind."

"Then, this may be the last time I see you." Emilen turned and walked away.

The soldiers quickly grabbed her, lifted her off the ground, and took her away.

Struggling the entire time, Avanda never gave up her fight for freedom. She hated to be under someone else's control. Vesik had finally given her the ability to be independent and free of fear about others taking advantage of her. Ever since Lucian had violated her in Rava'Kor, she couldn't stand to be touched by anyone, except Thorik. He was the only one she could trust, but even he had fallen to Emilen's ways. Now she had no one and was truly alone. Her world felt so small and suffocating. Every touch from the men carrying her caused her to feel sick of the thought of their dirty, dry fingers touching her soft skin. Every finger was a defilement in her mind. *"If I had Vesik, I'd teach them a lesson,"* she thought. *"They would never be able hurt me or anyone ever again."*

Dropped in the center of a large circle of tents, Avanda landed next to a roaring fire.

Hundreds of soldiers came and left the area to gather food and supplies. Others played music while a few danced to old folk songs. This was the central hub of the camp.

One of the men who had carried her removed her restraints before walking away.

She immediately jumped to her feet and tried to run away, but was quickly blocked in every direction she tried. When she attempted to push her way out of the open area, the crowd of men tossed her back into the center.

Not giving up, she ran for one of the tents, only to find a large man inside sharpening the blade of his weapon. She backed out quickly into the music-filled center.

Dancing to the music, one of the men snatched Avanda up from behind and began swirling her around.

She kicked and screamed and finally broke free, ripping her dress and falling against a table, knocking drinks onto those sitting around it.

"You idiot," yelled one of the men who was now wearing his drink. "You'll pay for that." Standing up, he reached over to grab her.

A quick kick by Avanda's boot stopped the man in his tracks, giving her time to roll to her feet.

Blood poured down from the man's lip before he spit out a tooth that had been broken off. "That's going to cost extra."

The music went silent and the men stopped what they were doing in order to watch the event unfold before them. An eerie sound of soft whispering voices gave way to the crackling of fire and the grunting and coughing of the soldiers surrounding her.

The man missing a tooth stepped forward, causing her to step back. A second step was made by both of them, before they broke out into a run around the bonfire, over and under tables and cooking equipment. Avanda had the advantage of her size and speed, but she had nowhere to escape to. The crowd prevented her from leaving the area.

Hands reached out to grab at her dress and hair while she passed by the onlookers. An occasional push or trip by the spectators caused her to fall, slowing her down. Slaps on her rump and heckling became more intense as time went on.

More violent words of hatred and bigotry were made against the Num. Drinks were then tossed at her before the occasional rock. It no longer became a race against the man she caused to spill his drink. This was now a mob who blamed Polenums and other species for their problems in the world.

More rocks were thrown, one hitting her hard in the leg and then another in the back. She fell and then stood back up, only to take another rock to the forehead, sending her to the ground again.

Blood poured down her face as she looked out at the screaming mob. Searching for any options, she saw Emilen standing in the crowd with a smile, before she turned her back on her and disappeared in the mob of angry soldiers.

On her hands and knees, she was taunted and screamed at while still looking for an option to escape. It was then when she noticed one of the tent flaps was moving. Peeking out of the tent was Pheosco, waving her to him.

Standing up she made it obvious that she was weak and hurt, stumbling back and forth and wiping the blood from her forehead across her entire face. It wasn't difficult to act hurt seeing that she really was. She was just playing on it even more.

Chanting and yelling continued toward her as she attempted to block any more rocks from hitting her head.

Swaying back and forth she made her way toward the tent. Once just outside the tent, a man splashed his drink at her face, knocking her backward into the tent. The sight of her falling again brought on cheers and laughs. With the tent surrounded, there wasn't a risk of her escaping, so they waited for the man who had been chasing her to approach the tent entrance.

Grabbing a drink from one of the other soldiers, he chugged it down, half of it landing on his shirt. Wiping his face, he smiled at the crowd and rubbed his hands together before opening the flap and entering the tent.

A high pitched scream could be heard from within the tent, causing the mob to cheer with delight. However, this quickly changed once the man came running out of the tent with his clothes on fire. Shocked at the sight, it took them a few seconds to start helping him douse the flames.

It was then that they looked back at the tent as the flap snapped open and Avanda stood before them with a fistful of magical items in one hand and a large old book open in the other. Blood was still pouring from her head, but she no longer looked weak and scared, she looked menacing and dangerous.

Vesik gave her strength greater than she could ever feel on her own. Its power fed her anger and filled her mind with revenge. She had fully opened herself up to the book of magic, and Vesik was now ready to unleash its own powers through Avanda.

Before the crowd could react, Avanda finished reading the spell from Vesik and handed the book to Pheosco, who stood just behind her. With a few verbal commands and physical gestures, fire raced from her fingers out towards the crowd.

Men ran from the area as they were lit on fire in their retreat. Those directly in Avanda's blast were instantly incinerated into charred flesh and bones. Those luckier ones where only set ablaze as they ran away.

Anger and fear festered in Avanda to a point that she had lost control of her mind. Implanted by Vesik, her thoughts were only about destroying anything and anyone that had done her wrong. In this case, that was nearly everything and everyone.

Within seconds, the area had been cleared of soldiers, leaving flaming tents and tables to brighten the vicinity.

Pheosco scanned the destruction with an evil grin. "Well done. They deserved it after what they had done to you." Glancing to the north, he nodded his head. "The coast is clear. We can safely exit the camp and return to Rivers Edge." However, by the time he turned back, she had already started marching south, deeper into the Southwind camps. "Avanda? Where are you going?"

She ignored the small green dragon. Her eyes darted back and forth from within her head that was locked in a stationary position on a single mission, to find Emilen.

Every movement caught out of the side of Avanda's eyes was immediately blasted with a shower of fire from her fingertips. Men hiding in corners, animals tied to stakes, and even the helpless Myth'Unday in their cages were burned alive. With each and every step she took, the power of Vesik drove her to a new level of rage. Nothing would stop her from confronting the woman who had done her wrong, and nothing would stop the fury within her until the deed was done.

Approaching the Southwind camp, Thorik and Chug watched an area toward the middle suddenly go up in flames. The two had left the victorious battle north of Rivers Edge, in order to save Avanda. After seeing the explosion, the Num questioned who needed saving.

"Chug, land near the highest flames. My guess is that Avanda will be there."

The brown dragon nodded and flapped his wings one more time before gliding down the camp.

Upon landing, the entire camp was a scene of chaos. Explosions and fire was breaking out on one tent after another. People were running for their lives, many of them on fire.

Thorik hopped off of Chug. "If everyone is running that way, that means Avanda is most likely the opposite way." As he looked beyond the tents, he noticed a smaller dragon heading his way.

Pheosco flapped his wings hard as he carried Avanda's sack toward the two. "I wouldn't go near her if I were you. She has lost control and is destroying everything in sight."

Chug's eyes widened and tongue drooled at the sight of Pheosco. He was overjoyed to see the smaller dragon.

Thorik nodded. "Then you two stay here. I have to try to stop this."

Setting her sack next to Chug, Pheosco rested next to it. "You're going to get yourself killed."

"She's worth dying for." Heading toward the flames, Thorik dodged the various people who ran past him, all of which were on fire.

It wasn't long before he found the root of the problem. Amongst the fiery tents, Avanda could be seen in the center of all the chaos. Her hands were glowing red from the flames that surrounded them without causing her any pain.

Before her was Emilen, cowering on her knees. She was begging for her life as Avanda stood over her listening to her pleas.

Hate of the woman and love of the power she now felt, she was overcome with revenge. Raising up her hands, she prepared to put Emilen out of her life once and for all.

"NO!" shouted Thorik from the outside of the ring of fire preventing him from approaching her. "Don't give into your anger."

Thorik's voice was enough to make her hesitate. "She has worked against us all along. She doesn't deserve to live," Avanda yelled back without moving her eyes from her victim.

Thorik tried to get closer, but flames increased as he approached. "You're a good person inside. Your anger at her actions has turned you into something evil. Don't give her this power. Let her suffer the life she's created for herself."

Avanda did not respond. Instead she stared deeply at the other Num, fighting the temptation to blow her into thousands of little pieces.

Emilen turned to Thorik in a last ditch effort to save her own life. "Thorik! She's gone crazy. We were both captured. You saw this to be true. We were both taken away by the Southwind soldiers. But then I learned she was working for Darkmere all along. She has been feeding him notes in your coffer. Think about it, Thorik. How else has he always known your plans? I wasn't there most of the time. She is the *only* one that could have helped him."

The flames in Avanda's hands increased in size and heat after hearing the lies.

"Thorik!" Emilen said, knowing he was the only one that could save her. "Save me, Thorik! You are my true love!"

A blaze of fire roared out from Avanda's hands at those words. The flames engulfed Emilen's head, racing down her throat and then out of her pores. She was burning from the inside out.

"Stop!" Thorik shouted, watching the execution.

There was no response from Avanda. She was so engrossed with her actions that she not only continued to pump fire into Emilen's now skeletal head, but she was intensifying the heat behind it. She literally couldn't stop herself from growing more and more angry at the woman before her.

Thorik didn't know what to do. He couldn't reach her and he couldn't convince her to stop. Vesik had made her so powerful and angry that she was dangerous even to herself.

It was then that the thought hit him.

Turning from the unsettling scene, Thorik ran back to Chug & Pheosco. Grabbing the book out of Avanda's sack, he hopped onto Chug.

"You can't take Vesik!" Pheosco complained. "It belongs to Avanda. Without it she could have been killed."

"With it, she definitely will end up dead by her own hands or those of the many enemies she makes. This book needs to be hidden forever." Kicking the sides of Chug, he yelled, "Up!"

Pheosco was not going to allow this to happen so easily. Flying over to Thorik, he grabbed at the book, fighting to get it away from the Num.

Thorik bucked and pulled away. In doing so he accidently steered Chug directly into one of the tents during his lift off. The fabric of the tent covered the Num and both dragons as the two of them fought for the book. Back and forth they pulled on it while Chug lifted into the air.

Eventually, a ripping sound broke the fight up and Pheosco fell backward, accidently wrapping himself in the fabric while pulling it off of Thorik and Chug.

Thorik looked down in his arms, where Vesik still rested. Several pages looked to be ripped out, but the mass majority was with him.

Pheosco fell the twenty feet to the ground before landing on another tent and then rolling off it. He had survived the fall.

Thorik was glad to see the smaller dragon was safe. "Okay, Chug. We need to hide this book where no one will ever find it. We're heading to Govi Glade."

After the flames ended and the smoke was slowly rising in the air from the remaining ashes, Grewen walked along the remains of a burnt camp, carrying Brimmelle in one of his enormous hands. "What do you suppose happened here?" he asked.

Landing on his shoulder, Gluic snapped her head back and forth as she assessed the damage. "Revenge."

They continued toward the center of the abandoned camp until they found Avanda and Pheosco sitting in the center of an open area covered in ashes.

"Avanda?" Grewen said as he approached. "Are you alright?"

Her head stayed tilted down, looking at the charred ground. "Thorik has taken Vesik and flown off on Chug."

Brimmelle and Grewen looked at each other, both thinking that it might have been for the best.

"Where did he go?" Brimmelle asked, as Grewen set him down. "Is he going to destroy it?"

Pheosco stood near Avanda, guarding her from anyone, including Brimmelle. "No. He said he would take it to a place where no one could find it."

"Hmm," Grewen stroked his chin. "Do you think he is going to return it to the Govi Glade?"

"That's it!" Avanda shouted. "We need to go to the Govi Glade to stop him."

Grewen chuckled at the thought. "He will get there and back long before we travel a small portion of the way there on foot. He is flying on a dragon, and unless Pheosco can carry us, we're walking the entire way."

Avanda raised her head, showing a devilish smile. "No, we don't need to walk anywhere."

"Avanda, what's going on with you?" Brimmelle demanded to know.

Pheosco handed Avanda two pieces of paper, which he had ripped out of Vesik prior to Thorik leaving. "Your spell," he said with a slight bow.

She glanced over the papers and opened up her purse of magic and a tan leather sack which contained white sand along with a few dead beetles from the Govi Glade. "Gather around, we are headed to the Govi Glade. Master Bryus Grum taught me this spell."

Chapter 40
# Time

Thorik pushed Chug to fly as fast as he could over Rivers Edge and the Kiri Desert, toward the distant Govi Glade. His eyesight was keen as he watched the horizon at the distant forests where he would get rid of the book of magic once and for all.

He was sure that its powers were just too strong for a Num to control and it had corrupted his love, Avanda. She would never had killed anyone out of anger without being pushed by some external control.

Glancing back over his shoulder, he didn't see her following him. He had no idea how she would do such a thing, but with her abilities anything was possible no matter how ridiculous they may seem.

Before looking forward again, he watched the gravity shifts from the Lu'Tythis Tower crystal still play havoc on the ground and water. Sandstorms erupted out of nowhere and then died off just as fast. Huge waves splashed one way and then another while vortexes in the lake spun out of control.

Beyond the tower and the lake was a mighty mountain range to the west, broken up by an opening sealed off by the Weirfortus Dam. It was a great distance away. Too far for Thorik to see, and yet something didn't look right in that general direction. He couldn't figure out why but, even with Polenum vision, he couldn't see forever.

Thorik turned back to see which way they were heading before patting the side of the big brown dragon to give him encouragement. They were still on course.

In response, a large glop of Chug's saliva struck Thorik's leg.

Thorik grinned at the thick goo spraying off in the wind. He knew it was a friendly gesture from his speechless friend.

Sighing at the current journey, Thorik felt he had betrayed Avanda, when in fact he was just trying to save her from the control of the magical book. In one sense he was very thankful that she was now safe and free of Vesik, and yet in another he feared for his own safety from her once they would meet up again. Hopefully Vesik's influence would fade away and she would return to the Num he fell in love with. "I wish I had had a chance to explain my actions before I left…if she would have been willing to listen…if Vesik didn't have full control over her. I hope she will forgive me."

Chug nodded to his statement as he worked hard to keep their speed up.

"Yes, I know. *You* would forgive me." Chuckling at the brown dragon's response to a statement meant for Avanda, Thorik pointed northeast. "You're doing great. Once we get to the north end of O'Sid fields, you can stop to rest."

A simple shake of the head was given and the two continued flying until the purple native grasses of the area appeared. The large soft hills and prairie land opened up before them as wind made flowing patterns in the grass fields. Eventually, they lowered to take a rest.

Nearly knocking Thorik off, Chug landed with a thud and immediately began eating the purple flumes on the tips of the prairie grass.

A long time ago, Grewen instructed Thorik on what plants in this region were nutritious, so he collected a few of the ones he saw nearby before enjoying their sweet and salty flavors. Doing so reminded him of when he and Avanda had traveled these lands with Grewen in an effort to save Brimmelle from being taken to the Southwind's prison mines. It seemed like a lifetime ago.

His time of rest and relaxation was unexpectedly interrupted by a loud crack and explosion.

Snapping his head to the northwest, Thorik watched the distant White Summit Mountain explode with enough energy to make the ground shake under his feet. A giant thick ash cloud flumed up and then rolled to the east toward the Govi Glade. Lightning immediately sparked from the ash cloud down upon the entire mountain range, giving the event an even greater ominous feel.

The distant mountain itself was of no immediate threat to the prairie and the two standing within it watching the destructive force. However, it could easily destroy the Num's hometown. "Farbank," Thorik said softly, hoping the little village would be spared from the volcano's wrath.

Again the ground rumbled beneath their feet as they stood there watching. These vibrations continued without intervals of calmness.

Chug stopped eating and gave a concerned look toward the Num.

Tightening his lips, Thorik spun around to see if there were any local issues. He had felt this rhythmic rumbling before. "Chug! We have a herd of chuttlebeasts heading this way."

Chug began running, causing Thorik to chase after him.

"Wait for me!" the Num yelled.

Hundreds of chuttlebeasts stampeded over the hillside and down toward the two. Stricken with fear, the beasts weren't charging toward something, like they usually do, but instead they appeared to be running *from* something.

"What could scare an entire herd? Was it the volcano's eruption?" Thorik said to himself, trying to reach his big brown friend before the dragon took flight.

Racing down the side of the soft slope, the chuttlebeasts quickly caught up to Thorik and Chug. Fortunately for the Num, he was close enough to hop onto the dragon's back. "Fly!"

Taking a few more steps, Chug lifted off the ground just as the chuttlebeasts demolished the grasslands Chug had been feeding on.

"What could have caused that?" Thorik asked, once safely in the air. Turning back the west, he got his answer. A wave, well over a thousand feet in height, was heading their way. Weirfortus dam had broken open and the ocean water was flooding the entire valley, which had been resting over two thousand feet below sea-level since the ancient times of the Notarians.

"Fly faster!" Thorik shouted. His mind raced on what this event meant. Had the wave already crushed the battlefield and the Southwind camp, killing all of his friends? He had helped win the war but failed to save the land they fought for. If he had left Vesik in Avanda's hands, could she have saved everyone? Had he single-handedly allowed all of this to happen just to destroy a simple book? What had he done?

Sweeping over the Lu'Tythis Tower, the massive wave had driven the tower's chuttle-sized crystal deep into the ground, but the gem's influence continued to be seen. The crystal's powers pushed flumes of water miles into the air in random directions and intervals. The storm clouds that had been controlled by the crystal broke into various small storms with openings of sunlight between them. These smaller dense storms gave birth to hail storms and tornadoes across the valley.

The wall of water had raced to the east, engulfing cities and tall hillsides as though they were anthills. Even the mighty Dovenar Walls had been swept away and rolled over without affecting the wave's direction or speed. Stone blocks from the blown away walls rolled in the churning water, acting as projectiles, destroying more in the wave's path.

Thorik didn't know what to do aside from hanging onto Chug, as the dragon forced himself to fly faster. The Nums last course was for the Govi Glade, so this was still the direction the dragon focused on.

Trees and soil were stripped from the landscape, while buildings were blown apart from the massive power of the oncoming wave. Nothing could stand in its way. Regardless how fast Chug flew, the wave was still catching up to them.

Thorik considered flying above it and letting it pass underneath, but he came up with an alternative idea that could potentially allow him to save all of his friends and the land itself. If they could still make it to the Govi Glade before the wave did, then they could jump into one of the spheres. He had done this once before and met Ambrosius back in the time of the E'rudite and Alchemist War. Perhaps he could go back in time again and alert Ambrosius of the destructive wave. If so, Ambrosius would stop it from happening, thus saving his friends. He would most likely never see his friends again, but it was his only chance to save them.

"Give me everything you have!" he yelled to the dragon.

Chug nodded and stretched out his neck and tightened up his back legs. A quick burst of gas out of his backside may not have helped speed them up any more, but it made him feel better.

Off they went, racing the wall of water toward the Govi Glade. The closer they were to their destination, the closer the wave was upon them. A background noise from the violent wave rang in the Num's ears as it approached.

Lightning continued to streak across the sky, flumes of water shot in random directions from the submerged tower crystal, the mighty White Summit Mountain was spewing magma and hot gasses tens of thousands of feet above their heads, hail storms and tornadoes sprang up out of nowhere, and the wave would soon be lapping at their heels.

Thorik attempted to block out his worry that too much was stacked against him. Repeating Gluic's words of wisdom, he ignored the obstacles and focused on his goal. "There it is!" Leaning forward he pointed at the Govi Glade in order to guide his dragon down.

Bowing his neck, the dragon dove toward the edge of the glade and landing, once again, with a thud. This time, Thorik fell off and rolled to a stop, as Vesik was stripped from his grasp upon impact.

Shaking his head clear, he realized he was lying on his back in the actual glade as clear spheres rolled in and out of the ground around him. Appearing like enormous bath bubbles, these giant globes slowly wandered within the glade, each one filled with a semi-transparent scene from another time or another place.

Lightning shot across the ash cloud and the wall of water could now be seen beyond the tops of the trees that surrounded the glade. There wouldn't be time to wait for just the right sphere to jump into. He would have to take the first one he could reach.

"Thorik!" The scream came from behind him, next to Chug. To Thorik's surprise and then horror, he saw Avanda, Pheosco, Grewen, Brimmelle and Gluic standing alongside the glade, just outside of the boundary where the spheres populated.

With arms crosses in front of her chest, Avanda was obviously still very angry about what Thorik was trying to do. "Hand it over, Thorik!"

Thorik watched the wall of water over the trees race toward them. "RUN!" he yelled, pointing at the wave.

It only took a moment for them to see the incredible sight before they did as he said. Avanda and Pheosco sprinted forward, followed by Brimmelle, Gluic and then Chug. Grewen was always slow to get started, and did his best to catch up.

Even with all of them moving the best they could, it was too late. The wave struck with a tremendous force, pushing Grewen off his feet and into Chug as the two of them tumbled forward toward the rest.

The water crashed down upon them as two of the Govi Glade spheres opened up in front of their path, sweeping everyone into the mystic globes before the clear bubbles of magic went back under the ground, out of sight.

The wave had no effect on the spheres in their endless paths through the glade that immediately became buried below the ocean inlet.

Now underwater, the location of the E'rudite and Alchemist War continued to bubble as it had for thousands of years. Thorik and his companions were nowhere to be found.

Choking from the water in his lungs, Thorik found himself lying in an open windy field on a dark moonless night. His clothes and gear were completed soaked. Nevertheless, he was pleased to find he wasn't missing anything.

Unfortunately, there was no sign of anyone else. Then again, his vision was poor in the faint starlight. To make matters worse, pockets of fog rolled past him, playing tricks with his mind, causing him to think people were moving past him before all would go pitch black.

Coughing a few more times to clear out the water, Thorik sat up and began to yell for his friends, but the howling winds easily absorbed his attempts.

After a few minutes of coughing and yelling, he noticed a distant light. It was the only light he could see, so he began making his way toward it. Perhaps everyone else would do the same. Perhaps they have already gathered and built a fire to attract Thorik. Either way, he was heading toward it.

"I hope we were all swept into the same sphere," he said to himself, squinting to focus on the light through the fog.

Each wet sluggish step forward was an act of faith. He didn't know if he was going to run into a large rock, or fall down a ravine. He simply took one step at a time toward the light which began to sharpen up in the Num's view as it slowly shifted from potentially being a bonfire to clearly being a light in a window.

"A structure? Here in the Glade?" Thorik slowed his approach. "A lit lantern inside means someone is home." He cautiously continued forward.

Easing up to the structure, Thorik leaned up against the wooden side of the building and listened for any noise inside. He heard shuffling of feet and then some yelling before it toned down to some mumbling.

"How far back in history have I gone? Did the Del'Unday still rule the lands at this time?" he asked himself. Thorik had to find out who or what was inside, so he eased himself up to the window and began to glance inside.

Just then, the door on the side of the structure opened up and then slammed shut.

Thorik immediately shot back from the window and slapped the back of his wet shirt up against the wooden wall. Breathing hard he waited to hear something more or, worst case, see someone come around the corner.

Neither happened. Instead the occupier of the structure came around the other way, from behind the Num. "Intruders? Uninvited guests?" yelled the gruff voice of an old man over the howling winds.

Thorik just about jumped out of his skin from the unexpected encounter. Leaping away, he turned to see who had sneaked up on him.

The resident of the structure stepped into the faint light shining through the window. It was a very old and tall thin man with long chaotic hair which covered most of his face. "Who's there? Give me your name?"

Squinting in the dim light, the Num kept his distance. "Thorik Dain of Farbank. And who are you?"

The wrinkly old man stood silent for several seconds. "Thorik?" he asked, pulling his scraggly hair from his face. "It is I, Ambrosius."

*Pronunciation Guide*

# *CHARACTERS*

**Ahzvietaweh:** ahZ-vE-tO-wAY
**Ambrosius:** aeM-brO-zee-ahs
**Asentar:** as-en-Tar
**Avanda:** ah-Van-Dah
**Bakalor:** Bah-Kah-Lor
**Bredgin:** Brehd-gehn
**Brimmelle:** Brim-'ell
**Chug:** Chug
**Darkmere:** Dark-Meer
**Deleth:** deL-'eth
**Emilen:** ehM-il-eN
**Ergrauth:** erR-gRahTH
**Ericc:** ehR-iK
**Feshlan:** FehSH-Lahn
**Gluic:** Glu-iK
**Grewen:** Gru-'en
**Irluk:** uhR-luhK
**Ovlan:** ahV-lahN
**Pheosco:** Fee-ahs-kO
**Rummon:** Rum-mahN
**Santorray:** sahn-ToR-rAY
**Thorik:** Thor-iK
**Vesik:** Ves-iK
**Wyrlyn:** Wer-Len

# *LOCATIONS*

**Corrock:** koR-RahK
**Cuev'Laru Mountains:** Koo-ehV Lah-Roo
**Cucurrian River:** Koo-kuR-ee-uhn
**Doven:** dO-ven
**Govi:** Gah-Vee
**Kiri:** kE-rE
**Lu'Tythis:** Loo-Tith-is
**Pelonthal:** peL-ahn-THahl
**Trewek:** trU-ek

*Pronunciation Guide*

# *SPECIES*

**Blothrud** (AKA Ruds): BlahTH-Ruhd
> *7' to 9' tall; Bony hairless Dragon/Wolf-like head; Red muscular human torso and arms; Sharp spikes extending out across shoulderblades, back of arms, and back of hands; Red hair covered waist and over two thick strong wolf legs. Blothruds are typically the highest class of the Del'Undays.*

**Del'Unday:** DeL-OOn-Day
> *The Del'Unday are a collection of Altered Creatures who live in structured communities with rules and strong leadership.*

**Fesh'Unday:** FehSH-OOn-Day
> *The Fesh'Unday are all of the Altered Creatures that roam freely without societies.*

**Gathler:** GahTH-ler
> *6' to 8' tall; Hunched over giant sloth-like face and body; Gathlers are the spiritual leaders of the Ov'Undays.*

**Human:** Hyoo-muhn
> *5' to 6' tall; pale to dark complextion; weight varies from anorexic to obese. Most live within the Dovenar Kingdom.*

**Krupes:** KrooP
> *6' to 8' tall; Covered from head to toe in black armor, these thick and heavy bipedal creatures move slow but are difficult to defeat. Few have seen what they look like under their armor. Krupes are the soldiers of the Del'Unday.*

**Mognin** (AKA Mogs): MahG-Nen
> *10' to 12' tall; Mognins are the tallest of the Ov'Unday.*

**Myth'Unday:** Meeth-OOn-Day
> *The Myth'Unday are a collection of Creatures brought to life by altering natures plants and insects.*

**Ov'Unday:** ahv-OOn-Day
> *The Ov'Unday are a collection of Altered Creatures who believe in living as equals in peaceful communities.*

**Polenum** (AKA Nums): Pol-uhn-um
> *4' to 5' tall; Human-like features; Very pale skin; Soul-markings cover their bodies in thin or thick lines as they mature. Eyesight is better than most species.*

Made in the USA
Charleston, SC
19 September 2014